THE
THIRD
PRINCE

A Novel

I0564560

PHIROZ H. MADON

JAICO PUBLISHING HOUSE

Ahmedabad Bangalore Bhopal Bhubaneswar Chennai
Delhi Hyderabad Kolkata Lucknow Mumbai

Published by Jaico Publishing House
A-2 Jash Chambers, 7-A Sir Phirozshah Mehta Road
Fort, Mumbai - 400 001
jaicopub@jaicobooks.com
www.jaicobooks.com

THE THIRD PRINCE: A NOVEL
ISBN 978-81-8495-140-0

First Jaico Impression: 2010
Third Jaico Impression: 2011

Printed by

Agra, 1603

The wooden wheels of the bullock cart turn as it clatters along the road. The iron rims of the huge wheels bump over the irregularities in the path. It is a bruising ride. The bull, a dirty white beast with huge horns, is comfortable, settled in its pace, which it has kept up all night. The driver holds a little stick with which he incongruously controls the huge animal. He has difficulty staying awake.

The cart is silhouetted against the dawn sky. It is a big north Indian sky, loud and splashy like the people themselves. Extravagant swaths of pink and orange streak halfway across the sky to mingle in passionate swirls above the rising sun.

Inside the covered cart are two passengers. Parvati Devi, called Paru by all who know her, is already too old to begin her career. She is fifteen. Her head is covered with her *odhni*, a combined veil and shawl. She is asleep. The other occupant is a turbaned uncle. They are already bone-tired, and it is hot.

The cart is caught up in the morning rush to get goods to the *bazaar*. In front of them is a milk-cart drawn by two bulls, the milk frothing in the narrow necks of the earthenware pots. A heavily-laden camel plods along, looking sour and resigned as camels do. A noble lady, with two guards, rides by in the opposite direction. She is covered from head to foot in an orange *burkha*. She looks out at the world through a small rectangle of gold netting. The guards are dressed as warriors, sporting turbans, long colourfully patterned skirts, and well-used swords that hang casually from their waists. The riders vie with innumerable peasants making their way to the market on foot — men and women carrying baskets on their heads, piled improbably high with coriander, mint, chillies, and lemons.

The bullock cart enters the city of Agra through enormous gates. Mughal sentries in resplendent uniforms stand on each side, although their presence is largely symbolic. The days when the City could be realistically protected by walls surrounding it have long gone. The economic boom of the last forty years has caused an explosion in size and sprawl that has outstripped the capabilities of any defensive wall.

The cart struggles through the crowded Agra *bazaar.* The uncle stirs from his sleep and peeps out from under the covers. The cart is following a road that skirts the swampy bank of the Yamuna River. It zigzags through a maze of alleyways and finally comes to rest in a quiet side street of artisans' shops and houses.

It has stopped outside a dance class. The uncle shakes Paru awake. She looks up groggily not knowing where she is. Still half-asleep, she automatically gathers her bundle of clothes and her copper *lota* and gets out of the cart. The uncle ducks under the cart and unties a small bundle of coins. Then, he goes to the back of the cart and finds a rolled-up document.

Hesitantly, they enter the dance class. They find themselves standing in a large shabby room with a threadbare carpet and cushions pushed against the walls. In typical Indian style there are no chairs. A fat woman, Amma, is sleeping in a corner of the room.

"She is asleep," the uncle says to no one in particular, "we have to wait." He and Paru squat on the floor, waiting for Amma to wake up. An hour goes by. They wait patiently, in the manner of village people who can sit in one place for many hours.

Amma stirs. She opens her eyes. Noticing the visitors, she struggles to sit up, and regards them balefully. Uncle and Paru spring to their feet.

"What do you want?" Amma demands.

"I brought this girl," Uncle says. "There is a document." He holds it out.

Amma formally unrolls the document. She stares at it for some time. She turns it upside down to see if it makes more sense that way. She throws it aside irritably.

"What does it say?"

"It says..." he starts, "it says, that she is related! Related to the most illustrious and noble Lady Nasreen! Fourth wife of the most illustrious and magnificent noble, Jaswant Shah. Now Jaswant Shah..." Uncle closes his eyes, the better to remember, "...is the second cousin of the most royal Princess Waheeda. And Princess Waheeda..." His closed eyelids flicker with the effort, "...and then I forget. I am sorry..."

"Do you have the money?" Amma demands.

"Yes! Yes. I have the money." Uncle hands over the bag of coins.

Amma opens the bag and counts the coins. Then, making sure Uncle understands, she speaks slowly and carefully, "I will take twelve *rupiya* from you, for six months. We will teach her to dance and to sing. After that, she will work. For six months, a year, as long as it takes. She has to pay us hundred *rupiya* before she can leave."

Uncle nods. Amma looks at the girl. "What is your name?"

Paru looks down, unable to speak. "Parvati!" Uncle says, glad he knows the answer to this one. "She is, Her Nobility, the most Illustrious Lady, Parvati Devi!"

"I need to see her face," Amma says.

The *odhni* falls off Paru's head.

Amma looks at Paru for a moment. "And your body."

Paru does not understand.

"Here," Amma says gently, removing Paru's *odhni* entirely. She exposes a three-day-old unwashed *choli*, the short blouse that all peasant girls wear. There is a patch of sweat under each armpit. Paru's waist is slim and perfect.

Amma pushes up Paru's chin, so that she is looking directly at her, eye to eye. "I always ask my girls this — would you really like to dance and sing?"

Paru manages a nod.

Amma professionally checks the swell and feel of Paru's breasts. Paru's eyes are beginning to fill with tears.

"Open your mouth. I want to see your teeth." She looks suspiciously at the Uncle. "Any scars on her body? Deformities?"

"Oh no! Nothing like that," he replies.

"She does speak, doesn't she?"

"Oh yes! A lot! On and on!"

"I need to—" She looks behind her. "Pithu!" From a room off the main hall comes the sound of a dancer's anklets. "Pithu!" Amma calls again. Pithu emerges wearing only a *choli* and a *ghagra*, a colourful dancer's skirt. She moves sexily, without thinking.

Amma goes to a wooden chest in a corner of the room and rummages inside. She finds a cloth. "Hold this," she says handing one corner to Uncle. She hands the other corner to Pithu. Pithu looks bored.

Amma takes Paru's hand. "I need you to come behind the curtain and take your skirt off."

They spend a long time behind the curtain. Uncle stares off into the distance, a frozen look on his face. Pithu stands, looking resigned.

They emerge from behind the cloth. Paru is flushed. She

struggles to put her skirt on and regain some dignity.

"She will do," Amma says. "I need a guarantee."

"Guarantee?" Uncle says blankly.

"After six months, she will have to work and pay us hundred *rupiya*. If she decides to run away, or grow lazy... I need a guarantee."

"Guarantee?"

"Do you have anything of value? Money?"

"No, I have nothing more of value!" he protests. "I already gave you the twelve *rupiya*!"

"Then I cannot take her," Amma replies.

Uncle is devastated. Amma looks no deal. She folds the cloth and returns it to the chest.

There is a movement. Paru is fishing inside her skirt. She gets something out — a jewel.

Uncle's eyes widen. "Child!" he exclaims, "Where did you steal that from?" He tries to grab it from her.

"It's mine!" Paru says fiercely, holding on to it. Her fist clenched tightly around the jewel, she hands it past Uncle to Amma.

Amma takes one look at the jewel and her face slackens. It is not a jewel that one would expect little Paru to own. It is a gigantic ruby surrounded by medium-sized diamonds, laid in intricately patterned gold. In the gold framing at the bottom is an inscription in Persian.

"This is your guarantee?" Amma says, regarding the jewel in shock.

"Yes. Until I can give you hundred *rupiya*," Paru answers.

"I will keep it... till then," Amma says, suddenly short of breath. "Pithu. Will you show her to her quarters?"

"Where?" Pithu demands.

"Next to Khursheed and Sima."

"There is no place—"

"You can make place. Move them over."

Pithu scowls at Paru. "Follow me," she says walking out without looking back. Paru picks up her things hastily and follows her.

Amma looks at the Uncle. "Is there anything else?"

"No," he says. He bows ceremoniously and retreats, walking backwards out of the dance class.

Amma takes another look at the jewel in her hand.

Since the rented bullock cart has served its purpose, Uncle lets it go. He walks the forty miles home, taking the high road out of town, his belongings slung over his shoulder.

Paru gets a tiny corner in the girls' dorm. There are about twenty girls spread across the floor of the room on straw mattresses. The senior girls get spots next to walls. Some even have shelves built into the stone wall next to their mattresses. Paru tries to fold her clothes. She is not very good at it. The scroll is an odd thing for her to store with her clothes. Sometimes it lies on the mattress next to her at night.

The teacher of the dance class is an old man with white hair and a flowing white moustache. Everyone calls him Guruji. While he teaches, he sits on the floor with a small pair of *tablas*, with which he can play an amazing variety of beats. The twenty girls stand in front of him, each dancing in her spot. They do this from morning till noon. At noon they break for a small lunch, when they can thankfully bend their legs and sit. Then they continue, through the hot afternoon until evening, when the sky begins to darken outside.

Some of the girls are good, and others are bad. And Guruji knows exactly how to push each of them to the next level. He is like a God with eyes on everything. He can spot even the ninth girl in the last row who does a gesture incorrectly. He asks the senior girls to help sometimes, showing them the movement of an arm, a leg, or a facial expression. Sometimes, Guruji gets up and shows them a move himself, but only to the very advanced girls, and then with a special tenderness in his voice as if they are now his jewels.

They stand in front of him and dance and dance. As the hot, tiring afternoons drag on, their bodies sweat and smell. At the end of the day, Paru's feet are like stones. She lies on the mattress at night thinking she will never move. When the girls are lazy or inattentive or rebellious they are sent to Amma. Amma uses a riding crop, and you can hear the screams from the next room. Everyone prefers the kindness of Guruji to the meanness of Amma, so this does not happen too often. But when it does happen, it is like a death. The day is engulfed in gloom and no one says very much.

Paru struggles in her spot, hoping Guruji does not see her. The other girls learn so much faster. She is like the village idiot, standing in her corner doing foolish things. She is so bad that Guruji should have sent her to Amma several times, but he pretends not to notice her mistakes. The other girls seem to be punished for much less. Then something happens, and she doesn't know why, but she can dance as well as the other girls.

Guruji teaches them to seduce men. He tells them what men think when they look at girls. And he teaches them how to move their bodies to make them think those things. How to see themselves from the outside as if they are the men looking at them, and how a skilled courtesan can achieve a 'lock', the perfect unity between the man's gaze and her body. Her movements, her self, and the man's gaze are united in a single effusion of joy.

And it is in the course of these lessons that Paru experiences the act itself. The class is filled suddenly with young boys, high-caste boys wearing white *dhotis*. Paru is paired with a boy with dark, smoky eyes. He seems very serious. His movements are deliberate, well-considered. Guruji makes them sit opposite each other in the lotus position and asks them to be still. They remain still with their eyes closed for a long time, longer than Paru has ever been still. Then Guruji instructs each girl to be as the water in a great river to flow wherever her mind would flow and her body would flow. The boy, Guruji says, is as the branch in the river, hard, and guiding the flow of the current. But it is the woman who is the river.

The boy seems to know what to do. Paru finds herself close to him, his breath on her face. She is surprised, hesitates. Then she reminds herself to be as the river. He is gentle. She looks at the ceiling. She seems to hear the wind sigh over the sand on the bank of the river. She loves, she melts. It is a long time before it ends.

She lies next to the boy. She is tired, triumphant. She looks into his dark, beautiful eyes. "It will not always be like this," he says. "Sometimes it will be very harsh. And you will feel unpleasant. When that happens, you should remember how it can be. It is but an art, the greatest art. It can be whatever the artist brings to it. That is what Guruji wishes me to tell you." With that he gets up and starts wearing his *dhoti*. Paru curls up on the mattress trying to hide her hurt. She looks up again and he is gone.

Paru stands on the verandah of the dance class in the evening gloom, thinking of her home. Sometimes, as now, she misses it. The girls are inside, gossiping about Guruji, speculating why he does not have his students like the other teachers do. A girl says it is because he is great man and does not want his desires to come in the way of his art. Pithu says it is because he is too old.

Paru stares at the trader's shop across the street and pretends it is not there. Instead she imagines the rice fields and the mud huts and the cows and the dung fires in the evening. She stares, and stares, and stares at the trader's shop, and thinks of her cousins, who are not really her cousins, and her aunts and uncles, who are not really her aunts and uncles. She thinks of the big village across the *bajra* field, where she and her cousins dared not go and the well they could not drink water from, even when there was a drought and there was none in their own little patch of land. She is free here. Of that she is grateful. There are no castes in the City.

None that matter.

And then she thinks of that of which she dare not think, because it is too painful. And yet it is uppermost in her mind, like vomit that has not come out. She thinks of that, and the tears come rolling down.

Amma hurries through the *bazaar*. The jewel is in a little leather pouch that she carries firmly under her arm. She cannot believe it, she just cannot believe it. It must be a fake. She knew that girl was no good. But it does not *look* fake. Everything she knows about jewellery... it just seems so real. And so beautiful! Each time she looks at it, it takes her breath away. Each time it looks better than before.

She is at the jeweller's, the most expensive and reliable one in the *bazaar*. She hands the jewel to the man. He is a seasoned old coot. He takes it to the back of the shop and examines it for a long time. Amma's attention wanders to the other jewels on display. Some lovely gold earrings she would like to have. But they do not compare. Nothing does.

The jeweller comes back. She knows from his suppressed excitement what the answer is going to be. He tells Amma that the jewel is the real thing, owned at one time by the Emperor Akbar and perhaps gifted to a nobleman. Amma is stunned. Her hand shakes as she takes it from him and puts it carefully back in its leather pouch.

A camel walks slowly by, picking its way expertly over baskets of goods for sale. A boy runs through the *bazaar* carrying a message.

Bengal, 1601

A lone mansion nestles in the woods. A long, muddy road leads up to it through the jungle. When it was built, it was grand, but now it looks neglected and overgrown. Carriages and horses are parked in the driveway. It is dusk. A tide of sound — of crickets and frogs — rises from the jungle and flows over the house.

Inside, a room is brightly lit. By Mughal standards it is modest, but has been artfully decorated. Sher Afghan is entertaining three friends. He is a large bearded man, a soldier and an officer. He has the privilege of being an *amir* — a nobleman — of the Empire.

The room is littered with hookahs and booze. Servants flutter about. The hookahs create a cloud of smoke that remains suspended in the middle of the room. Sher Afghan's friends are successful landowners and traders. They are better off and more self-assured than he is. The men pore over a board game of *pachisi.*

A friend called Munirji rolls a set of shells that, depending on how they land, yield a number. Munirji moves his pieces on the board. "I am afraid, my friends, I will have to charge each of you a *jizya* of two *rupiya*," he says with satisfaction. He is the type of person every group of friends should have — large and reassuring, capable of shepherding them through awkward silences.

Coins are handed over. Sher Afghan has the smallest pile of coins in front of him.

"The commission is six hundred," says Imran Das, a man who is always cautious and correct. He is telling them about some property that has recently been granted to him. "But the land is so far north, I have to send a troop of twenty men just to collect it. It costs me a hundred *rupiya* just for the collection party."

"Is it worth it?" asks Munirji.

"Oh yes! Very worth it. The people are *junglees*, but they work hard."

Imran Das throws the shells. The conversation pauses as they watch his turn.

"But I have to say it is all too tiresome at times," says Abhijit, a friend who has a sleepy, dishevelled look about him. "The first tax officer, the second officer... is there no better way?"

"You could acquire a sailing vessel," says Munirji. "If there is a way to become fabulously wealthy, it is to own a ship."

"That would be nice," Abhijit says dreamily. "How do you acquire a sailing vessel?"

"Your turn," Imran Das reminds him.

Abhijit throws the shells onto the carpet. The friends watch.

"I had invited a troupe of local dance girls tonight," Sher Afghan says abruptly in an overly-loud voice. "But sadly, the entertainment is not to be. They were at the house of the Governor yesterday, and it is a day's journey. And they could not make it here."

"We should hardly worry!" Munirji reassures him. "Our own Sheikh Abhi's verse here," slapping Abhijit on the back, "can put a trellis on the night as artful as the finest dancer."

"You are too kind," Abhijit murmurs, fiddling with one of the pieces.

There is a pause. The friends watch as Sher Afghan rolls the shells and moves his pieces.

"What about you, Sher Afghan?" Munirji asks. "You seem quiet today."

"Quiet, am I?"

"I heard you were involved in a little to do recently. What was that all about?"

"I killed a man."

There is a startled silence.

Sher Afghan tries to look nonchalant. "It's all right," he says. He takes a long puff from his hookah. "There was an argument. An aggravating little official, with whom I have had some business in the past. He was promoted recently, and was transferred to the District. And his first act on coming here was to summon me.

"When I went there, I found him waiting for me in front of a troop of twenty men. Friends, it did not look good. I thought I was done for! He walked towards me by himself. I saw my chance and attacked, knowing it would be hopeless otherwise. In an instant, his men were on me. I barely escaped with my life! But I am afraid I killed him."

The others look stunned. "Well, you are quite the *kharus ustaad*!" Munirji says finally.

"It was not my fault. I was being attacked."

"For your sake, I hope there are no consequences," says Munirji.

"All been dealt with," says Sher Afghan taking a long puff from his hookah. He lets the smoke out. "I spoke with the Governor. In any case, I think the other officers in the area are thankful. This man was not liked. There will be one less squirrel taking his cut from the rest of us."

"Is this squirrel, you speak of, the officer Qutub Uddin?"

"Yes."

"I would be careful," Munirji advises. "He has many friends in the Province."

"It is of no consequence!" Sher Afghan says dismissively. "I do not mean to spoil this fine evening with my problems." He looks around and signals to Ramji, a servant. "Dinner will be served shortly!" he announces.

The game is concluded. The men pack up the board and the shells and move to seat themselves in the dining area. Imran Das discreetly reminds Sher Afghan that he owes him twelve hundred *rupiya*. "Of course!" Sher Afghan says in a loud voice. "How can I forget?"

They are to dine at a low table placed over a strikingly red carpet with loud floral designs. The table sports place-settings with silver plates and little silver cups for each guest. The men seat themselves cross-legged around the table.

Three people enter the room in single file, carrying trays of food and wine. The first is Sher Afghan's head servant, Ramji.

The second is a woman, Nur Jahan. She is dressed in a red and gold *burkha*. Her face is exposed although her head is covered. She has the kind of beauty that makes a man look twice and not think of much else thereafter. Not the least of it is that she carries her beauty as if she is unaware of it. Her gaze is direct, disconcerting. When she speaks it is as if she is ready to touch.

She tries to meld in with the servants, but this is impossible. The men stare, distracted into silence. They watch as she puts down her tray, unloads two jugs of wine and pours them into glasses. A little unsteadily, she places a glass full of wine in front of each man.

"Allahi Akbar!" says Sher Afghan.

"Allahi Akbar," repeat the friends.

Sher Afghan motions to Munirji to start. The men serve

themselves and start to eat. But almost, immediately it is evident something is wrong. Imran Das takes a bite, suppresses a grimace, and washes the food down with a large gulp of wine. Munirji takes a bite of food and freezes in consternation.

It is Sher Afghan's turn. He puts the food into his mouth, then grimaces and sputters and coughs, spitting the food out across the carpet. "What in Allah's name is this? Ramji! Ramji! What have you put in this food?"

Ramji was trying to exit the room as quietly as possible, but now he freezes. He turns around slowly. "The lamb *shahi* —" he manages. "*Begum Saheba...* the lamb *shahi* —"

"I made the lamb *shahi* myself," Nur interjects.

Sher Afghan is incredulous. "This is lamb *shahi*? Why... why did you prepare it yourself? Why didn't you let Ramji make it, as always?"

"Because you often say you want me to cook for you. I made it as they make it in Persia."

The men suppress smiles. "They don't make food like this in the Persian court," Munirji says gently.

"They do, actually," Nur replies. "It is very plain food compared to ours."

"Yes!" Sher Afghan roars. "The Emperor Shah Abbas eats raw meat for dinner! Woman, what *shaitan* possessed you?!"

"Do you not like it? I am sorry. I thought it would be a nice surprise."

"We are surprised," Sher Afghan says. "We are all very surprised indeed! Now take this away!" He hurls the lid of the platter across the room. It hits the wall with a loud clang. Nur jumps. "And bring us some proper food!" Sher Afghan roars. Munirji puts a restraining hand on Sher Afghan's shoulder.

Nur looks flustered. "There's... there's nothing else, I'm afraid!"

Sher Afghan closes his eyes to calm himself. "Go. Just go! I do not want to see your face in here! Ramji you too! All of you! Leave me alone with my friends!"

"*Huzoor*," says Ramji. "I could quickly cook—"

"Leave! Leave! Leave! Leave!"

Nur walks over to the fallen lid and picks it up. She does a *salamat* to the men and leaves. Her retreating figure looks small and sorry.

There is a long silence.

Sher Afghan starts laughing. There is a touch of hysteria in his voice. "When she cooks a piece of meat," he sputters, "she succeeds in making it taste like a shoe! Friends, I think I have married a man from Persia! She has no womanly graces whatsoever. You know... you know we have not made love in two years!" Sher Afghan slaps his thigh as if the joke is too precious for words. "Whenever I am with her, she is always standing two yards away. When I hug her, it is like hugging a block of marble!"

"Surely, she must have some accomplishments," Abhijit says.

"Accomplishments! Yes, yes! She does have accomplishments. She knows how to spend good money on these—" He picks up a clay statue of Shiva and hurls it across the room. The statue hits a wall and shatters. "Ungodly idols that she scatters about the house like rice in a field."

The Hindus among the friends pale at this affront, but they stay silent.

"What else... what else!" Sher Afghan goes on. "She knows how to ride a horse. I will give her that. And she knows how to block access to her father. You must think, friends, that I am very lucky indeed, being married to the daughter of Itimad Ud Daulah! You must think I am in a position of high privilege being married to the daughter of the Prime Minister, must you not? Friends, look at me!" says Sher Afghan beating his chest excitedly. "Where am I?"

The friends look at one another trying to hazard a guess.

"I am in Bengal! The Toilet of the Universe!"

Munirji tries to choose the words with which to protest, but Sher Afghan has moved on. "The Prime Minister's own daughter and son-in-law have been relegated to Bengal!"

"But surely—"

"This is my reward for being married to her! But does she speak to her father about it? No! No! No! We cannot do that! The Prime Minister has to dispense justice. With objectivity! He has a position to maintain. His mind cannot be disturbed by thought of kin, not even his own daughter and son-in-law.

"So we live in neglect, in deepest darkest Bengal. Because the great Prime Minister is too busy, doing his prime ministerly duties!"

The others are silent. The room appears to ring with Sher Afghan's voice.

"Well," Munirji says finally. "I suppose we shall have to do without the lamb *shahi*. The others laugh, relieved. "Abhiji, your mind must be working. But I believe... something is coming to me. Wait, wait—" He closes his eyes.

"Dancers that might have been...
To enliven the night,
Lamb shahi returned to Persia
Ere it could take flight..."

"What do you think?" Munirji asks proudly.

Abhijit stares sleepily at the rug in front of him. Then abruptly he recites:

"Men with long faces
Sit wistfully dreaming
That ships filled with gold
Might give them some feeling."

The others look surprised, offended. Then as the words sink in, their looks turn to ones of grudging admiration.

"*Wah wah!*" Munirji says softly.

"*Wah wah!*" Imran Das echoes.

They do not sleep till late. The night's events have wound them up, rather than tire them out. It is one o'clock in the morning. Nur is folding clothes. Sher Afghan is sitting up in bed and writing. The room has two low beds against opposite walls.

"You embarrassed me tonight," Sher Afghan says.

"You embarrassed me," Nur replies without looking up.

Sher Afghan shakes his head. He decides to be generous and let it go. "Here is what I want you to write." He reads from the letter he has been composing. "'Dear Father. We are suffering here in our post in Bengal. The land is barren, the yield is small, and the country dangerous. When we married, the dowry that was due to us should have been at minimum 50,000 *rupiya* with a rank of one thousand *zat*—'," he corrects himself, "'one thousand *zat* for my *husband*. Instead, you gave us no money and just a few trinkets in jewellery. You have wronged me. And you have wronged my husband, Sher Afghan. You can easily right this wrong by providing some redress in the form of a token sum, but, more importantly, by recommending my husband for a higher rank to the Emperor. It is not much we ask...'."

Sher Afghan pauses, looking over his handiwork. "Then add, 'Further, we are most desirous of being closer to Agra. My husband will *benefit* from being close to Court, where his true talents will show, leading to rapid advancement and promotion!' What do you think?"

Nur has been avoiding his gaze. She looks up now from the clothes she has been folding. "I have already told you. I cannot let my father compromise his position with the Emperor, just because it suits us."

Sher Afghan puts down his writing and stands up. Nur retreats a little, lowering her hands.

"Mehrunissa," he says, using her familiar name.

"Yes."

"Are you my wife?"

"Yes," she whispers.

"Then why can you not do this for me?"

"Because our wedding is over and done with. I cannot keep asking my father for favours on its account."

With a practised movement Sher Afghan moves across the room and seizes a riding crop that has been hanging on the wall. "Do you consider..." he swings the crop, a loud whack resounds as it hits her skin, "...depriving me of my— WHACK — birthright, being over and done with?! Or would you rather fulfil your duties as my —WHACK — wife?!" Nur is not surprised by the violence. She bears the lashes stoically, bracing herself each time.

"What have you done with our money so far!" she cries. "We are twenty thousand *rupiya* in debt!"

"Exactly! If I had my correct and dutiful dowry right now, we could have wiped out our debt and made a real start in life. But I cannot do that with a wife who does not—" WHACK "—cook, or—" WHACK "—obey, or—" WHACK "—make love!" The blood shows from a welt from under her clothes. More than anything she is embarrassed, humiliated.

"Why don't you divorce me!" she shouts. "I dare you! Divorce me right now!"

"Divorce you?" His voice is silken. "I will kill you first, my dear. Long before I divorce you."

They look at each other like opponents.

"Leave this room," he says picking up the letter. "I don't want you sleeping next to me."

She is glad to do this. She picks up a pillow and blanket and rushes out of the room.

The morning mist rises as the house sits still in the woods. There is a faint sound. A door has opened. Nur emerges from the house. She walks through the woods along a barely visible path. The path twists this way and that. There is no hesitation in the way she walks. She knows her way well.

Abruptly, the woods end. She is at the edge of a grassy meadow.

There is a little clearing. A turbaned man with a trim moustache is squatting on the ground next to two saddled horses. Jagat Singh is making himself a *paan*.

Nur walks past him without looking at him. She breaks into a run, mounts a horse and is off.

Jagat Singh drops his *paan*, runs to the other horse and follows Nur. They set off with a shower of stones, their horses galloping across the lush Bengal countryside. The meadow is interlaced with an open swamp. Bordering it is a dense jungle, marked by the tangled trunks of sprawling hundred-year-old trees. Leopards hide in the undergrowth. There is a sudden flash of red as a flock of rosefinches rises from the meadow. They fly low in an undulating red cloud that skims the water and disappears into the trees.

Jagat Singh is a little behind Nur. Nur clears a fallen tree trunk. Jagat Singh follows. She comes to a wide pond and spurs her horse to jump across the pond. They do not make it. The horse lands in the water. Nur struggles to get to the other side. Jagat Singh is more circumspect. He gives the horse a good clean run before the jump. The horse's legs stretch across the pond and its hooves just barely make it to the soft mud on the other side. He is over. He starts gaining on Nur, crowding her.

Nur disturbs a herd of spotted deer. The deer break into a run, making springy leaps across the misty grass. She comes to an abrupt halt in a clearing. From the side of her horse, she draws a shield and a wooden stick. Jagat Singh overshoots, comes back. He draws his own stick.

Without pausing, she attacks him. She swings the stick hard. There is a loud clack as her stick hits his. She swings again. Another clack as he defends himself. Jagat Singh swings. His stick hits her shield with such force it pushes her backward.

Undeterred, she attacks fiercely. She is almost on top of him. He dodges the blow, and hits her with a loud thwack across her shoulder. She winces in pain.

They pause, squaring off. She regards him warily. A feint, and a surprise attack. She lands a blow on his arm. He cries out and drops the stick. She swings again, trying to finish him off, but flails in the empty air. He has ducked below his horse, and, amazingly, having picked up the stick, has moved away

She passes by him, turns after twenty feet, and begins a fearsome charge. He ducks and gets a clean shot with his stick across her ribs. Her horse stops dead to keep from colliding with his. She flies through the air, somersaults, and lands, hitting her head on the ground.

She is knocked out cold. Blood wells up through her clothes, from the base of her shoulder. A fallen branch has cut her, leaving a deep gash.

Jagat Singh gets off his horse and runs up to her, horrified. "*Begum Saheba*! *Begum Saheba*!" He is afraid to touch her. Finally he dares to put his hand on the wound, trying to stop the blood. He runs to his horse, gets a goat-skin filled with water. He sprinkles this on her face; then tries to make her drink some, all the time trying to place his hand on her wound.

She splutters, starts coughing, and opens her eyes. "Oooowwww! Uuuh!" She sees the blood on his hand. "Did you get hurt?"

"No, *Begum*. This is from you."

"Uuhhh! My head hurts. Feel if my head is okay." He hesitates, not sure if it would be proper.

"Chha-chha!" she says impatiently, and, taking his hand, makes him feel her head. She releases his hand, and touches her shoulder. Her hand is covered with blood. "Oh Allah! Give me your turban."

"What?"

"Give me your turban."

He hastily removes his turban. She tries to tie it around her shoulder. He comes to her aid and manages to fashion a bandage.

"Help me get up." With his help she stands up shakily. She

20

starts walking painfully back to her horse with Jagat Singh supporting her. She looks pale from the shock. "You won," she says.

"*Begum*?"

"The battle. If we had swords, I would be dead right now."

"*Begum*, don't say that! What will we do! How will we explain this to *Huzoor Sah'b*!"

She looks amused. "Don't worry. I won't tell."

"But he will see this!"

"Oh, I will blame it on him. He beats me when he is drunk. I will say he hurt me last night, does he not remember?"

Jagat Singh helps Nur onto her horse.

The house is soaking in the monsoon rain. The rain is relentless, falling straight down hour after hour. There is a sound of galloping hooves along the driveway. A postman comes to a noisy halt near the front door. He takes a leather pouch out of the saddle-bag and removes an official-looking sealed letter. He hands it to the servant who opens the door.

A shout of excitement emerges from within the house. Sher Afghan has opened the document. "Ramji! Jagat Singh! Everyone! Come here! I have news for you!" The servants file in, forming a straggly audience. Nur hangs back, standing behind Jagat Singh.

Sher Afghan passes his hand over the letter as if he cannot believe it exists. "There has been a *firman*!" he says looking around at them. "It is from the Emperor! I have received it. I shall read it to you."

Reverently Sher Afghan holds the letter up. "'By order of His Imperial Majesty'," he reads. "'His Divine Grace, the Emperor Akbar, Ruler of Ajmer, Punjab, Allahabad, Marwar...' it goes on, 'You! Sher Afghan! Have been commanded to provide, in the service of the Emperor, a cavalry of a hundred and fifty horses...' it goes on, 'Your duties and obligations...' It goes on. 'As compensation for the performance of your forsworn duties your Rank has been Raised to —'," Sher Afghan looks disappointed, "'Two hundred *zat*. To this extent you shall collect revenues from the district of Mirzapur...'," He looks up. "Mirzapur! Where is Mirzapur! Mehru, bring the map!"

"It is three days journey from Agra," Nur says.

"Three days journey from Agra! Three days journey from Agra!" he says excitedly. "Ha Ha Ha!" he roars, "Friends, I am going to Mirzapur!! Mehru! Pack up the household!" He looks from face to face, surprised at the servants' ambivalence.

"When do we have to leave?" Nur asks.

He has not thought of this. Feverishly he fumbles with the document almost dropping it. He reads it rapidly. "Immediately!" he cries exultantly. "We have to leave immediately!"

Something catches his eye. He turns the document over, looking at it from different angles. "This *firman* is from your brother, Asaf Khan. Not your father." He frowns puzzled. Then the mystery clears itself up. "I forgot! I had written to him a long time ago."

A strange, unreadable expression crosses Nur's face. Sher Afghan does not see it. He is looking at the servants wondering why they are still standing around. A thought occurs to him. "We will take Ramji with us. The rest of you should find work elsewhere."

He claps his hands dismissively. "Mehru, let us make preparations!"

Nur turns to Ramji. "Bring the carriage out to the front," she orders.

"Where are you going?" Sher Afghan asks without much interest.

Nur twirls around smiling. "To the bazaar. There are preparations to be made."

"Good!" Sher Afghan says distractedly. "Good! Good! Make your preparations. Let me see—" He looks around, knowing he should be doing something.

Outside, it is misty. The rain has receded to a drizzle. A masked figure dressed in a black cloak, emerges from the woods. The figure draws a sword, and slips into the house through an open window.

Nur and Ramji are seated in a *tonga*, a two-wheeled horse carriage. Its leather and wooden parts make loud creaking sounds as it sets off down the driveway.

The house sits alone in the woods, now visible, now hidden by the mist. More masked figures emerge from the dense vegetation. Each man enters the house through a different window or door, as if to surround and contain their quarry.

From inside the house, there erupt the sounds of a violent fight. Men collide and struggle. Swords clash, steel on steel. "Somebody! Help!" The voice of Sher Afghan is desperate. "Aaaaghhh!"

A man screams loudly as he is sent to his death, a sword driven through his body. Someone is slammed violently against a wall, bringing down shields, swords, and a bronze statue. The collective crash of metal objects hitting the stone floor seems to explode into the forest air. There is the loud, crisp clang of a sword on sword.

"Somebody! Help!" Sher Afghan shouts again. There are more sounds of a scuffle. "*Help!*"

A sword hits human flesh. A man groans as he is stabbed in the abdomen.

"Aaarrrggghhh!" Sher Afghan roars. His voice is angry, defiant. Not one of the earth's meek denizens, if he is to go to his death, it will be with the noise and commotion of a lion.

"Aaarrrggghhh!" he cries again. The sounds of the scuffle continue. Another clang of sword on sword is heard, as the wounds accumulate. "Aaaarrrgggh!" he cries, his voice weak.

Silence descends over the house, almost as suddenly as the noise had begun. Mist rises from the ground. The sound of rain dripping down the clay tiles and gurgling through the copper gutters seems louder than ever.

The road to the *bazaar* is twelve miles long. Nur and Ramji ride in silence, the *tonga* creaking over the bumps in the rough country lane. Presently, they hear a horse coming at them at full gallop. That strange, unreadable expression crosses Nur's face again.

Jagat Singh comes to a noisy halt next to the *tonga*.

"*Begum Saheba*!" Jagat Singh calls sternly. "Sher Afghan is dead! Killed! By swordsmen. In the house!

Nur covers her mouth with her hand, suddenly nauseous.

"Dead?" says Ramji.

"Dead!" Jagat Singh repeats sternly. "Murdered! By swordsmen!"

"Ramji!" Nur gasps. "Back, to the house!"

"*Begum*, it is not a good sight," Jagat Singh says. "I will call the soldiers—"

"No! I have to see. To the house!"

Some twenty minutes later, the half-ajar door to the house creaks as it is pushed open.. Nur, Ramji, and Jagat Singh walk silently through the rooms. The house is destroyed. Large parts of the carpet are soaked in blood. A trail of blood, marks a spot where someone was killed and the copiously bleeding body was dragged away.

Next to a wall, surrounded by an enormous pool of blood lies the body of Sher Afghan. His head is nearly separated from his body. Only the back of his head still seems attached. His eyes are open.

Nur covers her mouth with her hand. She looks down at Sher Afghan for a very long time. The two servants stand silently watching her. At length, she reaches over and closes his eyes.

She straightens up and continues to look at him.

"*Begum*," Ramji interrupts softly. "What will happen now?"

She looks away, suddenly remote. It is as if she has become a different person. "My husband is dead," she says. "My life is over."

Allahabad, 1604

The city of colourful tents that is Jahangir's Army of thirty thousand, covers an area of twelve square miles. To the kites that circle busily overhead, looking for scraps, it must seem like a vast checkerboard spread over the countryside. The tents are laid out in a precise pattern forming a grid of alleyways through which it is easy to ride. When the army moves camp, the tents at the new location are laid out in precisely the same pattern, so that one is never at a loss finding one's way through the camp. Each block of tents is marked by a set of flags that indicate the type of unit, the signature of the *amir* or noble who commands the unit, and the rank of the *amir*. Even the colours of the tents have meanings.

Towards the front of the checkerboard, is the complex of immaculately coloured tents and bright flags that make up Jahangir's camp. His commanding officers' tents are close by, as are the open areas laid out with straw and feed for their animals — twenty-three elephants, standing, kneeling, or lying on the ground, and a hundred and fifty Arab horses. The elephants are being scrubbed and readied by their keepers. Large, decorated harnesses are cast over their shoulders by the men. There is something in the air. A hint of impending action.

Immediately behind the area reserved for Jahangir is the royal harem. When the army is on the move, the highest-ranking royal ladies ride atop elephants with closed *howdahs*. Lesser noble-women make do with horses or camels, wearing *burkhas* that cover them from head to foot. Lower-caste female help, who provide crucial and heroic support to the army at all levels, are crammed into bullock carts and ride at the back. The rising cadence of women's voices can be heard outside the harem tents. The morning is hot and the women are quarrelsome.

Expanding outward from this core are blocks upon blocks of fighting units — mounted archers and lancers, infantry men, and artillery. Each artillery unit is armed with a single-cast bronze cannon mounted on a special carriage, and pulled by two enormous bulls. The mounted archers, most of them Afghan horsemen, are practised at riding in front of the enemy at high speed while shooting arrows with deadly accuracy.

The back of the checkerboard is for supporting this city-on-the-move. Vast fires cook meals for thousands. A haze of thick smoke rises, even now, into the bright, blue sky. A mile-and-a-half of drying clothes attest to the upkeep of the soldiers' full-skirted uniforms.

Most of the fifteen thousand fighting men of the army are Rajput warriors. An overlay of Muslim adventurers — Afghans, Turks, Persians — act in key roles. The Afghans form crack cavalry troops, the Turks are world-class gunners, and the Persians fill the upper ranks of nobles and generals. The Persians notwithstanding, there is no particular bar for a talented officer to advance. Some of the highest-ranking and most respected commanders are Rajputs. It is a diverse army.

The elaborately decorated elephants stand out above the checkerboard. The mid-morning sun beats down on the parched central Indian plain. In front of Jahangir's tent complex is a makeshift stage, ten feet high. Jahangir's personal flags fly from each corner. In front of the stage are assembled Jahangir's three hundred *mansabhdars* — captains. They stand attentive, facing the stage, perfectly outfitted, ready for battle.

A band starts playing, so loudly and abruptly, some of the men start. Eight enormous drums and four long battle-horns beat out a fierce marching tune.

Jahangir, surrounded by his commanding officers, steps onto the stage. He is a slight young man with a darkness about him. There are so many dignitaries on stage, it is hard to tell which one is Jahangir. To his immediate right is Mahabat Khan, the commanding general of Jahangir's Army. To his left is Asaf Khan, a civilian advisor. In the hot sun, the men look sweaty and grim.

The band stops playing. Mahabat Khan steps forward. He is handsome and dashing, to the extent that his good looks make him seem frivolous. "Amirs! Captains of the Army of Hindustan!" he shouts. "His Highness! Ruler of Gujarat! And of Ajmer! Prince Salim!" Mughal custom allows a person of royal birth to have more than one name. Jahangir's present name is Salim.

"*Salamat!*" shout the assembled captains.

Jahangir steps forward and regards the captains. "Comrades-in-arms," he says casually. "Today is the day. The stars favour us."

He pauses, looking at the sweating faces. "My father, the Emperor, spends his days in religious fantasies. He neglects the work of the Empire. He calls himself Allah. My fellow soldiers, there is no Allah, but Allah! No Shiva, but Shiva! No Vishnu, but Vishnu! No Brahma, but Brahma! Some say my father is losing his mind. I say he is getting old.

"It is time for us to free ourselves from the shackles of the past and march into the future. New conquests await us. Bountiful lands! Gold! Silver! Pearls! Riches such as you have never seen! They all await us.

"Today, I proclaim a new Hindustan! One free of my father's illusions and his strange fancies! One that will spread its golden magic and its riches over all lands! Praise be to Hindustan! Empire of the Sun! Empire of Allah!" Jahangir pauses.

Mahabat Khan steps forward again. "Soldiers in arms!" He points to Jahangir. "I proclaim! Before you! Our new Emperor! Emperor Salim! Sultan Salim *zindabad*!"

There is no reply. A confused murmur sweeps through the assembled men.

Mahabat Khan repeats assertively, "Sultan Salim *zindabad*!"

"*Zindabad*," the captains repeat softly, hesitantly.

"Sultan Salim *Zindabad*!" Mahabat Khan shouts in a strong, rousing voice, raising the call to rebellion.

"*Zindabad*!" the captains repeat, louder, but still reluctant.

The high-ranking commanders on the stage simultaneously draw their swords and raise them above Jahangir's head, as if anointing him.

"Sultan Salim *Zindabad*!" Mahabat Khan shouts forcefully to the hesitant captains.

"*Zindabad*!" the captains repeat loudly, obediently.

"Sultan Salim *Zindabad*!"

"*Zindabad*!"

"Troopers!" Mahabat Khan shouts. "We march to Agra! We capture the Treasury!" In his commander's voice he shouts, "All! De-camp! Forward! To Agra!"

The eight drums beat in time. The assembled captains disperse rapidly, suddenly burdened with the task of de-camping.

With the practice and speed of a lifetime on the move, the army prepares to march. Entire blocks of tents seem to collapse all at once. Elephants are lined up, their harnesses tightened, their passengers ready. Troops of cavalry arrange themselves in marching order. The cannon crews place rope harnesses on the bulls that will pull the bronze cannon. Trains of bullock carts are loaded with supplies. The train of supply carts, several miles long, containing gigantic bins of animal feed, food, weapons, ammunition, repair-kits, even cisterns full of water, are readied for travel. Flocks of birds feast on the scraps on the ground and rise skywards, with a great fluttering of wings.

In short order, the army starts marching. The troops in the front start moving, expanding forward in a broad phalanx, half a mile across. It is six hours before the rear, consisting of long columns of bullock carts, trains of burdened donkeys and herds of goats, is also moving.

They move through fields and farms. The drums beat loudly, rhythmically, setting the pace. They march from early dawn, through the day, and late into the evening until it is too dark to see. As night falls, they camp temporarily in line, ready to march again in a few hours.

Only Jahangir's tent has been fully pitched. It glows like a large Chinese lantern in the dark. Inside, Jahangir and Mahabat Khan are poring over a map. Jahangir is in a hurry to get to Agra. "We can go through Chattarpur," Mahabat Khan points on the map. "But the country is very rough—"

They are interrupted. A captain and a guard enter with a prisoner, Balaji. "Your Highness! The prisoner," the captain announces.

"Ah yes!" Jahangir stands up. "I was looking forward to seeing you. You have displeased us."

The prisoner is quaking with fear. "Your Highness, forgive me!" He prostrates himself at Jahangir's feet. "Please forgive me! I will repay! I will repay!"

"You can get up," Jahangir says. Balaji gets up apprehensively. "I suppose we could fine you and make some money — what is your name?"

"B-Balaji."

"Balaji. This is not the time for some silly rumour to be going through my army about the master of supplies putting away a little on the side. You understand me, do you not?"

"M-mercy, your Highness!" Balaji blubbers. "Mercy!"

Jahangir turns to the captain. "Tie him to the leg of an elephant and have him walk behind." He sits down and picks up the map.

"Your Highness!" Balaji protests in terror.

"The short route," Jahangir says to Mahabat Khan.

"Your Highness!" Balaji begs. "You are condemning me to my death!"

Jahangir looks up, annoyed at being interrupted. The captain and the guard grab Balaji. They hold his arms in a ruthless lock and start dragging him out of the tent. Balaji struggles trying to use his legs to stay inside the tent. "You are condemning me to my death!" he cries. The Captain and the guard pull him roughly away. Balaji's shouts turn into screams. "You are condemning me to my death! You are condemning me to my death!" His screams fade as he is dragged swiftly, to his extinction.

There is silence inside the tent.

"Chattarpur," Jahangir reminds Mahabat Khan.

Mahabat Khan is looking at Jahangir. "There was no need for that," he says.

Jahangir returns Mahabat Khan's gaze with one of his own. "It is not you who is going to be king."

Early the next morning, the march resumes. By nine o'clock, the sun is already very hot. Balaji is being dragged behind an elephant with a long rope attached to its harness. Practical by training, the Captain has re-interpreted Jahangir's order to mean the elephant's harness, as opposed to its leg. Balaji's head and shoulders stir up the dusty earth as he is dragged. To all appearances, he is already dead.

By afternoon, the army has to negotiate a rocky ravine. This is one of the hazards of taking the short route through Chattarpur. The ravine is long and narrow. Its bottom is strewn with small boulders. The massive phalanx of Jahangir's Army narrows and elongates. Elephants, horses descend slowly, picking their way cautiously among the boulders.

A bullock cart is stuck, its wheel broken, jammed inside a

crevice between rocks. There is nothing to be done but to push it out. Ten soldiers get off their horses to help. But the cart does not move. A soldier runs to get an elephant.

By evening, the army is still crawling slowly along the ravine. The drums mark the pace, pushing the marchers along.

The huge sun sets behind a ridge bordering one side of the ravine. At the centre of the sun on the ridge, sword drawn, is the silhouette of a lone horseman.

It seems that within the blink of an eye, the single horseman has become six men. Each of the six is armed with a long matchlock. The marchers below take a second unbelieving look at the silhouette of the ridge against the setting sun. Now it seems the entire ridge is covered by a line of horsemen. The line has gaps. At the centre of each gap is the ugly shape of a cannon, its barrel pointed directly at them.

The drums fade. Jahangir and his commanders look around in consternation. The opposite ridge, the one with the sun fully lighting its face, is empty. Nobody there. They look ahead. Their path is blocked by a line of infantry with long lances bristling through the scrub. Mahabat Khan wheels his horse around and draws his sword. Jahangir grabs his matchlock and stands up on his elephant.

Suddenly, they hear distant music. An elephant is walking across the valley floor, coming straight towards Jahangir's troops at a leisurely pace. It carries an enclosed red *howdah* on top. Surrounding it, is a small troop of cavalry, arrows drawn, matchlocks pointed. Something about this new army makes Jahangir's look amateurish.

The elephant stops. The music stops. There is silence across the valley floor, as if the events unfolding are too important to disturb. Attendants run up to the elephant carrying a set of steps. Akbar descends slowly from the red howdah. He is burdened with a gastrointestinal problem and is in evident pain. He has difficulty walking. He starts the long walk towards Jahangir, alone and unarmed.

Slowly Jahangir lowers his musket. He slides off the elephant and walks towards Akbar.

Akbar has a genial smile. He extends his arms wide.

Warily, Jahangir approaches. Father and son hug.

"I have something to show you," Akbar says. He fishes in his pockets and takes out an English chronometer. It is large and round with a polished wood casing. Inside, it is all metal and glass. It ticks crisply.

Jahangir looks at the strange object.

"The *firangis* use it to guide their ships across the ocean. Ingenious! But I have thought of another use for it. You see, it tells you the time. It tells you *English* time. Now who but a madman would want that?! But I have changed the setting on it, so that it tells you *our* time.

"Now when you send your scouts over the hill, you look at the time. And then — you check this — if two hours later, they have not returned, you group your army, surround it with cannon, and prepare very seriously for an attack... from the direction in which your scouts have disappeared..." Akbar has a way of making words trail away into the air, and then sink slowly. "Don't worry," he reassures Jahangir. "We did not kill them. Man Singh is too kind."

He grabs Jahangir's sleeve. "Sit down."

Jahangir does not understand. Inside, the emptiness he dreads is returning.

"Here, on the ground! Sit, sit!" Akbar moves to sit on the ground with some difficulty. He is seated at last. They sit cross-legged on the ground across from each other.

"It is a beautiful evening, is it not?" Akbar says. A small flock of egrets choose this moment to fly over the ravine. White, and dainty, they look incongruous as they flap their wings over the bristling lancers, archers, and cannon. "I believe that is a family of cranes going home to supper."

Akbar picks up a twig and starts drawing a map of the valley in the mud. "Your first mistake was to announce to your troops that you were going to be Emperor when they, poor fellows, were feeling very tired. Never tell tired men something new. They cannot absorb it. They get irritable.

"Your second mistake was to bring your troops through this particular valley. Now granted, you were in a hurry. After making your rash announcement that you were going to be Emperor, you had to move quickly. But to come through at sunset! Without first securing that hill over there? *Oaf! Oaf!* How many men do you have?"

"Thirty thousand," Jahangir says out of the emptiness of his soul.

"Thirty thousand! Take away ten thousand for the help and the harem. Another five thousand for your generals' lies, and you have fifteen thousand actual fighting men. Do you know how many men I brought?

"Ten thousand."

"I brought just five thousand men. Now you—" Akbar draws with the twig. "What do you have to the rear of your army? Cooks? Women? How many men do I need to stop your cooks?"

Jahangir is at a loss.

"I put just three hundred infantry, add a few cannon, to your back. Now from the western slope with the sun in your eyes—" Akbar draws again. "I launch my main attack. How many men do I place on the other slope? None! It is a steep slope, and you cannot escape by running up a slope. So where will your men run, while being rained upon by my arrows and cannon?"

"To the front," Jahangir says to please his father.

"To the front. So that is where I put my lancers. Two thousand of them. As you run forward into my prickly lancers, my cavalry charges down the hill with such force, they cut you in—" Akbar draws with the twig, "—half!"

Jahangir is silent. He stares at the drawing.

"Help me get up," Akbar says. Jahangir gives him a hand. They walk towards Akbar's elephant. Helpers start to approach, but Akbar motions them away.

"Ugh! Don't get old," Akbar says, struggling to walk.

"Those birds. They were not cranes. They were egrets. From the Sariska forest."

Akbar does not reply.

Jahangir presses his point. "You were wrong."

"I have been wrong about many things," Akbar replies mildly. "As part of your punishment, I am relieving you of the Governorship of Surat."

"Surat!" Jahangir says in alarm. "You cannot do that! Surat is mine!"

Akbar slaps Jahangir with such power that Jahangir staggers back. "Yours, is it? What else is yours?" He slaps Jahangir again. Jahangir falls to his knees. Akbar grabs his hair and picks him up. "Is all of Hindustan yours also?"

Jahangir scrambles, looking like a little boy being punished.

"I heard you just announced that." Slap! "*Harami*! Pig! Call yourself fit to be king! Do you know what that means! Do you have the slighest idea what that means?" He lets go of Jahangir.

Jahangir stares at the ground on all fours, not daring to get up. If he gets up, he thinks, he will have to face his father.

"I could have you executed for treason!" He kicks him ineffectively. "You shame me! You shame me in front of my soldiers! In front of my family!! "Guard!" he shouts, "put this wretch on a horse and bring him to court!"

Akbar strides off.

Jahangir remains where he is. The men move deferentially to arrest him.

It is a high-class public house, one where a noble, a soldier-of-fortune, or a well-heeled trader may slip away and enjoy a few hours of anonymous bliss. It is on a street, which is part of the *bazaar.* Crowds of people walk past the entrance. At this late hour of the evening there are stalls doing a brisk business yet, selling fortunes, weapons, jewellery, and fruits. The oil-lamps lighting the shops glow like large fireflies in the dark.

There is a hint of excitement in the evening, as the patrons climb the steps into the Public House. Inside, the cavernous room has a large open space in the centre. The customers settle into the cushions propped up against the walls. They let out extravagant puffs of smoke from *hookahs,* and are served wine by prostitutes dressed in brightly-coloured *ghagra-cholis.*

Two musicians sit to one side of the room, playing the *tabla* and *sarodh,* filling the air with a slow anticipatory beat.

A compère walks to the centre of the room. He is a young man with a slight beard that has refused to grow. He is dressed in white and wears a white girdle, so that he might stand out. He raises his arms for attention. "Nobles! Lords! Esteemed guests! Pandit Chandra on the *tabla*! Ustad Dalayat on the *sarodh*!"

There is absent-minded applause. The din of conversation in the room continues. The open space remains empty. The music continues.

Four dancers enter the room. They walk to the centre of the floor and take their positions. Their sexuality lights up the room. Their waists are exposed, their *cholis* light, translucent. There are no smiles. They are scowling from the hostility and the competition. Paru has a knot in her stomach. She can sense Pithu just two steps from her. She looks so perfect with her makeup; her classically chiselled features, her perfect dancer's stance. How can Paru possibly match up to her? The audience is hooting in anticipation.

The music quickens. The girls wait. They stand still for so many beats that the audience gets impatient and claps and hoots.

Then suddenly, the girls join the *tabla*'s beat. The four sets of feet move in perfect unison. The anklets add a loud *chhum, chhum, chhum,* to the music. The excitement is gut-level. The *tabla* starts to colour its beat with virtuoso variations. The girls do likewise with their feet. The dance is a free-form variation of *kathak.* Towards the end, the beat quickens even more. The girls spin rapidly across the floor, their feet and anklets moving in rapid question-answer, their hands and upper-body movements in surprising symmetries.

The dance climaxes. They spin eight times in the interstices of a single beat, again, and again, and again, and again. They come to a stomping halt, each back in her original spot, breasts heaving from the exertion.

The compère steps forward, raising his arms once again. "And now for the competition! The winner gets everything."

The girls stand still in their spots. The compère and an assistant use a chalk to draw a circle around each girl.

The *tabla* starts a new *taal.* The girls start dancing. But as the *taal* progresses, each colours her classical moves with an indefinable seductiveness. The moves seem deceptively like the old moves, only now the audience can think of nothing other than their arousing bodies.

The coins start landing in each girl's circle, in ones and twos at first. The girls step up the seduction. More coins are thrown into the circles. Pithu opens her mouth and touches her tongue to her lip. Her hips undulate with a fluidity that seems impossible for a human. Paru sways her hips, but cannot reach the total sexual abandon that Pithu achieves. The other girls are just as strong. It is hard for the gratified audience to decide who is better.

Occasionally a coin hits a girl's body. This is the source of much glee. The girl uses this distraction to engage the thrower in a look.

Paru does not get a single coin. She makes a supreme effort. Moves her breasts in rhythm with her waist, makes a connection from her breasts to the hungry men a few feet away.

A single coin lands in her circle. She steps up the seduction. She gets an idea. With her red-painted lips she makes a circle, as if she is kissing the boy in the white dhoti with whom she first made love. She moves her mouth rhythmically back and forth, closing her eyes imagining the boy's body close to hers, his breath on her cheek, swaying her hips, moving her legs still to the choreography of the dance moves.

There are hoots and claps. A rain of coins pelts down into her circle. Coins hit her waist and breasts. She is surprised at how much the heavy coins hurt.

Suddenly, Pithu leaves her circle and punches Paru very hard in the stomach. The air leaves Paru's lungs. She doubles over. The crowd roars its approval.

Pithu is back in her circle, a look of ruthlessness and triumph on her face as she sways her hips to her hungry admirers.

Paru stares at the floor for a few seconds. She feels sick. The compère stands between them, ensuring no counter-attack. Slowly, Paru straightens herself. She resumes dancing, tentatively at first, more seductively as she regains her strength. Gasping, she makes an enticing face, hoping the patrons find it attractive.

She is moving her feet in sync with the choreography, her anklets going *chhum, chhum, chhum*. She feels the sweat on her brow. She gasps, struggling a little desperately for each breath. She is behind in her collection of coins. But they start pouring in again, perhaps out of sympathy. She sways her hips feeling bolder. She gets another idea.

Slowly she reaches behind her back and starts undoing the ties of her *choli*.

The other girls look uneasy. The compère lets her continue, then has second thoughts. He walks to the side to confer with some patrons about the rules.

Paru has loosened all the ties of her *choli*. She sees the audience's rapt attention and feels emboldened, triumphant.

She raises her arms. She stamps her feet with force. The *choli* slips slowly, and deliberately, off her body. The patrons roar their approval. Her small, succulent breasts are on perfect display, sending a thrill through the bright lights. Still she dances, classical and correct. She does not smile, focusing instead on a pure sexual connection with her audience.

A shower of coins lands in her circle, hitting her body, breasts, legs. She braces for the pain, knowing it is good.

The music stops. The girls stand still, struggling for breath. The compère and his assistant start counting the coins in each circle. Paru picks up her *choli*, puts it on again.

The compère has finished the count for the third girl. "Two *rupiya* twelve *anas!*" he announces. The crowd applauds.

The assistant stands up with the count for the fourth girl. "Two *rupiya* two *anas!*" The fourth girl's face falls. The crowd makes a series of sighing sympathetic noises in her support. A drunk noble stands up, shouts something, and laughs loudly.

The compère has completed Paru's count. "Three *rupiya*, six *anas!*" There is a loud cheer. Paru's face lights up. She ventures a smile and raises her hands.

The compère's assistant has finished the count for Pithu. "Three *rupiya* eight *anas!!*" There is a house-splitting roar from the patrons. Paru is crushed.

The compère holds up Pithu's hand and displays her triumphantly to the audience. "And the winner is Devi Prithvirani!" he shouts. Pithu looks as if it is raining happiness. The disappointed girls have to rake up the coins in their circle and move them to Pithu's circle. Pithu sits on the floor and fills a large leather bag with the coins.

The compère raises his hands again. "It is time to show your love for the beautiful ladies." The fourth girl steps forward. "What do you say to the beautiful — Seva!" The girl sways her hips and teases the audience.

"Eight *anas!*" shouts a patron with a white beard.

"Eight anas. Do I hear more?" calls out the compère.

"Ten *anas!*" shouts the drunk noble who had laughed loudly.

"Ten anas. The beautiful Seva going for ten *anas*—"

"One *rupiya*," shouts an earnest-looking captain, still wearing his turban and soldier's uniform.

"One *rupiya*. Going for one *rupiya*, do I hear more — going for one *rupiya*." The compère claps his hands conclusively. "Sold! For one *rupiya*!" The captain takes the fourth girl's hand and leads her away.

Paru is up next. She steps up expectantly to the compère. She pouts. The patrons laugh and clap for her.

It is late. Paru and Pithu are walking home, each to the temporary quarters she has found after graduating from the dance class. The moon is three-quarters full, dominant and bright in a cloudless sky.

Paru is in a great mood. "He was fat!" she says. "Almost crushed me! I said I would only do it if I could sit on top of him."

"Did he let you?" Pithu, by contrast, is quiet.

"Yes. He was so drunk. I just pushed him, and he rolled right over!" Paru giggles, recalling. "Halfway, he got tired. But I kept going and going! He had to beg me to stop! How was yours?"

"He smelt of garlic. I could not stand it after the first five minutes." Pithu looks away. Paru does not notice. She smiles to herself thinking of her overwhelmed lover.

"That was a mean trick you played," she says remembering another part of the evening.

The statement cheers Pithu. "Yes," she smiles. "It was a mean trick."

"Another night, another fight," Paru challenges.

Pithu's smile widens. "We'll see."

They part at a crossing of two alleys. It says much for the governance of the city that an oil-lamp still burns at this late hour, casting its light across the crossing. Paru walks alone through an alley with high-walled houses. A few shrubs and creepers grow out of the dirt in the walls.

There is the sound of footfalls behind her. She assumes it is a passerby. A man seems to be following her. He is huge and fat.

Paru increases her pace. The man continues to follow, not bothering to hide his intentions.

Paru walks faster.

The man closes in, walking barely four feet behind her.

"Paru," the man calls out softly, like a suitor. "Parvati Devi."

"Go away," she says.

"Paru."

Paru walks as fast as she can. She is alarmed now. She is almost running. The man keeps up. She turns a corner, then a second corner. She seems to have lost him. She slows down.

She finds herself in a narrow lane with ten-foot high walls on either side. There is only a small square opening at the end of the lane, where it intersects another alley. The air in the opening is blue and misty. She feels a cold stab of terror. She sees his large form silhouetted against the blue air.

"Paru Devi," the man draws a sword.

She regards him, her eyes wide open. "You're not getting my money," she says.

"I do not want your money."

She looks incredulously at him as he leaps at her swinging the sword. Instinct makes her fall backward. The wind from the blade tickles her neck. She falls down and hits her head on the ground. She is looking straight up at him. She sees him readying for another swing. She screams, rolling in panic. The scything sword kicks up mud next to her face. He is almost trampling her, thrown off balance by the swing.

She rolls in the opposite direction from the one he expects. She is up. She is face to face with the mud wall bordering the lane. She runs, sliding painfully along the wall, away from him. The sword hits the wall, making a deep gouge next to where her shoulder would have been.

She turns and tries to run, but trips over a branch, and falls into a shrub. The fall saves her from his next swing. He cannot see her inside the shrub and he swings blindly, lopping off a thick branch. She forces her way forward. The branches scratch her viciously. She is up and away, in wild panic, only a few feet ahead of him.

She is running back in the direction she came from. He lumbers behind her. She runs through an alley with closed shops and push-carts. She jumps over a push-cart hurting her shin painfully on the wood. He goes around the same cart and is on top of her. She dives forward, hitting the ground and rolling. The sword rips through her *odhni*.

She is up again, just three feet in front of him. She runs straight ahead, and to her surprise, gains a little. She twists this way and that, through streets and alleys. He follows doggedly, ready to kill her the moment she stops.

She is nearing the bank of the river. A thought crosses her mind and she dives into the thick brambles at the river's edge. He immediately closes in, but she is far enough by the time he reaches the bushes' edge. The sword scythes through the bushes, barely missing, again. They struggle wildly through the shrubbery. Her clothes are in shreds, her *odhni* is gone. Her body is scratched all over, but she feels nothing in her desperation.

But, the bushes form less of a barrier to her thin body than to his larger frame. She bursts out of the brambles into the open swamp next to the water. Her feet sink into the mud. She increases her pace, running flat out over the muddy, shallow water. He runs behind her. But he cannot keep up while running straight. The gap between them increases.

The moonlight forms a long shimmering pattern over the water. He watches futilely as her slight, splashing form recedes in front of him. He comes to an aching, winded stop.

His size seems to have got the better of him. He pauses, trying to recover his breath, which comes in huge wheezing gasps. It is a few minutes before he is able to stand straight and breathe with some semblance of normality.

The water fans out on either side of her feet, giving her the appearance of a blue bird skimming the surface. Her tiny form is quite some distance away now, disappearing into the rippling cadences of river and moon.

He looks after her, breathing heavily. "Don't worry," he says aloud. "I will get you. Where will you run?"

Agra, 1604

Jahangir's palace is but one of the many royal residences that are contained within the complex of brilliantly designed buildings that is the Agra Fort. As a rule, the rooms inside the fort are open and airy, the walls decorated with colourful Persian and Hindustani carpets. But the great hall of Jahangir's palace seems to be the exception. It is vast and gloomy. The red sandstone walls are adorned with magnificent carvings, but the general effect is claustrophobic. In the door and window spaces, Jahangir has hung carpets of especially heavy and morose designs — designs, he is certain, his father would disapprove of.

The hall is almost empty, barring little servants whispering in corners. The light is dim. Jahangir is sitting by himself on a divan.

A fan man stands behind him, holding an enormous fan on a long pole, with which he moves the still air slowly back and forth.

Jahangir is brooding, drinking wine from a jade cup. There is a map of Hindustan thrown on the carpet in front of him. A row of wine cups stands ready and waiting on the low marble table.

Also, there is a hookah by his side, should he feel the need for opium.

A servant approaches. "Your Highness, the musicians are here."

Jahangir gazes glassily at the servant for a long time. It appears as if he is not going to say anything. "Show them in," he says at length.

It is the same two musicians who performed at the public house the previous night. They bow to Jahangir. They seat themselves at a discreet distance and start playing. Unlike the previous night, they commence with a classical piece, one which starts slowly and contemplatively.

There is a movement in the wings. The servant approaches Jahangir again. "His Excellency, Asaf Khan," he announces.

Jahangir raises a finger in assent.

Asaf Khan enters the hall and seats himself in front of Jahangir. His demeanour is one of diplomatic caution. As soon as he sits, he checks the hall, looking warily around to see who might be listening. His attention returns to Jahangir. He notices the row of waiting wine cups. "Can you talk?" he asks.

"I can always talk," Jahangir replies.

"I put myself at some risk coming here."

Jahangir regards Asaf Khan with his glassy gaze. "Is my father dead yet?"

"No. He would like you to attend the Religious Bazaar tomorrow."

"Tell him, I have searched in vain for a God to whom I can pray for his death. It has not worked."

Asaf Khan checks the hall one more time. "I have news," he declares.

"You put yourself at some risk coming here," Jahangir says.

"Your brother Daniyal is quite incapable. He drinks twenty cups of wine a day."

There is a pause as Jahangir waits for more. "That is your news?"

"That is my news. There are spies who have informed the Emperor of this. Some of those are my spies."

Jahangir picks up the map impatiently and opens it.

"What about the others?" he demands.

Asaf Khan takes his time to reply. "There is just the one child," he says at length. "The girl. She poses no threat."

"I want her taken care of," Jahangir says.

"Why?" Asaf Khan challenges.

"Why?!"

"It is only a girl."

Jahangir's gaze causes Asaf Khan to feel a stab of fear. "Evidently, Minister, your understanding of women is as pitiful as your knowledge of Hindustan. Have you not heard of the Queens of Licchavi? The Amazons of Chandra Gupta? I hope you have not been neglecting this?"

"No," Asaf Khan replies truthfully. "My man is on it."

Jahangir puts the map down. He knows there is more. "I shall listen to my musicians now," he informs Asaf Khan. He draws his knees up and starts listening to the musicians while stroking his beard.

Asaf Khan waits patiently for an opening. Jahangir ignores him. The musicians begin to feel appreciated and try to make eye contact with Jahangir. Something about the gravity of Asaf Khan's gaze catches Jahangir's attention.

"What!" he demands.

"The Emperor is casting his eye further afield."

Jahangir is suddenly anxious. "Where?"

"The Writer."

Jahangir sits bolt upright. "What has the Writer done?"

"He has taken control of Daniyal's army. Daniyal no longer has any say."

"And?"

"He is about to invade Ahmednagar."

"I already know that!"

"He has taken the fort at Maligarh."

Jahangir gasps. Asaf Khan is too taken with what he is about to present to notice.

"He even wrote his own success up in the court record," Asaf Khan fishes out a document that he has been carrying all along. He opens it up and reads. "The glorious Emperor, in his great wisdom, bestowed upon the Writer a force of three thousand. With that small number of troops, the Writer faced the mighty Sultan's army. The number of the enemy at first struck fear in the hearts of our warriors..."

Jahangir starts having an asthma attack.

"...But the Writer came up on his elephant, and the enemy was soon dispersed..."

"He refers to himself—" Jahangir gasps, "—in the third person!"

"The Citadel was captured thereafter. The Writer himself led the charge, and bravely scaled a long ladder over the Citadel's walls."

Jahangir's breathing is laboured and he is gasping for air. He clutches the edges of the table to steady himself. He looks at the table's inlaid marble pattern and concentrates on taking one long wheezing breath after another. His eyes are fixed, unseeing as he stares at the pattern on the table, holding on for dear life.

Asaf Khan sees Jahangir gasping, but knows better than to call for help. He does not want to be found thus with Jahangir. He sits, watching him suffer, waiting for the attack to pass. All of a sudden, Jahangir looks vulnerable, exposed. Asaf Khan considers reaching out to him in some fashion, but his caution gets the better of him.

Jahangir's breath is more regular now. He still holds the table, as if afraid he will fall. He closes his eyes to calm himself and concentrates on each breath. The wheezing stops. The attack begins to recede.

"I have been thinking about the Writer," Jahangir gasps as soon as he can speak. "The Writer must be...," he gasps, "...eliminated."

"That is a grave thought," Asaf Khan replies. "The Emperor thinks highly of him."

"The Writer has to go!"

"I can have no part of it."

"Do I have to explain to you," he gasps, "as to a child, what will happen when my father dies?"

Asaf Khan thinks. Then cautiously, "The Emperor is not keeping well. I hear he is summoning the Writer back to his side."

Jahangir looks up with excitement. "Has the letter been sent?!"

"It is being sent as we speak."

Jahangir picks up the map and drops it without looking at it. "Orchha! He will be riding through Orchha. I need a man who can ride faster than the post!"

Asaf Khan chooses his words carefully. "I have a spy who is very good." He pauses. "But you must approach him on your own."

"Who is this spy!"

"He is standing right behind you."

Jahangir turns around startled. His eyes meet the Fan Man's. The man's gaze is cold, deadly. His eyes lock with Jahangir's with an animal-like intensity.

A little smile crosses Jahangir's face.

The musicians' *raag* is in the midst of a gorgeous climax. As Asaf Khan leaves, Jahangir picks up his second cup of wine. He starts to follow the music. He feels much better now. The musicians look surprised and pleased.

Jahangir smiles kindly at them. He raises his cup in acknowledgement.

The kingdom of Ahmednagar, which lies along the south-west border of Hindustan, is a source of unending frustration to the Mughals in general, and to the Emperor Akbar in particular. It is one of three kingdoms to the south, each more fabulously rich than the next. Each is the perfect candidate for annexation under the extremely generous terms offered by the Emperor — central control, a required presence in the court at Agra, common weights, measures and taxation — in return for almost total autonomy, military security, and the chance to participate in the world's richest and most powerful free market.

Instead of ceding quickly to what should be an un-refusable proposition, the Sultan of Ahmednagar manages to stay one step ahead of Akbar's plans for annexation. Lately, he has employed an African slave, a six-foot-tall black man, with the adopted Indian name of Malik Ambar, to lead his army. As a general, Malik Ambar happens to be a genius. He has re-fashioned the Sultan's army to take advantage of its defensive posture and the mountainous terrain of the Deccan. Cannons, deep fighting capability, elephants, supplies for the long haul have all been jettisoned. Instead, the army consists of small light units of horsemen who can stage surprise attacks from different angles along the contours of the mountains.

It is this difficult enemy that engages the energies of the Mughal Army of the Deccan. While there are large forces dispatched by Akbar all across the Empire, as far north and west as the Persian border, and as far east as Bengal, it is the Army of the Deccan that is easily the most seasoned and that occupies central attention from the court at Agra.

The road from Agra to Bahranpur, headquarters of the Army of the Deccan, is broad and well-used. It is 800 miles long. A royal postman and four guardsmen are riding along this road as quickly as they can manage. They have been travelling for five days.

They reach a horse-exchange point. The need to provide five fresh horses, all at once, strains the resources of the point. A rider takes off at a gallop to the nearest village. The royal postman frets and curses loudly.

The Fan Man has been pushing his pace even harder than the postman's party. He has the advantage of riding alone, and the promise of a large reward if he succeeds. He has been lengthening his days, riding deep into the night, braving bandits and leopards, then waking up well before dawn to continue on the relentless miles.

So intent is he on maintaining his pace, he almost runs into the postman and his guards at the horse-exchange point. The postman looks up, thinking it is the messenger with the extra horses. He sees a horse's behind disappearing into the bushes a mile or so along the path that they have just traversed. He scowls, and returns to his own problems.

The Fan Man scans the scrubby terrain behind the bushes where he is hiding. He thinks he can discern an alternative path through the scrub that may run parallel to the main road. He decides to take the risk and urges his horse along the path. He is in luck. The path widens. The Fan Man pushes his horse to a full gallop. He races along the path, deep into the scrubland. Soon he loses sight of the road. He stops, confused. The path seems to have petered out. He stands up on his horse and tries to peer above the bushes. He can see the main road heading at an angle in the far distance. But, in between is a patch of dense scrub with no apparent way through it.

He gets off his horse. Drawing his sword, he starts hacking his way through the bushes, pulling his horse after him. The horse whinnies and protests. The Fan Man pushes on, relentlessly.

He is finally back on the road. He has wasted so much time with the detour he thinks he has failed. He looks back. To his shock, the postman and the guards are heading straight at him. He utters a loud cry and slaps the rump of his tired horse forcing it into a full gallop down the road. The postman and his guards ride through the dust raised by the Fan Man, oblivious of its import.

Two more days of intense riding go by in a blur. The Fan Man's horse is standing at the edge of a vast, manicured meadow. In front of him stretches the long, russet-brown palace of the Raja of Orchha. Its ornate battlements give it the appearance of a toy castle in the clear morning light.

Unlike the Sultan of Ahmednagar, the Raja has long since ceded his territory to the Empire. He has little to do now besides live in style and pay occasional subservience at the Mughal court. What is not as well known is that generations of pride cannot be undone by a political treaty. The sense of heritage remains, and the bitterness remains.

The Fan Man lets out a blood-curdling war cry and smacks the rump of his horse. At a dead gallop he charges across the meadow towards the palace's drawbridge.

The camp pitched by the Army of the Deccan sprawls untidily over a flat area between low-lying hills. It is an experienced, battle-hardened army. This morning it is still flush from its victory at Maligarh. The men have been rewarded with extra pay, and there is a sense of quiet accomplishment in the air. The skulking African, Malik Ambar, will have to come up with new strategies.

The man widely known as the Writer because of his many years as Akbar's official biographer, is in the commanding officer's tent. He is dressing himself with the help of several attendants. Ever a judge of character, Akbar has recently made him commanding general of the Army of the Deccan, replacing the alcoholic Prince Daniyal, with instant success.

The Writer preens himself carefully in front of a mirror. He is as one recently promoted to a high rank, conscious of presenting the right appearance. Although he was physically present when the fortress was captured and has been to it several times since, he has decided that a formal taking of possession is called for. He intends to make a ceremony of it, riding across the drawbridge with full guard, drums, and fanfare.

"Give me that other scabbard," he tells an attendant, unbuckling the sheath he has been trying on. The attendant hands him a sheath more ornate than the first. The Writer inserts his sword into it, to see if the design of the handle matches the sheath as well as his glittering tunic. He buckles it around his waist, all the time regarding himself critically in the mirror.

The royal postman bursts into the tent, followed by a clutch of guards. "*Huzoor*, a dispatch from the Emperor!"

The Writer glances at the postman to make sure he is the real thing. He breaks Akbar's red seal on the document and reads the letter swiftly.

"His Majesty is not well!" he exclaims with genuine concern. He turns to a soldier. "Tell Karan Singh to gather twenty horses. Any more and we will be too slow."

He takes one final look at himself in the mirror, then regretfully abandons his plan for a formal taking of possession of the fortress.

The Writer and Karan Singh ride briskly at the head of a cavalry troop of twenty. At this point, the long road from the Deccan back to Agra cuts through the territories of Orchha. They are riding through flat, dry scrubland. It is punctuated by enormous granite boulders, some of them so large they qualify as tiny hills. The road curves around a rock a hundred feet high.

Their path is blocked by a cavalry troop of five hundred.

They are mostly mounted lancers, their long lances at the half-ready position, pointed menacingly at the Writer and his guard. Their uniforms are different from the Mughals'. Each soldier wears a tin helmet with mail armour hanging down his shoulders. The helmet covers most of the soldier's face and he peers out through a slit. The effect is to instil terror.

The Mughals stop. "There are too many of them," Karan Singh whispers fearfully. "They will take us."

"Let me talk to them," the Writer says. He stands up in his saddle and shouts, "Troopers! I represent his Imperial Majesty, the Emperor Akbar. What is your intent?"

The leader of the Raja's troops barks an order in a dialect that the Mughals do not understand. A portion of the troops draw their swords. The rest lower their lances.

"This is not wise! This is not wise!" the Writer shouts, standing in his saddle. "An attack on me and my troop is an attack on the Empire. There will be no mercy shown to you, or your leader!"

The Raja's troops stand impassively with their lances in position, regarding the Mughals through the slits in the iron helmets.

Karan Singh whispers urgently to the Writer, "If we turn around now, and make a run for it, they will not be able to catch us!"

"I will not turn around," says the Writer.

"It's the only way out!" begs Karan Singh. "They will slaughter us!"

"I will not turn around," the Writer insists. He stands up in the stirrups once again and shouts to the Raja's troops, "In the name of the Emperor, I command you to lower your arms and give us passage! There will be no consequences, if you do as I say!"

The leader of the Raja's troops shouts the order to charge. The army of five hundred, lances lowered, swords drawn, charges at full gallop towards the Mughals.

The Writer yells at his troop to charge. The twenty men draw swords and arm their bows with arrows, riding at full gallop towards the Raja's army.

The distance between the two armies closes rapidly.

The mounted archers among the Mughals perform commendably. Ten arrows are released at full gallop. Ten of the

Raja's troops fall, creating a mass of fallen bodies that slows down the enemy's charge.

But there are too many of them. The battle lasts only a few minutes. The Mughals are slaughtered. Karan Singh is pierced by a lance. His horse rears up on its hind legs and he falls.

The Writer ducks an enemy soldier's swing and thrusts his sword at the man's torso, killing him. But there is an armoured trooper standing right behind him. The trooper swings his sword at the Writer's neck.

The Writer's head, decapitated, flies through the air, blood spurting from it as it rotates. It flies several feet, till it hits a rock, and falls to the ground, rolling before it comes to a standstill.

Akbar thinks of his religious *bazaar* as being so central to his reign that he has built a special hall for it, the *Ibadat Khana*. It is made of red sandstone and — with its breathtaking carvings, elevated balconies, perfect acoustics, and design for convection currents that lets the building cool itself in the heat of summer — is an architectural masterpiece.

Akbar's purpose is noble, and utterly unprecedented. It is to bring together the highest priests of each of the religions of Hindustan; to treat them equally; and to let them discuss their philosophies over many sessions and many days. Over time he hopes to evolve an understanding of God. He wants his subjects to do this together. The *Ibadat Khana* is open to the public and draws intense participation. And he wants the religious philosophers to hold their discussions with cooperation and mutual support.

Lately, the religious *bazaar* has been marred by Akbar's own idiosyncrasies. Jahangir's accusation that Akbar thinks that God speaks through him, has a grain of truth.

It is early evening. Akbar is seated at one end of the hall. His demeanour is self-effacing, and attentive. He is flanked by his aging, but eminently mature corps. Man Singh is the *Khan-e-*

Khanaan, General of Generals of the Imperial Army. Itimad Ud Daulah is Akbar's Prime Minister. Birbal is mostly himself, minister-at-large and advisor. With his intense intellect, he is free to assume any role he chooses. While the others are dressed in the formal manner of Mughal courtiers, Birbal, with his *kurta* and *dhoti,* could easily pass for a peasant who has just walked off the fields. The men secretly wish they were somewhere else.

At the centre of the open space stands Sheikh Mubarak, the Empire's highest cleric. He radiates that glow of goodness that seems to come from old men who have spent most of their lives ruminating about God. He is the Writer's father.

Surrounding Sheikh Mubarak are the religious representatives, two to a sect — two Hindu Brahmins; two members of the Muslim *ulema;* two followers of the poet Kabir; two Catholic priests who have travelled from the Portugese trading-post of Goa; two Buddhist monks from Tibet; and two Zoroastrian priests. Each pair of representatives gets a staff. When a representative wants to speak, he taps his staff on the floor.

Along the walls and in the balconies are the people.

It is the turn of one of the Brahmins to speak. "One God, many Gods," he says. "Why is it even a question? I ask you, esteemed colleagues, how many pieces of air are there in this room? One? Three? A thousand? All answers are correct. Sometimes, when I am about to breathe, it is a little puff of air that is of interest to me. And at other times it is all the air that surrounds me. I know that they are one and the same—"

A Muslim cleric and a Kabirite tap their staffs at the same time. With the air of one giving in to a trouble-maker, Sheikh Mubarak motions towards the Muslim cleric. He is an intense old *imam* called Badauni. "You have missed the point completely," he growls. "When the Prophet Mohammed proclaimed 'There is no God but God', he was not quibbling with the definitions of ignorant infidels such as yourself—"

"I would ask my Colleague to preserve decorum in this room!" Sheikh Mubarak interrupts. "We have been brought here for but one holy purpose. To discover the true nature of God. We shall respect all religions in this room."

"I was only suggesting that the Prophet Mohammad knew God," Badauni protests, softening his tone. "Look at you standing there, esteemed colleague. I know you. Do I ask if you are divided into a thousand pieces?"

There is a murmur of approval from the balcony.

The Kabirite taps his staff again. Sheikh Mubarak motions towards him. The Kabirite has a friendly, inclusive way of speaking. "Friends, as you know, the poet, Kabir, had no quarrel with any description of God. He was content to find joy wherever he could — in the wings of a butterfly... the song of a bird. The poet, if he was alive today, would sooner invite a bird to this gathering, and have its song explain to us that which we seek. For if we sit perfectly still and open ourselves to the Earth, the sky, the flowers... God comes to us."

There is a flurry of tapped staffs from different directions.

"The Christian Fathers from Goa have not had a chance to speak..." Akbar says.

"I had not forgotten," Sheikh Mubarak gestures cordially towards the two priests. "Please sir, go ahead."

One of the priests steps forward. His name is Aquaviva. He smiles and surveys the audience with a confident, pitying look. "Repent ye!" he booms suddenly, making the audience jump. "And be converted to the path of Jesus Christ, that your sins may be blotted out! For YOU, God has the lake which burneth with fire and brimstone! Which is a second death."

There is an astonished silence.

"Is that your speech?" Sheikh Mubarak asks.

"That is my speech," Aquaviva responds.

There is laughter in the gallery.

"Why... why will God burn us in the lake of fire?" asks Sheikh Mubarak, puzzled.

"For your sins," Aquaviva replies. "All of you are heathens. All are hell-bound sinners!"

"But we have done nothing wrong!" Sheikh Mubarak protests.

"You were born with sin!" Aquaviva booms.

There is bolder laughter from the gallery. "Brother," says Sheikh Mubarak, "I only ask you these questions so that through you we may better understand God."

"You understand nothing!" Aquaviva tells him. "repent! And accept the blood of Jesus Christ that your soul may be saved!"

Before the audience can decide what to make of Aquaviva's statements, there is an interruption. A courtier bearing grave news enters and whispers something into Itimad Ud Daulah's ear. Itimad Ud Daulah leans forward to confer with Akbar. The religious debate is silenced. Birbal and Man Singh lean forward to join in the muted conversation. The religious *bazaar* watches.

Abruptly, all four of them get up and leave.

Sheikh Mubarak looks after them and has a premonition. A Buddhist monk taps his staff gently. Sheikh Mubarak turns to the monk, his heart suddenly filled with agony. Instead of insisting on his turn, the monk merely gazes back at Sheikh Mubarak. His peaceful features seem to offer Sheikh Mubarak support, something to hold on to, until he can breathe more easily and understand the gloom that is in his heart. Sheikh Mubarak looks at the calming gaze of the monk for a long time.

Akbar and the others have retired to the seclusion of the *Diwani Khaas*, the hall of private audience. This is a large room a little smaller than the *Ibadat Khana*. There is an elevated stage at one end where Akbar sits during formal sessions. But at present the group is seated casually, as though they were family. They have been joined by Akbar's mother, Hamida Begum, and by Ruquiya, his wife. Hamida Begum is tiny, wrinkled, and ninety years old. Ruquiya is middle-aged, and a little younger than Akbar. Her smooth skin, and the sense of self-containment that she radiates, make her seem younger than she is.

Birbal has finished reading from a dispatch. Akbar's face is chalk-white. "We have to stop the discussion," he says. "We have to tell him."

Itimad Ud Daulah whispers to a servant, who leaves the room to fetch Sheikh Mubarak.

"It would take an army of a thousand men to arrest the Raja," states Man Singh.

"There is no need." Akbar turns to Itimad Ud Daulah. "Write the Raja a letter. I need a confession. By return post."

"It will be done," Itimad Ud Daulah says with the understanding of one who has served the Emperor for forty years.

"In the letter..." says Man Singh, "we need to understand why the Raja did it."

"I know why he did it. I know who is behind this," Akbar says.

"Who?" Birbal asks.

Akbar does not reply.

"Salim?"

Akbar nods. There is silence. The tears start to well up in Ruquiya's eyes.

Itimad Ud Daulah sighs. "What should we do, Your Majesty?"

"Kill him," Akbar says matter-of-factly.

Before the others have a chance to react, the servant who has gone to fetch Sheikh Mubarak opens the door cautiously. He shows Sheikh Mubarak in. Sheikh Mubarak advances, looking into the faces that speak volumes.

Akbar goes to Sheikh Mubarak and takes his hands in his.

"What has happened?" Sheikh Mubarak asks.

"Your son," says Akbar. "Killed. Murdered."

"Who... what...?"

"My son," Akbar holds Sheikh Mubarak close. Sheikh Mubarak is stunned.

"All I can say to you," Akbar says, "is that there will be justice. I need to hear from the Raja of Orchha. After that, Prince Salim shall be tried for murder, for treason, and executed."

"What are you talking about?" Ruquiya protests. "He is your son!"

"He is a traitor. He is a murderer. He murdered our Writer. What further discussion do we need?"

"But, he is your son! You love him. Are you a man, or a demon?"

"This business is not for you, woman. If I pardon Salim, what does it say to those out there, who place their faith in me? That we allow murderers and traitors?"

"Not murderers and traitors," Birbal says suddenly, and forcefully, "but people at war. We do allow people at war. We understand those very well. And when there is a war, the rules change."

Akbar looks at Birbal surprised. "What is the matter with you? What war?"

"The war to succeed you as Emperor," Birbal's gaze is intense. "Forgive me, *Huzoor*, but I urge you to think. Salim is engaged in a war of succession. It drives him in sleep and in waking. And in a war, the rules change. One may kill one's enemies. You have done this yourself."

"Are you trying to confuse me?"

"Not any more than I have to, Your Majesty. If you should... pass away, we cannot let Daniyal succeed you to the throne! Salim is all we have."

"If Salim is all we have, I do not see a future for Hindustan," Man Singh interjects. "His only talent is to drink as much as Daniyal, and still remain standing. That is why we needed the Writer."

"But the world has changed," Birbal says. "We no longer have a Writer."

"And we will no longer have a Salim," Akbar responds. "If he is at war, as you say, then let him pay the price of war. A fine beheading it shall be! We shall carry it through the streets of the—"

"Your Majesty! I know my argument fails. But, we need some time to think with cooler heads—"

"You are not going to kill your son!" Ruquiya bursts out. "I am not going to allow it!"

"And I too forbid you, my son, from carrying out such a hasty action," Hamida Begum says. "You may live to regret it."

"Who said I asked any of you your opinions?" Akbar scowls.

There is silence. After the flurry of protests, the group is at a loss for words.

Akbar looks from one reproachful face to the next. "Advisors only," he says unexpectedly. "And you too, Sheikh Mubarak. General."

The faces turn to Man Singh. "I agree with Your Majesty," Man Singh pronounces carefully. "Prince Salim is not above the law. He has committed crimes against the state, and he should be tried like any other criminal. And be executed."

Akbar turns to Birbal. Birbal takes his time. "I submit, Your Majesty, that because of the special circumstance of your poor health and the question of the succession, we take some time to investigate this crime."

"Sheikh Mubarak."

Sheikh Mubarak looks straight ahead and is silent.

Akbar waits. The others are quiet. "Sheikh Mubarak?" Akbar repeats.

"What Allah gives, Allah takes," Sheikh Mubarak replies at length.

"Do you wish for a speedy trial for the murderer of your son?"

"I have other matters on my mind."

Akbar regards him, hesitating. One of the oil lamps lighting the hall crackles loudly, sending up a snaking wisp of smoke. Akbar decides to leave Sheikh Mubarak alone. "Prime Minister," he says, passing over the women.

"I have to agree with the honourable Birbal," Itimad Ud Daulah responds, "that we use some circumspection. A death cannot be undone. While Salim is alive, we still have options."

Akbar looks at Birbal with the cumulative frustration of years of being bested in argument. "Once again you get your way," he says, his nostrils flaring. "But for a short time! Only for a short time!"

Birbal bows, "There will come a day, Your Majesty, when you will see the good in Prince Salim."

"Good? Do you not remember that he led an army of thirty thousand to try and kill me? You talk of good! Did I not see good in him then? And then he rewards me with... this?! By killing our beloved Writer? Who is this creature? Who is this creature?"

A shadow seems to pass in front of Akbar's eyes. He looks up at the high, sculpted ceiling. "Why do you torment me so!" he shouts. "Why do you torment me so! I am cursed! I am cursed! I am cursed!" Akbar's throat catches and he starts coughing.

It looks harmless enough at first. But the cough continues. Man Singh holds Akbar's arm and puts a hand on his back. But the coughing turns into vomiting. Brown bile emerges and starts to trail down Akbar's mouth. As he coughs, it turns into a gush of red. Ruquiya screams and dives forward, trying to stop the flow of blood with her hands. Akbar collapses slowly to the floor, sitting down helplessly, his face white with shock. Man Singh and Birbal try to hold him upright.

He vomits again. A second wave. More blood. He stares stupefied at his soiled clothes.

"Somebody call a doctor!" Ruquiya screams. Pandemonium ensues as a rush of attendants and guards come forward to help. Man Singh sits with Akbar on the carpet, holding his head up, trying to speak to him in a calming voice.

Outside the *Diwani Khaas* the great sandstone courtyards of the fort are empty. The cicadas are chirping amongst shrubs and trees growing from the spaces left between the flagstones. A crescent moon has risen, yellow and warm, and has climbed some distance above the horizon.

Sheikh Mubarak walks slowly out and into the courtyard. He is beset by the strangeness and uselessness of things. The light of the moon hits his face, lighting every feature in the pale light. It is not a sad face, or a grieving face. It is simply an astonished face. Stunned by the ways of Allah.

Paru is practising in secret with a Snake Charmer. At this time of the afternoon the dance class is deserted. The room with the threadbare carpet looks vast and empty. In the middle of the room is a closed basket.

The Snake Charmer squats about four feet to one side of the basket. He is grunge personified. He is naked to the waist, his body the colour of dark chocolate. His long hair, which has grown to half way down his back, is matted and dirty. He has not had a bath in many months.

Paru stands about ten feet in front of the basket, looking scared. Save for her thick dancing anklets she is in her street clothes. She is absent-mindedly moving her feet to a dance rhythm. The *chhum chhum* of her anklets is muted.

"You have to come closer," the Snake Charmer says.

Paru takes a small step forward.

He points to a spot that halves the distance to the basket. "Over here," he says.

Paru steps forward, but invisible strings seem to pull her back.

"Come on. I don't have all day... more forward... one more step," he says encouragingly. "Here," he points. "Paru Devi, I said here, don't break your rhythm. Maharaj hears it. Through his body. You are now within his reach."

Paru has crept to within three feet of the basket, a pit of fear in her stomach. She is still moving her feet.

"Stay there... keep your rhythm. He is listening. He has to get used to it. Come closer. One more step..."

She complies. Smoothly he reaches over and removes the top of the basket.

Nothing.

"Keep your rhythm... whatever you do, do not change your rhythm."

The snake's head seems to leap up from the basket. Suddenly she is dancing less than three feet away from a fully-fanned out King Cobra. The snake hisses at her. Paru draws her breath in sharply.

"Stay right there... don't worry, nothing will happen. He has to get used to you."

A soldier on a horse is passing in the street. The horse snorts and bucks. The soldier's shield catches a bright flash of sunlight and reflects it into the dance class.

The cobra strikes. A stream of venom flies across the room. Paru jumps with fright.

"It's all right! Stay right there!" says the Snake Charmer sounding a little unsure himself. "Don't change anything."

She keeps dancing.

"That is the poison you requested, Paru Devi. I have not removed it... Maharaj is a fully poisonous cobra. But he will not hurt you. Because you love him. And he loves you... don't change the rhythm."

Paru looks sick with fear. She keeps dancing.

The Snake Charmer swiftly grabs the cobra's head from the

back, pushes it into the basket, and slams the lid shut.

Maharaj thrashes inside. The basket's lid moves up with the force of Maharaj's attempts to get out. The Snake Charmer sits on the basket, using his full weight to hold the lid down.

Paru's eyes roll upwards. She collapses in a dead faint.

The Snake Charmer laughs.

It is three months later. The public house is packed. The patrons sit in a vast circle. The evening is lit with a buzz of excitement. There is the anticipation of the unexpected.

The musicians are present, the same ones who had played earlier for Jahangir, and earlier still for Paru at the public house.

At one end of the vast circle is a closed basket. Almost twenty feet away at the other end is Paru, dancing to an intoxicating beat on the *tabla*. She looks confident, sexy, teasing.

The Snake Charmer reaches forward and removes the lid of the basket.

Paru continues to dance where she is, which seems too far away. It looks like a safe performance.

Maharaj, the snake, emerges from the basket. He uncoils and slithers towards Paru. He is so long that there is a good bit of him left in the basket as he continues to uncoil himself. He is finally fully stretched out, all twelve feet of him.

His head is now a short distance away from Paru. He rises from the floor and fans himself out. Paru keeps dancing.

The Snake Charmer has crept up from behind. He is holding a cane. He slaps the cane sharply on the floor. Maharaj turns and strikes. A stream of venom flies across the room.

The audience murmurs.

Paru starts edging forward. She is about three feet away from Maharaj. She is swaying her hips sensuously. There is no fear on her face, just adrenalin-filled seduction. The audience's murmurs increase.

Paru lowers herself to the floor. She lies on her stomach, her head raised, mimicking Maharaj, swaying as he sways. The *tabla* keeps the rhythm. She inches forward. The distance between her head and Maharaj's decreases to two feet... one foot... six inches. Paru recalls her Guruji at the dance class asking her to go still. She is still. As still as she has ever been in her life.

She pouts as if embarking on a long and passionate kiss. She darts her tongue, mimicking Maharaj's. Snake and woman sway together, head to head, tongues flickering.

Slowly, the audience breaks into admiring applause. Paru stands up again. Her feet resume the rhythm. She is three feet away. Her eyes dart towards the Snake Charmer.

Maharaj slithers forward and starts coiling himself up her leg as she dances. Up and up he coils himself. He coils himself around her thighs, which are still moving to the rhythm of the dance. He coils himself up around her hips. He touches her bare waist and proceeds to coil himself sinuously around it. Then up over one breast, and over her shoulder to coil himself around her neck. It is all she can do to carry his weight.

He is entirely off the floor. Her feet continue a small step with the beat.

Maharaj's head appears over Paru's shoulder. He fans himself out completely, his head rising well above hers. To all appearances, she is the Goddess Parvati. With the cobra over her shoulder.

The audience roars its approval as she holds this position and dances with Maharaj fanned out over her head. Paru recalls her mother. She would be proud.

The Snake Charmer pushes Maharaj's basket out in front of Paru. "Gifts for the Goddess!" he proclaims. "Gifts for Parvati Devi!"

The bronze coins shower into the basket in a golden arc.

Despite being at the heart of a vast and powerful Empire,

Akbar's private chambers are curiously mundane. The rooms are huge as expected, the walls alive with beautiful carvings. But they have a cluttered, lived-in feel, as if the affairs of state have moved too swiftly for the Emperor to have had much time to think about decorating. Akbar's own aesthetic sensibility is pedestrian at best, and embarrassing at worst. In the chamber, outside Akbar's bedroom, mismatched objects of great value are strewn about, as if lying in a warehouse. There is a massive granite statue of Shiva, to please Akbar's Hindu wife, Jodhabai. And a fresco depicting a scene from the Old Testament in the ceiling, for his Jewish wife, Miriam.

Amidst a mêlée of cushions and carpets on a raised level, Ruquiya and Hamida Begum are holding audience. Birbal and Itimad Ud Daulah are seated at a lower level with the casualness of family members. Asaf Khan sits awkwardly in a corner, with the air of a junior, privileged to be included in this gathering.

Man Singh is ushered in by an attendant. "Forgive me. I am late. How is His Majesty?"

"The same," Ruquiya replies, conveying with the mere inflection of her voice that she recognises the superficiality of Man Singh's concern and that, to a mild degree, she resents it.

"Is he able to speak with us?"

"No."

Man Singh paces awkwardly. "Begum. I am but an army man, and know little of civic matters. But this business has me lying awake at night. Last night I dreamed Lord Krishna came to me. I dreamed he was trying to tell me something, but I could not divine what he was saying..."

A slight smile crosses Birbal's face.

"I have served His Majesty now for forty years," Man Singh continues. "There is no one who wishes more than I that he should recover quickly. But we have to face facts. If he should... if he should..."

"Die."

"Yes. Then... then I do not believe Prince Salim should be king," he says, all in a rush. "The Honourable Birbal may disagree. But..." Man Singh trails off. The others regard him in silence.

"Please complete your thoughts," Birbal says.

"There are many nobles who are opposed to Salim. If we do nothing, those opposed to Salim will take up arms. There will be a bloody war. Each of us will have to take sides. I will have to take a side. I do not wish to make that decision."

"General, you are a great man," Birbal says. "How may we avoid such a conflict?"

"Choose another descendant of His Majesty," Man Singh replies.

"Would not Salim take up arms against this pretender?"

Man Singh is at a loss for words.

"Do not forget the nobles. Whoever is chosen, must have the support of the nobles," Itimad Ud Daulah interjects.

"Which leads us to the thought that perhaps the nobles should pick a successor," says Birbal.

"That will never work," says Ruquiya. "Each noble will pick himself."

"But if we give them only the Emperor's direct descendants to choose from, they will feel they have chosen. And they will not take up arms against their own choice," says Itimad Ud Daulah.

"Prime Minister, your wisdom shines through in the heat of crisis!" says Birbal. "Who might these descendants be?"

They look at one another. "I propose Prince Khusrau, Salim's son," Man Singh says carefully. "His Majesty himself has spoken favourably of Khusrau. He is a fine youth. Very unlike his drunken father."

"That makes one," says Birbal. "We need another. I would hope for Salim. He is dissolute, without scruple and ruthless. I fear we may need such a ruler to keep Hindustan together."

Man Singh looks unhappily at Birbal. "Is there such a need?"

"Certainly. If the nobles are to choose, they must have at least two descendants to choose from—"

"We need a third," Itimad Ud Daulah adds unexpectedly.

There is a long silence. They regard each other, surprised at Itimad Ud Daulah's readiness to embrace the idea.

"Does it have to be a direct descendant?" Ruquiya asks.

"Yes," Birbal says. "Else every noble will choose himself!"

"There is another," Ruquiya says.

"Another?" says Birbal.

"Another."

"Who?" Itimad Ud Daulah demands.

"In the Siege of Chittor," Ruquiya replies. "We had been camping on that hot plain for two years. It was the most difficult fortress in the world to take. The hot wind flew up in the afternoons and the dust got into everything... your eyes, your mouth, your throat—"

"But who is this third descendent?" Man Singh interrupts.

Ruquiya quells Man Singh with a look of quiet authority.

"At night," Ruquiya continues, "if you were not careful where you slept, the prickly cactus got into your skin and itched for days afterwards. The mountain with the fortress rose two thousand feet straight up above the plain. On the best of days it took many hours to reach the top.

"And yet, our men had to scale this precipice with the Rana of Mewar's cannon, matchlocks and arrows raining down on them. You can imagine how difficult it was! We lost five thousand men in the first year, and gained not an inch of the Fortress."

"But," says Itimad Ud Daulah, "what does that have to do with a third contender to the throne?"

"You will see," Ruquiya says, not to be hurried. "Shah Baba," she says, using the endearment with which she is used to calling

Akbar," was in deep despair.

"He could not give up. His honour, his respect, his legitimacy, all depended on it. If he lost Chittor, he lost the Empire. Yet day after day the Rana's men defied us, indeed got the better of us. We lost a hundred cannon, just trying to push them up the hill to the base of the fortress. They would wait for us to get close enough, then rain down the slaughter. I remember the disaster one day, I could see the men rolling downhill, with the bulls, the cannon, the rocks, all rolling and sliding at the same time. Then in desperation, we started to build the tunnel under the fortress. And it seemed like we would never succeed, and each day we lost a hundred men.

"It was at this time that we were riding through a nearby village... and Shah Baba saw her. If I remember General, you had a dispute with him. And it was to the point you and he and Sipahsalar were all shouting at one another.

"And then she walked by. I was on my horse some distance away. She was balancing four brass pots of water on her head. She had such poise, such grace, she caught even my attention. She walked without hurry, as if she was not afraid of us, as if she was ready to defy us. Shah Baba just stopped and stared! I know him all too well. When he sees a woman who attracts him, he has difficulty thinking of anything else. And this woman made him breathless! Time stopped for him. I believe you won your argument for the day, General. He just could not take his eyes off her.

"That evening he wrote a poem — a love poem. I could see the despair — the wretchedness of that wretched siege — lift from him. I was so happy for him..."

Ruquiya is silent, drifting back in time. The others watch her changing face in the lamplight. "I was so happy for him, I suggested he court her. It was a short courtship. I thought it would end as most of his courtships do, with a conquest, leaving him uplifted, sure of himself, in command," Ruquiya smiles. "That is the way I like him. The conquest that eluded him at

Chittor, would perhaps be realised in another way with the conquest of this woman. And he would be the better for it. Or so I thought.

"I was to regret my decision. He was absent the whole of that week. Suddenly, he was very busy. His conversations with me were brief, distracted. I knew he was sleeping with her. Secret trysts! As he conducted the siege of Chittor! That is when it must have happened. She was a fertile woman.

This man, who is my husband, who tried for his entire life to have offspring and failed most of the time, scored a bulls-eye with a peasant woman in the middle of a smoking battlefield."

"But I dare say," Itimad Ud Daulah interrupts. "His Majesty has made love to hundreds of women—"

"He married her," Ruquiya continues without stopping. "He married her. I said I wanted nothing to do with the wedding, or with her, or even with him. It did not matter. His head was in the clouds. He decided he would court her for two weeks. He could barely wait for the courtship to get over. On the wedding day I resolved not to go. I stayed in my tent and wept. Then I got tired of weeping. And I began to wonder what was happening on the battlefield. So, I slipped out, found a horse and rode through the trees. I stopped some distance away where they couldn't see me. And I saw them marry.

"The soldiers had built a little pavilion. There had been a raid on that village some days ago and one of the charred huts was still smoking. The air was filled with the smell of smoke. She was very beautiful. In her colourful clothes, she looked like a Rajput princess. Indeed, I found out later that that is who she was.

"You cannot organise a wedding without the help of a woman. And Shah Baba in his mad rush, and without any counsel from me, made a mess start to finish. He brought his General, Sipahsalar, to stand behind him to witness the proceedings. But he forgot to bring jewellery for the bride.

"The *Quaazi* had finished reading his blessings and it was time for him to take her for his. Shah Baba fumbled, looking for the gifts that were not there. Looking around stupidly he realised he had his turban pin. He took this out and gave it to her.

"Her fingers closed around it, and she looked at him with innocent doe-like eyes. Shah Baba held her hand which was holding the jewel and looked into her eyes. He was madly, totally in love.

"Then something strange happened. She started to run. Shah Baba looked at her in astonishment, and set off in pursuit. That is when the matchlock was fired. Sipahsalar, who had been left standing in Shah Baba's place, was hit and died instantly. We heard an explosion. A fireball landed on the roof of the pavilion and set it on fire. A fusillade of matchlocks opened up. Arrows came flying from all around us. Several of the men fell. The *Quaazi* died. My horse almost threw me off. I rushed through the smoke looking for Shah Baba, I saw no sign of him. As for the woman — she had disappeared. She disappeared from our lives. We never saw her again.

"I saw him later that day, emerging from the smoke in one piece. I will never forget his face. The love was gone. Instead there was the cold rage of the warrior. A rage that knows no rest until it has avenged itself! She had been sent by the enemy. It had been a trap all along. To kill him, and to win the siege. And he had fallen into the trap head first. It was only by the blessed hand of Allah that he was still alive!

"It took six more months for the siege. Then the tunnel under the fortress was finally completed. But you know what he did in the end."

"Killed," says Birbal.

"Forty thousand. Mostly women and children. Families. The suicide fires were already going when the soldiers stormed the fort gates. The sky was alight from all the burning bodies. That killing has always been a great regret in his life, albeit done in the heat of war. But, he had never ordered such a killing before, and never one since. Now you know at least what drove him to it. They left no one alive. Not woman, not man, not child."

"Would not this woman have died too?" asks Man Singh.

"That is what we thought. There was no sign of her in the fort when we went in. But how could she still be alive? All had been killed, all destroyed.

"And now all of a sudden, just a week ago, I hear rumours from the *bazaar*. That she escaped after all. Perhaps because she knew she was with child, she chose not to sacrifice herself on the *sati* fires. I hear she died much later. And a child was born. And this child is alive."

"How can you believe rumours like that?" asks Man Singh.

"Have you ever known a rumour from the *bazaar* to be false?" Ruquiya replies.

The men are silent at this.

"If this boy were to exist," Birbal asks, "how would we know him?"

"From the jewel in Shah Baba's turban. I am sure she kept it. Also, it is believed there was a record of the marriage."

"You say the Emperor is not able to speak to us?" asks Itimad Ud Daulah.

"He is not awake."

Itimad Ud Daulah sighs. "I will start a search for the boy. But how can I find a child from a turban pin, and a marriage document? It may be too late." He comes to a decision and stands up. "I shall summon the nobles, as quickly as they can get here. And we shall have this... choosing of a successor. We shall present them with Prince Khusrau, and—" He looks at Birbal, "Prince Salim. If by some miracle we find this other boy, we shall present him as well." He turns and looks at Man Singh. "General, I would like you to place Prince Salim under immediate custody. We do not want any more strange accidents occurring before this Choosing."

The meeting disperses. The men drift out into the courtyard. The sun is bright. A lone cloud floats above, making the electric blue sky seem deep and infinite. Alert helpers see the men and instantly bring up horses for Man Singh, Itimad Ud Daulah, and Asaf Khan. As each man rides out of the courtyard, mounted guards appear mysteriously from the recesses of the fort as escorts — four guards for Itimad Ud Daulah, two for Asaf Khan, eight for Man Singh. The horses' hooves clatter loudly on the red flagstones.

Birbal walks by himself towards the palace inside the fort that Akbar has lavished on him. He is barefoot. In the palace he sleeps on a straw mattress in a corner of one of the vast rooms.

Ruquiya and Hamida Begum are left by themselves in Akbar's antechamber. "I have to check on Shah Baba," Ruquiya says getting up.

Hamida Begum puts out her hand. "Stay awhile. And have some tea. Shah Baba is asleep. He will not miss you," she looks around and over her shoulder. "Mehrunissa!"

There is no response.

"Mehrunissa!" she shouts again.

Nur makes a hurried entrance. She is dressed in a black, mourning *burkha*. Her movements are awkward. After two years of being Hamida Begum's attendant she has still not learnt how to conduct herself as a servant. There is a carefree air about her, as if she is quite happy to be a widow in mourning. She bows to Hamida Begum.

"Why don't you answer when I call you?"

"I am sorry, *Begum Saheba*."

"Ruquiya Begum and I will have some tea," Hamida Begum says.

"I have it ready, Begum." Nur goes behind the curtain and returns almost instantly with a silver tray laden with a serving of tea. The pot is made of gold, the cups of light green jade. Nur pours out the tea, a trifle unsteadily. Hamida Begum and Ruquiya busy themselves with their cups.

"Did you make it yourself?" Hamida Begum asks suspiciously.

"No, *Begum*," Nur says.

Hamida Begum sips the tea tentatively. "No. It's good tea," she says with satisfaction. She looks up at Nur. "Did you listen to everything behind the curtain?"

"Yes, *Begum*."

"In the future, please withdraw to a suitable distance. It is not your place to listen to matters of state."

"Yes, *Begum*."

"Since you listened, what do you think?"

Nur pauses to consider this. "No King has asked his nobles to choose a successor. The men will be flattered."

Hamida Begum is secretly pleased at the answer, but she does not show it. "Open the curtains, will you, and let some sun in here. It feels like a tomb."

Nur complies. The bright afternoon sunlight streams into the airy room. The two women look out across the courtyard. The shrubs and small trees that decorate the courtyard sway and sigh in the light breeze. The unmistakable call of a *koyal* rises above the chirping of sparrows.

Ruquiya has been staring off into the distance. "Hamida Begum! I made a mistake. The spy who told me about this child... he said it was a girl, not a boy!"

"Is that so?"

"That makes him... her, out of the question. I should summon the Prime Minister and tell him immediately!"

There is no answer. Hamida Begum's leathery face looks out across the courtyard as if she is searching for the *koyal* who is calling.

Ruquiya turns to her, puzzled.

"Why don't you wait a little," Hamida Begum says finally. "Let these men first find this... girl... boy contender. Let them come face-to-face with the fact that it is a girl. Then I would like to see their faces as they try to argue she should not be allowed. It will be interesting to see how they make that conclusion."

Ruquiya looks at Hamida Begum startled. She smiles.

Paru is planting rice seedlings. The day is still, and very hot. The mosquitoes are unbearable. The muddy water around Paru's ankles feels warm. Her mother is almost a field away, on the other side of a slight rise in the ground. There is no one about. Paru splashes the water loudly with her feet to make sure she can be heard. Then ever so silently, crouching low, she steps across the rice paddy. Then across the next paddy and the next. She is crossing the *bajra* field. It is deserted. The field is silent. And scary. Her clothes brush against the forbidden stalks. She is at the open land next to the big village. She crouches amongst the legs of the crowd getting ready to watch the travelling dance troupe. It is to be a big dance drama about Gods and Demons.

But she is in for a surprise. Into the performance space a band of enraged villagers drag her mother. They are armed with sticks and clubs and they start beating her. Paru covers her face with her hands and screams.

The scream wakes her up. The hot sun is shining straight into her eyes through an open window. Her hands are shaking. She is drenched with sweat. It was a dream, only a dream. Her mother did not die because she had crossed the *bajra* field, she has to remind herself. She died from an illness. The fevers. When you wake up, it is real life that appears manufactured and your dream that seems real. It takes some time to get used to the events of real life again.

The sunlight from the open window is beginning to bother Paru. She covers her face with her arm and closes her eyes again. She hears the loud voices of whores in the cavernous room that she shares with eight other girls. As usual, the whores are engaged in a loud argument. Paru tries to shut their voices out.

"Come on! Wake up!" somebody says. Paru keeps sleeping. Somebody kicks her. "Come *on*!"

Paru opens her eyes. It is Pithu. She is fully dressed.

Paru sits up slowly. Her hair falls forward. "I had a big night last night," she says, tired.

"So did I," Pithu replies, unmoved. "Let's go!"

The wall next to Paru has a hollowed-out *gokhla*, a space in which she can store things. Paru's *gokhla* is crammed with clothes. She picks a *choli*, from the tightly-packed clothes and pulls. All the clothes fall out.

Paru's scroll flops onto the straw mattress along with the rest of her clothes. She picks it up and attempts to read it. Failing, she rolls it up and puts it back again into the *gokhla*.

"Come on!" Pithu says.

The two of them walk through the *bazaar* with the anticipation of wealthy ladies who are about to spend a lot of money. They are demurely dressed, lest there be any recognition from the night-time suitors. Their *odhnis* are wrapped around their upper bodies and drawn tightly over their heads, covering half their faces. Their *cholis*, although glittering with tiny mirrors, are solidly opaque. There is a scarcely thin line of skin between the *cholis* and the *ghagras*.

They come to a stall selling cloth. Cottons and muslins flow in oranges, reds, greens, across the shop's *bazaar* front. Paru passes her hand over a red *odhni* that hangs prominently outside. It seems to glow. When her hand passes over it, it has the feel of butter.

"What is this?" she asks the shop-keeper.

"Silk," he scowls.

"What is silk?" Paru asks, her mouth half-open with wonder.

"It is made from worms," he says.

"Worms?"

"Comes from Kashmir."

"How much?" she asks.

"More than you can afford."

"Come on," she insists.

"Ten *rupiya*."

"You're a thief!"

"It's silk."

Deliberately, under his disapproving gaze, she takes the *odhni* down and holds it across her body. She spins, showing it to Pithu. "What do you think?"

A black lump of fear fills her stomach as she recognises her assailant from the other night. He is standing in the crowd some distance away from her. She tries to keep her expression unchanged, as if she has not seen him.

The man's name is Bhir Das. He seems to have acquired a helper, a slim, twenty-year-old youth. The two of them are in earnest conversation. The men look up, and realise that Paru has seen them. They quickly part, blocking Paru's retreat from either side of the shop.

Paru hands the two ends of the *odhni* to Pithu. "Can you hold this up for me?"

Pithu holds it up. "It's too—"

Paru's head disappears behind the *odhni*. The garment shop shakes as she dives forward through it. There is a convulsion of fabrics and falling things. Paru emerges two shops down breaking through a shop selling doves. The doves burst upwards flapping their wings as Paru dashes out.

She comes face-to-face with Bhir Das. He swings his sword. It barely misses Paru's head as she dives head first into a cart of tomatoes. She slides across the cart over the rolling tomatoes and falls to the ground on the other side. Tomatoes go cascading across the *bazaar* dirt.

Bhir Das swings again, awkwardly, over the cart. Paru runs. She gets a slight lead as he has to go around the cart. They are both engulfed by the dense crowd. Paru pushes forward frantically. He follows close behind, holding his sword above his head ready to use it the second he gets a clear swing.

A camel blocks her path. She runs under its legs only to collide with a large man on the other side. She struggles past the man, but a wall of people get in her way. By the time she emerges, Bhir Das is waiting for her. Paru drops to the ground and rolls. Somebody trips over her. There are angry shouts and a knot of people who are losing their balance and falling. Paru emerges through them not daring to look back, certain that the Bhir Das's sword will come scything down. But somehow the blow is held back. Perhaps there are people in the way.

Paru is off and running, dodging through the crowd. The crowd thins. Bhir Das is just six feet behind her. She catches a glimpse of the Youth, who seems further behind. The crowd clears. She breaks into a sprint. Bhir Das is running hard. He has dropped a little behind, but only a little.

Then, her way is blocked. She has come to a part of the *bazaar* that is filled by a sea of empty push-carts and shopping stalls. Bordering the far end is the high wall of an officers' barracks. The top of the wall is covered with rocky shards designed to discourage any intruder. The wooden push-carts and stalls are crammed together all the way to the wall offering no path through. In desperation, Paru jumps onto a push-cart.

She starts to run over the carts. She jumps from cart to cart. Each cart is unsteady, and rolls under her feet. Bhir Das is right behind. There is no time to look up.

She is almost at the wall. It seems Bhir Das has her cornered. She sees the long, tall counter of a stall. She jumps to the top of it. She runs its length with no idea about what to do next. The counter ends. At the other end is a two-wheeled push-cart. It seems to afford a little space towards the wall. She can hear Bhir Das's feet pounding behind her.

She jumps onto the push-cart. Her legs jolt painfully as the end on which she is unexpectedly gives way and she falls to the ground with a jarring thud. Paru runs across the push-cart. The other end gives way with a thud. She is trapped. The wall is in front of her.

Enthusiastically, Bhir Das launches his huge body from the counter-top onto the push-cart. The effect is astonishing. Paru feels herself being catapulted up into the air. Up into the blue sky, as if a benevolent God has decided to pluck her into the heavens. She rises twelve feet. She sees the top of the wall with its rocky shards flowing beneath her. Then she is falling. Falling into a large, dry brown bush. She falls through the nettles into the centre of the bush.

She lies still, winded from the fall. She is amazed that that she is still alive. She hears birds chirping. She wishes she could stay here in perpetuity, stuck in a brown bush in a deserted garden. But Bhir Das is outside, planning even now to storm in and trap her.

She moves, instantly the brambles scratch her, drawing blood. She sees that she has other scratches. Her clothes have been ripped. She tries to move the branches aside, struggling her way out of the shrubbery. There are more scratches across her body. She is covered in sweat.

She falls out of the bush to the ground. She lies on her back for a moment looking up at the sky, wishing she could rest. But she cannot. She gets up and looks around. The garden is a small oblong space, firmly enclosed by the surrounding wall and the front of the barracks. She looks at the barracks. They stretch across the entire back of the garden. She walks delicately past the front door, wondering if she can go in and hide.

Then her blood freezes. There are voices coming from inside. Men's voices. She hears movements, as if one of the officers is about to come out. Untold horrors await her if she is found intruding. She looks around quickly. In the far corner there is a tree growing next to the wall. She runs to it. One of the branches offers a handhold. She pulls herself up. She finds another branch and climbs up further. She is two feet from the top of the wall. She is lucky. This is a portion of the wall where the sharp rocks seem to have worn off.

She leaps and grabs the wall. She almost falls, but hangs on with both hands. The rocks make her cringe with pain, but she has to hang on. She struggles to pull herself over the wall. After some attempts she manages to swing her leg over. She is standing, crouching cautiously on top of the wall.

Bhir Das and the Youth are at the far end, near the push-carts. Paru looks down. It is a twelve foot drop. But if she could make it to the ground there is a path out, into an open side-street. But, she has to jump. She stops herself from thinking. Still, she will be still. Paru jumps. Her legs buckle underneath her. Her behind hits the ground with a jarring thud. She falls backward and rolls. She sits up, checking her hands and feet gingerly. She is in one piece.

She hears a shout. The Youth has spotted her. She gets up and takes off down the side-street. The men have to navigate across the sea of push-carts. But this time they have learned. The Youth jumps onto a push-cart and runs from push-cart to push-cart at an amazing speed. He reaches the side-street just in time to see Paru dashing off to the left at the far end.

Paru runs as fast as she can. But the streets now seem curiously empty. They are broad, deserted streets. Designed for military use, they lead towards the entrance of the great fort.

It turns out the Youth is a runner. Paru is almost a block ahead, but each time she turns down a side-street she finds the gap is shrinking. She twists and turns desperately through the empty streets. The Youth comes closer. She turns corner after corner, her breath bursting out in sharp gasps, her tired body slowing. The Youth comes closer.

She is face-to-face with the gates to the fort. A drawbridge crosses a broad moat. On the other side, the fort walls tower above her, stretching for miles in both directions. A stark curving red road leads up to the entrance, with the drawbridge. A troop of twenty men stands guard under the command of a captain.

Paru slows down. She looks back. The Youth is slowing down too, some hundred feet behind her. Bhir Das is rounding the corner. She looks ahead at the forbidding-looking troop.

The captain barks an order to his men, ignoring Paru.

Paru takes a tiny step towards the captain. There is no response from the troops. She takes another step. She wills herself to walk forward towards the armed men. She is all alone on the empty road.

She is within hearing range of the captain. "*Huzoor... Huzoor!*" she says nervously. "Those men over there. They are after me. Could you... let me stand next to you until they go away?"

The captain looks straight ahead, barely moving his lips. "Get out of here before I have to kill you."

Paru does not budge.

The captain's hand closes on the hilt of his sword.

Paru looks back at Bhir Das and the Youth. They are edging closer.

Paru composes herself for a second. She smiles and puts on her best seductive look. "*Huzoor.* Do you know who I am?"

The captain considers this. "No. Who?"

"I am a concubine," says Paru. "I fuck people for a living."

The captain looks straight ahead.

Paru moves a wisp of hair from her sweaty face. Turning on her charm she looks at the captain. "I could fuck you for free. Tonight."

The captain looks stonily ahead, standing very still.

"Please," Paru says tender, desperate. "Those men are trying to kill me."

There is a long silence as she regards the captain. He seems unmoved.

"Go stand near the wall," he says unexpectedly.

Paru obeys.

The captain barks a series of orders. Six men step forward. They space themselves evenly across the breadth of the road. They lower their lances.

They start advancing down the road towards Paru's pursuers.

Bhir Das and the Youth stop in their tracks, unable to believe their eyes. The captain barks another order. The lancers increase their pace, charging towards them in double-quick time.

Fear crosses the faces of the assailants. They flee down the road as fast as their surprised feet can carry them.

Bang! The shot kicks up dirt near the tiger's foot and startles it, causing it to get up and walk in a nervous circle. *Bang!* The second shot falls four feet short, but ricochets with a noisy burst of pebbles. The tiger decides to take off. It walks at a hurried pace, gathering speed. *Bang!* A third shot hits a fallen tree branch nearby with a loud thud. The tiger soars into the air in full flight. Its twelve-foot length is stretched above the ground as if suspended. Its forty-foot stride hits the ground with unimaginable force leaving pug-marks that will bake in the earth for the next ten years. Its muscular body flexes into a tight ball just above the ground. Then another magnificent stride aimed nimbly at the top of a flat rock. *Bang!* The shot flies uselessly below the tiger's outstretched body.

Jahangir is red with rage. He, Asaf Khan, and a servant are in the *howdah* of an elephant. Before them, stretch scrub and open jungle. Jahangir is aiming his matchlock at the tiger, some five hundred feet away.

"A Choosing, is it? They are going to choose between me—" *Bang*! "And my sixteen-year-old imbecilic son." *Bang*! It is at this point that the tiger starts its sprint. "I have an army!" *Bang*! "I have defended the Empire! I am the only son capable of ruling! The only son!"

Asaf Khan sits as far away from Jahangir as is possible in the cramped confines of the *howdah*. It is the servant's unenviable task to load a spare matchlock and exchange it with the one Jahangir has just fired. The man loads as fast as he can, sweating in his panic.

"But these Buffoons—" *Bang!* "are going to choose between me!" *Bang!* And an idiot!" Jahangir holds his hands out for the next matchlock. The servant is too slow. The man fumbles desperately, his sweating fingers slipping on the ball and the gunpowder. Jahangir looks at him. The servant cowers, certain Jahangir is going to shoot him next. He hands the loaded matchlock over. *Bang!* Jahangir shoots after the sprinting tiger. The tiger has gone down a shallow gully, traversed its bottom, and is now sprinting up the opposite side. In a few seconds it covers a distance that a man would take an hour to trek. It reaches the top of the rise, disappearing behind thick bushes that merge into jungle.

Jahangir fires at the bushes. He puts his hands out for another matchlock, and fires again. And again.

"What are you shooting at?" Asaf Khan asks curiously.

Jahangir makes a peculiar sound and throws the spent matchlock to the ground far below. He takes a deep breath. There is silence in the *howdah*.

"Did you get rid of the girl?" he asks unexpectedly.

"I put two of my best men on it," Asaf Khan replies uncomfortably.

Jahangir looks at Asaf Khan. "This cannot fail."

"Yes," Asaf Khan says, attempting to retreat further from Jahangir and pressing his back hard into the wooden rail of the *howdah*.

"Use the fan fellow," Jahangir says.

"Yes," Asaf Khan replies, glad for the advice.

"Go back," Jahangir orders the *mahout*, who is perched up front, riding on the elephant's neck. They turn around.

About twenty beaters have been strung out in a long line on either side of the royal elephant to assist with the hunt. One of them calls out, his voice echoing through the woods. "Your Highness! What animal would you like to hunt next?"

There is no reply. The elephant proceeds silently through the jungle.

The hunting party is on the high road leading back towards the city. Four guards ride ahead and clear all traffic as Jahangir and his entourage approach.

Their path is blocked. Some thirty cavalry under the command of an official-looking captain have arranged themselves across the road, in the form of a 'V'. Their colourful flags speak as no words can, of their high official business and their close proximity to the Emperor. As they approach, ten troopers from each of the arms of the 'V' ride ahead and block Jahangir's rear.

The captain has a long waxed moustache that extends to the sides and curls absurdly into circles. "Your Highness!" the captain calls. "By order of His Majesty the Emperor, I have been sent to place you under arrest! You have been commanded to be placed in close custody until further notice!"

Jahangir looks at the captain, his eyes wide with shock and outrage.

The courtyards that lead up to the top of the fort walls are especially beautiful. One of these lies within the bounds of the harem. On one side is the precipice of the great wall, plunging into an enormous moat at the bottom. Crocodiles and large turtles inhabit the muddy waters below. The wall overlooks a flat, open vista dominated by the Yamuna River, which curves lazily past the fort, disappearing on its thousand-mile journey towards a hazy blue horizon.

On the opposite side of the courtyard is a walkway. There is light traffic on this, consisting mainly of women, some of them scantily clad. A tall Russian woman, serves as a female guard, standing at an intersection of the walkways. She wears a sword, which she knows how to use. Through the centre of the courtyard runs a two-foot-wide marble canal with a waterfall at the end. It empties into a large, shallow pool, which is scented and has rose-petals floating prettily over its surface. Chirping sparrows and bulbuls flit through the shrubs and trees that have been planted amongst the red flagstones.

At the pool are Gossibai, one of Jahangir's nineteen wives, and two concubines, Saheli and Ritu. Gossibai is in her thirties. She has a plain, angular face, pock-marked from a childhood disease. She is Jahangir's main wife, the one he sees most often and shows the most affection to. The concubines are stunning eighteen and nineteen-year-olds. All three women wear harem dress, their tits showing loud and erect through their translucent *cholis*.

Saheli sits at the side of the pool, playing the *veena*. She sings to herself as she plays. Gossibai has her legs crossed and is lying on her back completely immersed in the pool. Ritu sits behind her, a comb in her hand. Gossibai looks up at the sky through the water, her eyes open, her body still. She seems dead. Saheli sings. Gossibai cannot hold her breath any longer. She sits up slowly.

"How does it feel?" Ritu asks.

Gossibai takes her time answering. "It feels... like nothing in your life that you have ever felt before. A kind word from my Prince, a glance, and I am in heaven. Everything feels—" She closes her eyes and draws her breath in ecstatically. "Hannhh! Food feels—Hannhh! Water! The air—Hanhhh! I would do anything for him. I would jump off that wall over there and feed myself to the crocodiles below, if he asked me to!"

"And if he should show his love to another?" Ritu asks, straightening Gossibai's hair with her fingers.

Gossibai does not answer. Her face is still as she slides into a sad reverie. Ritu caresses Gossibai's back with her fingers. She runs her hands down her arms and hugs her from behind, resting her head against Gossibai's shoulder. Gossibai is stiff, unmoved. Ritu releases her and runs the comb through her hair. A pair of peacocks appear from nowhere and prospect in the cracks between the flagstones.

"You have lice in your hair," Ritu says.

Gossibai screams. She turns around and looks at Ritu in horror. There are tears in her eyes.

"I was just making fun of you, Gossibai," Ritu says. "Your hair is beautiful. And I love you."

Gossibai wipes her tears. Saheli is unaffected. She continues to sing, plucking at her *veena*.

Nur appears on the walkway, holding a sketch-book and charcoals in her hand. She is glancing around, not at the people, but at the stone courtyard. In her head she is imagining, drawing.

"Here comes the serving lady," says Saheli.

The attitude of the three women changes instantly. They become stiff, hostile, alert. They examine Nur covertly for several seconds. "Look at her!" Ritu exclaims, breaking the silence. "A widow, and not even her face covered!"

"If my husband died," Saheli says softly, "I would jump into the funeral fire and die with him. Any self-respecting woman would!"

"Have you seen how she sneaks out each day?" says Ritu. "What does she do when she goes to town?"

"I would really like to know..." Gossibai muses.

"How does she get away with it?"

"She is the Prime Minister's daughter," Saheli informs them.

"The way she struts around, she is more the Prime Minister's daughter than the serving lady!"

"She's staring at us!" Saheli says excitedly.

Nur seems to be looking directly at the concubines and drawing in her pad as she sits at the edge of the walkway. She is using her free hour to indulge a fantasy in which she is to architect a fabulous new citadel, one that is impregnable in war, but breathtakingly beautiful otherwise. Nur has an idea all her own that she has shared with no one. The key she thinks is marble. She has been inspired of late by tales of the Persian architects who have built amazing mosques in Isphahan entirely out of marble. And yet, Nur knows, the best marble in the world is to be found in Hindustan, at Makarana. If only it can be transported the two hundred miles to Agra. The Hindustani marble is hard, unlike the Persian marble. It is difficult to work with. But when finished it has a texture that makes your heart soar. And it is known to last a hundred years. Nur's idea is not just to make little table-tops and statues out of the hard Makarana marble, but to make entire buildings.

"She's spying on us!" Ritu is outraged. "This is the limit!" She walks over to Nur. "Hey serving lady! *Salamat.*"

Nur stands up hastily and bows deferentially to Ritu.

"You're not allowed to write things about us in your book," Ritu says.

Nur looks surprised.

"Hand me that book."

Nur hands the pad over to Ritu. Ritu is taken aback by Nur's willingness. She looks surreptitiously at the pad. It contains a drawing of the courtyard in perspective. There are no people in the drawing. She scowls and hands the pad back to Nur. "Don't spy on us."

"No, *Begum.*"

Ritu returns to the other two. Nur, her reverie disturbed, decides to continue down the walkway.

"It was a stupid drawing," Ritu says.

Gossibai is looking at Nur through narrowed eyes. "Why would a widow walk around looking so happy? Unless... unless she is happy that her husband is dead?"

"Happy?" Ritu says.

"You know... if she didn't want her husband to live. And had a hand in his death. She would be happy."

Ritu stares at Gossibai. "I'm going to find out!" she says, springing up out of the water. She grabs Saheli's hand. "Come on!"

Ritu runs down the walkway after Nur, dripping water on the flagstones. Saheli follows close behind. "Hey serving lady! serving lady!"

Nur stops. She bows again, half-heartedly.

Ritu comes right to the point. "You're a widow, aren't you?"

"Yes," Nur says.

"How did your husband die?"

Nur's face changes. She regards Ritu for a moment. "Run away, little girl," she says her voice pleasant. "I'm in a good mood." She starts walking again.

Ritu follows determinedly. Saheli follows close behind. "How can you be in such a good mood when your husband is dead?" says Ritu.

"You seem so happy!" Saheli calls out timidly.

Nur ignores the remarks and keeps walking.

The concubines follow her. Ritu half-runs until she is almost at Nur's side. "I am talking to you, serving lady. You have to stop and obey me."

But Nur keeps walking.

"What do you do when you sneak into town all the time, serving lady?" Ritu demands.

Nur keeps walking.

"Do you meet your husband's murderers?"

Nur turns and grabs Ritu and twists her arm with such violence that Ritu almost falls. She cries out in pain. Saheli jumps back appalled. The coldness in Nur's face is frightening. She speaks softly into Ritu's ear. "See that guard there? He cannot tell what I am doing. I could break your arm right now. And the guard would not be able to tell I did it. And you would not be able to do your sexy dances any more... Please do not talk about my husband... or his death again."

Nur releases Ritu pushing her into Saheli. Ritu looks ill. Nur picks up her fallen sketch-book and charcoals and strides away. She crosses the large, front courtyard of the fort going past the *Diwani Aam* towards the fort's gates.

The girls remain where they are, terrified. They find shelter behind a stone grill and watch Nur's retreating figure through the safety of the stone netting.

Nur speaks briefly to the sentry at the gate, who lets her out through a small side door.

Paru has never been to this part of town. It is on the outskirts of the city, a large collection of nondescript huts built out of straw, bamboo, and wooden posts stolen from other houses under construction. The shantytown stretches haphazardly to the muddy flats that edge the river, until the mud becomes too soft to build on.

When her fat assailant first attacked her and chased her down the bank of the river, Paru, with the optimism of youth, chose to try and forget him. Maybe it would be all right in the morning, she told herself. She mentioned the attack to no one, and assured herself that the man would not come again. And so it was for some days, until this, her very recent brush with death. Suddenly her instincts are on the alert. She recalled what happened to Bahu's daughter in her village. Bahu's daughter was a wild and silly thing. Paru thought she was slightly off in her head. But one day she crossed the *bajra* field into the big village and made love to a man there. Nothing happened for a few days. Then one evening when Bahu's daughter was walking through the woods to collect water, four men attacked her with machetes and killed her. Paru recalled hearing the faint screams from the woods and not knowing what they meant. But then next morning she heard, and her heart started pounding as if it was she and not Bahu's daughter who had been attacked.

And now there are men after Paru, as there had been men after Bahu's daughter. But, she cannot divine what she might have done to deserve this. There are no *bajra* fields to cross in the City. With a heavy heart, Paru concludes that these men are serious and that they may come again. All she wants to do is dance and make money... and now, this!

The girl is about Paru's age. She says very little. She leads Paru through a maze of narrow spaces between the huts until she comes to one with an open door held in place with jute rope. She opens the door and goes in. Paru follows and looks around the hut.

"Where?" Paru asks.

There are two sets of straw mattresses and women's belongings strewn across the floor. There are clothes, a copper urn, which stands out because of its solidity, and a wooden spoon. The girl points to an area of floor next to the wall. "There," she says pointing to a straw mattress.

Paru looks at the straw mattress.

"She never comes," the girl explains. "You can take her place."

Paru steps outside. A thick bank of river weeds, eight feet tall, grows behind the hut, giving it a measure of seclusion. Paru looks out at the area in front of the hut. She sees other huts closely crowded in. The maze of little passageways through the spaces between the huts is indeed bewildering. The girl has followed her outside.

"How much?" Paru asks.

"Two *rupiya*," the girl says hazarding a number she knows is too high.

Paru looks around one more time, glancing again at the bank of river weeds. "All right," she says, to the girl's surprise.

Akbar's chief attendant wears a bright red turban, which projects a cockscomb of stiff red cloth that makes his six-foot five frame seem even more imposing. He towers over Badauni, the Shia cleric who spoke for Islam at the Religious Bazaar. The attendant has a private method of showing his estimation of people who visit Akbar's chambers. The higher the person in the attendant's opinion, the more he slows his gait to match the visitor's. For Badauni he slows just barely enough to let him maintain a fast walk. Badauni has to break into a little run sometimes.

Akbar's bed chamber is gloomy. The curtains are drawn. The sword of Humayun, Akbar's father, hangs on the wall. Badauni recalls the sword from almost thirty years ago when Akbar was in his late twenties. And now here it is. This is the first time he has been in Akbar's bed chamber. Akbar looks very sick. In the few months since his illness, he has grown shockingly thin. His face looks bony, almost white. Ruquiya is sitting on the pillow next to him stroking his hair.

When the men enter, she stands up. "It is the Imam Badauni," she tells Akbar. "He has just started talking," she cautions Badauni on her way out. "Do not tire him."

Akbar and Badauni are left alone in the room. Badauni stands a little distance away from the bed. His hands are folded tightly behind his back. "Badauni..." Akbar says with difficulty. "How are you?"

"I am quite well, Your Majesty," Badauni replies. It is a measure of Akbar's distress with his own body, that he misses the tightly-coiled formality in Badauni's response.

"And your family?"

"My family is quite well also."

"Badauni... we have known each other... for thirty years." Akbar contemplates. The silence hangs heavy in the room. "Badauni, I am going to die."

"We all meet the Angels of our Lord some day, Your Majesty."

"I have searched for God all my life," Akbar says warming a little to his subject. "I have explored the great religions. But I realise now that there is nothing so simple and so sweet as our own Islam."

"Indeed, Your Majesty," Badauni says, still standing a little away from the bed with his hands behind his back.

"The reason I called you, Badauni... I need your help. I want to ask Allah for forgiveness... for my... for my evil deeds."

"Which evil deeds might those be, Your Majesty?"

Akbar has difficulty getting the words out. "At Chittor, when the fort fell. We killed everybody. The women, the children. They were not *amirs*, they were not soldiers. They were just people. Ordinary... village people. We killed them... I think about that every day."

"Your Majesty," Badauni says. "You ask my help to get Allah's forgiveness? Is that your request?"

Akbar nods.

Badauni looks around the room to see if there is anyone within earshot. He steps a little closer to Akbar. "Perhaps Your Majesty's Quran has grown a little rusty? But when one is facing the moment of death, like this, it is too late to ask for forgiveness."

"How can that be?"

"Your Majesty, it seems to me you have been spending too much time with those Christian missionaries from Goa. They do so babble on about forgiveness. But our own Quran is very clear. It is too late, Your Majesty."

"Then... what am I to do?!"

Badauni looks around the room again. He leans closer, so that his face is only a few inches from Akbar's. "You will have to go to Hell, Your Majesty."

Akbar is too stunned to reply. Then his face hardens. He looks up at the ceiling. "You disappoint me," he says finally.

"What do you wish to do, Your Majesty? Order my death? If I have angered you, you have angered me tenfold! You have made us ...of the *ulema*, we who have given up everything to uphold the word of Allah, you have made us stand in a corner like embarrassed children! You with your Religious Bazaar! Where you cavort with infidels of every description! Hindus! Christians! Kabirites! Everyone but us! Asking them about their gods! As if that is of more import to you, than the word of Allah. At every turn you have shown your preference for them over us!"

"You misunderstand me, Badauni. I only wish to know Allah better. Therefore I ask other religions, other people—"

"Is there a need to ask! When you know the One True Path? If you had to ask, you are not a Muslim! And if you have to keep three hundred concubines for your carnal pleasure, you are not a Muslim. And if you have to have a school of artists make paintings of yourself and your fawning courtiers, you are an idolater, and you are not a Muslim!"

"You do not understand—"

"Oh, I understand perfectly, Your Majesty! I am, as you say, your friend. Do you even know what you have me doing right now? Do you know what that idiot Sheikh Mubarak, who you esteem so highly, has tasked me to do in your name? He has me translating the Mahabharata! Into Persian! I, an Imam of the True Faith, a lover of Allah! I am forced to translate that puerile rubbish of the Hindu non-believers into Persian!" Badauni seems to stand on his toes in white-hot rage. "Under your orders! By your tasking!"

He pauses for breath. "To us in the *ulema*, Your Majesty, you are an infidel." He leans closer. His dark, pockmarked face looms over Akbar's in the gloom.

"We hate you. You may have been the foremost of men in your time. But on Judgment Day you will be the most pitiable of stragglers, in line behind the concubines. And we! We of the *ulema*... will watch with pleasure as you suffer in Hell!"

Ruquiya walks in. Badauni springs back returning to his previous stance of standing some distance away from Akbar. Ruquiya looks around in surprise. "I forgot to mention..." she says. "You should call me when you are finished."

"Oh, we are quite finished already, Begum," Badauni replies. "His Majesty and I had a very good conversation."

Ruquiya looks at Badauni's flushed face warily. Badauni turns and leaves.

Stunned and devastated, Akbar fixes his eyes on the ceiling. There are few times in his life that he has felt entirely alone. This is one of them.

Paru climbs the steps to the dance class with a sense of quiet expectation. Inside, she sits opposite Amma across a low wooden table.

She takes the bags of coins out from a small cloth pouch she is carrying. There are many of them. She places the bags all to one side on the table. She starts emptying them out onto the table one at a time. It takes some time to count. The bags contain one-*rupiya* coins, as well as coins of smaller denominations. Paru has to make up some *rupiyas* by stacking a number of small coins together. The pile of counted coins grows larger and larger.

"Ninety-seven..." Paru counts. She picks up four four-*anna* coins. "Ninety-eight... Ninety-nine..." She picks up the last four four-*ana* coins. "Hundred!" she says triumphantly. The bags are empty. The coins form a large pile on the table.

Paru looks at Amma, a little smile on her face. "Now, can I have my jewel back?"

Amma's jowls have been working as Paru counted. She has difficulty speaking. "It's gone," she says.

"What?" Paru asks.

"It's gone... it's gone," Amma says going pale.

"Where did it go?"

"Some men took it. Took it. They came here and threatened me with swords... asked me where it was... and took it."

"But... how did they know you had it?"

Amma is shaking. "I took it to the *bazaar* one... one time. To the jewellers... I am sorry. I am very sorry."

"You're sorry?" Paru says incredulously. "You took my jewel to the *bazaar* and you're sorry?" The tears start welling up. "Where is my jewel?" she asks, barely able to speak. Her breath is shallow. "Where is my jewel?"

"I was very frightened... with the men!" Amma says shaking. "They threatened me with their swords!"

"Where is my jewel?

"Forgive me. I am sorry. I am very sorry. You... you can keep the money."

"I don't want your money," Paru says springing up, her eyes blazing. "I don't want your money! Here take it!" She picks up a handful of money and throws it at Amma. "Take it! Take it! Take it!" she screams, throwing the money at Amma. Amma covers her face with her hands.

"I want my jewel! I want my jewel!" Paru screams. "Why did you give them my jewel! I want my jewel!" She runs out of the room, crying.

She stops on the verandah, not knowing where she's going. She stands for a moment, then crumples, sitting on the steps. My jewel!" she sobs. "My jewel! My jewel! Where is my jewel! Where is my jewel!"

She sits on the steps and sobs. They are great heaving racking sobs, inconsolable sobs, as if her heart is about to come out. She sits that way on the verandah, as Amma cowers inside.

A shadow falls across her. It is the Snake Charmer. "Hey! What's this?" he demands. "What are you crying about?"

"They stole my jewel!" Paru cries. The pain in her voice is unbearable. "They stole my jewel."

"What jewel?"

"My jewel!" she screams. "They stole my jewel!"

"Who stole your jewel?"

"The men! The men!"

"What men? What are you talking about?"

"The men who are trying to kill me! They stole my jewel!"

"There are men trying to kill you?" the Snake Charmer asks, incredulously.

"All the time!" Paru cries. "They come at me with swords! And they try to kill me!"

"Then why aren't you dead already?"

"Will you get away from me!" she screams. "You stink anyway!"

"Okay! I'm sorry, I'm sorry. Listen. If there are men bothering you, I can protect you. Look. I'll show you. Look." From his loin-cloth he unsheathes a six-inch dagger. He swings it with a stabbing motion as if in a fight. "I'm really good with it," he says unconvincingly.

"My jewel," Paru sobs, her voice aching, plaintive. "I've lost my jewel!" It is as if she has lost a loved one.

The Snake Charmer puts his arm around her shoulder. Paru lets him. He is awkward and tender. They sit like this while she cries.

The high road into the city is clogged to the point of being non-functional. The parade of nobles and their attendant guards stretches for twenty miles. Each noble rides on an elephant or a horse with a guard ahead, and a guard behind. The size of the troop has been the source of some rancour, since each noble has wanted to bring as large a retinue as possible. But, the hand of Itimad Ud Daulah is long and the enforcement of his strictures steely. The nobles have had little option but to comply.

What the nobles' retinues lack in numbers they have made up for in show. Elephants and horses seem to be buried under saddle-cloths resplendent with mirrors, bells and glittering stones, extending all the way to the ground. Bands play a brisk march. Flags fly in such numbers they look like butterflies in a field of flowers. There is a collective roar that emerges from the shouting of orders, the pounding of hooves, the playing of bands, and the chatter of peasants pushed to the side of the road by the imperious mob.

At the fort's gates there is further evidence of Itimad Ud Daulah's steely hand. A Rajput noble and his troop of sixty are attempting to enter the fort. The noble is atop an elephant and is dressed in his best finery. His captain is trying to convince the Mughal guards at the gates to let the troop in. But the guards are unmoved. Eventually, only the *amir* and a small number of his officers on horseback are allowed to proceed through the gates. The rest of the troop has to return along the road they have just traversed, and camp on the outskirts of town. This causes close-to-impossible chaos on the high road, as the returning soldiers jostle with the unending procession of troops still approaching the fort. Swaths of countryside outside the city are now rapidly being appropriated by the tents of these spill-over troops.

Itimad Ud Daulah, Asaf Khan, and Nur ride down a side-street. They are alone and without guards. They stop outside the gate of a small, private garden, walled off from the noise of the street. A single sentry stands at the gate. He lets the three of them in, and closes the gate behind them.

The garden is perfect. It has red cobblestone pathways winding through perfectly manicured hedges. Benches made of inlaid marble and covered with intricate designs stand like jewel-boxes under exotic trees brought from the far reaches of the Empire.

In contrast to the garden's serenity, the demeanour of the three is agitated. They remain on their horses and canter nervously along the red pathways. "It is not like me to seek advice from you children," Itimad Ud Daulah says at length. "But this is unusual. I have never felt such fear."

"We will be safe, Father, if we play our cards right," Asaf Khan says.

"It is not for myself. It is for you people. The future of the Empire."

They ride in silence for some time. Nur is a little behind Itimad Ud Daulah and Asaf Khan.

"You have something on your mind, Father," prompts Asaf Khan.

"Yes. Man Singh is acting very strange. He is going to keep

Salim imprisoned through the Choosing."

"What is his reason?"

"Khusrau needs to be introduced. So Khusrau will get to address the nobles. But Salim will not."

"And what is wrong with that?"

"Wrong? It is not fair! I have no regard for Salim. But if he does not appear, they will assume he is drunk and the nobles will choose Khusrau by default. Salim should appear as well as Prince Khusrau!"

"Should? What is this 'should' you speak of, Father? You have such quaint notions."

"It is the notion of law! When there is law," Itimad Ud Daulah blusters, "the... the people are at rest. There is less... killing!"

"That law came from His Majesty. Now His Majesty is musing about the laws of Allah. He doesn't care any longer. If he doesn't care, why should you care?"

"You upset me, son."

"Upset or not, I am merely describing to you what is. It is obvious to me that Man Singh has become greedy. He fancies himself as Regent... for a King who will be a child. That will give him infinite power."

"I have known Man Singh for thirty years. People are not as low as you think."

"Oh they are, father. They are."

"Could you not speak to Man Singh," Nur interjects. "As to a friend—"

"Oh, I would not advise that, Sister. You do not understand these things."

Nur scowls, but says nothing. There is a long-standing sibling rivalry between Asaf Khan and her. Their relationship is perfunctory at best.

"Man Singh must not get the idea that we oppose him in any way," Asaf Khan goes on. "I have convinced Salim that I am his closest friend. Father, you must work with Man Singh and Khusrau and continue to keep a tight relationship with them. That way, we benefit, whoever wins."

Itimad Ud Daulah looks at Asaf Khan with distaste. "Any other advice for me... Son?"

"Yes," Asaf Khan says firmly. "This Choosing you have your heart so set on, father. It is a joke! A romantic notion of yours and Birbal's. A comic opera!" Asaf Khan stares back at his father's disapproving gaze. "Stay with the power, Dad."

That evening, Itimad Ud Daulah, and Asaf Khan are summoned to another urgent gathering, this time at Man Singh's palace. In his large reception hall, Man Singh has assembled Birbal, selected ministers from Akbar's court, and a collection of his close commanding officers. The sudden appearance with Man Singh of what appears to be a military contingent is not lost on the civilians.

In the centre of the hall stands Prince Khusrau. He is sixteen years old. His hair is long and tousled and extends to his shoulders. He has a pleasant face, and he looks painfully young. Itimad Ud Daulah allows himself a fleeting thought at the strangeness of it all — that this youth should be placed into the fire versus a man twice his age, one, moreover, who is his father.

Man Singh walks around Khusrau, appraising him. Khusrau stands as one on display. "Don't look up, look down," Man Singh advises.

Khusrau adjusts his gaze stiffly.

Man Singh appears to be in his element. "Too far. Look mid-level, into their eyes. Man to man. Who is the most important noble?"

"Raja Bihari Mal of Ambar," Khusrau replies.

"Who is the most talkative, and should be ignored?"

"Muzafar Shah of Gujarat."

"Who are you?"

"I am the direct descendent of His Majesty, the Emperor. His Majesty has chosen me to succeed him. I do not drink. I do not take opium. I am not possessed of pursuing women."

"What will you do?"

"I will not let difference of religion in a man affect my policy of his worth. I will improve protection of the roads, and provide free shelter to travellers. But most important, with General Man Singh's help, I will conquer Ahmednagar! Bijapur! Golkonda! To the glory of the Empire!"

Man Singh is not satisfied. He continues to walk critically around Khusrau.

"Mention that you follow the true path of Allah," Asaf Khan advises.

The *Diwani Aam* is an open hall, a roof supported by magnificently proportioned carved pillars. It overlooks a large lawn, which is now crowded with the assembled nobles and their retinues. Each noble has a pavilion of his own, where he is ensconced with his entourage. The noble, Rana Pratap Singh, has a wild and unkempt look, as if he has just emerged from the jungle. He has been allowed the largest entourage and is among the most powerful nobles. The *amir* Muzafar Shah, on the other hand, is bejewelled and well-manicured, but carries little clout. Raja Bihari Mal of Ambar is perhaps the most powerful noble. But he has a modest-sized pavilion and cannot be distinguished at all from the members of his entourage. A loud hubbub rises from the multiple conversations on the lawn.

The women sit behind a section of the *Diwani Aam* that has been cordoned off by an enormous, translucent curtain. They are looking out raptly at the men. Hamida Begum sports a pair of hand-held field glasses, of which she is quite proud. She is attended by Nur, who sits next to her.

Itimad Ud Daulah, Man Singh, and Birbal stand on the stage, on either side of Akbar's empty throne. The musicians start up with a burst of fanfare. Itimad Ud Daulah walks slowly to the front of the hall and faces the audience of nobles seated on the lawn. The music stops.

There is a long silence. The nobles search Itimad Ud Daulah's face. Their faces look alert. They seem apprehensive of what might happen next. Itimad Ud Daulah tries to hide his fear.

"My fellow *amirs*!" he announces. "We are here to stop a killing."

The palace hall in which Man Singh has imprisoned Jahangir is close to the harem quarters of the fort and was used by Akbar until recently for late-night parties. The room has the virtue of being well-enclosed. It has a thick wooden door. Jahangir looks longingly at this door. Four guards stand across it looking back at him. Jahangir sits opposite them, cross-legged and erect, with a yogic look on his face. The captain of the guard is the same man who arrested him, the one with the absurdly curling moustache.

Jahangir sees in the guards an extension of his father's long arm. They have been sent to try him. And it is his manifest destiny to brave their trial and win. Never mind that it is really Man Singh and Itimad Ud Daulah who have imprisoned him and that it is really Birbal who has laid the underpinnings of this absurd Choosing. Those are simple slaves of his father's will... goons in his employ. In the end, it is his father who is behind this. Jahangir has no illusions that his father would like to see him, Jahangir, being chosen by this Choosing. On the contrary, it is his father's fondest wish to see him fail. Akbar cannot tolerate a Salim who becomes as great as Akbar. Because there can be only one Akbar.

Jahangir feels strangely calm. That terrifying emptiness, where there is no support below, is absent. His yogic stance, which has been assumed for the captain's benefit, has an element of truth to it. He is indeed calm. He experienced that terrifying emptiness when Asaf Khan told him about the Writer, when it seemed for a moment as though manifest destiny would be flouted, and he felt himself falling in front of Asaf Khan's eyes. The chasm opened up under him, stretching for infinity. But it does not exist, the chasm does not exist. The world moves according to Allah's will, and Allah's will is manifest destiny. And the manifest destiny is that Jahangir will be King.

In his mind, Jahangir searches for ways to impress upon the captain the injustice of his situation. To be imprisoned in his own palace by the perfidious underlings of his father! "Are you sure I am not allowed to leave this room?" he demands.

"I am sure, Your Highness," the captain replies.

"Not even for a few moments?"

"My orders," the captain explains patiently, "are not to let you out under any circumstances. And to keep my eyes on you at all times."

Jahangir decides to look directly into the captain's eyes. He does this for several seconds hoping to elicit an effect. There is none. "You realise this whole ceremony is about me, don't you? It is to crown me King. Don't you think it odd, that I am not allowed at my own ceremony? There must be a mistake."

The captain does not reply.

"Show me those orders," Jahangir says casually.

"My instructions are not to let you see the orders, Your Highness. My instructions are not to even speak to you."

"Oh, how can you not speak to me? I am your future King! You and I, we shall start a great friendship." Jahangir gets up and extends his hand like a great monarch to a lowly captain.

The captain stares back, as one who does not take lightly to being trifled with.

"You realise," Jahangir says, beginning to pace the room, "that when I am King I will look kindly upon my old friends, but poorly on my enemies. You realise that don't you?" He glances at the captain. "I can even have people executed," he adds softly.

The captain's eyes meet Jahangir's. "Your Highness," he replies evenly. "I was warned that you would say that. If I was to open that door right now, there are eight guards on the other side who will kill both you and me."

At the *Diwani Aam*, Itimad Ud Daulah faces the nobles. "His Majesty, has taken the most unusual step of asking you to choose his successor. For each of you, your word shall carry the weight of your *jagir*."

The bejewelled noble, Muzafar Shah of Gujarat, sits in the front row as close as he can get to the stage. He now stands up, coughing noisily. He looks behind and to the front of him, massages his throat, and prepares to speak. "If I may... there is an inquiry about among the nobles... I speak not just for myself... but what if we like none of the pretenders?"

"If you like none of the pretenders, you may say nothing," Itimad Ud Daulah replies. "That is permissible."

Muzafar Shah looks for an excuse to say something else. Then sits down.

"His Majesty offers a choice of two pretenders. The first is his eldest son, Prince Salim. We all know Prince Salim.

"The second is the eldest son of his eldest son, Prince Khusrau. Most of you have not met Prince Khusrau. It is our intention at this gathering to present him—"

"What about the third?" A voice descends on the audience like a thunder-clap. The powerful *amir* Rana Pratap Singh is standing in front of his enormous pavilion at the back of the audience. With his wild beard and shoulder-length hair, he looks like an ancient prophet.

"What do you mean?" responds Itimad Ud Daulah, stunned.

"What about the Third Prince?"

"There is no Third Prince," Itimad Ud replies carefully. "There are only two princes. And you must choose from them."

Pratap Singh's eyes glow as one possessed of supernatural powers. They look straight into Itimad Ud Daulah's. "There is a

Third Prince!"

"There is no Third Prince."

Muzafar Shah jumps up. "If... if I may... if there are other pretenders to the throne, may their names—"

Raja Bihari Mal of Ambar stands up. He looks like a fat businessman rather than a steward of vast lands, populations and revenues. He speaks in a measured, plodding way. "I, too, have heard that there is a Third Prince."

There is a tense silence.

"It is true," Itimad Ud Daulah, relents. "There was a Third Prince at one time. But no one has seen him. He may be dead."

"If there was such a prince, Honourable Minister, why were we not informed—"

"The Third Prince is not dead!!"

"What do you mean?"

Pratap Singh's eyes glow with a frightening clairvoyance. "The Third Prince is alive! And is roaming the kingdom!"

"How do you know?" Itimad Ud Daulah protests.

"He is here! Among us!"

An *amir* called Sulaiman Karani leaps up from his seat. "I would ask the Rana to be quiet! We have hardly begun and he has to interrupt with his silly visions!" Sulaiman Karani has a sharp face with blazing brown eyes.

Pratap Singh ignores him. "The Third Prince is a princess!" he announces unexpectedly.

"I will turn *you* into a princess if you don't shut up!" shouts Sulaiman Karani.

"I speak the truth!" Pratap Singh thunders.

"Lies! You speak lies!" Sulaiman Karani responds.

At this, Pratap Singh draws his sword and charges across the courtyard at Sulaiman Karani.

Sulaiman Karani draws his own sword. A number of the nobles

stand up at once, their hands moving to their weapons. Four Mughal guards, distinguished by their gold and red uniforms, spring up from nowhere, deftly avoid Pratap Singh's sword, and bring him down in a flying tackle. Pratap Singh's tall frame crashes to the ground with the guards on top of him. Two other guards grab Sulaiman Karani from behind, trapping his arms in immovable wrestling holds. Suddenly, the square is filled with colourful guards in gold and red. Each noble who makes a threatening move finds himself shadowed by a guard, his arms ready to be pinned.

The commotion seems to calm Itimad Ud Daulah. "You are reminded that unruly behaviour during these proceedings may result in serious consequences. By order of His Majesty the Emperor," he reminds them.

Birbal advances to the front of the stage, his hand raised. The effect is dramatic. The *amirs* abandon their aggressive stances overtaken by curiosity at what Birbal might have to say. The many conversations quiet down gradually. "We shall make the Third Prince a pretender, as you suggest," Birbal says. "But we do not know where he is. If you choose this mystery Prince, and if he comes forward, His Majesty will recognise his own son and make him King. If he does not come forward, then we shall have to pick your next preference, be it Salim or Khusrau."

An excited buzz rises up from the lawn, as this new rule sinks in.

In his party-hall prison, Jahangir lies flat on the carpet, a row of wine cups balanced on his bare chest and stomach. He places a new cup on his chest and attempts to fill it from a jug. His hand is unsteady and wine dribbles down his belly on to the expensive carpet. Jahangir addresses the cup. "Three hundred *zat*, three hundred *sawar*, captain. That is my final offer. You could have an entire district to call your own. You would be... a small noble. An *amir*!" He picks the cup off his chest and drinks from it.

The captain stares back at Jahangir with a stony look.

"In each man's life, it is said, there comes a moment. A moment when destiny calls. And it is up to that man to call upon his Gods and to seize his moment! For the man who seizes his moment, there is no looking back. For the man who hesitates..." Jahangir sighs. "I know when my moment is going to be! It is the moment when I shall become King. When is your moment going to be, captain?"

There is no answer.

Suddenly, they hear the sound of the door being unbarred from the outside. The door opens a crack. The captain speaks to a messenger standing outside. Jahangir hears the captain protest. The captain glances over his shoulder at Jahangir. At length he turns to Jahangir. "The General has sent word that you are not to worry yourself about the Choosing, or its results. Instead, you should amuse yourself with wine, opium, and dancing girls."

Jahangir sits up red with anger. The cups go flying and wine spills on his clothes. "He has no right! He will rue the day!"

There is a sound from outside the quarter-open door. The captain turns and speaks to the messenger once more. At length he turns to Jahangir.

"You are to pick the best dancing girl," the captain says unbelievingly. "And make love to her."

Jahangir walks to the centre of the room and sits cross-legged, this time with his back to the captain.

"The girls are waiting outside," the captain reminds Jahangir.

Jahangir ignores the captain and regards a painting on a wall at the far end of the room.

Something clicks in his mind. "Send the girls in," he says abruptly.

Three dancing girls enter the party hall. They are accompanied by Saheli, carrying her *veena*, and the *tabla* player who had played for Jahangir earlier, and for Paru earlier still.

Jahangir picks up one of the cups fallen on the carpet and pours himself a new cup of wine. He sits solemnly to watch.

The musicians play. The girls dance. Saheli sings. Each girl does her best to win Jahangir. These are professional court dancers, skilled and sexy. They hold nothing back. One of the dancers removes her *choli* and throws it at Jahangir. Her perfect, succulent breasts seem to tease Jahangir with their nakedness.

The dancer on the left of the trio is Ritu. Jahangir is drawn to the breath-taking seductiveness of her body. He glances at her. Then, surprised at himself, looks again. Ritu moves her hips with a mastery that belies her nineteen years. She wears a thin, gauze *choli* through which her nipples stand erect. She sticks her tongue out at Jahangir her mouth half-open. Her body is poetry in motion, using the beat of the music to elevate Jahangir into a powerful sexual thrall. The dance comes to an end. The girls stand still, in various stages of nakedness. They pant slightly.

Jahangir solemnly raises his glass towards Ritu.

Ritu advances towards Jahangir her hips moving sensuously. Jahangir stands. They fix each other with their eyes. Ritu resumes her dance standing in front of Jahangir. The *tabla* and *veena* join in once again. Every few beats she sways her hips in rhythm. She inches towards Jahangir, aroused herself. She puts her hands on his chest and unbuttons his shirt. She passes her hands over his nipples, one hand descending to his belly and venturing lower. Jahangir places his hands on her back, caressing them forward till they are firmly placed on her breasts. All the while she is dancing, maintaining the beat, undulating her hips like an ocean's wave. She bends forward, puts her tongue on his nipple, and licks it.

Jahangir pushes her back, breathing heavily. He stoops, picks up the wine jug and takes a long swig. He glances at the captain.

"We can go behind the curtain," Ritu murmurs. Jahangir looks at the captain again. Ritu pulls him into a small alcove hidden by a curtain. It is meant for just this purpose.

The minute they are past the curtain, Ritu is all over him. She tears his shirt off, kisses his belly, starts going lower. Jahangir drops the jug as she pushes him onto the floor. She is on top of him, naked, wild, forceful. She moans as she begins to climax.

Jahangir regards Ritu's ecstatic face and upper body. Her moans get louder. He looks beyond Ritu's ecstatic face. He sees a sliver of blue sky. Built into the ceiling is an architectural flourish, a little air vent about a foot to two feet square. Through this vent Jahangir can see pristine blue sky. For several seconds Jahangir regards the sky against Ritu's naked, rhythmically-moving body. Ecstatically, Jahangir's hand moves out clutching the carpet. Ecstatically, he feels the fallen wine jug. His fingers close around it.

He swings the wine jug savagely at Ritu's head.

There is a dull sound. Ritu collapses abruptly on top of Jahangir. Jahangir lies still for a second. He tries to crawl out from underneath her limp, naked form. It is harder than he expects. Parts of her continue to hold him down. He frantically shakes himself free.

He stands naked, thinking, glancing nervously at the curtain that shields him from the guard. He picks up Ritu's concubine clothes and starts to wear them. Another thought occurs to him and he breathes heavily as he dons Ritu's clothes, trying to hold up his end of the love-making.

"Hannhh!... Hannhh!... Hannhh!..." Jahangir moans. Jahangir examines the forbidding stone wall leading up to the vent in the ceiling. The climb looks arduous, to say the least. He throws himself at the wall trying desperately to scramble up. But he slithers down immediately. "Hannhh!...Hannhh!...Hannhh!..." He drags the fallen Ritu towards the wall, hoping to use her as a footstool. He quickly abandons the idea and drops her. He sees a wall-lamp, just out of reach. He throws himself at the wall again, trying to reach for the lamp. He misses by a foot.

He remembers that there has been no sound from Ritu. Bracing himself he tries to approximate her voice. "Hannhh!... Hannhh!... Hannhh!..." he moans in a credible falsetto. He pauses, out of breath. "Hannhh!... Hannhh!... Hannhh!" he moans in his own voice.

He casts about frantically. He sees his soft trousers lying on the floor. He uses them to make a loop. He jumps again at the wall, this time ensnaring the lamp in the loop. The lamp holds. The trousers hold. Jahangir hangs on with one hand. "Hannhh!...Hannhh!...Hannhh!" he moans in Ritu's voice.

He is standing on top of the lamp. Loop in hand he examines the wall further up.

At the *Diwani Aam*, Khusrau advances awkwardly to the front of the stage. His presence does not inspire much attention. A hubbub rises from the lawn as the *amirs* wander over to their neighbours' pavilions and indulge in side-conversations.

Khusrau adjusts his tunic. His hands shake as he does so. "I am the direct descendent of His Majesty, the Emperor Akbar," he proclaims. "His Majesty has chosen me to succeed him as ruler of the realm."

Man Singh nods slightly, watching him closely.

"I do not drink," he continues. "I do not take opium. And..." He forgets his lines. There is a long awkward pause. "And I hate women," he says remembering.

Laughter rises from the lawn.

"I will rule with justice. I will not let religion..." He forgets again. "I will follow the true path of Allah..."

Khusrau freezes. His fingers shake uncontrollably.

Behind the women's curtain, Hamida Begum regards the scene through her field glasses. Nur sits beside her. There are two empty spaces next to Nur.

On the lawn, Raja Bihari Mal stands up. "How will you defeat Malik Ambar?"

"Who——" Khusrau is blank.

"Malik Ambar. The man who is the scourge of the Deccan."

"That is not a fair question," Man Singh intercedes hurriedly. "He is but a boy. It is I who will lead a campaign against Malik Ambar."

"So that is your game!" says Sulaiman Karani. "To be Regent, and have all the power!"

"If it is my 'game', as you put it, there is little choice," Man Singh replies coldly. "Prince Salim is a drunk. Do you see another option?"

"The Thrid Prince!" Pratap Singh's powerful voice interjects. "The Third Prince is a choice!"

"General, I would like to intercede here—" says Muzafar Shah.

Birbal steps forward and regards the nobles. Gradually, the hubbub dies down. "My fellow *amirs*, you have come all this way to choose a future king. We stand here poised in a crucial moment between two epochs."

The nobles regard Birbal with a mixture of awe and curiosity. Only the smallest of murmurs rises from the lawn.

"There is a story that keeps going through my head, which I would like to share with you... my friend Bhishti Sen, the mason, has just finished carving the tomb of Saint Salim Chishti. If you have not seen this wonder, you must visit it at Fatehpur Sikri. Truly it is a work of art from the divine world.

"But when he started, my friend faced a problem. How to carve his beautiful designs with precious stones set into white marble? He had all the stones at hand. Malachite for green, onyx for maroon, lapis for blue. But when he laid the stones into the marble, they fell off. My friend needed a glue. One that did not exist. Where to find such a glue?"

Nur turns her head by chance, and finds to her surprise that Jahangir is seated in the empty space next to her. He is dressed in a concubine's clothes.

Jahangir's pink veil, which has been covering his face, now slips.

Their eyes meet.

"My friend went to great lengths in search of his glue," Birbal continues. "But he could not find it. As the days wore on, and his work was at a standstill, he grew despondent. He could not sleep at night. He lost his appetite, and grew thin and hollow in front of my eyes. The months went by. A year. And still he struggled. In despair he turned to his Gods. But there seemed to be no answer from them. And then one day — through a friend, of an acquaintance, of a relative — my friend heard about it! There was a tribe in a distant village, in the mountains of the Aravali. The people of this tribe knew how to make the strongest glue in the world, using herbs and substances that they found in the forests. I have seen this glue. It is ugly and grey. But once cured, it can hold together any stone for a hundred years."

Jahangir looks at Nur. He is revealed, vulnerable, sweating. There is blood on his arm from having grazed it on the stone during his climb. He waits helplessly for her to sound the alarm. She regards him seriously. She then turns her head forward and continues to listen to Birbal.

"When you see the tomb of Saint Chishti, you will not think of this glue. It is hidden. I dare say you will take it for granted. But it has brought together many beautiful stones."

Curious, Nur turns to look at Jahangir again. Jahangir looks at Nur's face, and has the strange sensation that he has known this face all his life. It is a calm, sensitive face. Its direct gaze shows such empathy, it seems to fill the secret chasm inside Jahangir. He knows, without having to say a word, that Nur will not sound the alarm. She seems to have a mind of her own. A man sitting next to her in women's clothes in the women's section of the *Diwani Aam* is simply something to observe with interest. It is the face, Jahangir thinks, of Allah's will. Their eyes meet. Jahangir's are filled with gratitude. Nur's are composed, enigmatic.

"My fellow *amirs*," Birbal says. "Let us not waste this precious moment. Let us instead spend it in thought... thought that may create future happiness, not just for ourselves, but for our brethren all across Hindustan. I, for one, would like you to think about glue."

Hamida Begum lowers her field glasses and searches for something behind her seat. "Where is my... handkerchief?"

she asks Nur.

Nur gets down on her knees, shielding Jahangir from Hamida Begum. She rummages among the Begum's things, blocking Jahangir from her view. She finds the handkerchief and hands it to Hamida Begum. Hamida Begum waits for Nur to sit down. Nur remains where she is, on her knees, hiding Jahangir.

Hamida Begum gives Nur a curious, upbraiding look. Finally, she turns her head to the *Diwani Aam* again, as if concluding that Nur is beyond redemption.

Nur sits down.

Birbal's speech has concluded. The nobles are silent.

"The Honourable Birbal gives us something to think about," Man Singh says. "I am a simple man, but does not alcohol dissolve glue?"

There are titters from the audience.

It is at this moment that Jahangir leaps onto the stage through the curtain. He is filled with a righteous fire. He snatches at his concubine's top and takes it off. He struggles furiously with his pink veil, but it refuses to fall off. Finally it just hangs on one side from his skirt.

"*So!*" Jahangir proclaims. His voice explodes over the *Diwani Aam* like a thunder-clap. "We have a gathering here, is it! Is the party warming up?!" He points a finger at the nobles, as if noting future executions. "You have betrayed me! All of you! You have betrayed me! Do you dare to doubt that I should be your king?! I, who am the eldest son? The only son who has defended the Empire?! Do you dare to boubt me!"

"Your Highness, this is quite improper—" Itimad Ud Daulah tries to guide Jahangir off-stage. Jahangir frees himself with such violence, he hits Itimad Ud Daulah hard across the face.

Itimad Ud Daulah reels back from the blow. There is a red welt on his cheek. The nobles look on in shock. "His Majesty has commanded this meeting," Itimad Ud Daulah says coldly.

Man Singh signals to the guards. Four gold-and-red guards

come up and surround Jahangir.

"His Majesty who!" Jahangir demands. "He has one foot in the grave! The man thinks there is a light shining out of the middle of his forehead! You call him your King? He is mad! mad! You call him your King?!"

"That is enough, Your Highness," says Man Singh.

"Enough? You are not my tutor, General. It is I who say to you! Leave this stage right now! I need to address my subjects—"

"By the powers vested in me by the Emperor Akbar," Man Singh roars. "I order you off this stage!"

The guards step forward, surrounding Jahangir. Seeing them threaten him, the *amirs* feel a curious kinship. The gold-and-red guards have reminded the *amirs* once again of their subservience to the Empire.

"You should let him speak!" Sulaiman Karani shouts defiantly.

Raja Bihari Mal stands up with surprising intensity. "Yes! Why don't you let him speak?"

Man Singh gives the signal. The four guards pounce on Jahangir. He tries to dodge and run away from them. But they catch him and push him violently to the ground. Jahangir slips out from one side and begins to rise. A guard kicks him in the side. Jahangir grunts, and falls. Two guards grab his arms and pin him to the ground.

"Prince Salim, you are under arrest—" says Man Singh.

"You want us not to choose him, so you can keep all the power!" shouts Sulaiman Karani.

"He is under arrest!" Man Singh insists. The guards pick Jahangir up.

There are scattered shouts of protest from the nobles across the lawn.

"He's a pretender, isn't he?" Pratap Singh thunders. "If he is a pretender, you should let him speak!! And you should bring the Third Prince out and let him speak as well!"

Birbal looks amused. He signals to one of the guards.

"If I might address the assembly—" says Muzafar Shah.

The guard approaches Birbal. Birbal leans over to speak into the guard's ear. He indicates Jahangir. "I want you to hit him very hard where it hurts."

"By order of the Emperor," says Man Singh. "Prince Salim is placed under custody!"

"As future Emperor of Hindustan," Jahangir countermands, "I order you men to keep me here! As future Emperor...Aauuffff!" Jahangir doubles over in pain, as the guard punches him hard in the stomach.

A number of nobles simultaneously shout their protests at Jahangir's mistreatment.

"Guard! Take him away!" shouts Man Singh.

The guard who has hit Jahangir looks at Birbal, perplexed. Birbal nods approvingly and signals him to do it again.

The guard knees Jahangir in the groin.

There is a roar of protest as the nobles jump out of their seats.

Man Singh hastily orders the guards, who almost run, carrying the struggling Jahangir off the stage.

Birbal steps forward and raises his hand for silence. The nobles continue to protest excitedly. The guards press in threateningly. The noise gradually subsides. "By now both pretenders — who are present at this assembly — have had a chance to speak," Birbal says. "We shall proceed with the Choosing."

An unidentified noble speaks up. "One of them hates women," he says. "The other likes to dress up as a woman."

There is derisive laughter.

The sword of Humayun that hangs innocuously on the wall of Akbar's bedroom occupies a special place in the psyche of the Empire. In appearance it is an ordinary sword, one that bears the nicks and scratches of much use. But in the transcendental plane, it is the single object from which all power flows. It is the sword that went all the way to Persia when Humayun was forced to flee the conquering forces of the Afghan, Sher Shah Sur. And it is the sword that returned in triumph when, with fresh forces supplied by the Persian Emperor, Humayun returned to reclaim his capital. The only living connection now with that humiliating, near-death flight across the desert is Hamida Begum. She was the one who chose to walk with her husband, so that the camels might be able to carry water for the few remaining men. And it was she who one night in Sindh, under the brilliance of the desert stars, gave birth to Akbar.

With the Mughals, the near-God-like reverence for Humayun is not for his power, or for his war-fighting ability, but for his kindness and his strange vulnerability. Humayun's brother betrayed him and tried to seize the throne, not once but twice. Humayun's response, against all advice, was to forgive his brother and hope that love would cure him. He was wrong. But his very wrongness inspires a feeling of fierce protectiveness among the Mughals. It hides the chord of a collective humanity that runs through Mughal society, a secret too embarrassing to display, hidden carefully under the bravado and feats of military daring.

At the moment, the sword is all but forgotten on the wall as Ruquiya sits next to Akbar on his bed. The room is dimly lit. She is smiling, because he looks better.

"Ruquiya," says Akbar. "Am I a bad person?"

"Shah Baba—"

"Imam Badauni said I will go to hell."

"Imam Badauni is a bitter old man."

"Ruquiya, I am cold. Hold me."

She gets into the bed and lies next to him and holds him. Akbar moves his arm slowly and places it on Ruquiya's arm.

They lie still and content for a long time.

"I still think of Chittor," he says suddenly.

She is silent.

He gives a little laugh. "Remember my marriage?"

"How can I forget?"

"I think of it more often than you might expect."

"I know."

"I have never been so completely bamboozled by a woman. You saw her did you not? You saw how she ran from me!"

Ruquiya does not reply.

"You saw how she betrayed me, did you not, Ruquiya?"

"Yes. I saw how she betrayed you."

"That is what I do not understand. How she could do that. I can read people better than anyone. But this was... different. Granted she was sent by the Rana. But she loved me so! I was convinced of that. And I her! We had the supreme trust of love. And yet she ran!"

"Even when you are sick, you can think of nothing but your women."

"I still regret it. That she ran so, to leave me to my death. And the tragedy that followed..."

Ruquiya turns away. He tries to move his arm to place it tenderly on her, but is too weak. A tear rolls down her cheek.

"Ruquiya?" Akbar calls.

She sits up, looking away. She stands, as if about to leave.

"Ruquiya?"

"Why does it always have to be about you!" she explodes.

He is too taken aback to reply.

"All the time it has to be about you, you!!"

"Ruquiya, oh Ruquiya! Oh my love... come here. Please come here!"

She relents and moves a little toward the bed. He makes an effort and raises his arm weakly. She moves a little closer.

"Oh, Ruquiya! What would I do without you! After all these

years, do you still not understand? I can love her, but that does not take one breath away from my absolute adoration, my total devotion to you!"

She shakes her head. "No! I do not understand. Sometimes I do not." She wipes her tears with her hands. She gives him a reassuring pat. "You are tiring yourself out. You need to sleep." He watches with misgiving as she leaves the room.

Outside, it is dusk. Ruquiya walks rapidly along the deserted walkway, thoughts streaming excitedly through her mind. She can feel for him. Allah knows, she can, the jackass! That is the strange thing. She can even understand his selfishness. That is how much she loves him! She has nothing against this woman. But then, perhaps she does. She has her own feelings too! And he, oblivious as ever! A man, after all. A great, big self-obsessed pig! Steals your heart and moves on. Steals your heart and dies. Leaving you with a hole where your heart used to be, a hole in your life. After all these years, it is still the same. Nothing changes. They are both still the same... him and her...

At the far end of the corridor she sees a figure in the gloaming hurrying towards her. It is Itimad Ud Daulah. He is sweating with excitement.

"Begum! The nobles have chosen! They have chosen the Third Prince! And if we cannot find him... they have chosen Prince Salim!"

It takes a moment for Ruquiya to absorb the news. "They chose well," she says.

"Personally, I think they found neither Salim nor Khusrau to their satisfaction. So they chose someone they had never seen! I have to speak to his Majesty! He has yet to hear about the Third Prince! This is going to take some explaining. Allah knows what his reaction will be!"

Ruquiya makes a sudden decision. "His Majesty is not conscious," she tells Itimad Ud Daulah. "He cannot speak."

"But... I thought he was awake, and feeling much better!"

"He has relapsed again. He was coughing a little blood just now."

Itimad Ud Daulah looks for a way to get past Ruquiya. But she stands firmly in his path blocking the walkway.

"You look tired," Ruquiya says tenderly. "You should get some rest."

Itimad Ud Daulah hesitates, still trying to get past Ruquiya.

"The nobles have chosen well," she reassures him. "Let it flow as it is destined, Prime Minister. You need some rest."

Reluctantly, Itimad Ud Daulah turns back. Ruquiya is left alone in the dusk to contemplate the courtyard, the palace, and the fort that are all so rightly hers.

Jahangir has been taken to a new prison, a window-less dungeon deep in the bowels of the fort. He has spent the last two days in solitary confinement.

The captain with the curled moustache, accompanied by two guards, walks along the underground passageway to Jahangir's prison. The heavy wooden bar across the thick door is stuck. It takes the strength of all three men and some banging to knock it loose. The door creaks open. One of the guards holds up a flaming torch.

Jahangir looks up listlessly.

The captain unrolls an order and reads carefully and precisely. "By order of His Majesty the Emperor Akbar, Your Highness is free to leave this room." He looks at Jahangir. Then he reads on. "By order of His Majesty. Your Highness is to remain strictly confined within the walls of Agra Fort until the Third Prince be found. Or, until such time as a decision is made by His Majesty with regard to the succession."

Jahangir looks uncomprehendingly at the captain.

"You are free to leave this prison, Your Highness," the captain repeats kindly.

It is a week of uncertainty, of Jahangir walking like a ghost within the confines of the fort, and of a Prince who exists nebulously beyond its boundaries. The spies fan out with their mission; to the *bazaar* in the City, and to Delhi, Lahore, even Kabul. Has anyone seen a young man with a jewel, and a marriage document? Itimad Ud Daulah struggles with the notion of a more formal search, one that uses the help of the Army. But he can imagine nothing practical. He is barely on speaking terms with Man Singh. A barrier has developed between the two men since the Choosing.

To make matters worse, Itimad Ud Daulah is inundated with work. Since his pre-occupation with the Choosing, a massive backlog of the minutiae of his court duties has developed. He is overwhelmed by petitioners from all corners of the Empire with land disputes, justice complaints, revenue calculations, and on and on. He sits in the *Diwani Aam* trying to catch up. He is surrounded by a throng of courtiers, and advocates. There is a loud hubbub in the hall. His problem, as always, is that the humble petitioners are invariably elbowed aside by the moneyed and the high-and-mighty. He makes a point of randomly picking smaller petitioners from out of the crowd. But it is a losing proposition. He has asked Asaf Khan for his help. A smaller group sits to the side, centred around Asaf Khan. The two men toil till late in the evening. The hubbub around them remains constant.

Jahangir enters the hall unobtrusively and sits at the edge of Asaf Khan's group. Asaf Khan feels his presence. "That is all for today, gentlemen," he tells the courtiers around him. "I am sorry. Come back tomorrow... come back tomorrow."

He walks out surrounded by advocates. Jahangir follows him at some distance. "Come back tomorrow," Asaf Khan repeats, refusing to engage any further. The courtiers start to drop away. Jahangir catches up. Asaf Khan has a knot in his stomach.

"You said she was dead!" Jahangir whispers.

"I said no such thing!" Asaf Khan responds hotly. "I said my men were on it. We have the turban pin," he adds hopefully.

"That is cold consolation," says Jahangir. His voice is ice. "She has to be dead."

"She will be," Asaf Khan replies. "Tonight."

Jahangir blocks Asaf Khan's path. Their eyes meet. Asaf Khan can feel the sweat on his brow.

"Use the fan fellow," Jahangir advises.

"Yes," Asaf Khan replies.

Paru is at a weapon shop. She is looking at a display of evil-looking Mughal daggers. The shop is festooned with knives — double- and triple-bladed *kukris*, thin sharp blades, broad flat blades, blades with saws, heavy balls on chains with blades. Each weapon seems designed to hurt and mutilate its victim more creatively than the next. Paru puts her hand out tentatively towards the handle of a plain, sharp dagger.

"What are you looking for," the shopkeeper asks.

"Something small that I can hide on my body," she says.

The shopkeeper shows her a small dagger with a four-inch blade.

"No. Bigger than that."

He picks out a dagger with a six-inch blade.

"No," Paru says.

He reaches for a long, crisp instrument with a nine-inch blade.

"Yes," Paru says.

The shop-keeper takes the dagger out of its mount and hands it to Paru.

Paru holds it up trying to get the feel for it. The blade glints in the sunlight.

"If I had to stab a man with this, how would I do it?" She makes an inept movement forward. "Like this?"

The shopkeeper looks at her curiously. "No," he says taking the dagger from Paru's hand. He aligns his body, uses his other arm as counter-balance, and moves the dagger forward in a smooth, strong upward stabbing motion. "Like this."

Paru takes the dagger from him and tries to imitate his move. "Like this?" She muffs it.

The shopkeeper takes the dagger back and repeats his motion. "Like this."

She tries again, with a semblance of the right motion. Her hand closes comfortably around the handle.

Satisfied, she picks out a paper-thin leather sheath for the dagger. She ties the sheath around her bare waist, slipping it under her *ghagra*. She adjusts the *gaghra* to hide the dagger, then arranges her *odhni* over it. The dagger is barely visible under her clothes. She pays for dagger and sheath.

She walks away from the shop and is soon lost in the crowd.

A large yellow moon hangs above the horizon. It lights a black line of clouds underneath it. The night sounds of insects, arising from the bank of river weeds outside Paru's hut, is almost deafening.

Melting in from the darkness is an assailant. His sword glints in the moonlight. He is followed by another. And another. One by one, the assailants appear through the small passages between the huts that adjoin Paru's hut. There are nine assailants, their swords drawn and at the ready. They are led by the Fan Man. Bhir Das, and the Youth are both present. They act as his second-in-command.

The assailants surround the hut from all sides. They go around the back from each side to cut off any possibility of escape into the river weeds.

Bhir Das positions himself outside the window on the left side of the hut. He lights a torch. The area outside the hut is suddenly filled with light. The Fan Man stands on one side of the front door.

The Youth moves to the other side. He trips over someone sleeping in front of the door. It is the Snake Charmer.

The Snake Charmer awakens. He looks bewildered for a second, then realising the danger, he rolls away. He is on his feet in a trice. Snarling, he draws his dagger and lunges at the Youth.

The Youth barely manages to dodge the attack, the knife grazing past his waist.

The Snake Charmer lunges again. He stops stiffly in mid-thrust as the Fan Man delivers a professional blow to his head with the back of his sword. He falls like a log.

The Youth draws his sword ready to finish him off.

The Fan Man grabs his hand from behind. The Youth looks at the Fan Man, his eyes wide with aggression. "Only when it is necessary," the Fan Man says.

The Fan Man steps away from the hut to check the position of each man. The nine assailants are crouching in a tight circle around the hut, their swords ready.

The Fan Man signals to Bhir Das.

Bhir Das goes in through the window with the torch. Simultaneously, the Fan Man goes in through the front door, with the Youth close behind.

In the torchlight, the Fan Man sees the sleeping form of Paru's roommate. He swings his sword.

There is a small ugly sound from the roommate. Blood sprays upward, splattering his light shirt. The roommate's eyes open wide with surprise, fade, and go still. Her mouth remains half-open as if waiting to scream.

Bhir Das holds the torch up and looks at the dead girl's face. "That's not her," he says. He looks around the room.

Paru has been sleeping in the far corner, a blanket covering her. Now she wakes up.

"That's the one," Bhir Das says.

It takes Paru a moment to register what is going on. Then she screams.

The Fan Man starts walking across the room towards her.

Paru sits up holding the blanket screaming helplessly. In terror, she tries to push her body back into the wall.

There is a basket between the Fan Man and Paru. The Fan Man kicks it out of the way. The basket rolls and opens.

Maharaj, the King Cobra, springs up hissing. He fans himself out in full glory. He sees the large shape of the Fan Man advancing on him. Quick as silver, he is across the room. He strikes. His fangs sink into the Fan Man's thigh.

The Fan Man screams as his leg collapses under him. He drops to the floor, clutching his leg, screaming and writhing in pain.

Maharaj hisses and turns to attack Bhir Das. A stream of venom darts at Bhir Das missing him by a hair's breadth. Bhir Das yells in terror falling backward in his haste to reach the window. The torch goes out, plunging the hut into darkness. He claws his way out of the window, falling head first onto the grass outside.

The Youth, with surprising presence of mind, grabs the Fan Man's leg and drags him screaming, out through the front door.

"Cobra! Cobra!" Bhir Das shouts in the darkness. "There's a cobra in there!"

The cry is taken up. "Cobra! Cobra!" the men shout, with the primordial fear of men who find themselves with an angry snake in the dark. They have but one thought, to put as much distance as possible between themselves and Paru's hut.

One of the men helps the Youth and holds the Fan Man up by the arm. Together they carry him, running as fast as they can in the dark. The Fan Man is still screaming as the poison begins to course through his veins. It is some time before the cries of the men and their thrashing through the bushes dies away. Paru sits in her corner, the blanket up to her chin, whimpering in terror. The moonlight falls on the dead girl's face.

Maharaj wanders about the hut, pleased with himself.

An unused room in the fort is the rendezvous. The men have been let in through a side entrance. The Fan Man, carried by Bhir Das and the Youth, is brought in front of Jahangir. He is in a state of shock and is barely conscious. He looks grey. His bare leg is tied tightly with a cloth bandage to restrict circulation above the snake-bite. The men set him down on the floor, against the wall. Jahangir kneels next to him. Bhir Das slaps him to prevent him from passing out.

"There was a snake," the Fan Man says faintly. "Nobody told me about the snake."

"What about the girl?" Jahangir asks with surprising gentleness.

The Fan Man opens his mouth, unable to reply.

"We killed the wrong one," says Bhir Das. "Her roommate. She was sleeping in the same hut. Then the snake attacked. It was a cobra. The men would not wait."

Jahangir draws his breath in sharply. He springs up and paces nervously. He stops dead, his back to the men. He turns around. "The girl you killed. How old was she?"

"About the same," Bhir Das says, after giving it some thought. "But I did not kill her." He points to the Fan Man. "He did."

"Give me the turban pin," Jahangir says.

"What?" says Bhir Das, taken aback.

"The turban pin! The jewel you took from her. Where's the jewel!"

Bhir Das looks unwillingly at Jahangir. Jahangir stares coldly at him. Bhir Das reluctantly takes the jewel out of a hidden pocket. Jahangir snatches it from him. He holds the jewel up, examining it, tossing it up once. The jewel sparkles.

"You have done well," he tells the men unexpectedly. "You will be rewarded for your efforts." He indicates the Fan Man. "Take him to a good doctor. You may leave."

"What about—"

"Leave!" Jahangir abruptly walks out.

The men look at one another, perplexed.

Out in the courtyard, the same full moon that had hung above Paru's hut is now higher in the sky.

Clutching the jewel in one hand, Jahangir half-walks, half-runs along the deserted walkways. His lightly-coloured clothes stand out in the moonlight. He is headed towards the fort's gates. He stops short as he comes face-to-face with the sentries at the gates. He turns and runs back before the sentries see him. He runs across the fort, unable to stop. It helps his thoughts, which are flying at breakneck speed.

He is in a courtyard that adjoins the top of the fort walls. The moon hangs over the river in the distance, making it gleam. Nur stands on the wall, looking out. She seems to be waiting for someone or something.

Jahangir stops abruptly. She seems to calm him. He takes a

measured step forward.

Nur continues to look out, apparently uninterested in the source of the footsteps that have now stopped. Jahangir and Nur stand against the sky, the moon and the river behind them. Finally, Nur turns her head. She sees Jahangir and bows deeply.

"Who are you?" Jahangir says.

"I am Hamida Begum's attendant," Nur replies. Her voice is unhurried, contemplative.

"I am Prince Salim," he says, also calmly.

Nur nods slightly. They gaze at each other.

"It is very late, Hamida Begum's Servant. What brings you out here?"

"Forgive me, Your Highness. It is a full moon night. The animals are restless in their stables... and the lunatics."

"Yes..." Jahangir says. "The lunatics are especially dangerous." He thinks for a second. "The animals will calm down when the sun starts to rise. But the lunatics can start chains of events that refuse to stop."

"I was afraid of that, my Lord. When I came out here."

"I am afraid too," Jahangir says. "It makes me shiver. I can barely keep my breath straight."

Her gaze is soft, empathising. "I would wish to share your burden, Your Highness. But it seems every soul is alone with its destiny."

A thrill runs through Jahangir. It is as if she can divine every part of him. They look at each other unable to stop. He has the same pleading, apologetic look as at the Choosing, as of one in too much trouble to explain.

"I have often seen you leave the fort with a sketch-pad and charcoals, Hamida Begum's Servant," Jahangir says at last. "What do you do when you go out like that?"

"I take pleasure in the shape and the form of the houses," she says eagerly. "I draw the houses. I especially like the *bazaar*. The way it flows and causes new houses to be built. Sometimes I draw the people. And the animals."

"You draw animals?"

"Sometimes."

"The guards at the gate must know you very well," Jahangir says.

"Yes, they do... but I have permission. From Hamida Begum. And... from the Prime Minister..." She gestures, embarrassed. "He is my father..."

"Alas," Jahangir says. "I do not have the same permissions that you do, Hamida Begum's Servant. Though I would like very much to do what you do... visit the city and draw houses... but unfortunately my movements would cause a stir. I... I wonder if I could borrow your clothes?"

"My clothes?" she says surprised.

"A spare set of your clothes. Yes. If you should have them, somewhere."

Nur regards him seriously. "That should not be a problem."

"And... and a sketch-pad, if you would. With charcoals."

Her eyes search his. "Of course," she says. "Follow me."

She walks in front along the walkways. He follows in silence. They reach the edge of the dense living quarters of the harem.

"These are the... harem quarters," she says. "If Your Highness would wait."

"Of course." Jahangir waits. Nur returns with a folded black *burkha*, a sketch-pad, and charcoals.

Jahangir awkwardly unfolds the *burkha*.

Nur watches him struggling with it. "If Your Highness should need a horse to ride up to the houses — in order to draw them — you can hire one not three hundred yards from the gate.

"Ah yes, I forgot! A horse would be very useful," Jahangir says gratefully.

"The man's name is Sandhu," Nur says. "Your Highness can wake him up."

Jahangir fumbles with the *burkha*, dropping the sketch-pad.

"If I may take your leave, Your Highness," she says.

"Yes, yes!" Jahangir says, wearing the *burkha*.

Nur bows, and slips into the darkness.

Some time later, a figure carrying a sketch-pad, looking like Nur in her *burkha*, arrives at the gates. The guard barely looks up. The figure emerges into the street, through the side-door next to the gates. The *burkha*-covered figure makes its way to Sandhu's stable. It jumps onto a horse and takes off at a gallop. The horse's hooves clatter on the empty streets.

In Paru's hut, the moonlight comes in through the partially ajar door.

The dead girl is still lying there, her eyes peering questioningly into the darkness.

Paru's corner of the hut has been completely emptied. Paru, Maharaj, the Snake Charmer are all gone. The shelf Paru had crammed her clothes into has been emptied. The scroll is gone.

The door creaks open. Sword first, the figure in the black *burkha* enters the hut.

The high road out of the city has long since become a muddy track. The sun is almost directly overhead. Paru and the Snake Charmer carry their belongings on their backs, with more luggage on a donkey in tow. Maharaj, whose basket is very heavy, occupies pride of place on top of the donkey. The Snake Charmer has a cloth bandage around his head. It is splattered with dried blood.

"How much longer?" Paru says.

"Four days," he replies. They need to preserve their breath. The Snake Charmer has been setting a brisk pace.

"Where are we going?"

"I already told you. The village of the snakes. You will be safe. Only the snake people dare to go there."

"I am not one of the snake people."

"You are, now."

Paru is unimpressed. There is a new seriousness in her manner.

The Snake Charmer takes them on a path that is west, and south from Agra. The road soon peters out completely and they cross open countryside, lush and green at first, and then, as the days progress, increasingly brown.

Small brown hills with sharp edges and fantastic shapes scour the distant horizon. They start encountering sand and sand dunes. Miles of brown grasses rustle in the hot afternoon breeze.

Through entire days, Paru says very little. She lets the Snake Charmer lead, following silent and unquestioning in his footsteps. After some attempts at conversation, he too walks in silence, sensing her need to be alone.

At one point, she breaks the silence to say "I like you too much." The afternoon wind blows hot and dry. They are both panting from the effort of walking.

The Snake Charmer looks at her.

"You have to leave me," she says.

"What!" he replies, surprised.

"People close to me die."

"I'm not going to die!"

"She shared the hut with me. Now she's dead." Paru looks at him.

He laughs. "Don't worry. I can take care of myself."

Paru neglects to mention that she was thinking, her mother, too, had died. Her father she has never seen, although her mother claims that he is alive and about somewhere... he might as well be dead. But her cousins, her aunts, her uncles, her entire village, as her mother told her, had died. Victims of the cruel conqueror, when he took that ancient fort and killed everyone inside. The conqueror had a unique face, marked by a mole on his lip. It was said that the very sight of this man on his horse was enough to strike terror in the hearts of any resisting army. Many a ruler capitulated to this Conqueror with a Mole without a fight. Not so, the ruler of her mother's village. They stopped him, they fought him, and they won. They held him back from an ancient fort for two years. But, when he broke through, his vengeance was terrible. And he killed Paru's mother's family.

Then her mother died of the fevers. Then her roommate. Then.

She looks amusedly at the pitch-black back of the Snake Charmer as he trudges in front of her. No, never. She feels a hundred years older to him. He is so whole. So unspoiled. Which is why she has declared war. When she bought the dagger, she did not realise it at the time, but she had declared war. And declaring war can be good sometimes, because it can protect you and take you to places that you have not been. As when she overcame her fear of what had happened to Bahu's daughter and crossed the *bajra* field herself, to see the dancers in the big village. She had declared war then too. She crossed the field in direct defiance. Direct defiance.

The land opens out to large vistas. It is at once bleak and beautiful in the way that only Rajputana can be. In the evenings, a massive orange sun obscures the horizon, melting into a welter of shivering mirages and hilltops. In the cold nights, the waning moon dominates a spotless sky.

The Snake Charmer's estimate of four days was overly optimistic. After five days they are still trekking. They encounter a trading caravan headed south towards Surat. There are twenty camels, their black silhouettes standing out against the orange evening sky. Four soldiers guard the caravan riding on either side on tough, worn-out Arab horses. The Snake Charmer makes furtive contact with a porter on one of the trailing camels. He gets much-needed supplies in exchange for bribes. They part ways with the caravan and press on relentlessly toward the west.

On the sixth day, they round a corner past scrub and rocks, and are surprised to find two figures on horseback blocking their path. Paru and the Snake Charmer try to turn around. Two more men on horseback block their retreat.

The Snake Charmer curses and draws his dagger, readying himself for a fight.

Paru puts her hand out. "Stop, stop! It's not the same men."

The Snake Charmer lowers his dagger. The men seem to be

bandits. The leader has a flowing, black moustache. He is handsome and greasy.

"What do you want?" Paru calls.

"What do you think?" the bandit leader replies.

Paru thinks he wants her body, and her hand rises self-consciously.

"I want everything to come off," the bandit leader says. "Your necklace, your bangles, all purses, hidden money pouches, bags. Everything. I won't make you take your clothes off... if you're honest."

"Go fuck your mother!" the Snake Charmer says, ready to charge.

Paru puts out a restraining hand. "What are you going to do," she tells him. "They'll kill us." She starts removing her necklace and bangles. "Come on!" she urges the Snake Charmer. "Take out your money." She takes a leather pouch out from her waist and drops it onto the sand. Scowling, the Snake Charmer removes his own pouch and drops it next to Paru's.

"You can put the dagger down," the bandit leader advises the Snake Charmer. "The donkey," he says motioning to the basket atop the donkey.

The Snake Charmer unties the basket. It is heavy. He struggles to lower it to the ground.

"What's in the basket?" the bandit leader demands.

"A King Cobra," Paru says eagerly. "About twelve feet long. The poison has not been removed." She smiles shyly. "I can dance with the snake. Want to see it?"

The bandit leader looks at the basket for a long time. "That's all right," he says finally.

The bandits make them sit in the sand. They search every last corner of Paru and the Snake Charmer's things, giving the basket a wide berth. A bandit finds Paru's scroll. He opens it curiously and tries to read it.

Paru tenses. Her hand moves stealthily towards the knife hidden under her *ghagra*. The bandit looks at the scroll for a long time. Paru measures the right moment. Then he drops the scroll indifferently onto the sand. Paru relaxes.

The search concludes quickly. There is very little besides the two money pouches and the Snake Charmer's knife. The bandit leader tries to hide his disappointment. "Take your *choli* off," he says impassively to Paru.

Paru takes her *choli* off defiantly and drops it in the sand. The bandits regard Paru's breasts.

She sits, waiting for the next step.

The leader looks at Paru's small enticing breasts. "I want you to sit there the way you are, until you cannot hear our horses anymore," he says unexpectedly. "We will be watching. If you move too soon, we will come back and kill you."

He turns his horse abruptly. The men give Paru parting looks, then turn their horses after their leader. They raise a cloud of dust as they ride off.

Paru and the Snake Charmer sit silently until the sound of the horses recedes. Finally, there is only the rustling of the scrub and the buzz of a large desert fly.

Paru gets up and stretches. She picks up her *choli*. "Come. We have to get moving."

"Moving!" The Snake Charmer says outraged. "We have just been robbed, woman! We have lost all our money!!"

"I took care of that," Paru says. She opens the basket. Maharaj uncoils himself and heads out over the soft sand. Paru dips her hand into the basket. She takes out a handful of coins and lets them fall back.

"What... what is that!"

Paru looks at him seriously without answering. It is the money they made together from the dances with Maharaj.

They start moving again. The Snake Charmer decides to give

the bandits a wide berth. They head in the opposite direction, making their way across open country. The hours drift by.

By late afternoon it becomes apparent that the Snake Charmer is lost. They are winding through the small gullies and canyons of craggy brown hills, which are really sand dunes that have hardened over time. The Snake Charmer finds an animal track leading uphill. He decides this is his best bet, as the height will help him get his bearings. He looks back apologetically at Paru. But she is equable, trusting. They start following the path uphill. It quickly becomes steep.

The sun is setting by the time they reach a spot from which they can see some distance. The leeward side of the hill drops away sharply, opening up a vista of desert stretching for miles in front of them.

Suddenly, the Snake Charmer freezes. Directly below, the bandits have surrounded the caravan from which they had earlier bought supplies. The bandits have added to their numbers. There are ten of them now. Two of the bandits are armed with matchlocks, the rest carry bows and arrows. The bandit leader is saying something to the caravan members. Behind him stands a tall young man, who is apparently not armed. Paru and the Snake Charmer watch intently.

Abruptly, one of the soldiers guarding the caravan spurs his horse on and charges at the bandit leader, his sword raised, ready to swing. The tall young man seems to lower his arm. In mid-charge the soldier leans backwards, a knife through his neck. He slowly falls back and rolls off the horse, to lie dead on the ground. Paru feels her heart pounding.

The bandits disarm the remaining soldiers. The caravan members, men and women, start removing their clothes. They are made to sit and place their hands flat on the ground in front.

"Did you see that?" Paru says.

The Snake Charmer scowls. "Come on," he says.

The bandits start unloading the camels, throwing the goods

into piles. The dead soldier lies unheeded on the ground, his arms flung out, the knife sticking out of his blood-covered neck. Paru continues to gaze down at the scene, excited, enrapt. "Did you see that?" she says again.

"Come on," the Snake Charmer scowls. He pulls her by the arm and tears her away.

The work continues late into the evening. The lamps are lit. Exhausted, Itimad Ud Daulah watches the last of the ministers leave the *Diwani Khaas*.

Birbal has already been summoned for what is about to happen next. A captain appears and stands in front of Itimad Ud Daulah with an open box placed on a ceremonial cloth. Ruquiya is led in by an attendant.

Itimad Ud Daulah waits for Ruquiya to be seated. He then gets up from his divan and walks up to the captain. He opens the box, takes something out, and holds it hidden in his palm. He goes up to Ruquiya and opens his palm.

It contains Paru's jewel.

Ruquiya glances at the jewel. She looks expectantly at Itimad Ud Daulah. His expression is grim.

"I have bad news, Begum. The child is dead."

Ruquiya looks warily at Itimad Ud Daulah.

"Two nights ago. It was a girl. Not a boy. We found this on her person. Hidden inside her clothing." He looks up at Ruquiya. "Is it the one?"

Ruquiya inclines her head in assent.

"It is not what you think. The child was a *naach* girl... a common prostitute. There was a fight in the middle of the night with another girl, the one who boarded with her. She was stabbed to death."

"Salim," Ruquiya says.

Itimad Ud Daulah shakes his head disagreeing. "There were

witnesses who heard the girls screaming."

Ruquiya turns away angrily.

"Her roommate was seen purchasing a knife in the *bazaar*," Itimad Ud Daulah persists. "She asked the shopkeeper to show her how to use it. Now that girl has fled."

Ruquiya keeps her gaze turned away from Itimad Ud Daulah, looking out at the courtyard.

"It would not have mattered for the.... succession," Itimad Ud Daulah says softly. "The child was a girl."

Ruquiya gets up abruptly. "I have to be with my husband."

Itimad Ud Daulah makes as if to speak, then is silent.

Ruquiya departs. She walks by herself in the courtyard, a solitary figure in the gloom among the great carved pillars. Memories flood in. Mostly they are about an aching hole in her relationship with Akbar. Much as they were close to each other, there was some comfort, some love that was never there that she yearned for. Shah Baba must merely think that she was jealous when she was angry with him the other night. But her feelings are more complicated than that.

She feels a great love welling up inside her for this child that she has never seen, one moreover by a mistress — a wife — she has every reason to dislike. But she no longer feels the same animosity that she used to towards this woman. *The* woman. For whom he has displayed a passion he has shown no other. But the child... this child fills a void. A child always fills a void. In the past few weeks, when she learned about this odd prince of Shah Baba's, her feelings of love and hope welled up. Such a sense of renewal, and excitement! Rebirth. The void had filled temporarily.

But now this news! She walks some distance, then sits on the ground next to a pillar. The tears come pouring out.

Hiding two pillars away, very careful not to reveal himself, is Jahangir. From behind the cover of the pillar, Jahangir watches intently, as Ruquiya cries.

The pond nestles amidst a profusion of marsh grasses and scrubby vegetation. Soft mud leads into it. The water is pristine. An enormous *gaur* bull has been drinking the water. It watches Paru and the Snake Charmer suspiciously through the swamp-grass. It debates whether to charge, then decides not to, and trots away.

The Snake Charmer unfastens a leather water-bag from the donkey. He stands at the edge of the pond to fill it. He is fastidious about not getting himself wet.

Paru walks straight in. Her toes revel in the soft mud. The water is up to her thighs. Her *ghagra* is recklessly wet. "Come on!" she shouts. "You need a bath!"

He sits on the bank, on his haunches, watching her.

"Come on!"

He does not budge.

Paru falls backward into the shallow water. She splashes around, feeling its coolness. She straightens up. Her expression changes. "*Aiii! Aiii!* There's something in the water! *Ai!*"

The Snake Charmer rushes into the pond. "Where?"

Paru grabs his arm and throws him flat into the water.

"Hey!" he shouts, not amused. His arms flail desperately as he tries to get himself up.

Paru laughs. She grabs his neck and pulls him further in. "You really need a bath. You've no idea how you smell."

The Snake Charmer grunts unhappily. He stays for a few seconds to please her, moving his arms perfunctorily about in the water. Then he quickly wades back to shore.

Paru swims for a few moments going in deeper. The water is up to her neck in the centre. She takes off her *choli* and throws it to the shore, aiming for the Snake Charmer. It falls short and lodges among the reeds. She removes her *ghagra*, bundles it up and tosses it as well. Her aim is wide off the mark again, it lands in a cactus bush. Finally, she removes her leggings and tosses them as well. The Snake Charmer wonders sullenly how she is going to retrieve her clothes.

She swims naked and unselfconsciously. She dives and splashes, letting the coolness of the water flow over her. Tiring of this, she swims toward the shore. She stands up in the water, pushing her hair back.

She walks out of the water towards the Snake Charmer, standing naked in front of him. Then she pushes him flat into the mud and kisses him. Her thighs close around his. Her tongue seeks his, softly at first, then fiercely, passionately. He passes his hands over her smooth, young back, down past her waist to her buttocks. He is suddenly aroused as never before in his life. He turns her over and is on top grabbing her breasts with such force she winces. She spreads her legs wide, barely able to wait for him to enter.

She makes love to him, because she thinks he is pure and sweet and simple, and he is a surrogate... for the passion she feels deep within her, a passion that is suppressed and aching and ever-present, a longing for connection and family and self, a longing for love — things that she yearns for, but that she dare not think about, because of the black abyss of loss and loneliness that normally fills her heart.

Dusk falls. The air cools. As the night descends, they make a small fire. They lie down without clothes, hugging each other under a blanket, looking up at the stars. She puts her arm around him, snuggling close. Her leg steals between his.

The sun is high in the sky before the Snake Charmer opens his eyes. The blanket has been shielding his eyes. He must have been really tired. He reaches his hand out sleepily for Paru. It meets empty air. He sits up, groggily and looks around for her. She is nowhere to be found. He walks to the pond's edge and stands on a rock. He searches the banks of the pond calling her name. "Paru!... Paru! Paru!... Paru!"

She is gone. He sees Maharaj's basket, it is open. Maharaj is out.

He thinks of something and dives for the basket. He takes his hand out, it is filled with money. She left it all for him.

Motherfuck, says the Snake Charmer to himself. He throws the money to the ground. "Motherfuck! Fuck! Fuck!" he shouts. He picks up the money and throws it into the grass all around him. "Motherfuck! Motherfuck!" He jumps up and down in a frenzy of frustration, picking up more and more money from the basket and throwing it all around.

He stops. Looks at the ground. Scowling, he bends and starts to pick up the dropped coins.

The bandits are raiding another caravan. This one is smaller than the first. The perfunctory guard surrenders instantly. The caravan members are sitting in various stages of undress, their hands placed flat on the ground in front of them. The bandits have found a stash of swords, shields, lances and knives. They stack the weapons in a pile in one corner. They tie the loot onto mules and horses. They work unhurriedly and methodically. There is a desultory, sleepy air to the afternoon. Flies buzz about the sitting caravan members.

The bandits prepare to leave. They spur their horses, tugging at the cargo horses in tow. As they ride away, each of the bandits takes turns to fire warning shots around the sitting caravan members. A shot kicks up dirt near a man's foot. He yells in terror. Another shot hits a pot, making it jump with a clanging sound. A woman winces in fear as a shot kicks up dirt close to where she is sitting. The bandits ride over the crest of a low hill.

Paru emerges from behind a bush carrying her belongings. She stands directly in the path of the bandit leader's horse. The leader slows down. He picks Paru up with one hand. She scrambles and mounts the horse, sitting behind him.

The heavily-laden horse gallops away behind the others.

Birbal stands next to Akbar's bed. The two men are alone in

the darkened room.

Akbar's eyes are barely open. But, the friends can communicate without words. A tremendous bond, a sixth sense flows between them. An understanding has just been reached between king and statesman. Akbar has decided, with Birbal's support and concurrence.

Birbal reaches out and holds Akbar's hand.

Man Singh receives Birbal in the reception hall of his palace. He is drinking a cup of wine. He bears a sullen, defeated look. Birbal sits in front of him, cross-legged, attentive.

"It is over. I am finished," Man Singh says.

"We are all finished," Birbal says. "It is the passing of seasons."

Man Singh pours himself another cup of wine. "You won. You got your way. As always."

"I did not win. We decided something together, as civilised men. We avoided a bloody war. That is a great achievement."

There is a silence as Man Singh broods. "So... you will now become Salim's minister? Become his 'Birbal'?"

"No," Birbal says.

"What will you do?"

Birbal takes his time to answer. "I shall go for a long walk," he says. "I shall go by myself. To the forests of the Kodagu Valley many miles south of here. I have a friend there I would like to visit."

Man Singh looks at Birbal with the forbearance of one who has long thought the other to be nuts. He finishes his cup gloomily.

Akbar's tall chief attendant with the red cockscomb turban walks hurriedly in front. Jahangir walks two steps behind.

Behind him is a phalanx of dignitaries — Sheikh Mubarak, Badauni, Itimad Ud Daulah, Man Singh, Asaf Khan, Birbal, other clergy, a captain, and six guards. They walk with such urgency, they are almost running.

Ruquiya comes running from the opposite direction to meet them halfway. "Hurry! There isn't time."

The procession enters Akbar's bed-chamber. The women are already there, Hamida Begum, Akbar's three other wives, their attendants. Nur is squeezed into the far corner of the room, behind the women.

The room is overwhelmed with flowers — red roses and white lilies. There are oil lamps made of cotton wicks in little clay pots — two hundred of them. The effect is suffocating.

Akbar looks very pale, close to death. Only a slight snore shows he is still breathing.

Jahangir is on top of the world. It is all he can do not to laugh. But caution, he tells himself. This could be the most dangerous moment!

Sheikh Mubarak holds a Quran. "It was Allah who raised the Heavens without visible pillars," he says. "He ascended to the throne and forced the sun and the moon into his service. In the name of Allah, the Compassionate, the Merciful, I implore your Glorious Majesty, On whom doest thou shine thy light?"

Akbar is white as a sheet. He snores slightly.

"Your Glorious Majesty, in the name of Allah, the Compassionate, the Merciful, do you wish to give the Sword of Humayun to your son, Prince Salim?"

No response. Suddenly, there is great anxiety in the room.

Sheikh Mubarak picks up Akbar's limp hand. "Oh Majesty!" he says, a hint of desperation in his voice. "For the sake of all assembled in this room. For our sake, for your friends' sake, your subjects' sake, do not abandon us! Do you bequeath the mantle of the Emperor of Hindustan to your son, Prince Salim?"

Akbar's eyelids flutter half open. His eyes roll. It seems he sees Jahangir.

There is the most imperceptible of nods.

A huge release of tension engulfs the room. The slightest of murmurs, a happy murmur fills the air.

Sheikh Mubarak walks ceremonially towards the sword of Humayun, which has been hanging unnoticed on the wall for fifty years. He takes the sword off its stand and places it in a gold scabbard glittering with diamonds and rubies.

Jahangir looks at his father's face, stunned. Yes! His father said yes, to him.

Sheikh Mubarak faces Jahangir. "By the divine grace of Allah the compassionate. By the powers vested in me by His Majesty. I pass to you, Prince Salim, the sword of Humayun." He fastens the scabbard onto Jahangir.

An attendant hands Itimad Ud Daulah a magnificent robe, rich with gold and silver brocade. Itimad Ud Daulah unfolds the robe. The creases are still fresh in it.

He steps up to Jahangir. "By the powers vested in me by His Majesty, I adorn you, Prince Salim, with the mantle of the Ruler of Hindustan."

The murmur of excitement from the assembly is now audible.

Jahangir looks directly at Akbar with a pang of regret. Wait, don't slip away, he thinks to himself. Now that you have said yes to me, we have things to discuss! I barely know you. But it is too late. You fool, Jahangir thinks. You fool, it is too late. Aloud, he says the only thing that it is possible to say to his father at this moment. "I am better than you think," he tells him.

"By the powers vested in me by His Majesty," Itimad Ud Daulah announces dramatically, "I confer on you the title of *Jahangir!* Grasper of the World!"

Jahangir kneels by his father's bedside. Humbly, and with a respect he has never felt before, he says, "By the powers vested in me by His Majesty — my Father... my beloved Father — I proclaim myself, Jahangir, Successor to the Rule of Hindustan."

The men formally embrace one another. Jahangir embraces

Itimad Ud Daulah. Next in position is Sheikh Mubarak. Jahangir moves to embrace him, but the old man steps away. Jahangir is taken aback. His gaze meets Sheikh Mubarak's. He bows stiffly.

Jahangir looks again at the old man slipping away on his bed. There is a catch in his throat. He raises Humayun's sword in mock salute. "I am better than you think."

Paru has been with the bandits for nine months. The camp is scattered amidst the dry bushes surrounding a small hole, which marks a deep well. The bandits are sprawled about in the open, tired and asleep. Campfires burn low, on the verge of going out. A solitary bandit keeps a drowsy watch, whisking away the inevitable desert flies.

There is a movement among the sleeping figures. Paru is fully dressed. Staying low so that the watchman does not spot her, she gathers up her belongings, already packed into cloth bundles. She ducks low and ties her bundles onto a horse hidden behind a *khejri* tree. She leads the horse quietly out of the bushes. She rounds a corner out of the camp.

The stars burst forth in the desert night. She is alone and she is free.

Handling the bandits was easier than she had expected. She made love to the leader the first night, and for every night thereafter, until he tired of her. She knew how to make a man tired of her — a useful trick she learned at the dance class. The other bandits demanded desultorily to sleep with her. She always obliged. On the raids, she was more of a nuisance than a help.

She smiled at the tall young man one day. He was the bandit leader's son. He said very little and kept to himself. Paru guessed there was something wrong with him. She made a point of being kind to him, and kept asking him questions. At night, his passion surprised her. He challenged her with his love-making, which was unusual for Paru. Many nights, the men were asleep, the camp-fires burned down to embers, but the desert night was punctuated by Paru's little screams as the bandit leader's son clung to her, writhing with mystery and desperation.

One night, her hand slid down his leg and closed over the handle of his knife. He grabbed her wrist so hard she yelled out in pain. His black eyes, unknown abysses, glared into hers.

She smiled timidly. "How do you do it?"

"What."

"What you do... with the knives?"

In the late afternoon she runs into a sandstorm. Sand envelopes her. The wind is so intense she has to lie flat on the horse and hug its neck. Sand gets into her hair, her eyes her mouth. She is hot and parched. The ground swims in front of her. She hangs on, urging the horse on with growing desperation. She senses a dark shape through the wall of brown sand. She urges her horse towards the shape. She is filled with relief when she reaches the shape. It is a large granite rock jutting out of the sand.

She finds the leeward side of the rock and gets off. She makes the horse sit. He does so readily, looking to her for security. She curls up next to the horse in the sand, covering her head tightly with her *odhni.*

It is some hours before the wind slows. Finally it dies down to a whisper, as mysteriously as it had arisen. She and the horse are buried under a mound of sand. She struggles and manages to pull herself out. She pulls on the horse's reins. With some scrambling, he manages to stand.

The journey takes her fifteen days, much longer than it normally should. She gets lost and travels in a vast circle for two days. But finally she recognises the muddy track that is the long road back to Agra. She feels a little jump of joy.

As she approaches the city, it is dawn. A cart laden with earthen milk pots rolls noisily along ahead of her. There are people walking on the high road, a man carrying a vast basket of coriander, a camel. Paru is filled with excitement. It is home.

She is tired of running. The Snake Charmer misunderstood her when they took flight on the night of the attack. She was not running to abandon the city forever and live in another place. She was only running to return, to give herself some time, a measure of safety, so that she could think about a way to come back and make the city her home.

For, after all, when would it stop? She had spent her entire life running. She recalls her very first memories, being carried by her mother from village to village trying to find a home. Her mother was fleeing the cruel conqueror, the man with the mole on his lip. Paru recalls vast tracks of countryside that her mother covered on foot, the sky blue with soft threads of clouds, the grass smelling fresh and sweet after a burst of rain. She recalls the pangs of hunger as she and her mother wandered through endless expanses of brush and fields hoping to find a village that would take them in. And she remembers the kindness, the relief of food and rest. And she also remembers the times that people shooed them away, the little crowds of boys and men who stood throwing rocks at them until they turned; to undertake another long, hungry trek to another uncertain destination.

Paru could tell that her mother too got tired of running. And it was a relief to both of them when she stopped finally and they found a home with Paru's new cousins, and new aunts, and new uncles.

She stops the horse on the side of the road and unloads her belongings, which consist of her bundles of clothes (she still has too many), and her copper *lota,* which reminds her of her Uncle. She gives the horse a final affectionate rub across his neck and body. Then she slaps his rump hard, pushing him towards the field by the side of the road. "*Hatt*!" she says. The horse trots a little into the field and starts grazing. He is on his own.

Paru walks through the gates of the city past the sentries. She is a face in the crowd, dirty and poor. As she wends her way through the *bazaar,* the memory of her lost jewel comes flooding back, and her excitement fades. The Snake Charmer could not have known how close to Paru's heart the jewel was. The city is where she lost her jewel. The City is where she will return until she finds it. But now that she is here, it seems overwhelming. A sadness settles over her.

She makes discreet inquiries. It is afternoon by the time she finds herself on a quiet side-street. She is outside a prosperous captain's town-house. She sits on a rock by the roadside. To wile away the time, she picks up little sticks and throws them into the dirt.

A square, covered carriage drives up to the entrance of the town-house. Three women get out and enter the house in single file. They are covered head-to-foot in colourful *burkhas*. Their faces are hidden behind the netting. Paru looks absently at the women as they enter the house.

One of the women stops. She turns and walks up to Paru. She crouches so that she is staring through the netting into Paru's face. Pithu lifts up the flap of her *burkha*. She studies Paru with cautious amazement. Paru looks back.

"What are you doing here?" Pithu says.

"I am looking for you."

"Where were you..." Pithu looks over her shoulder. The other women have stopped. They are looking back at Pithu and Paru. "Where are you staying? Come on," she says, grabbing Paru's hand. The two of them hurry down the side-street away from the women.

Pithu leads the way silently. They walk back through the *bazaar*. On one of its crowded thoroughfares, they come to a decrepit whores' boarding house. Prostitutes go in and out of the doorway. There is a loud argument going on inside. Paru and Pithu find a spot on the steps. They sit to one side, allowing room for the traffic to go through the doorway.

"Where were you!" Pithu finally bursts out.

"I joined some bandits," Paru says.

"Bandits!"

"I haven't killed anyone," Paru says drily.

"You didn't even tell me when you left!" Pithu complains.

"People close to me get killed."

The explanation does not register on Pithu. "Why did you join the bandits?" she demands.

"I had to get away. From the men who were trying to kill me."

"What men?"

"The men. Who were trying to kill me."

"Why are there men trying to kill you?"

"I wish I knew," Paru says.

"You're making this up."

"There are men! Eight or nine of them. With their swords drawn! They surround me. Then they come at me... trying to kill me!"

Pithu thinks for the first time in her life that she is witnessing a truly crazy person.

"You saw them yourself!" Paru says urgently. "When we were in the *bazaar*. The fat man with the sword! What did you think that was?"

"That was a fat man with a sword," Pithu says trying to sound reasonable. "Did he make love to you? And then was he jealous because you avoided him?"

"This is different," Paru says. "I never made love to that man."

"How would you remember?" Pithu asks weightily.

"I am telling you, I never made love to that man! He just wanted to kill me! From the start. Like the others!"

"You look tired," Pithu says holding Paru's hands. "Perhaps you should rest—"

Paru knocks Pithu's hands away in a spurt of anger. "You're giving me a headache! Go away! Why don't you just go away!" She clutches her head and looks at the ground. She puckers her lips, trying not to cry.

Pithu regards her for a moment. She takes Paru's arm in hers and strokes it gently. "You came looking for me. Why?"

"I need work," Paru says sullenly.

"Oh! There is a famous dance troupe. I can—"

"No. No dancing. Something where I cannot be seen. Sweeping the floor, maybe."

"That's beneath your station."

"Nothing is beneath my station. Do they need a servant in that big house?"

Pithu touches Paru's chin trying to raise her head. "What happened?"

"I don't know. I feel so tired!" Paru says. "Everything goes wrong for me! I wish I could just live an everyday life like other people."

"You can just live your everyday life."

"They'll come again."

"Who?"

"The men! The men! Pay attention!"

Pithu makes as if to speak, then stops herself.

"I have to find them first," Paru says. "I cannot keep running away. And I have to get my jewel back."

"What jewel?"

"My jewel. I gave it to Amma as a guarantee when I started at the dance class. The men stole it."

"What will you do when you find these men?"

There is a movement, a flash. Paru is holding a dagger pointed at Pithu's chest. Pithu jumps. Paru smiles shyly and puts the knife away. Pithu is looking at her in amazement. Paru reaches over and brings the *burkha* flap down, covering Pithu's face.

"You shouldn't be seen with me. It's dangerous."

Pithu defiantly uncovers her face again.

Paru is touched. "I need a place," she says. "What are you doing in that big house?"

"I am married," Pithu says.

It is Paru's turn to be stunned.

"He's a captain," Pithu says. "He has three hundred men under him."

They hear the sound of doors slamming in the distance. The sound becomes louder and louder, approaching down the street like a wave. "He's been very good to me. But he's away a lot, and he leaves me with those other two wives of his. And I don't like them very much. I don't think they like me very much either—" She breaks off, noticing the sound.

The shopkeepers on the street in front of them look up apprehensively. There is a rush of rumour, people hurrying down the street, looking backwards, looking at open doorways. Men call out to each other. The vendors start packing up their carts in double-quick time. As soon as they are packed, they take off down the street. They seem to be running ahead of the wave of slamming doors. The entire *bazaar* is packing up and leaving.

Suddenly, prostitutes from everywhere come crowding in though the doorway. Paru and Pithu stand up baffled, resisting the rush.

"Come on! Get in!" a prostitute shouts at Pithu.

"What happened?" Pithu says.

"Stop blocking the doorway! Get in!" another woman screams.

Paru and Pithu are swept into the dark passageway by a wave of women who come pouring in. The inside of the whores' boarding house is dim compared to the bright sunlight of the street. They cannot see anything.

"What happened!" Pithu asks again in bewilderment.

"The King is dead. There is going to be a massacre!" someone replies.

"Prince Salim is advancing on the city with a huge army," someone else shouts.

"There is going to be a massacre!" the first woman screams.

"Massacre!!" the cry is taken up by the panic-stricken, jostling women.

The door-slamming is upon them. It is now very loud. They hear shouting and running in the street outside.

The last of the whores squeezes in, and the door of the boarding house is slammed shut. It is pitch dark.

Outside in the sunlight, the *bazaar* street is broad and eerily empty. Two dogs walk casually along. Presently, an old Mughal town-crier appears, advancing on foot down the centre of the street. He carries a big brass bell, which he bangs loudly.

"The Emperor has passed away!" the town-crier cries. *CLANK*! *CLANK*! "Allahi Akbar!

"The Emperor has passed away!" *CLANK*! *CLANK*! "Allahi Akbar!"

The town-crier passes the door of the boarding-house. Unable to contain their curiosity, the whores open the door just a crack. They peer out breathlessly.

"The Emperor has passed away!" *CLANK*! *CLANK*! "Allahi Akbar!" The town-crier walks down the empty street, repeating his call.

The dogs wag their tails.

December 1605

The ministers, officers, royals, and nobles, are seated in an evenly spaced arrangement, each according to his rank, each dressed in full splendour. The air has cooled for the first time in months, in anticipation of the coming winter. The lawn of the *Diwani Aam* has been perfectly groomed. The sun glints off the dazzling abundance of the courtiers' jewellery. Itimad Ud Daulah stands one level lower, and to the side of Akbar's throne. Birbal is gone.

Jahangir sits erect on Akbar's throne.

Only six days were allotted to the formal mourning for Akbar's passing. The fear of rebellion, secessions, new wars was preeminent. After those six days, there were five more confused days of coronations and late-night entertainments, during which Jahangir was watchful of everyone around him and did not drink too much.

But this morning, for the first time, he feels calm. That the *Diwani Aam* has assembled and the courtiers are sitting in their appointed places is in itself a triumph. It is perhaps believable.

What has occupied his thoughts while sleeping and waking for as long has he can remember, as long as he has been alive — it is perhaps believable.

Musicians burst into triumphant fanfare. Asaf Khan formally approaches the throne and bows deeply. Jahangir stands above him. Jahangir is at ease, in command. He is enjoying himself.

"To the post of Prime Minister of the realm," Jahangir says, "I appoint the Honourable Asaf Khan."

Asaf Khan bows, touching his head. He takes his place beside Itimad Ud Daulah.

Mahabat Khan approaches the throne.

"To the post of *Khan-I-Khanaan*, General of Generals," Jahangir says. "I appoint General Mahabat Khan."

Mahabat Khan bows. He stands beside Asaf Khan. Jahangir nods to Itimad Ud Daulah.

"The Honourable Itimad Ud Daulah, has served my Father for thirty years in the highest post of the Empire. Words cannot describe the debt we owe him. Sir, I humbly ask if, in your more contemplative days, you will accept the post of Grand Vazir of the Empire."

Itimad Ud Daulah has not been expecting anything. He is pleased with this honour, and bows deeply. "I will, Your Majesty."

"I summon the Honourable Man Singh," Jahangir commands.

Man Singh approaches the throne apprehensively.

"When the nobles were assembled to choose between myself and Prince Khusrau," Jahangir says, "General Man Singh decided to lock me up! But he had the grace to send dancing girls for my amusement." Jahangir's voice sinks to a murmur. "I found one of them quite endearing."

The courtiers burst into laughter.

"General," Jahangir says. "We have had our differences. But in the end, I have the utmost respect for you, as a great general, and as a loyal servant to my father. I humbly ask you to accept the post of — Governor of Bengal!"

There is a rustle of surprise. It is all the assembled courtiers can do to not shout their approval. Man Singh is touched beyond reason. He accepts the honour, bowing deeply to Jahangir.

Jahangir smiles, pleased with himself.

Asaf Khan steps forward. "All stand, and pay subservience to the King of Kings, Grasper of the World, the Emperor Jahangir!"

The fanfare trumpets across the sky. The courtiers rise in unison and bow deeply to their new and unfamiliar monarch.

The meadow stretches out in front of them, bordered at the far end by a jungle. Jahangir and two colourfully-dressed attendants are mounted on horses waiting at the edge of the trees.

Nur emerges from the cover of trees, at full gallop. She rides like a man, with surprising strength and speed. Jahangir sets off in hot pursuit. Nur increases her speed. Jahangir increases his, unable to catch her. She zigzags across the field with Jahangir in hot pursuit. She comes up against a broken stone wall. She clears it with her horse. Jahangir follows, clearing the stone wall too. She comes full circle. The trees and the mounted attendants block her path. She slows down. Jahangir finally catches up.

"Your Majesty!" one of the attendants shouts anxiously. "The ministers are waiting for you at Court!"

Jahangir's horse frisks and rears up on its hind-legs. He smiles at Nur. "Justice calls," he shouts to her. He spends some time calming the horse. "Justice is sweet," he says.

Nur smiles back at Jahangir.

Paru emerges from Pithu's house with a broom. She vigorously sweeps the area in front of the steps raising a cloud of dust that makes her cough. She goes back in and brings out an earthen pot filled with water. She dips a *lota* into the pot and commences to throw water out in front of the steps in a fan-shaped pattern. The water will settle the dust and cool the house during the midday heat. Paru picks up the broom again.

There are people walking past the house on the street. She looks longingly at them. It has been five months since she has danced. The city is about people, about being at the centre of things and performing. But she dare not do that now. It is the easiest way to be seen. Being Pithu's servant is a good disguise. Most of the time she hides in the house. As a servant, she is almost invisible. Even Pithu looks through her. Pithu has acquired a new haughty air, as if she is a big house-mistress. But Paru understands that she is going through a lot. There is tension between Pithu and the other wives. Add to that, she is the junior-most wife. The captain is never home. Paru has yet to see him. When she and Pithu are in the same room and one of the other wives is about, Pithu simply ignores her. And Paru disappears into the walls.

In the late evenings, Paru has made up a routine of slipping out by herself for a walk. She covers her face tightly with her *odhni* and walks rapidly, roaming the dark streets among the shopkeepers' lamps that interrupt the night like large glowworms. She tries to look closely at the people she passes and she scours the streets methodically, searching a larger area around the house each day. But she sees nothing. After a month, the walks have become discouraging.

How she yearns to be done with this and be able to dance again! Paru recalls that first great realisation when she was crouched amongst the legs of the villagers, having crossed the *bajra* field, when that gorgeous man of the dance troupe came out into the cleared space surrounded by the crowd. In a single moment he transformed the space into a sculpture of his own making. And then he changed it as he moved. An ethereal living form that evolved itself, from moment to moment. Paru gasped in wonder. Forget that the man assumed the role of a God in the drama that was to follow. He was a God himself! How could anyone do that!

And then the women entered, two of them, soft and delicate as butterflies, expanding the space created by the man, until it filled the world. Paru squealed with excitement, almost giving herself away to the grownups whose legs towered over her. At that moment she knew what she was going to do. She was going to become one of these women. She was going to take the world in those slim expressive hands and turn it into a place of magic and beauty and joy, instead of one of suffering, and anger, and guilt.

Paru has been absent-mindedly sweeping the steps of Pithu's house until every last particle of dust has been swept away and the steps have become squeaky-clean. She stops and stands up straight. She looks longingly, as a man walks by in the mid-morning heat. She comes to a sudden decision. She tosses the broom into a corner near the steps, and walks rapidly away from Pithu's house.

The crowds are in the *bazaar*, as always. It is as if the panic of a month ago never occurred. She walks past shops looking for something, she does not know what.

A crowd is gathered around a Street Orator. Paru joins to listen.

The Street Orator is a half-naked *sadhu*, covered in white ash. He has a pot of burning incense next to him, from which a thick stream of smoke emerges. He is framed in the smoke, appearing mystical, magical. His voice is dream-like.

"...so when Shiva's wife died," he says, "Shiva was very distraught... this is the worst thing that can happen to a man — to lose his wife. Shiva's mind was filled with anguish. He decided to undertake a penance, to come to terms with his grief.

"There are parts of the Himalayas so high and remote, only the Gods live there. And it is here that Shiva found an ice-covered cave and plunged into a deep meditation. A meditation so deep that no one could rouse him from it.

"At this time, the devil Taraka saw his opportunity and arose from the underworld. You see, Taraka had pleased the God Brahma in a past life. In return, Brahma had given him two gifts.

The first, that no one would be more powerful than he, Taraka. The second, that he could only be killed by a son born of Shiva. Seeing that Shiva was occupied with his meditation, Taraka had no fear that Shiva would ever have a son who could kill him."

The spell-bound crowd looks at the Street Orator.

"Within a short time, Taraka wrought havoc upon the world. He drove the Gods out of the Heavens. He made the Angels his slave girls. He took delight in cruelty and in murder... And a sadness fell upon the people. They took to drink and opium, like Taraka himself. They feared for their lives, from Taraka's cruelty. There was a rumour in the *bazaar* that Taraka would impose a new Tax on the people..."

"When will this new Tax come into being!" demands a crowd member.

"Nobody knows," the Street Orator says. "But it is rumoured."

"Why is it that Taraka rose to the throne?" asks another man.

"It is a great sadness," the Street Orator says. "It was said that Taraka would usurp the rightful rulers of the land. And that is exactly what happened."

A conspiratorial look crosses the Street Orator's face. "Did you know, that the emperor Akbar, God rest his soul, summoned the nobles to a meeting in the Palace. To choose a new King! And who did they choose? The Third Prince!"

A subdued "Aaahh!" rises from the crowd.

"Where is this Third Prince?" somebody asks.

"Nobody knows," the Street Orator says. "But he is said to be roaming the land." He looks directly at Paru. "He has to get his strength up. It is not easy to defeat the great Taraka."

The Street Orator's gaze fixes on Paru. She looks attentively at him. Abruptly, she yawns. She tries to suppress the yawn, patting her mouth delicately with her hand.

The Street Orator continues to talk, but Paru's attention has wandered. By and by, she edges her way out of the crowd. She spends the rest of the morning among the fabric shops in the *bazaar* looking at clothes.

It is early afternoon and Jahangir presides over the *Diwani Khaas*, the Private Council. It is his first time with this select group — the highest governing body of the land.

He has a headache. One of Jahangir's miscalculations has been the fact that being Emperor entails waking up, dressing, and being ready at the *Diwani Aam,* the Public Council, by nine each morning. He is now tired from the morning and not ready for the *Diwani Khaas*. The entertainment of the previous night had a little more abandon than usual. Since his father's passing, the few evening ceremonies had been studied, formal affairs, with Jahangir ever watchful of those around him. But last night, his confidence had grown. In mid-party Jahangir stood up with a bottle of wine in one hand and announced that tonight was a blessed night, the dawning of a new age, and, to celebrate, every man should feel free to indulge himself to whatever extent he deemed fit. This little stolen interlude, a moment in which he abandoned himself to the pure pleasure of believing that he was actually Emperor, is now taking its toll.

The morning at the *Diwani Aam* was wearisome, with an endless stream of petitions and public judgments. Jahangir finds them overwhelming. He is feeling irritable. His entire being wishes to abandon this court and retire to his chamber, or, even better, to the woods. Yet this is how it is. This is Allah's will, and this is how he is Emperor. With a little fear inside him Jahangir faces the forty courtiers of the *Diwani Khaas*. There should be no questions in their minds, no doubts. He is the Emperor.

The men in front of him are royals from the Empire's conquered territories, *amirs*, generals, ministers, and court officials. They stand or sit facing him at progressively lower levels, depending on their ranks. They are all formally and resplendently dressed.

Jahangir is seated on his throne at the highest elevation. He gets a small thrill from the sheer physicality of it. In seating at least, he is the supreme monarch! One level below him stand Asaf Khan, Itimad Ud Daulah, and Mahabat Khan. Further down, are the courtiers, seated on the rich carpeting and divans. On the far side of the stage, stand four musicians with drums and trumpets.

All sit perfectly still, as if inhabiting a painting of the courtroom. The only movement is Asaf Khan's, who uses a side-table to sort through a stack of papers and ledgers. Asaf Khan takes some time to get ready. Jahangir sits expressionless.

"Your Majesty," Asaf Khan says in a businesslike manner. "We have a number of decisions to go through this morning. The turmoil of the last few months have, alas, caused a great deal of work to pile up...

"First, we have the case of the property of Karan Singh, who played a critical part in the taking of the fort at Maligarh, and who gave up his life. On his death, his lands and revenues reverted to the Emperor—" Asaf Khan looks up pointedly. "That is to say, to you, Your Majesty — leaving his widow and her three sons destitute. I should mention, the young men show great promise—"

"Let the widow keep her husband's lands," Jahangir interrupts.

Asaf Khan looks up again. "I would agree, your Majesty. Although it is not the Emperor's custom to forgo what is rightfully his, the special circumstance of this woman calls for an act of generosity and reward from the Emperor—"

"I intend to make it for everybody," says Jahangir.

Asaf Khan is startled, "I am sorry, Sir... I do not understand..."

"Everybody should be able to pass his lands on to his family after his death."

There is surprised silence in the courtroom. Asaf Khan and Itimad Ud Daulah regard Jahangir with consternation.

"I suggest, your Majesty, that we tread cautiously," Asaf Khan says. "We will lose a great deal of revenue if we adopt such a measure."

"The revenue will be paid for by the increased happiness of my subjects," Jahangir replies mysteriously.

Asaf Khan looks at him with unease.

"Perhaps Your Majesty, we should ask for a calculation first," Itimad Ud Daulah suggests smoothly.

"Please yourself," Jahangir replies "It will not change my decision."

"If I may say something your Majesty..." Itimad Ud Daulah ventures. "Your father was very careful with the rules he set up."

"I am not my father."

Itimad Ud Daulah looks discomfited.

Asaf Khan decides to move on. "Next... your son, Prince Khusrau, wants to visit his late Majesty's burial-site at Sikandra."

"No harm in that," says Jahangir.

Asaf Khan looks at Mahabat Khan. "I would advise caution, your Majesty," says Mahabat Khan.

"Caution? For what?"

"He was in line for the throne against... against you."

"I beat him fair and square, didn't I? The nobles chose me over him."

"Yes," Mahabat Khan responds. "But there are rumours... the late Emperor spoke approvingly of Khusrau. I request permission to send him under heavy guard, your Majesty."

"Permission denied," says Jahangir.

There is another awkward silence. It is evident from the demeanour of Mahabat Khan and Itimad Ud Daulah that this is clearly the wrong decision. Jahangir is unmoved. Asaf Khan leafs through his papers.

"Next..." Asaf Khan sighs. "There is a petition from the *ulema*. Requesting that at the Religious Bazaar, twice the time be allotted for discussion of the Quran as for other religions."

"There will no longer be a Religious Bazaar," Jahangir replies.

Asaf Khan is taken aback. "What should we state as a reason,

Your Majesty?"

"I find them boring."

Asaf Khan regards Jahangir hopelessly. "That may be a good reason... but... Your Majesty... your subjects are waiting for you to make some statement with respect to religion."

"The religion of the state is Islam. It has always been thus."

The court, which for fifty years has seen Akbar treat all religions with equal and passionate interest, greets this news in stunned silence.

"Not to seem stubborn, Your Majesty," says Itimad Ud Daulah, a note of desperation in his voice. "But there are some questions we need to debate, before we can lay such a topic to rest."

"What questions would those be, *Vazir Sah'b*."

"Well... for one thing, there has been much speculation as to your own religious beliefs... considering the somewhat confusing behaviour of your late father."

"My father thought he was God. I have no such illusions, *Vazir Sah'b*. I am but a humble and devout Muslim."

Abruptly, Jahangir stands up. "Five times a day, I turn towards Mecca—" He turns towards Mecca. "And bow my head in prayer—" Jahangir prostrates himself, "—to the one and only Allah."

Jahangir closes his eyes and prays. The court watches in dumbfounded silence.

Asaf Khan clears his throat. "There... there are some practical questions we need to discuss, Your Majesty..." Asaf Khan's voice squeaks involuntarily. He decides to let his words fade into silence.

Jahangir prays. His eyes remain closed for what seems an eternity. The praying gives him some refuge from his courtiers, he can sleep this way, while they watch him. His eyes closed, he luxuriates for a few seconds in the darkness.

The courtiers wait tensely. No one dares speak.

Jahangir opens his eyes slowly, smiling rapturously. "Wonderful!" he murmurs to himself. He shakes his head in amazement. "Wonderful!" He turns to Asaf Khan, his face filled with religious ecstasy. "You were saying, Minister."

"There are some practical questions we need to debate about religion—"

"I hope we are not going to do that today, Minister. We had planned a short session, if I recall."

"Er... yes," Asaf Khan says defeated. He shuffles his papers distractedly, not sure what to do with them.

Jahangir waits, his gaze on Asaf Khan. Presently, Asaf Khan gets the hint. He starts gathering up his papers. "Then that concludes this very short session of the Private Council, Your Majesty," he announces in a bewildered voice.

Itimad Ud Daulah steps forward, "All rise."

The musicians burst into a loud fanfare.

"Pay subservience to the King of Kings, Grasper of the World, The Emperor Jahangir!" Itimad Ud Daulah proclaims.

As one, the entire court bows low to Jahangir.

Jahangir stands alone, expressionless, the supreme monarch high above the uniformly bowed heads.

In a deserted hall in the far corner of the harem, Gossibai sits with Ritu and Saheli. The hall is little more than a roof supported by pillars. It has a broken-down, overgrown look. Gossibai sits in a corner, looking distracted and despondent. Saheli sits across from her with a *tabla* and a *sitar*. Ritu stands in front of Gossibai, wearing a see-through harem dress suitable for dancing. She has a white dove perched on her arm.

"Your Prince will be sitting over there—" Ritu says pointing to the spot where Saheli is sitting.

"Emperor," Saheli corrects her.

"What?"

"He is now the Emperor."

"Give me the beat," says Ritu.

Saheli plays the *tabla*. Ritu dances sexily with the dove on her arm. She moves towards Gossibai. "I come and give the dove to you—" She hands the dove to Gossibai. "And I keep dancing—"

She dances as Saheli plays. She undulates her hips, unable to resist showing off her body. "Now you hold it up—" she says to Gossibai. "Hold it up with both hands—"

Gossibai holds up the dove.

"And you let it go."

Gossibai lets the dove go. It flies up among the rafters, circling and hesitating. The women look up expectantly. It leaves the hall entirely and goes up, up into the bright, sunny sky. It flies over the perfectly laid out expanse of the fort below, with the river meandering in the distance. It looks as if it will never return. Ritu looks at the dove with chagrin. Abruptly, it makes a U-turn and dives steeply, back into the hall. Ritu holds her breath. The dove lands on the floor some feet in front of Saheli.

"It should have come right to you!" Ritu says, disappointed. "Anyway, when it lands on the Emperor — as if by magic — there is a beautiful jewel tied to its leg! A silver box! studded with diamonds. And in the box is a note. And on the note is a poem. A poem... about love! To the Emperor. Written by you! What do you think?" she asks triumphantly.

"It is nice," Gossibai whispers.

Ritu's expression changes. She sits down in front of Gossibai, taking Gossibai's hand in hers.

"He has not summoned me in three weeks," Gossibai says despairingly.

"Three weeks!"

Gossibai nods.

"But how is that possible? I see you together — at dinner, at the entertainment..."

"That is the only time we meet. In public."

"And then how is he?"

"He is gentle. And kind. And attentive."

"So?" Ritu says. "He loves you!"

Gossibai shakes her head, holding back the tears.

"Maybe he is very busy with state affairs. It must be difficult, to be crowned Emperor."

Gossibai shakes her head again. The tears come.

Ritu kisses Gossibai's hand, and hugs her arm. Gossibai lays her head on Ritu's shoulder.

Saheli is distracted by something in the courtyard. "Look! there's the serving lady!"

On the deserted walkway across the courtyard is Hamida Begum, followed by Nur. In one hand Nur holds a pile of folded clothes. With the other, she holds Hamida Begum's arm, helping her walk.

Ritu and Saheli stand up to watch, their demeanour suddenly tense and hostile.

"I am sure she murdered her husband," Ritu says.

"She frightens me," Saheli says. "She almost broke your arm that time! And the way she pushed you into me!"

"Why would the Prime Minister's daughter become a servant to Hamida Begum?" says Ritu, imitating as closely as possible Gossibai's suspicious look.

"She doesn't have a choice. She's a widow." Saheli replies.

"She is so shameless!"

Across the courtyard, Nur glances at them warily. They stare back at her. Nur ignores them and looks straight ahead.

"She will probably find some old noble to remarry," Saheli says.

"Then she will kill him and steal his money! Like the last one!" Ritu adds. "He will have to be a fat and ugly noble for someone as fat and ugly as she is!"

Saheli, the literalist, looks askance at Ritu. Her gaze catches Gossibai, who is also looking intently at Nur. "At least, Gossibai, she is in no danger of stealing your Prince!"

The clearing is a small open patch amidst dense bushes in the middle of an almost dry swamp. A *sambar* doe is giving birth. Jahangir is crouched low in the tall grass. He watches attentively through the thick leaves. "Do you see it?" he says.

"Yes," Nur replies. She is crouched beside Jahangir.

"She is about to give birth!" he says amazed.

"I see it."

"Are you drawing it?"

"I cannot draw in the mud over here." Her clothes are covered with mud.

"Where's your pad," he demands.

"I left it on the horse."

"You should always bring your pad!"

"It would get wet. I will draw from memory."

"I knew it would be the day!" he says enthusiastically. "The fawn is about to emerge. "Look... look!!" Jahangir cries excitedly.

The fawn is halfway out. Jahangir's face is lit with wonder and amazement.

Nur, tiring, turns over and lies on her back. She lets her hair fall into the mud.

He is still engrossed with the doe. He seems to feel the mother's pain. His face tenses as she struggles. The baby is finally out. Jahangir relaxes.

He breathes deeply, exhilarated by the experience. "Do you remember it, to be able to draw?"

"Yes!"

He looks down at Nur.

She reaches out to take his hand. Deliberately, she holds it on her belly. "Make me your concubine," she says.

Jahangir is taken aback. He looks down at her for quite some time, unable to reply. "That would ruin it," he says anxiously.

"Ruin what?"

"If you were to be the King's concubine."

Nur laughs. "You think too highly of me. I am too old. And too plain — and a widow moreover — to be the King's concubine." She takes his hand and moves it slowly till it comes to rest on her breast. Jahangir can feel her erect nipple. There is a slight smile on her face, daring him.

Jahangir bends to kiss her, hesitantly at first, then with a passion that surprises him. "I cannot—" he gasps.

Her mouth is jammed tightly against his. "Cannot what!" she demands between bites and kisses.

"Make you my concubine—"

"Why!" she says holding him tightly.

"You're a widow," he says breathing hard. He rips open the front of her *burkha*, exposing her breast. He kisses her erect nipple. "Widows can't be concubines!"

"Are those the rules?" she says, her chest heaving.

He moves his hand across her breast down her body, kissing her again, over and over again, with increasing passion. He lies on top of her, kissing, biting, their mouths open, their bodies writhing, their bodies undulating against each other.

The mud engulfs them on the jungle floor.

There is an inquiry from the fort's housekeeping staff if His Majesty would be interested in a game of fire-polo. Calculating that he can avoid a day at court, Jahangir readily agrees. The fire-polo is a tradition set up by Akbar. The match is to be held at Nagarcin, a pleasure city about fifteen miles from Agra. The party sets out in the early afternoon with ten elephants and an entourage of a hundred.

The game is played in the dark after sunset. Jahangir, Mahabat Khan, Asaf Khan, and about forty royals and courtiers sit on an elevated stand at the edge of an enormous field. Bearers carrying torches stand around them, casting a dim light. The ball is made of burning wood-embers and glows in the dark. The riders are barely visible, as they swing long clubs and shout their plays to one another.

A rider gets hold of the fiery ball and races across the field. Two others gallop up, close behind. There is a collision in the dark. A rider falls and is dragged by his horse. A second rider gets control. The audience cheers and claps.

The second rider is immediately caught up in a mêlée of six riders, vying for the ball. Sticks are swung repeatedly. The loud *thwacks!* resound across the field amidst shouts and occasional cries of pain. A horse falls. Another stumbles over it. The courtiers jump out of their seats, cheering and shouting.

Jahangir remains seated, watching impassively.

A rider breaks free with the ball. Mahabat Khan jumps up. "Get him! Get him! Kill him! Kill him!" He catches sight of Jahangir sitting impassively by himself, and feels rebuked. He sits down meekly.

Jahangir glances at the torches lighting the audience. He signals to a colourfully-dressed attendant. The attendant approaches. Jahangir says something to him.

The attendant finds a vantage point in front of the audience, and holds two torches aloft waving them back and forth. "Nobles! Your eminences!" he calls. The courtiers fall into silence. "His Majesty has requested that we watch the game in total darkness. We shall be extinguishing the torches." The audience area is plunged into darkness. The fiery ball zigzags across the field amidst the cries and thuds of the riders.

Jahangir's seat is empty.

He walks alone in the moonlight across an empty meadow towards a copse of trees. The meadow is laced with white flowers.

Nur is waiting for him, sitting at the base of a tree. "What took you so long! I was getting cold."

Jahangir takes her hand and helps her get up. "Did you hear anything?"

"What?"

"The owls! The white owls! Come on!"

He sets off rapidly into the shrubbery. Nur follows.

"This is the most amazing little wood!" he says excitedly. "I used to sneak away here all the time. My father brought us to the arena to stage his elephant fights... and I would sneak away... this forest floor is full of rats. And snakes... who eat the rats."

"Snakes?"

"Shhh! Stay still!"

They stand still. Their lightly-coloured clothes glow in the dark. Their slight figures are dwarfed under an enormous canopy of hundred-year-old trees that enclose them like an ancient cathedral. The sounds of frogs, crickets, and cicadas envelope them.

A white owl descends wraith-like from the treetops, its wings spread out. It lands on the forest floor. There is a thrashing sound among the leaves and grass. The owl flaps its wings. It climbs back up into the treetops, holding a rat. Another owl descends. And another. The woods are lit up with the great white forms of the owls, descending and ascending. Jahangir watches the owls, as if watching a great event. He puts his arm around her shoulder. She snuggles close to him in the late-evening chill.

The spectacle ends as abruptly as it began. The last of the great white owls finds its perch in a branch high above them. And then all is still. Jahangir and Nur stand by themselves in the darkness under the canopy. She finds his hand and holds it, trying to warm her cold fingers.

"Initially... initially, it appeared I was afraid," he says into the darkness.

"What?"

"I did all right in the end. But I had to fortify myself with alcohol."

"What... what are you talking about?"

"The elephant fights. My father used to test our mettle by making us ride wild elephants. Here in the arena. Sometimes he would make two of us kids mount, one on each elephant and the elephants had to fight. I used to escape over here into these woods, because... because..." He stops himself. "That is when I saw the owls. I hid in these woods one entire night. They had to send out a search party for me.

"But then I discovered the secret. I filled myself with spirits and it turned out I had the mettle. I rode a truly wild beast, a huge rogue that it took ten men to keep in check. I was dizzy with the wine and flying atop the elephant, as it reared and trumpeted. And I caught a glimpse of my father in the spectator stand... he was laughing with pride. And it felt as if the beast would throw me any moment. But I did not care. I could fall to the ground and break my bones and be crushed to death and I did not care anymore. My father was so pleased! He immediately gave me a handsome reward, and was very nice to me for an entire week.

"And so I rode wild elephants for my father. The secret was to drink twenty cups of wine mixed with *arak* just before the event. I did that two more times. But it became apparent he wasn't noticing that much anymore. So I stopped. But I had proved I was worthy."

"Worthy!"

"Yes. Worthy to be King."

A shaft of moonlight finds its way through the trees and lights his anxious eyes. She touches his cheek with her fingers. "You would have been worthy even if you had not ridden a single elephant. And instead, come to these woods to see the owls every single time. You would have been worthy in my eyes even then."

He looks away unable to believe that she could be saying this, that anyone could be saying this. "Worthy to be King?" he asks.

"Worthy to be King."

He looks at her unbelieving. The firmness in her voice thrills him. He has never met a woman so clear, and so decided. "You really think so! That I am worthy?"

She runs her hand down his chest. "Yes."

"I mean... not just to be King."

She smiles in the dark. "Not just to be King."

"I have not told this to anyone," he tells her. "Nor brought them here."

She takes both his hands and holds them to her bosom.

Jahangir experiences a calm that he has never before felt in his life. The emptiness inside him fills up. It is as if he is held aloft — above the chasm. Above the chasm of uncertainty. Floating. He could fall asleep in this calm! There can be no chasms, he thinks to himself. There are no chasms.

The moonlight finds its way through the gaps in the canopy and speckles the forest floor. They stand holding each other in the darkness for a long time.

Ritu runs along the walkway to Gossibai's room. Her breath comes in gasps from news so shocking, she can barely contain it. "Gossibai!" Ritu screams. "Gossibai!" She rushes into Gossibai's room and grabs her, crying hysterically. "Gossibai!"

Gossibai's heart stops. "What is it!"

"Gossibai!" Ritu sobs.

"What is it child? Speak up!"

"The woman!"

"What!"

"The woman!"

"What woman?!"

"The serving lady!"

"What—"

"The Prince!"

Gossibai gasps. "My Prince?!"

Ritu nods, crying.

"Oh!... Ohhh!... Oh Bhagwan! Oh Bhagwan!" she cries.

Ritu hugs her tightly. The two women cling to each other crying.

Pale, stern, formal, Gossibai sits on an elevated divan in her reception room as Nur enters. Nur's manner is wary and deferential. She bows respectfully to Gossibai.

"Do you know who I am?" Gossibai says.

Nur nods apprehensively.

"I am Jahangir's main wife. The one he is most devoted to. The one he loves and cherishes the most." She regards Nur's bowed head. "Up to... oh, about two months ago, I used to see him at least three times a week. I saw him many, many times a week."

Gossibai waits for this news to sink in. "That makes me the Queen, does it not?" She smiles a small, ironic smile. "I am the Queen of Hindustan." Gossibai gets up from her throne. Sympathetically she takes Nur's hand. "Come. I have something to show you."

They walk through a passageway in the *zeenana* quarters and come to a door. Gossibai opens the door.

The room is similar to Gossibai's. There are divans along all the walls, and a large low-lying bed. Seated, or standing, are eighteen princesses. It is evident they have dressed up for Nur. There is an explosion of glitter — from jewellery worn by the women, and from sequins and little mirrors sewn into their flowing, colourful dresses. The room belongs to Man Bai, an older princess. By *zeenana* standards, it is large and luxurious. But it is so filled with women right now, it seems crowded.

The princesses have an air of melancholy, of resignation.

Nur enters and looks around at them.

They watch her looking at them.

"We are the wives of Jahangir," says Man Bai.

Nur recoils as if from a blow.

"We thought we would get to know you a little. And make you feel welcome," says a smart younger princess named Malika Jahan. She gives Nur a little smile of welcome.

Nur is nauseous. She is unable to reply.

"It's no use us wives fighting all the time," Malika Jahan explains. "It is better if we act as sisters. We thought, we would tell you a little bit about ourselves, and you could tell us too."

Nur does not reply.

"I'll start!" Malika Jahan says cheerfully. "I am Princess Malika Jahan. Daughter of Raja Kalyan of Jaisalmer. On my wedding day, I thought I had lost my tongue. I could not speak! But then he took a flower from my hair and tore it apart carefully, and told me the names of each of its parts. The petals, the stem, the stem inside... and for the parts that didn't have names he made up his own names—"

Nur is pale.

"I got so much jewellery that day, I could hardly stand. But the only thing I remember is that flower."

"You were married before?" Man Bai asks kindly.

"My husband died some years ago," Nur replies. Her voice is so soft, she can barely be heard.

"I am sorry to hear that," Man Bai says.

Nur looks at her in silence.

"I am Man Bai," she continues. "I was the first to be married to him. We don't see each other anymore. So I run a business, a trade route into Surat. Last month I made a hundred thousand *rupiya*... in one month!"

Next is a tall, willowy princess with mascara under her eyes and a mysterious remoteness about her. She lounges languidly across a divan. "I am Akhtar Begum," she says. "I like to study the stars. Someday I will show you the night sky. If you take a little opium... and let your eyes get used to the dark, it is amazing what you can see."

It is the turn of Saliha Banu, a pretty, giggly princess. "Oh!" she says. "I am Saliha Banu! Daughter of Qum Khan. I write poetry sometimes. And I love clothes!"

Nur is next. They look at her expectantly. "I am Mehrunissa," she says softly. "I am Hamida Begum's attendant. A servant."

She turns and flees, out of the room and down the walkways, trying to go as far as she can away from the crowded room of wives.

The typical time for the *mina bazaar* is the winter months. It is an occasion for the royals and the women of the fort to converse, meet, and flirt. This year, however, Jahangir has asked that it be arranged earlier.

The *bazaar* is held in a beautiful garden inside the fort. Stalls have been set up, making an oval around the garden. The 'shopkeeper' for each table is either an established royal lady, the wife of an *amir*, or a young concubine looking for an opportunity, or a husband.

An *amir's* wife has established herself at a stall selling highly-prized china brought from across the Himalayas. A stunning twenty-two year-old sells exotic perfumes imported from Europe. Ritu sells bejewelled tunics. Saheli sells hookahs. At the far end of the garden, Hamida Begum has a stall selling jade cups. She is barely able to stand in front of it. Crowding the walkways around the garden stand the courtiers and the fort residents, eager to watch the show.

By some accident, Nur has been ordered to participate. She has a stall selling jewellery. She stands facing her jewellery feeling out of place and miserable.

The men enter from one end of the garden ready to shop,

looking for flirtation. Jahangir is in his element. He is thrilled with the sheer beauty of the occasion — the women, the garden, the shrubs! This is fun! He is the Emperor! The men are overtaken by bashfulness. Mahabat Khan and Asaf Khan hang back with the rest of the nobles. Jahangir finds himself a few feet in front of them, trying to get the occasion going. He approaches Ritu's table and bows formally. "Madam. May I look?"

"Surely, Your Majesty! Ritu says breathlessly. She still nurses a bump on her head, where Jahangir had hit her with a wine jug. But now that is all a dim memory. Jahangir is at her table, charming and gracious. Ritu can hardly breathe.

Jahangir browses. Hesitates.

"Can I help you?" Ritu asks, unable to hold back.

"Yes. This tunic. No... this one."

"Would you like to try it on?"

"Er, yes. If you would—"

Ritu comes from around the table. She dares to be a little seductive as she walks, and steals a familiar glance at Jahangir. She helps him with the tunic, working from behind him. She comes around to the front and adjusts his collar. She takes a little longer than necessary.

Jahangir shows off the tunic to Ritu. "What do you think?"

"Oh! I think it looks very good on you, Your Majesty!"

"And... how much do you want for it?" he says, still posing.

"I think its price is ten thousand *rupiya*, your Majesty."

Jahangir starts taking it off. Ritu's face falls. "I... I'm afraid I cannot afford it," Jahangir says.

"Cannot afford it!" Ritu gasps. "I... I will give it to you for five thousand!"

"No, no," Jahangir protests. That's still a lot of money—"

"Your Majesty, that is what I paid for it! Please! Please take it! Especially... especially since we've... met!!"

Jahangir looks surprised. "Met! I don't think so, Madam." He adds mischievously, "Unless... unless perhaps in a past life our souls have met!"

Jahangir starts to retreat. Ritu is crushed. Jahangir bows. "It was charming making your acquaintance, Madam."

He escapes to the next stall, which has Saheli selling hookahs. "Hookahs!" he says. "The love of my life!"

Mahabat Khan has found an audience among the women on the opposite side of the oval. The group includes two of Jahangir's wives, Malika Jahan, and Saliha Banu. Mahabat Khan balances his sword on the tip of his nose. The women, who are without customers, watch with amusement. Mahabat Khan stands in profile to the ladies and pretends to swallow the sword. Except he fumbles, holding the sword hidden on the other side, and drops it. He quickly lays himself on top. The women laugh.

Asaf Khan is talking to Hamida Begum. He is absently holding a jade cup she has to sell and is talking earnestly.

Jahangir is at Nur's table. "You look familiar," Jahangir says. With perfect pitch, "You are... let me think... let me think..."

"I am Hamida Begum's attendant," Nur says evenly.

"Ah yes! Hamida Begum's servant! And what are you selling, Hamida Begum's Servant?"

Nur indicates the jewellery. Jahangir browses briefly. He picks out an incredible diamond-studded earring. "That is a very pretty earring! How much for these... Hamida Begum's Servant?"

"For someone else, Your Majesty, I would say twenty thousand for the pair. But for you, it is a hundred thousand."

Jahangir is shocked. "What! That is not fair!"

Nur looks at him, her expression one of stone.

"Why hundred thousand for me!"

"There are customers that a shopkeeper must turn away, Your Majesty."

"How so!"

"They browse for too long. As if they are going to buy

something. They touch this and that. They carry on a conversation. The shopkeeper is seduced... into believing in great things. And then it turns out they were just looking."

"That is fine, Madam. I do not see what it has to do with me!"

Nur does not reply. Jahangir determinedly examines the earrings.

"My wares are of a low quality, Your Majesty," Nur says coldly. "They are not suited to one such as you." She glances at the stunning twenty two-year-old selling perfumes downstream. "There are better shops down the road."

"How much for these earrings, Madam!"

"Hundred thousand, Your Majesty," Nur replies unmoved.

Jahangir has a look of challenge on his face. "Put them on me!"

Nur does not move. Jahangir holds up the earrings, so that she has no choice but to put them on his ears. She starts doing this stoically. The audience of courtiers in the walkways looks at them curiously.

"How do I look?" Jahangir demands.

"They do not become you, Your Majesty."

"Do not become me!"

"You are weighed down with your attire as it is. Your necklace does not go with your tunic." This is true. Jahangir is gauchely over-dressed. Each item of clothing is taken to excess. His tunic is encrusted with jewellery. A large necklace loaded with jewels sits on top of the tunic.

"A king who is confident of his place should dress lightly," Nur tells him. "Especially if he is to go shopping for clothes."

Jahangir goes red. He takes a moment to control himself. "But I do think these — very expensive — earrings will suit me, Madame," he says slowly and carefully. "They may offset the other aspects of my attire — that you find so tasteless."

"You will take the leap from monarch to buffoon, my Lord."

Jahangir makes an angry noise, snatches the earrings off, and places them on the table. He moves closer to Nur. "I have but to nod my head," he whispers, "to have you publicly executed in the public arena!!"

Nur bursts out laughing. "How can I forget!" She looks genuinely amused.

The courtiers see her laughing. Their excitement increases.

Mahabat Khan's audience has expanded to a full circle of ladies. Malika Jahan sits eagerly in front. Mahabat Khan gets up from the ground, where he is lying on top of his sword. He uses it like a walking stick pushing himself up slowly and infirmly. Then casually he twirls it with some breathtaking warrior moves. He takes a coin out of his pocket, tosses it in the air, and chops the coin in half. The ladies laugh and applaud. Malika Jahan stands up in her excitement.

Jahangir glances over his shoulder at them. Privately to Nur he says, "Why are you doing this?"

Nur shakes her head, suddenly on the brink of tears. Jahangir covers her from the watching courtiers by holding the earrings up to the sun to examine them. "I am a fickle woman, Your Majesty," Nur says. "Given to flights of fancy. The fever has passed. A king such as you. A woman such as I. You are only looking. How can it be otherwise?"

The courtiers are now watching with keen interest.

Jahangir is about to reply, then stops himself, aware of the eyes on them. Instead he says loudly and crisply, "I am not here just to look at your wares, Madam. I am very serious when it comes to my shopping. I would like to take these earrings." He picks them up and starts to move away.

"Do you have the money?" Nur interrupts loudly, and laconically.

Jahangir stops in mid-stride. He puts the earrings down again. He fishes in his pockets, finds two bags of coins, places them on the table. He realises it is too little. He checks futilely in his pockets. He is out of money. He looks at her. She is stone. He storms across the garden to speak to Asaf Khan. He returns with three additional bags of money. "Fifty thousand!... Seventy-five thousand!... Hundred thousand!" he says, putting the bags down on the table.

He snatches up the earrings, and leaves Nur's stall, heading towards Mahabat Khan and the ladies. Trying to regain his composure, he smiles and nods genially at the party.

Asaf Khan is looking at Nur in utter disbelief.

It is late evening. Asaf Khan does not deem it necessary to have many oil lamps burning in his living quarters and the spacious room that is his reception hall is engulfed in gloom. Nur stands before him half-deferentially. She still has her servant's manner.

Asaf Khan comes right to the point. "What did you think you were doing?"

Nur gestures, not knowing how to answer.

"Who let you into the *mina bazaar*?"

"It wasn't my choice. I was ordered," she replies.

"Never ever speak directly to him again! A few thoughtless words from you, Sister, and he would make decisions that would change our lives forever! We could be ruined! Do you realise what you were doing?!"

"He was speaking to the other women as well," Nur says mildly.

"They were concubines. Or nobles' wives. Or, they were Hamida Begum. What are you!"

The question amuses Nur. She thinks. "I am... the Grand *Vazir's* daughter. And the Prime Minister's sister!"

"Well then. You will let the Prime Minister do your talking for you. Should, by some chance, you meet him again, you are to only speak when spoken to. And then briefly. Be subservient —"

"Why."

"Why! Do I have to explain to you why? Because you're a

woman. You do not know the ways of the world. You have had no training in the arts of diplomacy—"

"How is it that I have had no training in the arts of diplomacy?" Nur asks him.

"Sister! You are trying my patience. Our father was a fool. He was a lucky fool, for his time. But for you to believe that his kindness to you as a child amounted to training—"

"How is it that you believe I have had no training?"

"I am wasting my time! I am going to move you. Immediately. Perhaps to the court at Lahore. You are... too exposed here—"

"Brother."

"In Lahore you can lead a quiet life. You can do your sketching—"

"Brother!"

Asaf Khan stops.

"You have not asked for my consent," she says.

"Your consent! I do not need to ask your consent, Sister! This is something I do! This is something we have to do!"

"His Majesty will not be pleased with your decision. When I tell him."

He moves as if about to strike her. "You hit me at your peril!" Nur warns. He stops.

"Have you taken leave of your senses?!" he expostulates. "Which would you rather do? Be punished for disobedience—"

They speak at the same time.

Asaf Khan "—or be locked up with the lunatics!"

Nur: "He has asked me to marry him."

She repeats, "He has asked me to marry him!"

Asaf Khan is stunned into silence. "What?" he says finally.

"He has asked me to marry him," Nur says in wonder.

"Marry him? Who, you?"

"Yes."

"How can that be?" he says baffled.

"You can ask him yourself. Or you can wait for him to tell you."

"But... you are already married! You're a widow!"

"I am a widow. And therefore I am not married."

"But... but this is impossible! Has he gone insane?!"

"No."

"You are thirty-one years old! He should be looking at women half your age! What about... what about all those women at the *mina bazaar*! Have you not told him your age?"

"I have told him my age. And I have told him I am a widow. And he has asked me to marry him."

Consternation overtakes Asaf Khan as the full impact of her statement sinks in.

"You have to tell him no!" he says in panic. "He cannot do this! You, Father, I... we have to make a plan!" He stops for a moment trying to think. "But first, I need to speak to him. And, I need to understand the circumstances that led up to this..." Words fail Asaf Khan. "...this disaster! Oh, Sister! What have you done to us!"

"I am going to say yes to him," Nur says.

Asaf Khan looks at her with horror. "You are going to say yes to him?" he repeats, unbelieving.

"Yes."

"I do not think you are going to say yes to him, Sister," he says his eyes glowing with outrage. "You are going to say no."

"I am going to say yes."

Asaf Khan closes his eyes for a moment to contain his anger. "Sister. Do not visit this tragedy upon us," he says trying to sound reasonable. "Out of consideration for our family and as your brother, you have to get a hold of your senses. You will say no to him!"

"I am going to say yes," replies Nur.

"Sister! You do not understand," he says in desperation. "This... this can be very bad. As your brother I could order a *fatwa* against you. I could have you killed!"

Nur does not reply. They regard each other as adversaries.

"So, one more time," he says slowly and emphatically. "I, your brother, under threat of a *fatwa*, am *ordering* you to say no to him!"

Nur looks at him with equal fierceness. "I am going to say yes!"

Paru returns to the *bazaar* unable to keep herself away. The crowd around the Street Orator seems to have tripled. There is a vast semi-circle of people now, leaving space in the centre for the Street Orator. Intrigued by their intensity, Paru is once again drawn in.

The Street Orator sits cross-legged and erect, like the Gods he speaks of. He sits on a six-foot-high wooden platform. His forehead is adorned with ashes symbolising the trinity. His hair is long and greying. The smoke from his pot billows in the slight breeze, sometimes covering him entirely, sometimes clearing to reveal him through it. His voice is once again mystical, dream-like.

"...and Shiva was deep in his meditation, a meditation such as the world had never known. Very few could even reach his remote, ice-covered cave in the high Himalayas. As we know, the God Kama, with the best of intentions, tried to rouse him from his meditation by shooting arrows at him. But Shiva's great Third Eye turned angrily on Kama, and burnt him into a crisp — a small heap of ashes! In no time at all! But that is a story for another time...

"What I have to talk to you about today is the devil Taraka. Seeing that Shiva was occupied with his meditation, Taraka had no fear that Shiva would ever have a son who could kill him. It was his chance to dominate the World.

"It takes a very short time for a Devil to cause destruction. And in a short time indeed, Taraka brought great misery. He drove the Gods out of the Heavens... he was cruel and intolerant. He hated love, charity, good deeds. Instead, he started a cult of violence and power. The people took to it eagerly because people will take to anything and they were mesmerised by Taraka's dark power."

Paru's assailant, Bhir Das, is scanning the crowd. Being large, he bumps into people and makes a pest of himself.

"A stream of sadness ran through the people. They took to drink and opium, like Taraka himself. They feared for their lives, not only from Taraka but from the ill-will that spread outward from him like a poison. Friends, look around you. What do you see?"

They stare at him, enrapt.

"Do you not see the age of Taraka?" The Street Orator pauses, giving them time to think. "I believe the Emperor drinks twenty cups of wine each day. As for the tales of his cruelty," he says softly, "we all know them."

Paru thinks of the night in the hut. The light of the lamp fell on the Fan Man's blood-splattered clothes. Bhir Das looked at the dead girl lying across the room. "That's not her," Bhir Das said. They looked around the room and saw Paru in her corner. "That's the one." Paru screamed, but in her mind the scream is silent.

"Why is it that Taraka rose to the throne?" a crowd member asks the Street Orator.

"It is a great sadness," the Street Orator replies. "It was said that Taraka would drive out the rightful rulers of the land. And that is what happened..."

"But there is hope?" asks another man.

"There is hope," the Street Orator says. "The hope is in Parvati. She was the daughter of the Mountain King, who ruled not far from Shiva's cave. Parvati had not only great beauty, but truth and loyalty. She had strength and resolve. None could sway her from doing what she deemed to be right.

"Most of all, she was devoted to Shiva. From her birth she had loved no one but Shiva. Now as Shiva was in meditation to resolve his grief, so Parvati was in meditation in her devotion to Shiva. Each day she brought fruits, flowers, milk, and left them outside his cave."

"And she won Shiva over?" a woman says wistfully.

"Yes. Shiva was at first annoyed that a young girl should be visiting his cave to distract him... He put her through many tests. He came to Parvati in the form of a young *sadhu* and tried to persuade her that only a fool would go after that awful Shiva! But Parvati dismissed the sadhu's arguments. Finally, one day, Shiva opened his eyes, and looked at her. With a love that only Shiva can show. And, as you know she became his wife..."

The woman smiles.

"So when will this son of Shiva be born who can defeat Taraka?" asks the first man.

"He is already here." The Street Orator's voice drops to a conspiratorial whisper. "Did you know that the Emperor Akbar, God rest his soul, called the Nobles to the palace for a secret meeting? To choose a new King? And who should they choose but the Third Prince!"

The crowd gasps.

"So, where is the Third Prince?" the first man asks.

"Nobody knows. But he is roaming the land." The Street Orator looks directly at Paru. "He is preparing. Growing. It is not easy to defeat the great Taraka." He looks around at the others. "But very soon friends, he will show himself. There will be signs. Unmistakable proof." He looks at Paru again. "And there will be a great battle..."

Paru is searching the faces in the crowd. She recoils as she spots Bhir Das.

The Street Orator regards her through the smoke. The smoke clears. The people who were standing behind Paru are still there. But Paru is gone.

Bhir Das scans the crowd suspiciously. Paru has dropped to the ground. She crawls through the crowd members' feet, trying not to touch anyone. She wants to get to a spot from which she can observe Bhir Das without being observed. But she soon finds this is a bad idea. She is lost among the feet. She stands up cautiously.

Bhir Das is gone. She looks around frantically, and catches sight of his receding back as he walks purposefully away from the crowd.

There is a fleeting moment in which Paru is tempted. A moment in which she sees Bhir Das walking away, and thinks that perhaps she too can walk away... in the other direction. And perhaps she and Bhir Das will never see each other again, and this will be over. But no sooner does she think of this than she knows it can never be. She needs her jewel. She is not whole without her jewel. And he is the only one who knows where it is. Her destiny is entwined with his. He is like a wrestler who will not let go. The thought of her lost jewel makes her frantic. She pushes her way roughly out of the crowd.

Bhir Das is rounding a corner past an area where large stocks of feed have been stored. Paru ducks for cover behind a pile of hay. But Bhir Das is walking quickly and she has to run to keep up. He mounts a horse. Paru hides. He starts cantering away. She follows.

The horse trots rapidly. She finds she cannot hide and keep up at the same time. Then she realises that Bhir Das is in deep thought and is not looking back. She decides to run out in the open, hurrying after the horse.

He rides for about three miles to an area on the outskirts of town, where she is surprised to find a vast swath of soldiers' barracks. The tents are laid out helter-skelter across a squalid field. Bhir Das rides past a well, around which soldiers in various stages of undress are drawing water and washing. They laugh and joke loudly. Bhir Das rides humourlessly past. He gets off his horse and enters one of the tents. His sword seems to jut out long and prominent on his side.

Paru lies low in the grass some hundred feet away. She is

panting — from excitement, as much as from the long run after the horse. She stays crouched for a long time, watching the entrance to Bhir Das's tent through the rustling blades of grass.

Pithu sits in the inner courtyard of her captain's house, buying vegetables from a hawker. There are three baskets of assorted vegetables spread out around her. An eight-year-old girl stands by to assist the hawker with the baskets. In a corner of the courtyard Paru squats next to an urn of water scrubbing pots and pans.

"Show me your green beans," says Pithu. "Your green beans were like dry sticks the last time." She examines the green-beans fastidiously, looking for all the world like a queen.

One of the captain's other wives comes out on the tiny balcony that encircles the courtyard. She glances at Paru, then glares angrily at Pithu. Pithu ignores her.

Pithu is done buying the vegetables. The hawker stands up. The little girl puts a basket on her head with the help of the hawker. The hawker places the other two baskets on his own head. The two of them depart. The captain's wife with the angry gaze has returned to her room. Pithu gathers up the vegetables she has just bought.

Paru abandons her pots and comes rushing over, excited and triumphant.

"I found him!" she announces to Pithu.

"Who?"

"The man! The man who stole my jewel! The man who tried to kill me! I found him!"

11

March 1605

The captain who has been assigned to guard Prince Khusrau is getting nervous. The jungle darkens as the canopy overhead thickens. The elephant plunges deeper and deeper into the undergrowth. The branches of the large old trees impede the party's progress. They are so low sometimes that the occupants of the *howdah* have to duck flat to pass from underneath.

"It's getting late," the captain says unhappily. "We have a long distance to cover before nightfall."

"Please, captain!" Khusrau says, pouting like a spoilt prince. "I have my heart so set on these cheetahs! I just want one shot at them. Then we can be on our way. Grandfather's tomb can wait!"

Small branches scratch their faces and have to be pushed aside as they forge their way through the canopy. Prince Khusrau talks nineteen to the dozen. "We used to go see saint Salim Chishti all the time... we would have a little picnic, and make the day a holiday just by ourselves as a family. It was the only time we were together — grandfather, my father, my mother, and us brothers. I cannot describe the joy I felt! At last, we were away from all the people surrounding grandfather. Oh, the people, the people... how I hated them! But then we were together. It was as if we were a real family! I used to feel so jealous of those farmers I would see in the fields. Just the farmer, his wife, his children, living together in a hut like a family. What bliss!"

Something about Khusrau is not right. He speaks just a little too fast, a little too nervously. The two guards in the *howdah* have been assigned to the captain's duty at the last minute. They look impassively ahead. Their turbans, moustaches and beards seem to be sculpted in the gathering gloom.

"And then the fights began," Khusrau continues. "My father would ignore something grandfather said — something completely friendly and innocuous, some request from father to son, from Emperor to subject, which any other man would jump up and do. And my father would act as if grandfather had not spoken. Grandfather would tolerate this for a few minutes, and then there would be another slight, something completely rude and hateful and angry from my father towards grandfather. And then Grandfather would explode with a fury that knew no bounds—"

Khusrau looks intently through the trees. There is a clearing ahead, a barely discernable area among the trees where the undergrowth is only chest high. "This is it! This is the spot..."

Khusrau freezes staring intently through the drooping leaves.

"Where are they?" asks the captain intrigued in spite of himself.

"Over there," Khusrau whispers. "Near that pond... they come out to drink in the evening... watch! Watch!"

The captain peers through the foliage at the clearing. Through a coincidence of clouds and tree branches, a bright bar of sunlight falls across the clearing. The captain sees the tall grass glisten in the bright, five o'clock sun. He sees the limpid gleam of water in the tiny pond that hides beneath the grass. He looks hard for the cheetahs that Khusrau is pointing to. But there is nothing there.

One of the soldiers in the *howdah* nods slightly. Without

turning around, Khusrau passes his matchlock quietly to the soldier.

For a moment, it seems the elephant is alone in the world, insulated from all else by dense jungle.

The shot echoes across the clearing.

The captain's body falls from the *howdah* like a pile of old clothes. It half turns on hitting the ground, twelve feet below, and faces the sky.

Khusrau's white shirt is splattered with little droplets of blood. The smoke from the matchlock engulfs the *howdah*. The *mahout* yells at the elephant and pokes it hard with his stick. The animal trumpets and rears up excitedly on its hind legs. It starts crashing back through the undergrowth in the direction from which it came.

The elephant bursts out of the jungle onto a dusty road where the rest of Khusrau's entourage is waiting. Only, there has been a mutiny. Selected troopers and attendants lie dead in the grass, the blood gushing red from their fallen bodies. The others hold matchlocks in their hands, their horses frisking nervously. A cloud of blue smoke rises from the recently-fired matchlocks.

The rebels are officers, gangsters. Their leader, Husayn Beg, is tall, dark, unshaven. His sword hangs casually from his waist and looks well-used. His cohort and second-in-command is Dalit Singh. He is a slight, neatly-dressed man with a pointy beard.

A soldier runs up to Khusrau's elephant with a freshly-saddled horse. Khusrau jumps dangerously and foolishly directly off the elephant onto the horse.

"Hurry!" shouts Husayn Beg. "There's no time."

Khusrau is white with shock. "What about the elephant?" he asks.

"It will slow us down."

"It will give us away!" Khusrau protests.

"We have to be fifty miles from here by nightfall!" Husayn Beg replies. He spurs his horse and gets onto the road without looking back. The others quickly follow. The troopers gallop away in a cloud of dust.

The elephant is left standing by itself. The royal *howdah* is still strapped to its back. It forages serenely by the side of the road. Presently it comes to a decision, and starts walking along the road in search of friends.

By nightfall, the rapidly moving rebels have covered twenty miles. Their horses, in for the long haul, are strung out along the road. The soldiers hold burning torches. The torches glow, a limpid stream of light floating through the darkness.

There is now a village procession following the abandoned elephant. Mostly children and teenagers, they trot by the side of the road next to it. A teenager grabs the elephant's tail and manages to scramble onto its back. He crawls into the *howdah*. A second teenager uses the help of the first and crawls into the *howdah* beside him. Somebody throws a garland of flowers, which lands on the elephant's head. The elephant keeps on walking.

Late into the night, a messenger bearing a torch runs in the direction of the broad, empty streets leading up to the fort. He is breathing heavily, pacing himself. He is covered with sweat. He approaches a group of drunk revellers, talking loudly and laughing.

"Danger! King's message! Danger!" pants the messenger.

The revellers stop in mid-conversation and stare at him as he runs by. One of them jokes drunkenly. The others laugh loudly.

The messenger reaches the drawbridge. He runs without pause up the draw-bridge. "Danger! Danger! Danger!" he calls.

The guards move to intercept him.

It is two in the morning in the *Diwani Khaas*. Jahangir, Mahabat Khan, Asaf Khan, Itimad Ud Daulah, have been dragged hastily out of bed. Jahangir is in his nightclothes. They look stunned. An open map lies untended on the carpet.

"How did we miss it?" Jahangir asks.

There is silence. "Prince Khusrau has many supporters among the nobles," Itimad Ud Daulah says at length. "Some of them are resentful that the Choosing did not go in his favour."

"Where is he?" Jahangir asks.

They look at each other. Nobody knows.

"Where is he?" Jahangir repeats, bewildered.

"He dare not go south," Mahabat Khan says, trying to think. "He will come up against the Sultan's Army. Malik Ambar will tear him to pieces."

Mahabat Khan picks up the map. They look at it. "He might go east, to Bengal, and seek refuge with Man Singh. Man Singh has but to nod his head to raise an army. And... with due respect, Your Majesty, he would crush us."

"What about north?"

"North? There are the wild tribes. The Oymaqs and the Uzbeks. And then the mountains."

"He could head for Kandahar," Itimad Ud Daulah suggests. "If he manages to reach Persia and get the support of the Persian Emperor..."

Jahangir draws a wheezing breath.

"Why would he go to Persia, when he could go east and join Man Singh?" Mahabat Khan says.

"I think he will go north and west," Jahangir gasps.

"Why," Mahabat Khan challenges.

"There are no big cities between here and Bengal," Jahangir replies. "He needs supplies."

"We have to be sure of the direction he will take," says Asaf Khan.

"We cannot be sure," Jahangir says with a gasp.

Itimad Ud Daulah notices that Jahangir is struggling with his breath. "Are you all right, Your Majesty?"

Jahangir's legs crumble. He kneels, looking at the floor, taking one desperate wheezing breath after another. He is having a full-blown asthma attack.

Mahabat Khan holds him by the shoulders. "Look up, Your Majesty!" he says urgently. "Give your breath some space."

Jahangir obeys.

"Get a doctor!" Itimad Ud Daulah tells an attendant standing by the door. The attendant departs running. Jahangir falls forward and lies face down on the floor.

"Your Majesty!" Itimad Ud Daulah shouts in consternation. "Your Majesty!!"

Itimad Ud Daulah's voice seems to echo in Jahangir's head. 'Majesty, Majesty'. He is falling, falling. It is all an illusion. It never was. He never was. There is only this chaos and savagery. Each cutting the other's throat. And he unable to breath, unable to cope. The darkness is enveloping him. Into nothingness. Nothingness. "Mehru!" he calls in desperation. "Mehru!"

"What—?" says Mahabat Khan.

"Mehru," Jahangir mumbles softly into the carpet.

Mahabat Khan is at a loss.

"He wants Mehrunissa," says Asaf Khan. The others look blankly at him. Asaf Khan turns to the remaining guard by the door. "Go and get the lady who is Hamida Begum's servant. Her name is Mehrunissa." The guard departs.

Mahabat Khan and Itimad Ud Daulah turn Jahangir over. His lips are turning blue. His eyes roll upward.

"Your Majesty!" Mahabat Khan says desperately. "Breathe!" He props Jahangir up and tries to hold his mouth open.

"Breathe!" Mahabat Khan exhorts. "Breathe... breathe... breathe..."

Jahangir appears to be trying to obey. Itimad Ud Daulah fans him hopelessly. Jahangir passes out.

"Where is the doctor!!" Itimad Ud Daulah shouts in panic.

Mahabat Khan lowers Jahangir's head to the floor. The men look at one another nonplussed. They are suddenly leaderless. For what seems like an eternity, they stand in front of the unconscious Jahangir in bewildered silence. Nothing in their book of experience has prepared them for this.

Mahabat Khan dares to look down at Jahangir again. With the loss of consciousness, the tensions in his body seem to have relaxed. Mahabat Khan thinks it is his imagination, but he sees a slight rise of Jahangir's chest. He is suddenly hopeful. The breaths are very light and sporadic, but they are unmistakably coming. Jahangir is returning. He seems to be schooling himself, slowing down, concentrating on each breath. He is breathing gently.

The moment of what might have been has passed.

Jahangir opens his eyes slowly. The men crowd around him, swept by a wave of relief.

"Help me up," Jahangir says softly. He can hear his heart pounding, struggling with the effort. He feels tipsy. But he knows he is not. The men hasten to sit him up on the cushions.

"I think—" He stops, closes his eyes, concentrates on his breathing again. "I think—" he gasps, "we should send scouts in both directions. North, as well as east. Light and fast." He pauses for breath. "Give the scouts plenty of money. They should inquire from the villagers along the route which way Khusrau's army has gone."

Nur rushes in following the attendant. She sees Jahangir sitting up with the men and stops herself from going up to him. Jahangir looks at her and takes a moment to collect himself. He turns to the men. "Mahabat Khan," he says without looking again at Nur. "You will go north with the scouts." He looks around. "*Vazir Sah'b*. You are to command Agra while we are gone. You are to protect the treasury with your life! I will go with the main army, when we have found out which way these people have gone."

It is a few hours later. Still in his night clothes, Jahangir stands alone on the fort wall overlooking the road leading up to the Gates. The sky is lightening. The men accompanying him have been dismissed and gone to rest. It has been a long night. He is tired, but he cannot rest. He puts his hand on the stone parapet and keeps his vigil alone.

The eastern sky is now a bright orange. The sun is about to rise. Light bathes the city sprawling in front of him. The sun touches the dome of the Juma Masjid making it gleam a molten gold. The sounds of early morning join themselves into a collective whisper that wafts its way up to Jahangir. He has never looked at the city in quite this way. Suddenly it seems very delicate — at once fragile and beautiful. It is his city. His to protect. In more ways than anyone can imagine, it is his. He feels a tenderness in his heart for it. Perhaps more than for any woman. It is the tenderness he feels for his Empire, for Allah's will.

A soldier at full gallop comes riding up the road towards the gates. He thunders up the drawbridge.

"North!" he shouts. "North! North!"

Jahangir leaves his post hurriedly.

The Mughal Army is stretched out as far as one can see, to the horizon. It is an army of thirty thousand trying to move in a hurry. Elephants and camels wade through crowds of infantry, cavalry, bullock carts, loaded hastily with supplies. Cannon crews try to urge their bulls on, pulling heavy, wheeled, bronze cannon.

The train straggles backward for miles, to the point that it merges into a great chaotic mass of the army that is at a standstill. A cannon is disabled, its wheels off, the bulls standing still. The crew struggles to repair it. A bullock cart crammed with lower caste female help passes them by.

Jahangir is at the front, on his elephant. It is hot and dusty. Jahangir is red with misery. Mahabat Khan comes riding up on a horse. He looks expectantly at Jahangir. "Too slow!" Jahangir calls out.

"We are going to break up at this rate!" Mahabat Khan replies. "We are not an army, we are a mob."

"Each day we are behind, he gathers more troops."

"I don't care!" Mahabat Khan says vehemently. "This is not an army. If they attack us now, we will get killed!"

"Too slow!"

Mahabat Khan turns his horse around in frustration and rides away.

Half a mile behind, Nur's covered *howdah* shakes from side-to-side as the elephant carrying her sets a bone-jarring pace. She is crowded in with two of Jahangir's wives, Man Bai and Saliha Banu, as well as two other women she does not know. It is hot in the *howdah*. The side-to-side motion of the elephant makes the passengers nauseous. Man Bai and Saliha Banu regard Nur coldly. After her meeting with the wives when she fled, there have been no words between them.

Nur looks through them. She has war-lust. She is on her knees, looking raptly through the thin curtains at the surrounding phalanxes of men and animals on the move. She mumbles softly to herself, making plans in her head. The *howdah* lurches. She almost falls into Man Bai. The leather and wooden fittings of the *howdah* creak loudly. The women hold on for dear life.

Seventy-five miles further up, the rebel army, now at a strength of two thousand, heads in a north-westerly direction. Unlike Jahangir's, this army is entirely cavalry. The horses move at a fast canter, crossing the countryside in a great racing rectangle. Also unlike Jahangir's army, the rebels are calm and organised. Their disciplined movement contrasts sharply with the chaos of the Mughals. Khusrau rides at the head with the rebel leaders.

Presently, a second much larger army of three thousand horse approaches from a westerly direction. This army is also all cavalry. The Oymaqs are fierce nomads, retaining their identity as they roam through Persia and central Asia, ceding sovereignty to neither Persians, nor Mughals. The Oymaq chief is wiry and old.

He has a flaming white moustache and wears a magnificent bejewelled turban and an ornate, colourful tunic.

The leaders greet each other with smiles and loud salutations.

"To victory!" Husayn Beg calls, his horse rearing exuberantly.

"To victory!" the Oymaq chief responds.

"To victory!" shouts Khusrau.

The leaders join and continue their ride northwest. Behind them, the mass of the Oymaq army merges with the rebels. The expanded army rides across the plain with a great thundering of hooves.

Night descends on the Mughal army. There has been no time for camp. The soldiers are sprawled out in the dark next to their horses. Camels and bulls sit on the ground surrounded by the supplies and belongings of their keepers. Campfires burn helter-skelter across the vast field on which they are camped. The stars emerge through the ascending smoke. The sound of crickets in the grass is almost drowned out by the shouts and collective conversations of the soldiers, and the squeals and whinnies of the animals.

Only a small cluster of royal tents have been pitched. They glow from afar, like Chinese lanterns. Jahangir, Asaf Khan, Mahabat Khan sit in Jahangir's tent poring over a map. They are tired and irritable.

"The gunners are still trying to catch up," Mahabat Khan informs them. "They will march through the dark for the next six hours. The supply carts are twelve hours behind. We are running low on water."

Jahangir shakes his head.

They hear a conversation at the doorway. Mahabat Khan gets up and speaks to a messenger. He returns, crestfallen. "The Oymaqs have joined Khusrau. The army of Abdur Rahim — the army of Mirza Beg — have joined Khusrau."

"How big does that make them?" asks Asaf Khan.

"Nine thousand horse," says Mahabat Khan.

"They will soon be as big as us."

"We cannot let them reach Persia," says Jahangir.

"It is a long road to Persia, Your Majesty," says Mahabat Khan, the realist. "A lot can happen before that."

"What?" Jahangir challenges.

"There is the citadel at Lahore. The citadel at Kandahar. They have to capture both."

"But as they go along, they will muster a huge army!"

Mahabat Khan has a sudden thought. He looks at Jahangir.

"What?" Jahangir demands.

"I am afraid to suggest it, Your Majesty. It will give you wild ideas."

"Man, you and I will be dead pretty soon! What!"

Mahabat Khan traces his finger on the map. "We are falling behind. If we take a small army — just one thousand horse — and ride rapidly, we could outpace them. But it means leaving the cannon behind, the elephants, everything."

"And then?" says Asaf Khan.

"And then Khusrau will turn around to engage us." Mahabat Khan traces his finger backward. "We will flee... backwards..."

"And that will take several days, by which time our main forces will catch up," Jahangir says excitedly. "I like it! I like it!" He is suddenly animated. "A thousand horse! General, you and I shall go in the advance troop. Asaf Khan, you will bring up the Imperial Army."

Mahabat Khan has doubts instantly. He regards Jahangir with misgiving.

At noon the following day, Jahangir's small army, consisting of a thousand mounted troops, with donkeys carrying supplies in tow, is in the last stages of departing from the main forces.

Jahangir stands on his horse looking back impatiently. Mahabat Khan comes galloping up.

"We're four hours late!" Jahangir calls. "And we haven't started!"

"There is a lot to prepare, Your Majesty." Mahabat Khan has been awake through the night.

He stands on his stirrups, raising his sword. He shouts, giving the order to march. The horses move forward. The small army elongates, still merged with the main army. It is almost twenty minutes before the last of the loaded donkeys and mules start moving forward.

Some of the donkeys carry the great bronze barrels and the mountings of dismantled cannon. Mahabat Khan could not entirely abandon his beloved cannon. He had the men work through the night to devise a way to take them apart and load the pieces onto the pack animals. Among the supply animals at the rear of the army there are now teams of four donkeys, each rigged together carrying the heavy brass barrels between them. The cannon crews have been given horses, and it is their job to urge the protesting donkeys on.

A gap develops between the small army and the main army. The gap widens. A cloud of dust hangs over the plain.

The sun is high in the sky. The horses move at a brisk canter. Jahangir and Mahabat Khan climb up the rise of a gentle hill. There is a panoramic view of the valley behind.

A scout comes galloping up to them. "Sir! We are being followed." They stand up on their stirrups and look back. The columns of the small army extend to the bottom of the hill. Behind that they can discern the speck of a horseman raising a trail of dust. It is Nur. Jahangir turns without comment and rides on.

Presently Nur bursts upon them, escorted by a trooper. Jahangir looks straight ahead and ignores her. The others follow his cue. Nur tries to get close to Jahangir, but is blocked by

Mahabat Khan and the trooper. Nur makes a determined effort. She scowls at Mahabat Khan and forces her way past him to ride behind Jahangir. Jahangir looks straight ahead. Nur rides behind him in silence.

"What are you doing here," Jahangir says finally.

"I am coming with you," she replies.

"I did not say you could."

"A future wife's place is at her husband's side."

"Go back."

Nur continues riding behind Jahangir.

Mahabat Khan tries to crowd her out, looking at Jahangir for a signal. Jahangir rides ahead without turning around.

"Madam, this is no place for a woman," Mahabat Khan pleads.

"I can ride better than most of your men, Sir... General," Nur responds.

"But we cannot spare soldiers to look after you—"

Nur lifts her cloak to reveal a sword. "You will not, Sir General. If I am a burden to you I will be the first to realise it. I will go back of my own accord."

Jahangir abruptly increases his pace, so that he is fifty feet ahead of the others.

The rebel leaders, Khusrau, and the Oymaq chief ride at the head of their army.

"When do we stop for supplies?" Khusrau asks.

"Very shortly, your Highness," says Husayn Beg.

They are approaching a village "Oh good!" Khusrau says. "We can buy supplies. I brought money—" He reaches for his pouch.

Husayn Beg puts his hand out to stop him. "Save your money for the soldiers, your Highness."

"What about the supplies?"

Husayn Beg raises his sword and shouts an order. The horses increase their pace. The army starts moving towards the village at a threatening canter.

"Wait! What's going on!" says Khusrau.

Husayn Beg shouts another order.

The troops break into a gallop, swords raised.

"Wait! STOP!" Khusrau yells. "STOP!"

Husayn Beg shouts the order to charge.

Khusrau's horse is almost run down. He rides with the others to keep pace. "I said stop! I did not give the order! Stop! Stop, I say!"

The horses thunder past Khusrau. He increases his pace, his face white with shock and misgiving. He keeps his sword raised, in a futile gesture of restraint.

A man is standing among the huts of the village, carrying a pot of milk. He sees the advancing horde and drops the pot. It breaks, and milk flows around his feet. A woman carrying a bundle of sticks on her head sees the charging troops, and runs away. The man is still standing in the same spot, frozen with panic. From one end of the horizon to the other, he sees the galloping cavalry of soldiers coming straight at him. There are no war cries, no shouts. The charging men are silent, businesslike. This is not personal. Something hits the villager's face and he is knocked down. He sees the sky for a second as horses' hooves thunder close to his ears.

The horsemen loot the village. Horses clatter between the huts, looking for produce, valuables. Doors, huts are knocked down. The soldiers bludgeon their way into each hut and ransack it, throwing the goods into a large pile at the centre of the village. An unseen woman is screaming somewhere, over and over again. The rebels work quickly. The few villagers who have not fled are killed with a swiftness and efficiency that leaves them unawares.

A horseman uses a torch to set fire to a hut. The other huts start catching fire. Soon a heavy column of black smoke rises from the entirety of the village. The horsemen ride out through the smoke onto the plain. It has only been a few minutes since they first approached the village.

Khusrau rides by himself, his heart pounding, his stomach churning.

It is almost three days before Jahangir's small army reaches the village. It is deserted. Jahangir, Mahabat Khan and officers search through the burnt ruins of the huts. The smoke has subsided. There is ash everywhere.

"General," Jahangir says, "pass the word down. Unlike the wretch, who is my son, we are to do no burning. No burning, no looting!"

Something catches Mahabat Khan's eye. He is inside what remains of the walls of a burnt down hut. He dismounts. With his sword, he carefully moves a piece of fallen wall aside. He sees rings of dust on the hard village floor, as if a pot that had been there a long time was recently moved.

Mahabat Khan looks up at Jahangir. "They're running out of money."

"Running out of money?"

"Yes."

"How do you know?"

"They have been stealing food."

Mahabat Khan takes a map out of his saddle. He lays it on the ground and pores over it on his hands and knees. Jahangir dismounts to look over his shoulder. With a stick, Mahabat Khan points to the north-west route out of Agra.

"The best way they can get money," he says, talking to himself. "The best way they can get money—" He traces his stick along the map until it comes to rest at Lahore, "—is to raid the treasury at Lahore." He looks up at Jahangir, suddenly excited. "Lahore! They will capture the fort at Lahore and hold it! And pay for their soldiers from the richest treasury in Hindustan! That is where they will make their stand! Come on!"

Hurriedly, the men mount their horses. The orders are passed down. The small army is on the move again, this time with renewed urgency.

Seventy miles ahead, the great phalanx of rebel horsemen, nine thousand strong, raises a spectacular cloud of dust that rises high over the arid plain. Khusrau is up front. He looks worn, desperate. He repeatedly stands on his horse's stirrups looking back. Far behind them, black smoke rises from a burning village.

A herd of heavily-laden donkeys brings up the rear of the rebel army. The slim long legs of the animals make patterns in the sun with light and shadows.

The small army pitches a weary camp for the night. The thousand troopers are sprawled out helter-skelter. The moon has yet to rise, but the stars are out in the evening sky. A water-carrier goes from person to person carrying a goat-skin filled with water. He pours out a small ration for each soldier.

Jahangir has dispensed with the luxury of a tent. He now sits like his troopers, around a fire, with Mahabat Khan and officers.

Nur hovers in the background not knowing what to do with herself. Her avowals to be no more than an ordinary soldier have not worked out. The captain, to whom she has been assigned, does not speak to her and is very far from giving her orders. For the most part, she has been left to ride alone. Whenever she gets too close to a group of men, they fall silent. In any case, silence has been the norm of the small army. The strain of setting the gruelling pace has taken its all from the men and animals.

A servant comes by and pours Jahangir a cup of wine from a jug. Jahangir takes the cup. Then he takes the jug from the servant as well.

"They are barely five days from Lahore," Mahabat Khan says wearily. "We cannot catch them."

"The cannons are slowing us down," Jahangir growls.

"Your Majesty!" Mahabat Khan responds with abrupt vehemence. "Without cannon, how will an army of one thousand men face a force of nine thousand? We will be slaughtered!"

Jahangir looks up at the smoke from the camp fires, rising orange-grey into the black sky. Whither Allah's will? Whither Allah? It was almost achieved. Manifest destiny was his. But it seems that Allah, if there is indeed an Allah, will not let him rest. It must be snatched away at the last minute. Spoilt and dispersed into petty struggles and burning villages. His father was the greatest ruler in the world and he is nothing. It always seems thus, in this strange Universe. All that is good lies scattered, broken, fragmented. The perfect pear rots. The auspicious child of a beautiful woman is stillborn.

Jahangir's chest is filled with despair. In truth, he can barely stay in the saddle on this long, brutal ride. A number of times during the day his lips opened to ask Mahabat Khan to order them to stop. Each time he closed them again and, instead, hung on, his bones aching, his muscles begging for reprieve.

Mahabat Khan is saying something. Jahangir finishes his cup in a single swig and glowers at him. "Our only hope," Mahabat Khan says, "is that Dilawar Khan at Lahore closes the fort's gates and defends it against Khusrau."

"He will do no such thing." Jahangir pours himself a new glass of wine. "Khusrau has my seal. He will be welcomed into the fort. Through open gates."

Abruptly, Mahabat Khan stands up. He goes to his saddle and gets out a prayer mat. He lays this out on the ground and stands solemnly in front of the mat, facing Mecca.

"What are you doing?" Jahangir demands.

"I am requesting Allah to make Dilawar Khan close the gates of the fort."

"You are requesting that tree over there. And it doesn't care."

Mahabat Khan is not amused. "I need to pray to Allah now,

your Majesty," The tone of his voice makes it clear he is in no mood for interruption. He closes his eyes and prepares to prostrate himself on the mat.

Jahangir throws the cup of wine into Mahabat Khan's face. Mahabat Khan's eyes widen with shock. "Wake up, General!" Jahangir snaps. "You are addressing that tree."

Wine drips down Mahabat Khan's face. "Your Majesty," he replies evenly, "you need to leave me by myself while I say my prayers."

With a power and fury that take him by surprise, Jahangir leaps up at Mahabat Khan, knocking him forcefully to the ground. Jahangir is on top of him with a knife at his throat. "You are praying to that tree!" he snarls. "Where is your Allah!" Mahabat Khan's turban has been knocked off. Jahangir half-rises, grabbing him by the hair. He swivels Mahabat Khan's head around. "Look! Look around you! Do you see him?"

There is a brief moment when Mahabat Khan thinks that Jahangir is about to sweep the knife across his windpipe. His chest heaves under the wine-stained shirt. Jahangir glares at him, his face barely six inches away. Then abruptly he drops Mahabat Khan and stands over him, still holding the knife.

"There is no Allah, General," he says casually. "Only the wine on your face. And the cold light of the stars. Which shines down pitiless. On you, and on me. And on the scorpions underneath your feet. That will bite you. And kill you, if you are not careful. You can puff yourself up with the fancies of little men. Little men who need to believe in their stories of Gods and infidels. Men like my father. Or you can see it as it is, General. The cold light of the stars. Which shines down without favours. Which at this very moment illuminates a commander in Lahore who does not know he has to close the fort gates."

Mahabat Khan regards Jahangir's knife carefully. "I have no way of telling Dilawar Khan to close the gates," he says. "Khusrau has your seal. Even if I was to send a messenger right now, he would not believe him."

"He would believe me!" says a voice. They turn in unison. It is Nur. She has been standing close by in the dark.

"Dilawar Khan would believe me," Nur says hurriedly. "I played with him as a child! We grew up in the fort at Lahore together. When my father served the Emperor!"

"And how would you get there?" Mahabat Khan asks.

"I will ride."

"Madam, you have lost your mind."

"No one will suspect a woman, Sir General. I will join the harem. I will ride through them!"

"They will catch you," Mahabat Khan says. "If you are lucky, they will behead you."

There is a silence. Nur stands in front of them, not budging.

"Do you have another plan, General?" Jahangir asks at length.

Mahabat Khan gives him a cold stare. "I would like to get back to my prayers."

Jahangir chuckles. He reaches down and picks up the jug of wine. He takes a long swig directly from the jug and looks up at the sky. He walks to his saddle and pulls out his matchlock. He tosses it to Nur, who barely manages to catch it.

"I cannot take it," Nur says. "It is too heavy."

"I did not say you could speak, soldier," Jahangir orders.

April 1605

It is that ambiguous time of day when the evening light starts to turn into night. There is brisk traffic on the street outside the public house. In ones and twos, the patrons filter in. With that odd demeanour that looks as if he is wondering vaguely if he is being watched, Paru's assailant, Bhir Das, climbs the steps of the public house and enters through the beaded, silken curtains. He enters the large room, which is not yet crowded. He is shown to a comfortable set of cushions in a corner. Prostitutes, beautiful with their bangles, anklets, and made-up faces, stand around waiting to be picked up. Some of the girls have already found clients. They sit on their clients' laps and make conversation with the sweet seductiveness of awkward youth.

Bhir Das is served a jug of wine and a hookah. He takes a puff and surveys the room through the smoke. Two girls are standing some distance away, talking to each other, waiting. He smiles to himself through the smoke. His eyes caress the girls' bodies. He hears a voice. "Beautiful, are they not?"

Bhir Das turns his head slowly. Pithu is breathtakingly

beautiful. With make-up and jewellery, she is the whore with experience, the one who can project soul. A single glance, and Bhir Das knows she can play a man with every trick. He looks knowingly at her knowing face. "Yes," he says, smiling in reply to her question.

"They are all made up, like little painted dolls," Pithu says. "But I find them beautiful underneath."

"You do," Bhir Das says.

"Yes. Look at them." Pithu looks raptly at the girls. Bhir Das, influenced by her, looks as well.

"Can I smoke from your pipe?" Pithu asks.

Bhir Das holds up his hookah. Pithu licks the pipe briefly with her tongue, then takes a drag. She lets the smoke out slowly through her mouth. "A man's beauty is very different from a woman's."

"Really?"

"Those girls have such pure and lovely bodies. But a man's beauty is who he is."

Bhir Das takes a puff from the hookah and looks at her with interest.

"You must be a *kharus ustaad* with that sword."

He looks at the sword and touches it. He is about to speak.

Pithu puts her hand to his mouth. "Don't tell me," she says huskily. "I want you to tell me very slowly... through the night... who you are. If you will spend the night with me?"

Bhir Das considers. "I don't have a lot of money."

"The pleasure is mine," Pithu says. "There is a power I feel coming from you."

Bhir Das is at once suspicious and hugely attracted. He looks warily at Pithu. Pithu unbuttons his tunic, and slides her knuckles over his bare chest. She is beginning to breathe hard. "Stop, stop!" she tells herself. She pushes him away. "Slowly," she says. "We must do this slowly. I would like to dance for you."

He smiles, his suspicions receding.

"Come." She stands up, pulling him by the hand.

He is a little surprised, but follows. He gives a last glance at the two girls, as she leads him to the doorway.

"Where are we going?"

"Where I can dance for you."

On the street Pithu walks in silence. She covers what she can of her body and head with her *odhni* and walks half a step in front of Bhir Das without looking back. Some ten minutes later they enter the large front room of the dance class. It is pitch dark. Pithu lights two wall-lamps across the room from each other. She smiles reassuringly at Bhir Das. Because of its size, the room is still only dimly lit.

Bhir Das looks around. "It is very quiet here," he comments.

"The girls are out for the night. They have to find lovers early." Pithu removes her *odhni* deliberately and drops it on the floor. "Do I scare you?"

Bhir Das looks startled. He shakes his head.

"Sometimes I scare men."

"It is very quiet here," he says again.

"It won't be for long. I am glad I don't scare you. She puts on a pair of dancers' anklets. The anklets make a sound as she walks. He looks at them. She sees him looking and taps out a flourish.

"Sit over there." She holds his hands and pushes him towards the wall cushions. She unbuckles his sword and throws it aside, so he can sit. She lights two more lamps illuminating him where he is sitting.

"I will show you magic."

She walks back to the first pool of light. "We don't have any music. You have to imagine the music in your head."

Pithu starts dancing. Her anklets seem to speak. They voice perfectly Pithu's dark and mysterious sexual tension. She is as one. Her hips, her clothes, her body, her jewellery, her face, her makeup — they emanate a single thrilling excitement to Bhir Das. She does some rapid flourishes with her feet. She moves her hips sensuously. She curls her tongue. She raises her arms and gets him to focus on her breasts.

She goes down on all fours and advances on him. He reaches out. She retracts, playing with him. He smiles appreciatively. Even on her fours she can maintain a rhythm, dancing skilfully, interlacing her sensuousness with snake-like undulations of her long, slim waist and hips.

She stands up again. She dances in one spot. Her movements become more studied, more formal, as if she finds herself going too fast again and wants his bursting penis to subside a little.

The one pair of anklets begins to sound like two.

There is now a magic trick. In front of Bhir Das's unbelieving eyes, Pithu turns into Paru.

It could have been that Paru was shadowing Pithu's movements exactly behind her, and Pithu abruptly disappeared into the dark and Paru appeared in the light. Bhir Das has no time to wonder how it was done. But Paru is dancing in front of him.

She wears a leather belt. On the belt hang six knives.

Paru continues to dance as Pithu did. Her moves are as seductive and expertly executed as Pithu's. Even after he realises it is Paru, it still takes Bhir Das some time for the change to fully register. His expression gradually changes to one of consternation.

He dives sideways to grab his sword, and yelps with pain.

Paru has thrown a knife. Blood gushes out from Bhir Das's arm. He grabs his arm screaming in horror and anger. He reaches desperately for his sword with his good hand, struggling to his knees.

"Stop!" Paru orders. She is holding another knife ready to throw. "This one will be through your heart."

Something in Paru's voice tells Bhir Das he is within a hair's breadth of death. He freezes. They stare at each other, adrenalin rushing.

"You stole my jewel."

He says nothing.

"I am going to kill you," she says with certainty. Her voice is calm, steady. "But first I will ask you some questions. You answer the question correctly, I go on to the next question. You answer it incorrectly, I put this knife through your heart."

Bhir Das glances at his sword.

Paru throws a knife. It sticks in the floor an inch away from his penis. Bhir Das's breaths come out in small gasps. He sits very still clutching the floor with both hands.

"Six knives," says Paru softly. "Six questions. On the last one you will lie, and I will kill you." The certainty in her voice sends a chill up Bhir Das's spine.

She circles him carefully. "Did you steal my jewel?"

"Yes."

"Is the jewel mine?"

"Yes."

"Who gave it to me?"

"Your mother."

Bhir Das moves his feet minutely, tensing them to dive forward.

"What else did my mother give me?"

"A scroll. A piece of paper."

There is a pause as Paru thrills with the information.

"Where is the jewel now?"

"The Prime Minister has it."

The answer throws her off balance. She hesitates, decides to go on.

"Where is my mother?"

"She died. Two years ago."

It is all Paru can do to conceal her excitement. "Where is the jewel?" she asks again, as if about to experience a great secret.

"The Prime Minister has it," Bhir Das replies, looking puzzled.

A door bangs open. The loud voices of girls talking and laughing suddenly breaks the quiet of the dance class.

Paru hides a small spurt of panic. "What does the scroll say?" she asks hurriedly.

Another door slams. The loud voices of the girls advance towards them.

Paru glances behind her.

Bhir Das lunges forward, knocking Paru off her feet.

She throws the knife. It sticks in the floor at the spot where he has been sitting. He is on top of her trying to grab her. She twists and tries to kick his balls. She kicks his lower abdomen instead. This stops him for a moment. He grunts. She writhes and rolls out from under him.

She is on her feet. He struggles to get up, hampered by his bad arm. She draws a knife and is about to throw it into him. But something flashes through her mind. Perhaps it is the power and mystery of the unanswered questions, but she hesitates.

Two girls enter the room. Paru disappears into the darkness beyond the lamps. There is a moment of shock as the girls regard the bloody Bhir Das. Bhir Das hastily retrieves his sword.

The girls scream. They make a dash for the door. But, Bhir Das is ahead of them. Bhir Das and the girls collide violently and bounce off each other. The girls shrink back into the room, screaming in terror. Bhir Das runs out through the door.

Holding his bloody arm and limping painfully from the kick, Bhir Das escapes into the night.

Pithu sits on the steps of the whores' boarding house. Paru sits a step behind her. Pithu stares ahead in a blue fury.

"Why did those girls have to come back?" Paru sighs. "Nobody comes back that early!"

Pithu looks straight ahead not replying.

"Stupid bitches!" Paru mutters to herself.

Pithu does not say anything. Paru looks at her apprehensively.

"They told him I had gone missing!" Pithu explodes suddenly. "They are all going to ask now, where was I, where was I? So I'm going to say to him, dear husband, I spent the evening in a whore-house. With my friend, another whore!"

"Maybe he won't ask," Paru says nervously.

Pithu purses her lips dismissively.

"I... I found out who has my jewel," Paru says hesitantly, hoping that will please Pithu.

"Who?"

"The Prime Minister."

Pithu turns and gives Paru a look that could kill.

"He seemed to be telling the truth," Paru says uncertainly. "I think he was..."

"Why is he trying to kill you?"

Paru looks at Pithu with a sinking feeling. "I forgot to ask."

Pithu stands up. "You forgot to ask?!"

"There was no time to ask! I only had a few questions. And then the girls came in—"

"All this! And you forgot to ask? Have you gone insane?"

"There was no time—"

"Maybe you didn't ask because there is no one trying to kill you!" Pithu explodes with rising passion and certainty. "Maybe there isn't even a jewel!"

"Of course there's a jewel—"

"I haven't even seen the jewel! Maybe you just like sticking knives into fat men!"

"Pithu! It's not like that—"

Pithu starts walking away.

Paru runs after her. "They want to kill me because of the jewel—"

Paru pulls Pithu's shoulder. Pithu shrugs it off angrily and keeps walking. "Don't you see?" she says desperately. "It's about the jewel! There's something about that jewel—"

"You leave me alone!" Pithu shouts, wide-eyed with anger. "You make me crazy. Then I do crazy things... like you!"

"It's not crazy!" Paru retorts trying to control the tears. "All these men, they are all very real!"

Pithu keeps walking. Paru follows, running to keep up. Pithu does not look back. Paru follows silently, refusing to give up. They walk a long time this way, Pithu making random turns through the *bazaar*, Paru following, trying to keep up.

"I need... normal!" Pithu says, as if explaining to herself. She does not look back. She stretches out her arms. "I need... children!" she says looking up at the sky with her arms outstretched. "I need... husband!"

Pithu keeps walking. Paru follows her silently and stubbornly. Pithu traces a zigzag path through the *bazaar*, past the dance class, past the whores' quarters, then back through the *bazaar* again. She does not once look back.

Paru tires, and stops. She walks slowly back to the steps of the whores' boarding house and sits down. There is a strange, isolated look on her face. She takes a lock of her hair between her fingers and twirls it absently.

Maybe Pithu is right. Maybe her assailant is just some strange, fat man and now she's thrown a knife at him. And the jewel was stolen because, well, it was expensive and someone could get a lot of money for it, and that is why it was stolen. And maybe the thief is gone a thousand miles from here. A hand seems to clutch at Paru's heart when she thinks of this. And the men in her hut with the swords? Well, maybe she imagined them, maybe a bad dream. And the blow to the Snake Charmer's head and the big cloth bandage he wrapped around it? Maybe she imagined that too!

She twirls the lock of her hair faster and faster. Maybe life is just a dream — a bad one. And crazy people like her cannot tell the difference where the dream ends and where the real begins—

No, no, no! She stops herself. The people are real, and they are really trying to kill her for some reason that she does not understand. And they took her jewel, and she will get it back. And now that Pithu is gone, she has no one to convince but herself. Paru's face assumes an eccentric look as she stares blankly in front of her. She purses her lips and her mouth becomes small, her eyes receding into isolation. Now that she's alone, she tells herself, she has to do this by herself. And she will get the jewel back and find out why these men are trying to kill her. There is no one to team up with. She has to get the jewel back by herself. With a slightly mad look on her face, she twirls the lock of her hair faster and faster and faster...

It is some hours later when she slips into Pithu's house unnoticed. She goes to her little corner and packs her clothes into a cloth bundle. She finds her copper *lota* and places it on the ground nearby. She picks up the scroll and packs it into her bundle with the clothes. Some minutes later she emerges from the house carrying the bundle and *lota*.

She walks aimlessly down the street.

The enormous orange sun rises over the horizon. It melts into the land in a great orange dewdrop of shimmering haze. In front of the dewdrop is a tiny black spot. It is Nur, on her horse moving at a fast canter. He *burkha* flies in the slight breeze. She has been riding eighteen-hour days, stopping to rest only when the exhausted horse can go no further. Since her childhood, riding has been Nur's talent. It is something she did with insolent ease growing up in Lahore. Riding with the boys as a child, she often embarrassed them. The boys extracted vengeance and ostracised her. But she was a boisterous girl and could not be brushed off easily. But now as she rides, the mission fits. Everything in the Universe fits. It is the destiny she has been waiting for. The moment.

The bag of ample gold coins in her saddle has been a great help. She exchanges two, sometimes three, horses in a day. She moves too rapidly for word to get out into the villages ahead, and she has to wait impatiently at the horse-exchange point for a man to scramble to a nearby village to get a fresh horse.

At night she does not bother with a blanket, let alone a tent. She simply rolls off the animal to lie on the ground beside it for five hours. Then it is time to move again, and she is riding in the dark, using just the starlight, long before the sun lightens the sky with dawn.

Smoke rises in front of her from a group of smouldering huts. It is another village the rebels have burnt. As Nur approaches, there is black ash everywhere. She gallops through the huts, scattering a shower of ashes.

The day seems to go by in an exhausted blur. It seems she is never as far as she wants to be. Evening falls and then night and then the orange moon rises. The moon is Nur's friend, giving her light by which she can ride till very late. Her mounted shadow flies rapidly over the shadows of the bushes and the trees.

And then late afternoon the next day, she sees them, raising a great dust cloud far on the horizon ahead of her. It is almost magical. She never expected to catch up. With a thrill of fear and anticipation, she rides the last few miles up close to the rear of Khusrau's army.

She approaches cautiously, using the cover of bushes and riding over grassy or rocky areas in order not to raise the dust. At this view, from the rear, the army is mostly mounted porters, each of them leading a train of donkeys and mules carrying supplies. There are many animals and few men. Nur abandons the cover of the bushes behind which she has been hiding and catches up with the animals. She rides among them, testing her ground. Off to the left in the distance she sees a group of mounted rebel women. She contemplates riding with them for cover, then fears they may see her in a way that the men may not, and recognise her instantly for the enemy.

Nur rides up to a train of donkeys. She pauses briefly next to the last donkey, draws a knife and cuts it from the train. She pulls the donkey by its rope, and spurs on her horse, leading the donkey behind her. The porter in charge of the train looks up at Nur. He checks his train of donkeys.

Nur hears a shout behind her. She increases her pace, losing herself among the numerous animals' bodies and legs. With one hand she holds the donkey's tow-rope, with the other she pulls the shawl of her black *burkha* tightly over her face.

Four turbaned soldiers are riding rapidly along the edges of the army. Nur feels a tingle of fear. They are checking on the supply trains at the rear. Two of them appear to be in command. The other two ride behind. They stop briefly near a porter, observing his train of donkeys and letting the animals pass by. It is only a matter of time before they see her.

Nur stops suddenly, and gets off her horse. She takes her matchlock and sword out of her saddle, runs to the donkey and hides the weapons hurriedly into its pack. Animals and mounted porters jostle past her. She looks up. The four rebel soldiers are riding straight towards her. She reaches quickly underneath the donkey and loosens the leather belt by which its load is fastened.

She goes back to the horse, mounts it and pulls at the donkey's tow rope. She is in full view of the men now. As soon as her horse pulls on the rope, the load falls off the donkey. She goes to the load and tries to pick it up. It is too heavy. She tries to drag it towards the donkey. She cannot move it.

The men ride up and surround her. Nur struggles with the load. The men watch her impassively.

Nur regards them with long-suffering impatience. "What are you waiting for?" she demands.

"Who are you?" asks the leader of the group, who appears to

be a captain.

"I don't have time for this," Nur says. "You," she orders one of the men. "Find a horse for me and tie this load onto it. Properly, this time."

The man draws his sword.

"Allah!" Nur says, exasperated by his stupidity. "I am Nafisa Begum," she explains to the captain. "Prince Daniyal's consort and third wife. Now I am a widow, because my husband drank himself to death! Prince Khusrau is my nephew."

"So... you are a noble woman," says a rebel, who appears to be the second-in-command.

"Yes!" Nur smiles brightly with a touch of sarcasm. "Now find a horse for me. I need to give the Prince his medicines. He is prone to convulsions, I hope you know that. If he doesn't take his medicines he may get a fit and die on you!"

"Begum," says the captain. "I have never seen you before. How do I know whether to believe you?"

"You believe me because you are talking to me," Nur says with a personal power and authority so sudden and overwhelming, the captain starts with surprise.

He hesitates.

"We should take her up front and check her out," whispers the second-in-command.

"We don't have time," the captain replies.

"Tie my luggage back onto the ass and I will let you go," Nur says, taking advantage of their indecision. "If you see the Prince before I do, tell him I am looking for him. And I have his medicines."

The captain glances at the fourth man in the group, who has stood by and said nothing so far. "Do it," he says.

The fourth rebel is a surly fellow. He gives Nur a truculent look, giving her body the once over. He gets off his horse reluctantly, places the fallen load back onto the donkey, and ties it down tightly. He picks up the rope attached to the donkey's harness and takes it to Nur's horse. He takes a long time to tie the rope onto Nur's saddle. They wait in silence.

"Begum," the fourth rebel says unexpectedly. "Why does your horse look so tired?"

Nur raises her eyebrows and looks away. The question is too out-of-place to even merit a response.

The captain looks at Nur thoughtfully. "Begum, answer his question. Why is the horse so tired."

"It is a bad horse," Nur explains. "Half the time it runs off by itself. The other half, it does not keep up."

The fourth rebel holds Nur's horse's head, and gives it a friendly rub. He runs his hand over its straggly mane and nuzzles his head against it. "Begum," he says, speaking out of turn once more. "This horse does not look tired as if it has just been running. It looks tired as if it has been running for a long time. Hours... days perhaps."

The captain looks expectantly at Nur.

There is a long silence. Nur is stricken, found out. "It is true," she says huskily. She clears her throat unable to speak for some time. "I have been riding all night." She starts crying. The tears roll off her cheeks. "I love him too much! I cannot bear it! I could not stay away!"

"Love who?

"The Prince! The Prince! Need you ask?" She wipes her eyes. "How is he? How is my child? My beautiful, sweet, gentle child?" She takes a corner of her *burkha* and blows her nose noisily into it. "Tell me, captain! Is he a big commander now? Does he command this army?"

"The Prince is sixteen years old," the captain says incredulously.

"True love does not wait on a man's age, captain!" Nur explains fussily. A wild look crosses her face. "Take me to him, captain," she begs. "I know there are all kinds of guards and such in the way, but you have the authority. I can tell. Please! I beg you! Take me to him!"

The second-in-command smirks.

"Please, captain!" Nur begs.

The captain is not amused. He wheels his horse.

"Captain! What... where are you going?!"

"Watch your step, Begum. You lead a dangerous life." The men start riding away.

Nur runs after them. "It's true about the medicines! He needs to take his medicines!" she shouts waving her arms.

The fourth rebel glances impassively back at Nur.

Nur walks back to her horse, and buries her head in its side. She clutches the saddle tightly. She is shaking. The shaking seems to get worse. She cannot control it. She hangs on to the saddle, her knuckles white, as she shakes like a leaf. She tries to cry, but her breath comes out in dry heaves.

It is some time before she feels in control of herself. She runs up to the donkey, takes the matchlock out, and attempts to load it. Her still trembling hands fumble with the powder. She spills it over herself, onto her *burkha*. She spends an absurd amount of time trying to brush the powder off her *burkha*. She tries again to load the powder. After what seems like an eternity, the matchlock is loaded. She holds it up, looking around, getting ready to defend herself. But the rebel army has passed her by. The last of the supply animals are already receding in the distance. She lowers the matchlock. She stuffs it into her saddle.

She remembers her sword and shield. She runs to the donkey again and retrieves them. She jumps onto the horse and lets the donkey loose.

She wills herself to ride once again towards the rebel army. She gives the horse rein and makes ground, catching up with the rear and ducking her way past the pack animals. She sees the four rebels again in the distance and rides slow and erect at a leisurely pace. They appear to be ignoring her.

She finds herself between two phalanxes of mounted archers. There are curious glances. She feels reckless, desperate. This seems to help because it gives her an air of brazen confidence and the men leave her alone. She noses her horse diagonally across the phalanx. This is behaviour altogether too curious to be normal, and she sees men glancing at her, on the verge of challenging her. She straightens out, ducks among streams of horsemen and animals, losing herself once again.

She finds herself at the army's flank. Off to the side, there is wild countryside, consisting of eight-foot-high shrubs and low trees. Abruptly she crosses the no-man's land that separates the riders from the area of shrubs. She is behind the bushes. She cannot be seen. Nur yells at her horse and races forward at full gallop.

She makes rapid ground past the rebel army. She and the horse improvise a slim, dangerous path through the bushes. The bushes come at her at fearsome speed, shaking and jittering. At any moment, it seems she will be blocked and thrown. But in the last fraction of a second she and the horse see a way. She feels at one with the horse, in love with him. She stands up in her saddle and yells. After a minute, Nur is relieved to see the path widen. In fact she can see quite some way along it.

Then she freezes.

The fourth rebel is waiting for her at the end of the path. His sword is drawn.

Nur pulls on the reins, coming to a noisy, panic-stricken halt. She is at a standstill. She regards the fourth rebel, her heart pounding.

She draws her sword, and pulls out the shield from her saddle.

He does not move.

Nur gives a fierce cry, and charges at him, her sword ready to swing. He easily sidesteps the charge. She charges again from a shorter distance. He sidesteps again. She attempts a third charge. She swings her sword wildly, attempting to reach him. He successfully sidesteps again.

She looks foolish, outclassed. He twirls his sword like a master, waiting.

Nur waits.

They both move simultaneously at each other. Nur misses completely. She raises her shield just in time, as his sword hits it with a crisp, expert *CLANG!* that is shocking in its force and jars her hand. She can barely hold on to the shield. He comes at her again, deliberately, comfortably. She makes no attempt to strike, but just raises her shield in time to stop his sword. Another *CLANG!* of such force that the shield moves sideways and slams into her body. An ice-cold part of her thinks that her playfights with Jagat Singh years back when her husband was still alive were for naught, because in the real battlefield a man is so much stronger than a woman and she is easily outclassed no matter what.

She swings her sword futilely. She misses him by a mile. She raises her shield bracing for the next strike, but he rides past without an attack. Then half a beat later he strikes her past the shield.

Nur yells and falls off the horse. The tip of his sword has made a cut on her chest. There is a long gash of red from her left shoulder across her chest. She rolls away, gets up, minus the shield, her left arm in pain, hanging useless. She can still move, the cold part of her thinks. That is good.

She stands facing him holding just the sword with her good hand, ready to fight to her death.

He plays with her, getting ready to finish her off. Nur sees her horse standing behind him. He comes at her and swings. She should have been killed, but for once she makes the right move. As he approaches she dives forward to the ground under his horse. She feels the air from the horse's hooves brush her ear, as the animal instinctively, and mercifully, steps over her.

She is still alive. She stands up. She is behind his horse and he has to turn around. She uses the gap to sprint to her own horse, mounting it in a single, desperate motion. Her sword has been abandoned. There is nothing left but to flee. She gives a desperate cry, slaps her horse on the rump and attempts to gallop away.

He follows close behind. Nur rides as she has never ridden in her life. The bushes jitter wildly, coming at her with fearsome force. He is so close, he seems to be attached to her back. She twists and turns through the bushes. She cannot shake him off. He is implacably behind her. She is surprised he has not reached her yet, that the strike has not come that will chop her head neatly off.

The ground seems to be ascending. They are going up the slope of a large granite rock. Nur does not see the sharp drop where the ground gives way. Her horse does not see it either. It misses its footing and falls over a small cliff at the edge of the rock, going at such speed it does a half-somersault. Nur is thrown to the ground, rolling. She finds herself being violently pummelled and then crushed as the horse rolls on top of her.

She feels a cry of pain, but it cannot emerge from her mouth because her breath has stopped. She is still conscious. She tries to move, but cannot. At first she thinks it is because she is hurt in some way and is about to die. But then it dawns on her. She is pinned under her fallen horse. Obviously the horse is hurt as well. It moves a little, but cannot get up.

The fourth rebel takes his time. He dismounts and walks up to Nur. He has to reach over the horse's body to face her; she is pinned between the horse and the rise of the rock behind her. There is still plenty of room to kill her.

Nur looks helplessly up at her saddle and at the sky. Awaiting her death. On the edge of her vision she sees a dark shape. The dark shape obstructs her view of the fourth rebel as he stands over her.

He is in his element. He seems to want to lengthen the moment. He twirls his sword once. He raises it deliberately getting ready to finish her off.

There is a loud *BANG!* as the barrel of Nur's matchlock blows a hole the size of a fist through the fourth rebel's chest. His face stiffens. His eyes stare absently into the distance, glazing. He collapses slowly on top of Nur's horse. His dead face hangs over Nur's. He gazes sightlessly at something near Nur's face. Blood runs from his wound, down the side of the horse, and on Nur's clothes.

Nur sits beside her horse. It has taken her almost an hour to get out from underneath it. She spent the hour making tiny movements with her body, pushing with her free hand, trying to wriggle first one leg, then the other. Inch by inch she moved, with the patience of choosing life over death.

The horse lies still on his side, his leg broken. He whinnies softly now and then, moving his limbs awkwardly. Nur strokes his long neck, looking tenderly into his large eyes. Flies buzz around the horse's head. Nur whisks them away.

There is a loud bang as she shoots the horse through the head.

An hour later, Nur limps painfully through the woods on foot, carrying what supplies she can on her back. Her ankle was twisted in the fall and she can walk only with difficulty. The wound in her arm and across her chest seems deep and swollen. But the pain is tolerable. She has abandoned the matchlock because of its weight, but still carries the sword. The front of her *burkha* is covered with dried blood and mud.

It is nightfall before she reaches a village. A boy is sent out to a neighbouring village to bring an ayurvedic, a doctor of herbal medicine. The wound is treated with neem leaves and other herbs Nur has never heard of. She is made to drink a bitter tea. She has been lucky, miraculously lucky. The doctor insists she rest for the night. She is too faint and tired to argue. Nur is overwhelmed by the kindness of the villagers. The boy who went to get the doctor has a thin, angular, smiling face. She is in a cocoon of comfort and relief.

It is late morning before she sets out again. A villager shows her a shortcut, a country path by which she can simultaneously avoid Khusrau's army and get ahead of it.

It is another two days of hard riding before she sees the citadel in the distance. It is sunset. The gaunt outline of Lahore Fort stands black against the orange sky. Nur's spirits surge upwards. Her horse is fresh and strong, her *burkha* flies, her arm is bound in cloth and poultices.

Nur gallops across the drawbridge. The sentries move to intercept. She thrills to announce herself.

It is late night before the order to close the gates is given. The intervening hours were used by Dilawar Khan, the fort's commander, for hasty resupply.

The drawbridge has lain open through years of peace and prosperity. Now, with a creaking of winches, the clank of chains, and the shouts of many straining solders, it is slowly raised. The glow of light emanating from the fort's entrance is gradually shut out as the drawbridge closes over it.

Khusrau and the rebel commanders look up at Lahore Fort in consternation.

The drawbridge is up. The fort is uncannily silent in the midday sun. There is not a soul to be seen, either on top of the battlements or in the intervening ground in front of them. Through the slits along the fort's wall the rebels see the stubby bronze snouts of cannon. The cannons are perfectly still. There is no doubt in the rebels' minds that there are crews hidden behind them and that they are loaded and ready to fire. The rebels have to approach with caution. The first line of five hundred cavalry stands by, well out of firing range.

A slight breeze disturbs the afternoon stillness. "Two mortars," says the Oymaq chief. "Two mortars to keep them busy inside. And two cannon to break through the gates."

"We left the cannon behind," Husayn Beg reminds him.

"The gates were going to be open!" protests Dalit Singh, the second-in-command. "And we were going to walk into the fort!"

They look at Khusrau. His mouth dry with fear, he shakes his head. "I have never in my life... This... this is outrageous!"

"It may be a nail in our coffins," Husayn Beg says matter of factly. "Let us try calling to them."

A troop of fifty is chosen to ride behind Khusrau. To show his trust, Khusrau rides a hundred feet in front. Husayn Beg and Dalit Singh ride as subordinates, bringing up the troopers. The fact that he is exposed and possibly in danger of his life is secondary to Khusrau. He is much more anxious to prove to the rebels that he can enter the fort.

He stands in his saddle. "Dilawar Khan!" he calls. "Commander Dilawar Khan! It is Prince Khusrau! Why are the gates closed?"

The fort is silent. The breeze creates little ripples on the broad, green waters of the moat.

"Open the gates! I have orders from my father, the Emperor!" Khusrau reaches into his saddle and pulls out a rolled-up document with a prominent red seal on it. He holds it up.

Behind one of the cannon turrets, there is a swift, fleeting movement.

"I have orders from my father!" Khusrau yells again. He stands in his saddle and holds up the document.

The minutes drag by. Khusrau's arm begins to ache. Tiring, he turns and rides back to where Husayn Beg and Dalit Singh are standing. He consults with them briefly. He returns to his previous position. He stands in his saddle again, holding up the document. "Dilawar Khan! I have an army of ten thousand! We have orders from my father, the Emperor, to regroup here, and then to move north! Please open the gates!"

The fort is silent.

Khusrau glances back at Husayn Beg and Dalit Singh. They nod assent. "Dilawar Khan!" Khusrau shouts. "This is an act of treason! I warn you for the last time!... open... the gate!"

A sudden flapping of wings from the top of the fort startles the soldiers. A flock of pigeons has taken off in the sunny afternoon silence.

Khusrau waits. Minutes drag by. He holds the document up as long as his aching arm permits.

He gives up. He turns his horse around and rides dispiritedly back to Husayn Beg and Dalit Singh. Wordlessly, the troop of fifty returns to join the main rebel force.

Husayn Beg shouts the commands. An attack is in the making. There is furious activity. Supplies are unloaded, plans are made, troops regrouped. At the end of an hour, a thousand mounted archers in two well-formed lines stand ready for battle.

Husayn Beg barks a command. The lines advance towards the fort at a wary canter. Without breaking stride the archers string their bows.

Husayn Beg shouts again. The two rows of mounted archers part in the middle. From behind emerges a troop of fifty. At the centre of the troop, trail two long lines of mules. Each of the mules is heavily laden with gun-powder. Burdened as it is, this phalanx breaks out in front, galloping urgently towards the moat.

When it is a good two hundred feet in front of the archers, Husayn Beg shouts the command. The first line of five hundred archers lets loose a flight of arrows. Five hundred arrows arch across the sky, making a great wooden parabolic arc over the phalanx of gun-powder-laden mules. But the arrows are out of range. They land in front of the fort and fall uselessly into the moat.

The column of mules rides on. The archers are now racing closely behind the phalanx, keeping a short distance. The second line of archers lets loose a wave of arrows. These hit the fort wall. Some of the arrows find their way through defensive slits. Many others fly over the fort wall and land inside. Through the galloping of horses and the shouts of men can be heard the faint cries of the wounded from inside the fort.

The moat is within reach of the phalanx of gun-powder-laden mules.

There is an orange flash from the fort, and a loud deep THUMP! as a cannon fires its charge. Smoke emerges from the cannon turret and swirls in front of the wall. The fire-laden cannonball misses and lands in front of the phalanx, kicking up a shower of dirt.

The phalanx keeps going. A flash and another THUMP! as a second cannon fires. The shot misses again, landing behind. The phalanx rides urgently on. The wall of the fort is shrouded in smoke.

A third flash and THUMP! and a fireball arches across the sunny sky and slams directly into the phalanx. Horses, soldiers, mules go flying from the impact. Then the gunpowder catches. A series of secondary explosions rend the air as, one after another, the gunpowder packs on the mules light up.

Where the phalanx used to be there is now an enormous fire. Thick black smoke rises into the blue sky.

Husayn Beg gazes at the burning phalanx and the screaming men and animals, with an ugly premonition.

Paru has walked the streets for four straight days. She has been traversing one long street after another, end-to-end, hoping to catch sight of her assailant before he sees her.

After leaving Pithu, she staked out his quarters in the barracks outside town, and spent long hours crouched in the grass observing the soldiers come and go. But he was nowhere to be seen. He seemed to have moved. She was disappointed.

She decided to try the *bazaar*. Sooner or later everyone in the city passed through the *bazaar*. She was surprised how large a place it was. She crisscrossed it several times, her *odhni* wrapped tightly around her head. It was tricky, because not only was it easy to spot other people in the *bazaar*, it was easy to be seen, yourself. Once in a while, somebody fresh would call out to her, "*Psst!*" looking for a tryst, an angle with a pretty girl walking by. Paru drew her *odhni* ever more tightly around her head and shoulders and strode on. She was cautious that the vendors in the stalls did not come to see her as a familiar presence, someone they remembered. Word got around quickly. Then again, that may be a way to draw her assailant out.

At night, Paru has become adept at finding cosy corners in which to sleep. At around ten o'clock the soldiers come to the *bazaar* for a sweep, clearing beggars and loiterers from the carefully governed streets. It is always good to be on one's feet and moving at those times. Sometimes they come around again, a surprise visit. But Paru has a keen eye for the odd angle between two walls, or accidental shrubbery in an abandoned space that hides a comfortable getaway from the dangers of the street.

For food, she dips into the small stash of money she has from her wages with Pithu. She uses this to buy an occasional fruit from the *bazaar*, or whatever food takes her fancy. In fact, money is the least of her problems. If she runs out she can make some from hustling. The hardest thing to do is to search without being found, to hunt without being hunted.

After leaving Pithu, she has been in a state of mild shock. She no longer has Pithu. She left the Snake Charmer. She no longer has her village. Or her uncle, who so kindly helped her come to the city. In fact she has no one. Only her mother remains in her heart, always her friend.

Paru sits on the road in the late afternoon, leaning against a wall, her bare toes defiantly pushing out the mud. She yearns for a bath. There is nothing to do. She decides to be brave. She dares herself to think about her mother.

She recalls the shouts across the rice fields. There would have been ten or more of them, her and her new cousins and aunts and uncles from the village, spread out across as many paddies. Each paddy was neatly enclosed by banks of mud and filled with water by the monsoon rains. They had to plant the rice seedlings quickly to give them sufficient time to grow before the water dried up. Paru loved being there. The warm, muddy water curled around her legs and toes, and she splashed and jumped, splashed and jumped. At first the mosquitoes bothered her. But then she got used to them, as did everyone else.

She spent many a blissful morning there splashing in the water and falling headfirst into it. Her mother was off in a distant field somewhere, and she was all by herself with the sun. Then her mother turned up suddenly, and scolded her for slacking off. And then both of them had to work very fast to make up for her foolishness. Even while scolding, her mother was gentle. She could not bring herself to be harsh.

There were late evenings when her mother was the only one left in the rice paddies, working rapidly by the light of the moon and the stars to make up for lost time. Too tired to move, Paru sat on the edge of the paddy and watched her. The moonlight caressed her face and her arms, which glowed luminescent in the dark. When she worked hard, she looked especially beautiful. The night hid the wisps of her grey hair, which were beginning to emerge. Paru liked to count them. "Three today!" she would report, or "I can see five!" Paru could hug her, and hug her.

When she was five, how her mother had carried her from village to village! For half her life it seemed her mother had been on the run, fleeing enemies Paru had never seen and knew nothing about. And now she too is on the run. Fleeing enemies she knows nothing about. How strange is destiny!

Her mother did not wait long to show her the jewel. And the scroll. From as early as Paru can remember, there were secret trysts in the dark of their hut, when they were about to sleep, when her mother dug into her belongings and brought out the jewel. It glittered in the lamplight. It contrasted so utterly with the simple things in their little hut, indeed, in their entire village, it made Paru gasp. The jewel radiated! The huge sapphire in the centre! Diamonds! Gold! "You must never sell this," her mother told her. "It must remain with you all your life. It is how you will find your father." Then her mother brought out the scroll. Paru looked at it every which way, turning it sideways, upside down, backwards. Her mother told her it was even more precious than the jewel. But Paru could not see the point. It was a stupid piece of paper! "Can't we find someone to read it!" Paru demanded. But there was no one, not in their village.

And it was at those moments that her mother thought of

faraway things. There would be a subtle change in her attitude. Paru can feel the goosebumps, even now. She would look into Paru's eyes. Sometimes she held her hands. Paru remembers those big gentle eyes looking into hers. "You can use these to find him. One day you will find him. And when you do, tell him that I still love him. I cannot forgive him. And he may not forgive me. But..."

"Forgive him for what!" Paru demanded.

Her mother shook her head. There were things she did not say to Paru. It was when she got that faraway look. "You are pure, and you are innocent. You are my innocent little girl," her mother said passing her fingers through Paru's hair. "One day you will find him. And when you do, give him a message from your old mother. Tell him I still love him. Even with his failings. I love him with all my heart. Every moment."

Paru trembled when she heard that. And she hugged her mother. And her mother hugged her. And they clung to each other for a long time in the dark.

Paru covers her face with both hands. She brings the tears down as if she is wiping her face with her hands and dries them on her *choli*. She finishes the job with her sleeves. This is not so bad, she thinks to herself. She can think of her mother.

But can she think of the fevers? Paru puts her head on her knees and shivers, as if the fevers were shaking her own body now. They swept through the village like a storm, a storm that lasted weeks, months. First, it was Chandni, whom they found leaning against a pole, an exhausted vacant look on her face. "My bones hurt," she said, as they carried her limping inside. Then it was Ganpat, his tall, already thin frame lying angularly across the straw mattress. As the bodies mounted, the village retreated into a stunned silence. There was nothing to do but go on. Expensive *kriyas* were conducted. Pandits were called. And with the smoke rising up around the fruits and the milk and the flowers and the statues of the Gods, the people lost themselves into a kind of numb faith — that somehow they would get past this, or that it would be all right in the end, or that it was meant to be.

At first her mother hid her tiredness. She sat down in the field one day. But then she got up and continued to do what she was doing. To Paru, the fevers were other-worldly, something that she and her mother just had to live through while others died around them.

But then there was alarm in the faces of the boys who called her. She went back to find her mother shivering violently in her hut. Some relatives stood around her. Somebody gave her a wet cloth with herbs to put on her head. Her head was as hot as a stove-top. "I'm cold," her mother said, shivering. They rushed about trying to find every sheet, every cloth they could lay their hands on, and covered her from head to foot. They took a moment to open her *choli*, although she was cold, and put poultices with herbs on her stomach and then covered her up again.

"Better?" Paru asked.

Her mother shook her head, trembling helplessly. She closed her eyes. She seemed to be sleeping. Paru lay down next to her, hugging her. Once in a while she trembled, and Paru hugged her tighter.

Paru must have dozed off, herself. It was dark when she woke up. Her mother was awake too. She was drenched in sweat. Paru's heart raced. She seemed better. Paru fumbled around and managed to light a small fire outside the hut. Her mother sat up. She smiled at Paru in the dim light. Paru beamed with happiness. Soon her mother was standing up and walking around. They made a nice meal, and her mother ate. It was going to be all right.

Her mother went back to work the next morning. Paru checked up on her a few times to make sure she was all right. But in the late afternoon, she caught sight of her mother walking back to the huts, and her heart sank.

It was always the late afternoons. Paru came to dread them. If only there was a day they could miss that the fever did not come back! But it always did. Her mother stopped trying to get up and go to work in the mornings. The cumulative exhaustion from the days was too much and she just lay on the floor. Paru could see that she was upset because the fevers stopped her from getting up and going to work. There was too much for her to do in her life, too much to look after. She struggled to fight the fevers, but it was hopeless. They were almost continuous now. Sometimes a blank look descended over her eyes, and Paru was paralysed with fear. She shook her mother then, placing the wet cloth frantically on her forehead, trying helplessly to do something, something. There were many relatives, many remedies, many herbs. Paru tried them all, and screamed at them when they did not work, and then the relatives had work to do, other responsibilities, and one by one they left.

And then the fever broke, for blessed minutes, hours, when they could be together again. And her mother smiled at Paru, and Paru smiled back and wiped the sweat from her brow. "Tell him I love him," she said, as if reminding her of a chore she should not forget.

Paru nodded vigorously. "I will."

"You know where the... jewel is?

"Yes!"

"...and the document?"

"For the hundredth time, yes! I will find him and I will tell him. But you will be there with me. And we will tell him together!"

A look of pain passed over her face, and she shook her head ever so slightly. She raised her arms for Paru, and Paru hugged her. Forever and ever.

She died one night in her sleep. And in Paru's sleep. There was something to be vaguely grateful for about that. The big black ball in Paru's stomach had been growing in anticipation of such an event, and now such an event had occurred and Paru could make no sense of it. The ball was still there, bracing for the strangeness of a new life, a life without her mother.

Paru remembers being fascinated by the wood flames. The weather had been dry for the past few weeks, and the wood burst into spectacular flames. Hot, holy flames, which crackled and bent the air, and let her mother rise upward, pure and spirited, into the sky. And out across the Universe, and into Paru's heart.

She went back to the hut after the funeral, and checked on the jewel and on the scroll, just to please her mother, although she knew they were there. She felt them in her hands in the dimness of the hut. She clung to them trying to hold her grief, trying to hold her mother. Some things remain. They really were her mother's jewel and scroll, much more than they were her father's. And they were Paru's. Now. But she would find him. And she would tell him, because that was what she wanted. That was her legacy.

It is getting dark. Paru's wall is along a quiet side-street with only one shop and with some genteel residences. A lamp is lit in the shop front. Another glows through the entrance of one of the houses. She has had the wall to herself these last two or three hours. She has been sitting against it, thinking and crying the entire time. No one bothered her, for that she is grateful. With her head over her bent arm and her legs tightly curled up, she looked as if she was asleep.

But she has to face the world, and she looks up now. She feels drained, exhausted. She sits for several minutes, looking ahead and taking in the stillness of the evening. She feels compelled to move. She stands up and stretches. Tired as she feels, it would be a bad idea to try to sleep against the wall just now. It is approaching the time for the soldiers to come by. She decides to go for a walk. There is nothing else to do. She may as well look for her assailant. She does not even know where he lives any more.

She threads her way through the *bazaar*, which is crowded at this time of the evening. It is easier than during the daytime. She can hang quietly in the shadows and watch the glittering goods being sold under the bright glare of the oil lamps. She drifts past shops stacked with beautiful fabrics, and one offering handsome jewellery. A hawker is selling fritters made of potatoes and chillies fried in batter. Suddenly, she is hungry. She decides to buy one. She takes her money out to pay and finds to her alarm that it is running low. She almost hesitates over the fritters, then decides to take the plunge and buy them anyway.

She slinks into a dark corner to eat. The fritters go down her gullet and into her stomach and make her feel good. She can think of something else now, besides food, or her mother. Suddenly, she feels very dirty. Grains of sand chafe between her fingers, and her arms. They are down her back, inside her *choli*, and they fill her hair. She cannot imagine how she must smell. She yearns for a bath! Her mother would not have approved of this dirtiness. She can get a bath if she takes up quarters in the whores' boarding house. And she can afford to rent a space there if she takes up hustling.

She comes to a decision. One last night out on the street. Tomorrow she will start to hustle. There are dangers to working the streets by yourself without being associated with a pimp. But she knows how she will do it. This is something she is good at.

In the meanwhile, she is the Queen of the hidden corners. Since it is her last night outside, she decides to take a special risk and find an audacious spot amidst the stones of a high-class graveyard. Usually there is a watchman there, squatting on the ground next to the entrance. Paru explores the graveyard surreptitiously. The watchman seems to be missing for the night.

The grass is soft underneath Paru's body. It caresses her head and her arms. She can hear crickets and frogs croaking in the neglected shrubbery around the headstones. They remind her of the sounds of her village at night. She is tired... so tired.

Itimad Ud Daulah has occupied the same palatial quarters in a corner of the fort for forty years. Like Akbar's, they are untidy and well-used. Itimad Ud Daulah is seated on a divan at one end of the reception hall. In front of him is a low table with an enormous expanse of inlaid marble. On either side, he has piles of ledgers and court documents. He is writing, making rapid, perfectly shaped letters with a quill.

He looks up at Bhir Das, who is escorted in by two guards. His manner is not welcoming. Bhir Das has a cloth bandage tied around one arm.

"This is the man, *Vazir Sah'b*," says the guard.

Bhir Das bows formally. "*Huzoor*, I will come right to the point," he says before Itimad Ud Daulah can challenge him. "There are rumours in the *bazaar* that a Third Prince will rise up among the people and defeat His Majesty. The rumours say that His Majesty is not the rightful ruler of the land. That the Third Prince is."

There is a silence. "Tell me something I don't know," Itimad Ud Daulah says at length.

"I believe I know where the Third Prince is."

Itimad Ud Daulah regards Bhir Das sceptically.

"It is a girl," Bhir Das says. "A prostitute."

Itimad Ud Daulah is unmoved.

"She is wanted for murder. For killing the prostitute she roomed with."

"You are standing there in front of me," Itimad Ud Daulah replies. "She must be fifty miles away by now."

"She stays in the city. She prefers the city."

Itimad Ud Daulah is impressed with the information, although the expression on his face does not show it. "I will have my men look into it. I suppose you want a reward," he says dismissively.

Bhir Das shifts his weight from one foot to the other. "Not exactly, *Vazir Sah'b*. I am offering my services to bring her in."

"And why should I use you, when I can call upon my own men?"

"I am the only one who knows what she looks like." Bhir Das pauses. "I witnessed the murder."

Itimad Ud Daulah contemplates Bhir Das standing in front of him. "You are the lowest piece of scum to inhabit the earth," he pronounces. "I will have my men bring her in. I do not need your services."

"*Vazir Sah'b*, I would urge you to think. His Majesty is already upset with his son's rebellion. He is not going to be pleased to come home to a city full of rumours about a Third Prince. He may be hearing those rumours even now, on the battlefield."

Itimad Ud Daulah chews on this for some moments. "If you bring her in, how will I know it is her?"

"She has a paper in her possession. A document. Only she knows what it is. And we do."

Itimad Ud Daulah experiences a feeling of distaste at Bhir Das's familiarity. He thought knowledge of the document was private. "You will get nothing from me until you bring her in," he says guardedly. "With the paper."

"You are a man of your word, *Vazir Sah'b*. I do not need money in advance from you. However, I will require a reward of thirty thousand *rupiya*, when I bring her in. And twenty troopers from Birbal's old guard."

"Those are our best men!"

"She is armed and dangerous, *Vazir Sah'b*. She needs the best... when I bring her in, she may be dead."

The conversation is concluded. Itimad Ud Daulah waits for Bhir Das to leave. "What happened to your arm?" he asks for want of something to say.

"That was a hunting accident, Huzoor," Bhir Das replies smoothly.

Itimad Ud Daulah nods slightly, acknowledging the fiction.

In the bazaar square, an expectant crowd stands in a large circle. The crowd members move forward eagerly, encroaching on the space in the centre. The Snake Charmer pushes them back. "Back! Back everyone!" he scowls. "This is going to be difficult. Difficult and dangerous! Back!"

Inside the large circle formed are two smaller circles, made up of charcoals soaked in oil. At the centre of one of the smaller circles is a closed basket. At the centre of the other is a pile of knives. A man bangs out a loud beat on a *dhol*, a fair drum.

The people have been pushed back to the Snake Charmer's satisfaction. He goes to the pile of knives and picks up two. He rubs them together holding them high above his head. "Nobles! Lords! Ladies!" he announces. "You are about to witness the greatest show on earth! This is not going to be pleasant. If you have a weak stomach, I would advise you to go home. In one circle of fire here," he points to the basket with one of his knives, "we have Maharaj! King of the cobras! King of snakes! A cheer for Maharaj!"

There are some absent-minded applause and some impatient hoots.

"Maharaj is a fully poisonous snake!" the Snake Charmer scowls. "His venom has not been removed. So far, he has killed nine men! I have seen it myself! I was sleeping. I was attacked by bandits. Maharaj woke up! He saw the men. And killed them all! A strike from Maharaj, and you are dead... DEAD!"

Paru is at the back of the crowd. She is in full hustling mode, bathed and groomed, with her sexiest make-up. She looks stunning. She can hear the Snake Charmer's voice and is anxious to get to the front.

"And with Maharaj!" the Snake Charmer continues. "Alone in the circle of fire! The beautiful! The lovely! Goddess! Sita Devi!"

Into the circle with the basket enters a young, pretty girl, about Paru's weight and height. She actually looks like Paru. But her mannerisms are very different. She is showy and demonstrative. She spins into the circle, her arms raised, rousing the crowd for a loud cheer.

Paru watches, amazed at the sheer brazenness of the imitation. A nine-year-old boy looks up at Paru in fascination.

"And at the same time," the Snake Charmer continues. "In the other circle of fire! You have... you have... me!... Why do you not cheer?! Lords and Ladies! I am going to juggle these knives in the air." He juggles two of the knives. "See?"

The crowd chatters, unmindful. The boy continues to look up at Paru.

"I will be in my own circle of fire! And I will juggle... not two... not three... not six... not ten... not twelve... but fourteen knives! fourteen knives, Lords and Ladies! Up in the air at the same time! If one should slip... you know what will happen to me."

Paru notices the boy staring at her. She looks back at him and gives him a small smile. The boy bursts into a sunny smile. Paru smiles back.

"Each in our own circle of fire! Sita Devi in hers with the deadly poisonous King Cobra," Sita Devi extends her arms and turns. The Snake Charmer opens the lid of the basket. The *dhol* becomes louder. He sets fire to Sita Devi's circle. Instantly, orange flames leap up, entrapping her in the circle with Maharaj.

"I in mine with my knives!" The Snake Charmer sets fire to his own circle.

The two circles of fire burn ferociously.

Sita Devi focuses on the open basket, standing as far away from it as the circle will allow. The *dhol* is now loud and hypnotic. She starts dancing rhythmically to the beat.

Smoothly, Maharaj uncoils himself from the basket, and slithers towards her. He stops some four feet from her. He raises his head and fans himself out to his full glory. With the seductive beat of the *dhol* and the snake-like movements of Sita Devi's body, Maharaj sways his head from side to side.

The two circles burn furiously. Heat from the flames wafts towards the fascinated spectators.

The Snake Charmer has been juggling two knives. He now bends and picks up a third knife. He throws the knives higher into the air. He picks up a fourth. Sita Devi sways her hips looking fixedly at Maharaj. She starts inching towards him.

Paru glances down at the boy. He is gone. She does a double-take and looks again. The boy has vanished. Alarmed, she looks around for him. He is nowhere to be seen. Highly alert now, she forces her way out of the crowd.

The Snake Charmer picks up a sixth knife. "Six knives, Lords and Ladies. Six blades spinning through the air!"

Paru is out of the crowd. She grabs her *ghagra* and feels for the knives she is wearing. She passes a bullock cart filled with straw. The bull sits unharnessed next to its cart. Paru rounds the cart and is out of sight of the square. She starts walking rapidly down a side street.

A quarter of a mile away, twenty troopers from Birbal's crack guard are assembled at a cross-roads. Half the troopers are mounted archers. The others are swordsmen, carrying great curved scimitars and prominent shields in their saddles.

Bhir Das comes riding up. "Wait for me to recognise her!" he calls to the troopers. The horses charge noisily down a street towards the bazaar. When they reach the edge of the square, Bhir Das stands up on his horse, looking frantically over the heads of the crowd. He cannot see Paru.

"She can't be far!" he shouts to the troopers. "Block the roads!"

The practised troopers fan out, going down each of the four main roads emanating from the square. When they reach an intersection, they split up further.

Paru walks, almost runs, down a road leading out of the square. There is a crossing up ahead. She sees the troopers' horses at the crossing. She stops, her heart pounding. Her instincts were right. She runs back, away from the troopers.

Two of the troopers turn and start coming towards her. Paru ducks out of sight into an alleyway, just in time. She runs down the alleyway, turns right, and then takes a sharp left onto another main thoroughfare.

There are troopers coming up this thoroughfare as well, straight towards her. She retracts just in time, back into the narrow alleyway. She runs down the alleyway and back left onto a roadway that had been clear before.

She comes face-to-face with Bhir Das. He is at the far end of the roadway.

Bhir Das draws his sword. He shouts, spurs the flanks of his horse, and comes charging down the roadway towards Paru.

Paru stays where she is, crouching slightly.

Bhir Das comes to a sudden realisation. He aborts his charge and pulls his horse to a skidding halt. He pulls hard on the horse's reins. The frightened animal takes several steps backward. Bhir Das keeps pulling the horse back, creating a healthy distance between himself and Paru.

Paru turns and runs in the opposite direction. She stops immediately. The other end of the roadway is blocked by a trooper — a swordsman with a long curved scimitar.

"That's the one!" Bhir Das shouts to the trooper.

The trooper smiles and draws his sword. Sword raised, he charges down the street at Paru.

Paru stands, waiting for the trooper.

"No!" Bhir Das shouts at the last minute. "No! Don't!"

The trooper thunders down the street. He is almost upon Paru.

There is the blur of her hand and a flash of steel. The knife lodges squarely through the trooper's neck. Paru recoils in shock.

The trooper starts falling forward, still attempting to swing his sword at Paru. Paru steps aside. The trooper falls off the horse, dead. His foot is caught in the reins, and he is dragged several yards before the horse stops.

Paru turns and runs up the road away from Bhir Das, feeling sick to her stomach.

Bhir Das spurs his horse and follows Paru.

She takes a sharp right back onto a street that seems clear for the moment. Bhir Das follows. Paru is halfway down the street. She senses Bhir Das behind her. She turns around abruptly and throws a knife. But the distance is too great. The knife kicks up dirt in front of the horse's feet. Bhir Das halts, keeping a safe distance between Paru and himself.

Paru walks, casting an occasional scornful glance back at Bhir Das.

At the *bazaar* square, an arc of spinning knives arches through the sky. The crowd is beginning to be impressed by the Snake Charmer. A smattering of applause rises against the beat of the *dhol*.

The Snake Charmer is sweating with the effort. "Fourteen—" he gasps. "Fourteen knives, Lords and Ladies! And now watch—"

Maharaj is fully fanned out, swaying aggressively. His tongue flicks in and out. Sita Devi is stuck. She is still dancing, about four feet in front of Maharaj. She looks sick. She takes a tiny step forward.

Then the fear hits her. She starts shaking. For several seconds she stands in front of Maharaj, trembling like a leaf, taking tiny dancing steps. Her face is white with panic. She takes a confused step back, while simultaneously trying to maintain her rhythm. Her feet are entangled within themselves, and she falls.

The crowd gasps. Maharaj closes in and coils his way onto the fallen Sita Devi. He is now fully fanned out above Sita Devi's face. He hisses aggressively. She is paralysed with fear.

Some streets away, Bhir Das follows Paru. At a crossing up ahead, a swordsman turns into the street, and sees Paru. He draws his sword.

"Stop!" Bhir Das shouts. "She throws knives!"

The trooper stops.

"Back off!" Bhir Das shouts.

The trooper's eyes meet Paru's. He pulls violently on the reins of his horse forcing it back.

Paru walks threateningly towards the trooper, her hand at the ready.

The trooper backs away in front of her.

"Get the archers!" Bhir Das shouts to the trooper.

The trooper turns his horse around quickly, and rides away.

Paru looks defiantly back at Bhir Das. She reaches a corner and darts left. She quickens her pace. This is the roadway leading back to the open square. There are passersby.

She comes face-to-face with a trooper, a mounted archer. The trooper reaches into his quiver.

Paru throws a knife. It lodges squarely in his chest. The trooper falls. Paru is pale with shock.

She feels in her *ghagra* for another knife. There are none. She looks back. Bhir Das has just rounded the corner. She starts running. Bhir Das maintains his pace behind her, keeping a healthy distance. Then he realises that she is without a knife. He shouts, spurs his horse and charges forward.

Paru sprints down the trafficked roadway. Bhir Das gains rapidly. She reaches the crowd surrounding the Snake Charmer's circle and pushes her way roughly into it.

The flames have burnt down low. The rings of charcoal glow red-hot in the afternoon heat. Maharaj is coiled across Sita Devi's panic-stricken body as she lies in the dirt. There is a buzz of apprehension in the crowd.

"Help the girl!" someone calls.

"You need to help the girl!" a man shouts at the Snake Charmer.

"Help!" Sita Devi calls softly.

The Snake Charmer senses disaster, but is unable to take his eyes off the knives. "I am putting them down, Lords and Ladies! I have to put them down one by one... there!" He drops a knife.

A chorus of shouts to help the girl rises from the audience. The shouts are getting urgent, insistent.

"I am putting them down, Lords and Ladies," the Snake Charmer says fearfully. "One by one. I have to put them down one by one..." He drops a knife. "There!"

All is not right with Maharaj's mood. He feels hemmed in by the crowd. He looks from side to side and hisses viciously. He opens his mouth showing two huge fangs.

Paru glances behind her. Bhir Das is forcing his way through the crowd towards her. She looks at Maharaj, measuring her distance. She looks behind again. Bhir Das is upon her, his sword ready to swing.

Paru dives into the open space. She rolls, gets up and jumps over the charcoals. She is inside the circle of embers with Sita Devi.

Maharaj strikes. A stream of venom barely misses Paru. She freezes. Maharaj hisses. His tongue darts in and out. Paru stands perfectly still. She locks Maharaj in her gaze. Maharaj waits for her, ready to strike. Paru does not move.

Bhir Das is now in the open space, his sword ready. He wills himself to enter the smaller circle with Paru, but seeing Maharaj, he stops short.

For several seconds Paru stands, her eyes locked deep into Maharaj's. Then smoothly, as if she has not moved, she moves. Her body starts snaking slowly from side to side. Maharaj watches. The *dhol*, which has been quiet, starts up again, softly, smoothly. Paru dances for Maharaj. Maharaj is entertained, fascinated by Paru's movements. His crabby mood calms, as he watches her undulating body.

Bhir Das is standing, sword raised just outside the circle. Several times he wills himself to jump in with Paru. Each time he stops.

Paru turns on her sexual charm. There is a maturity, a naturalness and professionalism to her moves that thrill her as much as they thrill the crowd. She edges closer to Maharaj. The crowd murmurs its approval. Her thin, muscular body is bathed in sweat. She feels a small triumph at reclaiming her lost territory from Sita Devi. It is rightfully hers. She has just killed two men and is fighting for her life. But she is the pro, the original one. The heat, the sweat, the danger elevate her into an ecstatic state. She goes down to Maharaj's level, her body moving like a summer wave. Her eyes are dreamy, seductive as they remain locked with his. She sways her upper body, he sways his.

She is on all fours. She edges closer to him. Two feet, a foot. Her face is six inches from his. She pouts and sticks out her tongue. Maharaj sticks out his. He is mesmerised.

Bhir Das still hesitates, unable to force himself to enter the circle.

Paru's mouth is close to Maharaj's. Her lips pout. It seems they are about to kiss. Somebody starts clapping. This turns into full, enthusiastic applause. With imperceptible slowness, Paru starts backing away from Maharaj. He follows, his head still barely a few inches from her face. Imperceptibly, as Paru backs away, Maharaj uncoils himself from Sita Devi, and follows her pouting seductive mouth.

He is entirely off Sita Devi. Sita Devi, who has been watching the exchange while frozen with fear, finds herself suddenly free. With the pragmatism of youth, she gets up, jumps over the charcoal embers, and runs into the crowd. She struggles furiously, forcing her way through. She is out of the crowd and running as fast as she can, away from the square, away from Maharaj.

Four mounted troopers thunder towards the square. Sita Devi comes running straight at them. "There she is!" one of them shouts. Sita Devi is upon them before they know it. She is going to run between the horses. A trooper dives off his horse and tackles her savagely to the ground. She is knocked unconscious.

At the square, Paru is holding Maharaj's head firmly from behind. He is strangely docile. Barely able to carry his weight, she edges him towards the basket. She sits next to the basket and places his head in it. His body follows obediently. She slams the lid shut and sits on it.

She glances at Bhir Das. Before he can move she darts to the

Snake Charmer and picks up two knives. She stands poised, ready to throw them. Bhir Das backs away hastily into the safety of the crowd. Paru throws a knife just for the fun of it. It lands near Bhir Das's toes. A woman screams.

"Six knives to go, Lords and Ladies!" shouts the Snake Charmer. "I have to put them down one by one! Or else, I am done for!" He drops a knife. "There! Five knives left!"

Paru edges her way into the crowd, holding a knife at the ready, aimed at Bhir Das. The crowd makes way for her. She runs to Bhir Das's horse, which is standing nearby, and jumps into the saddle.

She rides off in a cloud of dust.

The four troopers who have just captured Sita Devi approach Bhir Das. She is slung across a trooper's horse, trussed hand and foot. "We got her!" the trooper shouts exultantly.

"That's the wrong one," Bhir Das replies with a despondence that comes from the depths of his being.

The Snake Charmer uses a wooden scoop to shovel charcoal from a large pile outside his hut. His knives are piled in an unceremonious heap nearby. Paru is seated on a rock watching him. In repose now her body emanates a warrior-like athleticism. "She's good!" Paru says approvingly.

The Snake Charmer scowls at the charcoals as he shovels.

"She just has to be convinced in her heart that Maharaj will not harm her. It is a hard thing to learn."

The Snake Charmer continues to shovel.

"I like the way she came out so boldly and wasn't afraid of everyone watching."

The sack into which the Snake Charmer has been shovelling the charcoal is full. He ties the mouth with a coir rope.

"I was so happy when I heard your voice in the *bazaar*!"

The Snake Charmer carries the sack to a corner and leans it carefully against the hut. Paru watches him.

"Are you angry with me?"

"Angry? No!"

The Snake Charmer walks over to the knives. He picks one up and tosses it, catching it by the handle. He scowls at Paru.

Paru summons up the courage. "I am sorry I left you," she says.

The Snake Charmer squats and picks up a sharpening stone. The palms of his hands are covered with cuts.

"Actually... there are no words. I hurt you..."

He scrapes the sharpening stone over the edge of the knife, trying to make it blunt.

"...but I had to go," she explains.

"I know," he says.

"You know?"

"Yes."

She looks at him mutely, asking.

"Why did you come back!" he explodes.

"I think of you every day," Paru says softly.

"Don't come back. Stay away!"

"I thought maybe..." Paru looks at the ground.

"You're dangerous. You upset everything!"

Paru nods meekly.

"You upset me! Why did you come back!"

"I saw you. In the *bazaar*... I was so happy!"

"People around you get killed."

She nods, as if being rebuked for doing something bad.

"I don't want her to be next."

Paru nods again.

"I can look after her... maybe... I mean with you. I don't want to take her place dancing or anything—" This is difficult for Paru to say. "Just... be near you."

The Snake Charmer stands up, the blood rushing to his face. A part of Paru's thigh is exposed. One elbow rests casually on her knee. Her arms are lightly muscled. She sits confident in the space she occupies, like one who is capable of facing anything. Yet she is so vulnerable, so sweetly open to him. It is too much!

"You left me!" he shouts in frustration.

"I am back," Paru responds in a small voice. "I am living at the whores' boarding house in the bazaar."

The Snake Charmer does not reply. He turns his back on Paru and tosses the knife into its pile.

Huskily, afraid to ask, she steels herself: "Does she do anything... that I don't do?"

The Snake Charmer turns to face Paru. "Yes," he says, looking directly at her.

She makes love to me every night. And she wants to stay with me."

It is as if Paru has been hit by a blow. The Snake Charmer maintains his resolve. He stands in front of her, breathing heavily.

The makeshift door of the hut opens and Sita Devi comes out. She gives Paru an apprehensive, evaluative look.

Paru's face twists as she tries to hold back the tears. She seems to shrink back into herself. She makes a decision, and looks defiantly back at Sita Devi, wiping her tears, her face working with grief.

"I have to go in now," the Snake Charmer says. He and Sita Devi go into the hut. He does not look back.

The makeshift door swings shut after them.

Paru sits on the rock, looking at the closed door swinging back and forth. She sits that way, wiping her tears, for a long time.

There is grime and sweat on every part of their bodies. Jahangir is slouched low, hanging on to his saddle for dear life. The small army, with a thousand men, has been streaking northwest across the great plain of the Punjab towards Lahore.

Mahabat Khan rides up. "They have reached the fort. But the fort has held!" he announces exultantly. He looks at Jahangir. "The gates were closed."

Jahangir is pleased. "How many days, General?"

"Three." A note of anxiety creeps into Mahabat Khan's voice. "There is very little armour at Lahore Fort. They may not be able to hold it for long."

"We better hurry then," Jahangir replies.

They come within fifty miles of Lahore when the scouts report that a rebel force of six thousand has separated from the main group and is headed back, straight for them. Mahabat Khan takes the time to pitch a proper camp and let the soldiers get a good night's sleep.

The morning is bright and cool. Flags fly confidently in front of the small group of colourful tents. Right at the front are twenty well-spaced cannon, each tended by a busy crew. The army looks small and inconsequential. The plain is vast.

Jahangir sits in his tent examining a butterfly perched on his finger. This is not what his bones tell him, but this is how a monarch should seem, and how a monarch seems is all that matters. The butterfly's wings are resplendent, a bright orange with black and purple patterns on each side. He is a big fellow. Jahangir is surprised to find a tiger butterfly this far north.

A captain is waiting to speak to him. "your Majesty... the General asked me to inform you that the rebels are close."

"How close?" Jahangir asks studying the creature on his finger as it moves its antenna about guardedly.

"Four hours, your Majesty."

"Good. When they are one hour away, I want the cannon to start firing. Make them ten minutes apart."

"Your Majesty... that is a waste of shots."

"Not at all, Captain," Jahangir says pleased with himself. "We have to look big to them." He carries the butterfly to the entrance of the tent. "As big as possible." He releases it and watches it fly away. He walks back into the tent.

The captain departs. But there is another man waiting to speak to him, a cook. Jahangir looks up. "Ah, yes!" Jahangir tells the cook. "For lunch today, I would like a large pheasant *biryani.*"

"Very good, Your Majesty.

"They are easy to hunt around here, aren't they? Wild pheasants?"

"Quite easy, Your Majesty."

"And a cup of wine to go with it."

"Yes, Your Majesty."

"How many cups a day am I having?"

"About two or three, Your Majesty."

"You shouldn't say that. I am down to one cup. To keep myself fit for battle."

"Very good, Your Majesty."

The cook is about to leave.

"And—"

The cook stops.

"Red fried chillies on the side."

"Yes, Your Majesty."

"The ones from Kashmir."

"As always, Your Majesty."

It is some hours later that the cook arrives at the tent with a kingly dish of pheasant *biryani*. He lays it out on a low table in front of Jahangir. The promised red chillies are arranged in a pleasing pattern over the saffron and white rice. The dish glows. The aroma envelopes the tent with a warmth and hospitality that only a *biryani* can summon. The cook pours out a cup of wine. Jahangir watches with anticipation. He picks up the cup and takes a much-cherished sip.

The cook fills Jahangir's silver plate. He is done. He gives his creation one last satisfied look before departing.

Jahangir picks the red chillies off the rice and places them reverently in a little pile on the side of his plate.

Mahabat Khan bursts into the tent. "What are you doing?" he demands.

"Having lunch," Jahangir replies meekly.

"We are about to engage! They are almost here!"

Mahabat Khan regards Jahangir apprehensively, as one who needs to lay down the rules for an unruly child. "One more time," he fusses. "There are two things they want. They want the cannon. And they want your head. If we lose you, we lose the battle. You are not to engage with the enemy. No heroics, no swordplay. Stay to the rear. Use your guards' protection. You should be seen by the men. But, you should be difficult to capture."

"Yes," Jahangir acquiesces.

"And then when I tell you, you will give the signal—"

"Hold my sword up with both hands, and ride across—"

"Yes."

"General—"

"What!"

"I outrank you. Why do you get to have the fun?"

Mahabat Khan gives him an exasperated look and rushes out.

Jahangir eats, holding up his plate and using his fingers. There is an uneasy silence, punctuated by the shouts outside of the men preparing for battle.

A cannon goes off in the immediate vicinity of the tent. Jahangir jumps. A fusillade of matchlock fire opens up. Two or three cannon open up simultaneously. The shouting of the men outside the tent is now frantic, battle-intense.

Jahangir quickens his pace with the *biryani*. He picks up a red chilli and bites into it with great satisfaction.

The loud THUMP! of a cannon close by makes the dishes jump. The wine ripples in its cup. Jahangir eats faster.

In the vast plain, the small army is huddled in a tight defensive rectangle. Guarding the front are the cannon. Behind them stand mounted archers, followed by a line of bristling lancers. At the rear are three tents, one of which is Jahangir's.

In contrast, the rebel army is huge. Four rows of a thousand mounted archers and lancers stand at the ready. Between the two armies is a very empty no man's land. Immediately, the first line of rebel cavalry begins its charge. The vast line-up takes time to accelerate. But then it is at full gallop, thundering across the no-man's land. The ground shakes. A collective roar of battle cries rises up from the rebels.

The small army holds its fire. The gap closes rapidly. Then the twenty cannon fire in close sequence.

The effect on the charging rebels is devastating. The cannon balls plough through the riders. Horses fall, rolling with the momentum of the charge. Their riders go flying. Instantly, the troopers behind crash into the fallen men, making a chaotic heap of men and horses. The small army opens up with a fusillade of matchlock fire taking advantage of the knot of fallen rebels.

A second line of rebels steps forward. They too accelerate and charge. But, this time, the horses move forward in a more dispersed pattern. The cannon respond frantically. Once again the rebels fall. But now, the rebel mounted archers and sharpshooters are within range, zigzagging in front of the rectangle of the small army. They let loose a hail of arrows and matchlock fire at point blank range into the rectangle. Soldiers fall like flies.

A third line of rebels disperses across the plain. The cannon still manage to hold them at bay. But then there is a breach. Rebels enter the rectangle from one side. The small army soldiers rush to engage them in hand-to-hand combat.

Jahangir eats a handful of *biryani*, holding the plate up to his mouth. He feels an urgent need for a sip of wine and extends his hand. Matchlock fire shatters the wine cup from his reach. There is a hole the size of a watermelon in the fabric of the tent. Through the hole he can see bright blue sky and sunlight. Jahangir carefully takes his hand back from where the wine cup would have been. He eats quickly now. The collective noise of horses, men, matchlocks and cannon is deafening.

Several arrows rip through the canvas, shattering a hookah and sending the *biryani* platter spinning.

Jahangir stands up, protecting his plate. The tent fabric flutters uselessly.

The captain of Jahangir's personal guard bursts in, accompanied by a soldier. "Your Majesty! Come on!"

Jahangir takes one last quick bite. He puts the plate down carefully on the table and follows the men. On his way out he casts a regretful look at the abandoned *biryani*.

Outside, Jahangir and the two men sprint to waiting horses,

ducking the arrows and matchlock fire. Jahangir's personal guard of twelve soldiers is waiting. The guards are crack fighters. They include a Flag-Bearer, and a Horn — a soldier carrying a long, martial instrument. Jahangir leaps into his saddle. The flag flies high.

A cannon crew loads and fires. The air is filled with smoke. A soldier manning the cannon gets hit by an arrow and falls. Another of the crew is hit.

Jahangir and his guard ride swiftly past them. Jahangir holds himself high in the saddle, oblivious to the danger. At the breach in the defensive rectangle, rebel soldiers and small army soldiers engage using swords, lances, and battle-maces.

The breach widens. Rebels pour into the rectangle. They are immediately engaged by the defending Mughals.

Four rebels break through and ride straight towards Jahangir. A guard fires his matchlock killing one of the rebels. The other three keep coming. Four guardsmen move out to intercept them. Two of the rebels are lifted physically off their horses as they clash swords with the expert guardsmen. The last rebel is pierced through and through by a guardman's lance.

A wall of twenty rebels comes towards Jahangir and his guard. The guardsmen charge forward to engage them. Jahangir is suddenly alone with the Horn and the Flag-Bearer. Three rebels break through the fighting and come charging at them.

Instead of turning away as he has been instructed, Jahangir charges straight at the oncoming rebels. "*AAAGHHHEEE!*" Jahangir screams, leaving the Horn and the Flag-Bearer behind. He collides with one of the rebels with a massive clash of swords on shields. Unscathed, the rebel rides on with the momentum of his charge. Jahangir swings with a savage backhand, slashing the rebel from behind. Blood gushes out of a great red cut in the rebel's back. Jahangir skids to a halt, turns his horse, goes after the rebel, who is slumped forward in his saddle. Jahangir swings his sword once more into the rebel's back. He falls from his horse, dead.

The second rebel is suddenly right in front of Jahangir. The rebel hesitates. Jahangir swings his sword and chops his head right off. The rebel's head goes flying. Jahangir laughs maniacally, holding up his bloody sword in exhilaration.

But, the third rebel is behind Jahangir, sword raised, ready to finish him off. There is a loud shot from a matchlock. The rebel stiffens and falls off his horse. The Flag-Bearer is holding the flag in one hand and a smoking matchlock in the other. Jahangir looks back at the Flag-Bearer and grins.

The outnumbered guardsmen are still engaged with the rebels, trying to keep them at bay. A guardsman swings his sword and kills a rebel. A second rebel comes up from the side and buries his battle-axe into the guardsman's neck.

Mahabat Khan comes rushing up to Jahangir through the dust and smoke. "Why is the flag down? Where's the guard?"

The Flag-Bearer indicates the pitched battle between the guardsmen and the rebels some fifty feet away.

"All right, it's just us," Mahabat Khan orders. "Flag high! Blow the horn! LOUDLY! As loudly as you can!" He looks at Jahangir. "Now!... Now!... Now!!"

Jahangir stands in his saddle holding his sword up horizontally with both hands.

Jahangir, Mahabat Khan, the Horn, and the Flag-Bearer ride magnificently across the battlefield. The Horn plays a tap. The Flag-Bearer holds the flag up as high as he can. The Horn's music rises thinly above the noise of battle.

The tight group rides, apparently towards the fight between the guard and the rebels. But, at the last minute they avoid the fight, skirting it narrowly.

A rebel carrying a lance breaks through. He comes charging at them, his lance set straight for Jahangir. Mahabat Khan turns to intercept him. Ducking to the side of his horse, Mahabat Khan avoids the point of the lance. Using his sword he fetches a resounding blow past the lancer's shield to his neck and shoulder.

The lancer is knocked sideways and backward, rolling in mid-air as he falls off his horse, dead.

Four rebels have spotted them. They come chasing after the group. Mahabat Khan grabs the reins of Jahangir's horse pulling it in a sharp right turn, away from the rebels and into the main battle. Guardsmen turn up from nowhere to intercept the chasing rebels. Jahangir and his group manage to graze past them.

Mahabat Khan, Jahangir, the Horn and the Flag-Bearer zigzag through the field, past fighting men, past firing cannon. Their horses do sharp turns, deftly avoiding Mughals and rebels alike.

The horn blows its tune. The flag flies. Jahangir holds his sword up with both hands.

The members of a cannon crew look up, as Jahangir rides past. Surprisingly, they abandon the cannon and run to mount their waiting horses. A guardsman is engaged with a rebel. Jahangir and his crew ride by. The guardsman swings at the rebel. The rebel blocks the blow with his shield. The guardsman rides past the rebel. And keeps on riding. The rebel looks after him in astonishment.

In numbers now, the cannon crews abandon their cannon. They mount horses and flee, accelerating their mounts to ride after Jahangir. The cannon sit by themselves untended on the battlefield. The rebels overwhelm what remains of the small army's position. Groups of rebels quickly surround each cannon, capturing it.

The small army soldiers flee across the great, green Punjab plain, their horses galloping at full speed. The Horn, the Flag-Bearer, and Mahabat Khan ride on either side of Jahangir.

The rebels get out rope harnesses for the captured cannon. They surround what remains of Jahangir's tent. The bodies of the dead lie thickly across the battlefield.

Husayn Beg has his eye on Jahangir and the small army, which appears to be fleeing. He raises his sword. "They are getting away!" he shouts. Come on!" With battle cries of triumph, swords raised, the rebels chase after the small army.

The small army soldiers increase their pace. The ground vibrates with the thundering of five hundred horses. Jahangir tires of holding the sword up with both hands. He puts it back in its sheath, and spurs his horse on. The horses are now in full gallop, as if in a race. Their feet are a blur. Each man pushes his mount to the limit. The riders spread out with the faster animals developing a lead. A cloud of dust trails into the sky after the small army.

The rebels are in hot pursuit. Ahead of them the fleeing small army looks inconsequential in the wide expanse of the plain. The rebels are much larger. They are overwhelming, victorious, the mass of their army sprawling backward.

In between the two armies is a gap of two thousand feet.

A thick black line appears in the distance. It spreads across the horizon, a persistent dark shape that interrupts the green meadow of the plain. The rebels see the line only hazily behind the dust cloud of the small army.

The rebels ride up a slight rise in the land. Their view is limited and the shape disappears. There is only the dust of the small army against the sunny blue of the sky. The small army riders disappear over the top.

The rebels ride to the top of the rise. Then they see it clearly.

Stretching from horizon to horizon, covering their entire field of vision is the main Mughal army. Facing the rebels stand two thousand cannon and a thousand elephants. Filling the gaps between the cannon and sprawling backward without limit are dark lines of mounted archers and lancers, facing them and at the ready. At the centre of the vast expanse, barely discernable, is Asaf Khan, mounted on an elephant, looking very imperial.

The small army riders race to safety across the plain, taking advantage of their lead.

The rebels hesitate, slow down, and stop. Husayn Beg raises his hand vaguely, halting the charge. There is panic on his face.

A silence follows, a slow, eternal silence, punctuated only by the last of the small army riders merging with the dark shape that will kill them.

Then from across the horizon two thousand cannon fire simultaneously at the Rebels. The cannon balls seem to physically lift the soldiers and slam them backwards. There is a second of silence. Then the cannons open up again, taking turns, setting up a continuous barrage. The rebels fall in a dying, broken heap of men and horses.

Across the plain, there now are a series of deadly fireballs. Small pieces of brush catch fire all across the rebel army. The fire spreads and seems to take hold in haphazard patches across the plain. The cries of the dying men can be heard through the rising smoke.

Khusrau can hear himself breathe. He and Husayn Beg are on foot, crashing wildly through the tall weeds and bushes of a river bank. Khusrau carries a leather bag with some belongings. They both still have their swords.

After the disastrous defeat, the rebels dissolved, fleeing in panic-stricken groups. Khusrau and Husayn Beg took off by themselves in a different direction, separating themselves from the fleeing men. What they did not anticipate was the swiftness with which a hunting party was organised to descend on them. There was a long line of 'beaters', from the sound of it, almost two hundred men on horseback. And they corralled their prey inexorably towards the banks of the Chenab River. Khusrau and Husayn Beg's horses began to get bogged down in the soft mud. They showed up like sitting ducks above the tall grass. Desperate, they abandoned the horses and set off on foot, the better to hide.

They have stopped to catch their breath. They hear the galloping and shouts of men searching along the river bank. The shouts are frighteningly close. Kushrau can hear himself breathe.

He points. "That—" he gasps. He dives through a screen of shrubs and nettles, forcing his way through, getting thoroughly scratched. Husayn Beg follows close on his heels.

They break out of the river weeds onto a wide muddy bank. Their feet sink ankle-deep into the mud. There are two small boats on a spit of gravel jutting out over the water. A boatman sits on a rock, smoking *hashish* from a clay *chillum*.

Khusrau runs up to the boatman. "Take us across!" he gasps.

The boatman stands up. He retreats apprehensively from Khusrau.

There is a shout from close by and the sound of horses galloping. Khusrau claws in his bag and pulls out a bag of gold coins. "Five thousand *rupiya*! Take us across!" he yells.

The boatman retreats fearfully.

"Come on! I beg you!!"

The boatman keeps his hands to himself, not taking the money.

"Ten thousand *rupiya*!" Khusrau pleads. He takes out another bag and advances on the boatman, trying to press the money on him. The boatman retreats, almost falling into the water.

"They're here!" a rider shouts. "I see them!!" Instantly more shouts echo the discovery.

Husayn Beg uses his head and gets into the boat. "Come on!" he yells. Khusrau throws the money at the boatman. He pushes the boat into the water and jumps in. He grabs a pole lying in the boat and pushes off with it.

The boat leaves the shore. Khusrau pushes hard on the pole. It is submerged all the way in the water. Khusrau keeps pushing. His clammy hand slips. He looks up at Husayn Beg. His face is a pasty white. "I lost the pole."

Four soldiers cordon off the river bank behind the boat. Khusrau and Husayn Beg sit frozen in panic.

Jahangir is on his horse at the water's edge. He looks out at the boat drifting placidly down the river. He spurs his horse on, splashing into the water.

Khusrau's eyes meet Jahangir's.

"Hello, Son," Jahangir says.

The polo field at Nagarcin is being put to a different use. Asaf Khan, Itimad Ud Daulah, Mahabat Khan sit prominently in the spectators' stand, among the ministers and officers. They are trying to remain expressionless, but there is dark portent in their faces. In the women's stand, Nur sits by herself in a position of prominence slightly apart from the other women. Malika Jahan sits closest to her. The women are much more expressive than the men, gossiping anxiously in whispers. Nur looks straight ahead.

In the field, facing the stands, at regular intervals stand eight of the highest-ranking rebels. Each rebel is tied to a stake with leather thongs, and is made to stand on a short stump of wood so that he is at the height of a man on horseback. His feet are fastened tightly to the stake, and his arms are stretched around it and tied together at the back, keeping him standing stiffly. At the right end of the field is a large, colourful, tent. The entrance remains mysteriously closed.

The sudden fanfare of drums and trumpets shatters the afternoon stillness. A royal elephant, carrying Jahangir, Khusrau, and a guard, enters the field. The elephant is escorted by eight of Jahangir's personal guards on horseback. The two lead guards are executioners and carry long lances.

Khusrau's hands are tied behind his back to the *howdah*. There is a strange remoteness in Jahangir's eyes. "I hope you like it," he tells Khusrau. "I put some thought into this."

"My fault, Father," Khusrau says talking fast. "All my fault... I encouraged the men. Right from the start. Grandfather used to forgive the men, remember? That was the custom for Grandfather... even when you rebelled. Remember how you rebelled and Grandfather forgave you? He forgave the men too... you can... you can execute me if you like... I started it—"

Khusrau sees the rebels standing tied across the field and his voice fades. "What... what are you doing?"

Jahangir does not reply. The elephant advances towards the first rebel.

"Father... Father, what are you doing?!"

Jahangir nods slightly to the lead guard.

"These..." Khusrau says, his mouth dry, "these are all men with wives and families—"

There is a dull sound. Khusrau recoils as if in physical pain. One of the lancers has staked the first rebel through his heart. The lancer pulls his weapon out of the rebel's body. A flood of blood flows down the rebel's clothes. The rebel's wide-eyed horrified face stays fixed in death.

"I am enacting Justice, Son," Jahangir explains. "Treason is a serious crime." Privately, he hopes that through their father-son bond Khusrau understands the true meaning of this ceremony — that this is his, Jahangir's, response to the pettiness and stupidity, to the forces of rot and despair, which come in the way of manifest destiny. The forces must be shown once and for all! Without mercy. Only then can we be whole again. Jahangir revels in the crisp morning air. In the bright colours of the arena enhanced by a brilliant, blue sky. He enjoys a quiet satisfaction with the ceremony itself. It is clean, brilliant, just, imaginative, and perfect!

The elephant advances towards the next rebel.

"Father... Father, stop! The man has a family! I'm the one who's guilty of treason!"

"So is he," Jahangir replies.

"He's an ordinary fellow... he made the mistake. He's just like..."

Jahangir nods slightly.

The other lead executioner stakes the second rebel. There is a spurt of blood as the lance is withdrawn. It splatters down the dying rebel's clothes and onto the ground.

Khusrau is crying. "Stop, please stop!"

The elephant advances to the third rebel. "Mercy, Your Majesty!" the rebel calls. His tone is reasonable, trying to make a human connection with Jahangir. "I beg you. Spare me!" The rebel looks into Jahangir's eyes and realises it is hopeless. "Mercy," he mumbles hopelessly. "Mercy."

Jahangir nods. The third rebel is staked.

"Why don't you stop, you bastard!" Khusrau screams in sudden rage. "You monster! Haven't we killed enough? You and I! Haven't we killed enough?"

"You should save your temper," Jahangir says. "We are only on the third one."

Nur looks as if she is about to throw up.

"You are not my father!" Khusrau screams. "You are not my father!"

An officer sitting next to Asaf Khan smiles slightly, rather enjoying the spectacle. Asaf Khan is poker-faced. Itimad Ud Daulah is drenched in sweat, suffering.

Nur has her hand over her mouth.

The fourth rebel makes a sound of convulsive pain as he is staked.

"Oh Allah, why don't you STOP?" Khusrau begs.

"It's amazing," Jahangir muses. "A lunatic can sometimes cause the most random incident, which then starts a whole chain of events that refuses to stop."

Khusrau bangs his feet violently on the floor of the *howdah*. "You monster! You hideous monster!" He tries to kick Jahangir, who is out of reach.

Malika Jahan leans over to Nur. "He will listen to you," she whispers urgently. "Why don't you stop him?"

Nur pretends not to have heard.

The fifth rebel is defiant, brave. "You are the Devil!" he shouts. "The Devil Taraka! You are not the rightful ruler of the land!

Death to the Emperor!"

"Death to you!" Jahangir retorts spiritedly.

The fifth rebel is staked.

Nur leans over to Malika Jahan. There is an unreadable expression on her face, the same unreadable expression that she had when she rode in the *tonga* down her driveway the day her husband died.

"He has his own soul," Nur says to Malika Jahan. "Does he not?"

The sixth rebel is the Oymaq chief. His flaming white moustache and his wrinkled, weather-beaten face make him stand out among the rebels. He is silent, regarding Jahangir with defiant dignity. Jahangir, for his part, can say nothing to the Oymaq chief.

The Oymaq chief is staked.

The last rebel is staked. Across the polo field, the rebels' bodies stand drooping on their stakes, streams of blood running across their feet and over the stumps down into the earth.

The entourage is not done. They stop in front of the large, mysteriously closed tent.

"This part is the best," Jahangir tells Khusrau.

The musicians let forth another fanfare. Two guardsmen open the tent entrance. Husayn Beg and Dalit Singh, the two rebel chiefs, emerge from the tent. Each of them is mounted backward on a donkey. Husayn Beg is clothed tightly in the skin of a bull. The skin is wet. His head is covered with the bull's head, two curved horns emerging from the top. Only his face is exposed. Dalit Singh is similarly clothed in the skin of a donkey. The donkey's ears stand upright above his head.

Khusrau looks at Husayn Beg and Dalit Singh in utter despair. He is crushed, old, a shell of his former self. They look back at him in their humiliation.

Jahangir regards the scene appreciatively. "I believe the skins will shrink once they start drying in the sun," he informs Khusrau.

Husayn Beg and Dalit Singh cringe in fearful apprehension.

Khusrau's hysteria seems to have left him. "I swear upon Allah—" he says calmly to Jahangir. "If I have one breath left in me, I will destroy you!"

"You cannot," Jahangir replies. "I defeated you."

It is late afternoon by the time the procession reaches the street with the whores' boarding house. Husayn Beg and Dalit Singh are seated backwards on their donkeys. Eight guards ride in front, eight behind. A dense crowd lines either side of the street. It is, for the most part, quiet. A part of the crowd, mostly children, walks along with the procession, watching in hushed fascination.

A large bearded man, who seems drunk or high on opium, breaks out into the street. He flaps his arms and does a little dance in front of Husayn Beg and Dalit Singh. "Ha ha ha! Look at them!" he says addressing no one in particular. "One is an ox and the other is a donkey." The bearded man skips and kicks his feet. "How do you feel now, Ox and Donkey!" He points to them and tries to encourage the crowd to participate. "Ox and Donkey! Ox and Donkey!" he sings.

The crowd is not drawn. They walk along, silently watching. A trooper herds the bearded man off the street.

Paru finds herself standing next to the bearded man. "Who are those people?" she asks.

"Where have you been! Those are the two sidekicks of Prince Khusrau. Wait till those skins start to dry!"

"Has Prince Khusrau been executed?" another man asks.

"I don't think so. I bet we will see his head high on a pole when *that* happens!" The bearded man rubs his hands in anticipation. "I like this Emperor!"

Husayn Beg's face is crumpled in pain. The air is rent by his incoherent scream. "*Aaarrrnnngggghhh*"

"Sooner than I thought!" the bearded man comments.

Dalit Singh's face is also crushed in pain. He is silent.

"*Aaarrrnnngggghhh!*" Husayn Beg screams again. He starts writhing where he sits on his donkey.

Suddenly Dalit Singh drops like a stone from his donkey. He kicks a little, then lies still on the dirt road.

Paru looks on in shock.

The Street Orator sits on his platform, framed by a shroud of smoke. The crowd is almost a hundred people thick. It is highly charged, intent. The Street Orator is dark, portentous. "Now have you seen the cruelty of Taraka! Now have you seen the hand of Death!" He looks around. "Who lives in despair? And who lives in hope?

"As Shiva was in meditation, grieving for his lost wife, so Parvati was in meditation in her devotion to Shiva. In the heat of the summer, Parvati lit four fires on each side. And meditated in their midst. In the deluge of the monsoon, she sat on a rock in the pouring rain. In the howling winds of winter, she stood neck-deep in the freezing Himalayan lake. And she kept her thoughts with Shiva. Always the same purpose. Always the same goodness and strength." Hearing this soothes and comforts the crowd members. Paru is hustling the crowd. She rubs her shoulder against a man. The man turns to look at Paru. She gives him a seductive, how-about-it gaze. The man stares back stonily.

"Friends!" the Street Orator says. "It is love that saves the world. Always love. Shiva, who would be disturbed by no one, who was in the deepest grief, the grief of losing one's wife, was won over by Parvati. Her love. Her truth. Her devotion to the righteous path."

Paru sees the bearded man. She drifts up to him and runs her hand down his back and arm. Her breast touches him.

"It is said Taraka is going to impose a new tax—" a man calls.

"Yes! A tax. For religion," the Street Orator replies.

The bearded man turns. Paru smiles at him. He turns back to the Street Orator, preoccupied.

"When will one be born of Shiva," shouts a man, "who can defeat the great Taraka!"

The Street Orator does not reply. He closes his eyes and meditates.

"When?" the man persists.

The crowd waits breathlessly. The silence stretches as the Street Orator continues to meditate.

"When?" the man calls impatiently.

The Street Orator opens his eyes. "He is already born. He is here."

"You have been saying that for months, old man!" the bearded man shouts. "There is no Third Prince!"

"He is here," the Street Orator repeats calmly.

"Then why don't you tell us where he is, so we can see him!"

"He is here," the Street Orator insists.

"Where!"

A screen seems to pass over the Street Orator's face. Suddenly he is charged, clairvoyant. "I mean here. Among you. I feel his presence. Now! He is here!"

"What are you talking about!"

"The Prince is here! In this audience! I can feel him!"

A man in the front row suddenly shouts. "I feel him too! The Third Prince! He is here! He has come!"

"I feel it!" someone shouts from the back of the audience. "The Third Prince!"

An invisible, occult, electric jolt runs through the crowd. As one they move, as if the jolt has run like a streak of lightning through them. They look around in frenzied excitement, at one another and at the empty spaces between them.

"Where is he—"

"He is here!"

"Here!"

"Here!"

"Here! I feel it!"

"Third Prince!"

"Third Prince, *Zindabad*!!"

"Third Prince, *Zindabad*!!"

The bearded man looks at them incredulously.

As one, the crowd bursts out of the square, fanning out in all directions. A captain in full soldier's regalia is riding up ahead.

One of the men points to the captain. "There he is! The Prince! The Third Prince!" The crowd races towards the captain.

"Wait! Wait for us! You are the Prince!"

"The Third Prince! Third Prince *Zindabad*!"

They come to a halt, surrounding the captain.

"Third Prince *Zindabad*!" one of them shouts.

The captain looks blankly at them.

"*Huzoor*, we are yours!" someone explains. "We are your subjects! Long live the Third Prince!"

"Long live the Prince!"

They stand wide-eyed, looking at the captain.

The spell breaks.

The captain glares back at them, waiting for some sign of coherence. The men begin to look foolishly at each other. The captain spurs his horse dismissively, riding on.

At the square, the crowd is dispersing. Paru has her arm around the bearded man's waist. Her body is close to his, her leg caresses his.

The Street Orator is still seated on his platform. He looks

around, thoughtful, puzzled. He is as confused as anybody else about what just happened.

But he is sure it did happen. He felt it.

He glances at Paru and the bearded man walking away from the square, then his gaze moves elsewhere, searching the crowd for something he is sure he will recognise instantly when he sees it. He glances again at Paru and the bearded man. But he sees nothing there. His gaze moves on.

The bearded man has his hand around Paru's bare waist. She sways her hips playfully nudging them against his, as she walks.

Paru is fucking the bearded man. They are both naked on a straw mattress on the floor of a flop-house. He is on top of her moving to her rhythm. She looks into his face passionate, thrilled. She is writhing, moaning, "Haanhhhh! Haanhhh! Haanhhh!"

"Uuurrnhh! Uuurrnhh! Uuurrnhh!" the bearded man grunts simultaneously with Paru.

"Come on!" Paru screams, abruptly aroused. In a single facile movement she flips him and is now on top of him. She moves to a deep long rhythm. "Uuunnnhhh! Uuunnnhhh! Uuunnnhhh!" She reaches down and holds it preventing him from coming.

"*Aaaiii!!* That hurts!" he protests.

She lets go.

His face is lit with joy. He comes amidst a series of grunts. Paru screams loudly as she climaxes. He collapses. Paru keeps going, climaxing and screaming.

"Stop!" he pants after a while. "Stop! Please stop!"

She seems to notice him. Her eyes meet his. Her hair is plastered over her sweating brow. She lets him out. But immediately moves downward along his body.

"No, no, no! Stop! Please stop!"

Paru stops. She looks up at him from the area of his groin and smiles. Her body is covered with sweat.

She sits naked comfortably astride him, feeling the hair on his chest.

"That was..." he says, out of breath. "That was... I never..."

Paru gets off the bearded man slowly and stands up. She reaches for her clothes, lying beside the mattress.

"Two things I am good at," she says. "Fighting and fucking."

He sits up, looks at her.

Paru dresses.

"Where can I find you—" he says. "If I... again..."

"You won't. I'll find you."

"I have not seen you before," he says, interested. "Are you from out of town?"

"No."

"Where do you live?"

"In the City," she replies.

She pulls on her concubine's thin leggings. "That will be three *rupiya*."

The bearded man shakes his head. "That's three times what the other girls take. Two rupiya. Take it or leave it."

She pulls up her *ghagra*, and fastens it around her waist.

"You did not hear me just now," she says pleasantly. "I said I was good at fighting and fucking."

The bearded man's gaze falls on Paru's leather knife belt, which is lying on the floor. Paru picks it up and starts wearing it. He feels an inexplicable chill of fear. He tries to tell himself that she is only a woman, that he could overpower her easily. But his apprehension does not go away.

Slowly, acquiescent, he reaches for his money pouch.

It is night outside. A crescent moon casts a sliver of light from a cloudless sky. The flop-house door creaks as it opens. Paru steps out. The door closes behind her. She melts like a ghost in the darkness.

The door is old. The scars on its surface remain faintly visible in the dim moonlight.

Paru steps silently through the shadows towards her quarters in the whores' boarding house. After the big attack by her assailant, she has decided not to run anywhere, but to stay at the boarding house. In any case, he appears to have a knack for finding her whenever he wants to. What is more important is for him not to find out where she lives. She is afraid he will find the scroll, or catch her unawares in her sleep. She is careful not to be seen when she enters and leaves the boarding house. This behaviour draws strange looks and the occasional joke from her fellow prostitutes, who think she is crazy. Paru just smiles back at them.

The very transience of the boarding-house provides a kind of safety. Whores move in and out. Things are thrown all over the place. There are arguments, fights. Paru lives quietly in the midst of the chaos. She is very protective of her few things, and keeps them arranged methodically around her mattress. Her neighbours have noticed that she possesses more than one knife.

She comes and goes at odd hours, as do the others. When she wakes up from a mid-afternoon sleep, she bathes, dresses, and makes herself up until she looks perfect. Then she slinks quietly to the front door, looks cautiously both ways and steps into the street, disappearing for long hours. Days sometimes. She returns just as mysteriously and erratically. Before they know it, she is back. Her things remain undisturbed during her absence.

She makes some attempts to hide her scroll. Every few days, she moves it to a different place among her things, until she realises this is pointless. She considers finding a secret hiding place somewhere outside town in which to bury the scroll, a place only she knows about. But then, what if she returns to the hiding place and finds the scroll missing? Paru cannot bear the thought. She made that mistake when she parted with her jewel. She would rather keep the scroll with her and die protecting it.

What puzzles her about her assailant is, where he gets all his men. There must have been at least twenty the last time. With every attack the number of men seems to increase. Is there someone big behind this? If so, what could he possibly want? He already possesses the only thing of value that she has ever had — her jewel (which she will get back). But stealing her jewel did not stop the attacks...

The City is so rife with plots and conspiracies! The *bazaar* square has that orator, rambling on about a Prince who will emerge from hiding and save the land. Could she be mistaken for someone else? If so who? Paru recalls her assailant's remark after they killed her roommate. "That's not her," he said. And then he pointed to Paru. "That's the one." If anything, he seemed to be emphatic about knowing who she was. And what about that mysterious statement of his, "The Prime Minister has it." What Prime Minister? He seemed to think Paru would know what he meant. Was it a code? If so what did it mean?

Paru yearns to be rid of this nonsense, and dance again! She has made so many sacrifices already for this joke of an assailant. The very fact that she is reduced to hustling for a meagre living... she has no more patience for this! The next time she sees him, she is going to put a knife through his heart and be done with him! But then, he has her jewel. She has to get her jewel back. She has to find her father. Paru stamps her feet with frustration in the dark street.

And all she really wants to do is dance.

When she crossed the *bajra* field to see the dance troupe, the stalks were taller than her. The day was overcast, but very hot. Mist rose up from the moist ground past the silent stalks. There were ghosts in the *bajra* field. Gods, demons, and playful spirits that skirted the stalks through the mist and made her jump. The mist frightened her, but only a little. The spirits were more unnerving.

And then she was across the field, and crawling around in the big village, and was too excited to remember her fear. And then that beautiful man of the dance troupe came and changed everything. And those two women who danced with him. Wraithlike forms, delicate as gossamer, perfect instruments for the man and the space that he wove. At that moment, Paru decided she was going to be them! Her mother's death was just the precipitating event. But in reality she had made up her mind about dancing much before that. It was when she had crossed the *bajra* field.

After her mother died, Paru was deemed to be too young to live in the hut by herself. An aunt called Champabai took her in. Paru protested, but it was of no use. It was all somehow taken care of. Other people started living in her mother's hut, and Paru had to move with her things into Champabai's home. Paru felt vaguely taken, but at the same time they were so kind and sympathetic, she did not see what else she could have done.

She never showed them the jewel. Nor the scroll. She was careful to hide them when she moved her things. She also found seven *rupiya* under her mother's straw mattress. She was surprised at the amount. She packed it in sadly with her mother's clothes.

Champabai had two small children, a boy and a girl. They were noisy and bratty, and Paru had little patience with them. She had even less patience with Champabai, who tended to scream at her with the same frantic authority that she reserved for her children.

Instead of working in the fields allotted to her mother, she now worked in the fields that belonged to Champabai's husband. He was an odd man, large and mild. He told Paru to call him Uncle. Uncle disappeared for long intervals, leaving his fields for Paru and Champabai to work. The two brats pretended to work, but in fact were useless. They caused more harm than good. Paru could only guess where Uncle went, but she heard it was to villages and towns far afield. When he returned, Paru was grateful. His presence seemed to lift the dire mood of the household. He sat next to the door and said very little, but when he did, it was to interrupt Champabai, to say something whimsical, or something kind.

Paru could not pinpoint when it started. In the beginning when she entered Champabai's household, she was treated with a great deal of sympathy, almost like a guest. But as the weeks wore on, she started to become a burden, an extra mouth to feed. Champabai actually bought her clothes, an odd garment that Paru found too large for her size and too peculiar to wear.

Paru did not understand how she had given offence. But the complaints mounted. Champabai pointed out that she had to make larger meals every night because of her, and that food cost money. But worse, Paru took up too much space in their cramped household. There were a hundred things that Champabai could have done with that extra mattress and that extra corner. Now she could not, because of Paru. Moreover, Paru was not neat. She did not scrub the copper cooking vessels up to the standards held by all common decent people. She did not bathe properly, or groom herself properly. Champabai complained that she smelled.

Paru was not used to this. She had always been the centre of her mother's world. She had been the good child, the supporting child. Now, all of a sudden, according to Champabai, she was not good.

Paru's worst trait was her habit of waking up late. Nothing could equal Champabai's disappointment at the person who woke up late. That person cut the day short, and did less work in the fields, leaving all the burden on Champabai and her children. Paru tried to compensate by working late into the evenings, cutting the stalks by moonlight as her mother had done. But that did not seem to count. When Paru realised it made no difference, she grew defiant and gave up. But she continued to wake up late in the morning. Some mornings she was up with Champabai, well before dawn. On others, she was late. Some nights, she lay awake for hours thinking of her mother. Some nights she thought of her father. What sort of man was he, she wondered.

As the months slipped by, Paru's stature rose to that of being the greatest calamity to have ever befallen Champabai's family. She started to shout back at Champabai. The mewling children screamed and misbehaved and did terrible things, but they did not talk back to their mother. And Uncle never talked back. Only Paru talked back. She was a Problem. A Disaster! When Champabai flew into a rage, she beat Paru with a flurry of confused slaps and blows that did not hurt so much as they humiliated. Paru would raise her arms and sit in a corner. She found it was harder to be hit that way.

The arguments reached deadly proportions one day in the fields, and Paru flew into a rage. She walked off the field, afraid of what would happen next. She had never been so angry! This was something new. She did not recall having such emotions when her mother was alive. She walked by herself, away from Champabai. She did not care if the work was not done! She did not care if no one fed her, or looked after her, or if she died.

A God must have had his eye on her as she walked, because she encountered Ganpat's cow. After Ganpat died, his cow became an orphan. Ganpat's widow was a crippled old thing. She could not do much, and Ganpat's cow walked from house to house, looking for treats, making a nuisance of herself. Paru was good friends with her, and at a time like this she needed a friend. The cow was squatting serenely in the dusty space in front of the huts. Paru decided to sit with her. She leaned against her broad, generous body. She could use some serenity. She was numb, tired, angry, rootless. Perhaps it was time to die. What purpose did life hold? But then she remembered her father and the jewel and the scroll. There was too much she had to do.

She found herself looking into Uncle's eyes. He had apparently been at home, preparing for one of his long, mysterious journeys. In his hands he held a bundle, which he had been preparing. He looked curiously at Paru.

"How goes it child?" he called.

Paru struggled to keep back the tears.

Uncle could have walked on. But he continued to regard Paru. "How goes it?" he asked again.

"I want to dance!" Paru burst out.

"Dance!" Uncle said, surprised. "Oh ho!"

Paru nodded, the tears rolling down her cheeks. "I want to run away! I want to run away to the big village, and dance. Like, like..."

Uncle considered this deeply for some time. He closed his eyes the better to think. He opened them. "In my opinion," he said, "you should not run away to the big village to dance. That is not a good place. You should run away to the City."

"The City!"

"There is a big City. North of here." He checked himself to remember if he got the direction right. "That way..." He pointed vaguely, then gave up. "It is a three-day journey."

"How big a city?" Paru asked.

"Oh ho! Big! The biggest you have ever seen! If I am not mistaken, it may be the biggest city in the world!"

Paru's eyes were round with excitement.

"You would like it," Uncle said, amused at the thought. "At night, the lights! They drive you crazy! Lots of dancers in the City. They make good money."

"Uncle! How can I get there?"

"I was thinking about that. As I was talking to you..." This was apparently too much, and Uncle had to slow down. He closed his eyes again.

Paru waited breathlessly.

"In my opinion, you should join a good class that will teach you how to dance properly. A lot of dancers, they go heaahh, heaaah—" He waved his arms about, parodying bad dancers he had seen. "That is no good. You need a proper teacher. It is expensive," he added matter of factly.

Paru's heart sank. "Expensive! How expensive?"

"I don't know," Uncle replied. "But just now I am going. I can make some inquiries and find out for you."

"Please find out," Paru said faintly.

"Do you have any money?" Uncle asked.

"No." Paru's voice was small.

"Then that is a problem," Uncle said significantly. He started to leave. Then he paused, as he remembered something else. "In my opinion," he said, "when you go to the City, you should hire a cart."

"A cart!"

"Yes. A bullock cart. When you enter the City for the first time, you should do so in style. It is not good to enter on foot."

"Why is that?" Paru gasped.

"It looks bad."

She watched as Uncle's form receded towards his mysterious destination. A thought suddenly occurred to her. She ran after him. "Uncle! Uncle!!" she called. "I just remembered! I have some money!"

"You do?" Uncle said curiously. "How much?"

"Seven *rupiya*," Paru said, not knowing whether that was large or small.

Good," Uncle said. "I will keep it in mind."

He walked for some distance. Then he paused. Turning, he gave Paru a formal salute, bowing deeply.

Evening set in and, with it, crushing disappointment. The money was probably not enough, Paru thought anxiously. How was she to make money? Where could she go?

Champabai was oddly calm. It was as if the incident of the afternoon had not occurred at all. They ate the evening meal in relative silence. The mewling brats mewled, and Champabai called out to them, but without much force. Champabai smiled at Paru. "I have been thinking," she said. "When your dear mother... passed away, we took all the necessary steps to dispose of what little property she had. But I overlooked one thing. Did she, perhaps, give you any money to keep?"

Paru froze. "I don't know," she managed to reply sullenly.

"Was there not some money among her things? In the hut?"

Paru's mind raced. What was she to say? Yes? How could she say yes? She needed the money for the dance! What would her mother have wanted her to do? But her mother was not from this village. She remembered how her mother had wandered. How she had carried Paru from village to village! And how they had refused to help her! Direct defiance, she thought frantically, direct defiance!

"There was no money in the things I brought over," Paru said. She could hardly believe the words coming out of her mouth. "But I don't remember, maybe something is left behind in the hut. I was very confused—"

"Because that money may help with all the expenses we are going through, on your account."

"I can go and look tomorrow, if you like. If Babubhai will allow me."

A crafty look crossed Champabai's face. "I think I will go and look myself."

"Okay," Paru said, staring at her food.

That night she lay awake in the dark, her eyes wide open. She had thought she would have difficulty staying awake, but that was not a problem at all. Her mind was awhirl with thoughts. The hours crept by. She turned once and sighed, pretending to be asleep. Then she heard a soft and comforting sound. It was Champabai snoring. Inch by inch Paru's hand crept outward from her mattress. She felt the jewel in her fingers. Then the scroll. She had to search a little to find the seven *rupiya*. It was all there, all in her hands.

The night was moonless. Paru stepped softly into the light of the stars, as softly as when she had crossed the *bajra* field. She had already decided on the hiding place: a corner in Ganpat's hut.

Ganpat's wife would not know anything. The door to the hut was open. The wife was fast asleep. Ganpat's cow stood outside. Paru swept her knuckles across her soft brown back as she passed. In her head, she thanked Ganpat's cow. The cow turned her head, and her large brown eyes regarded Paru in the dark...

Uncle did not return for two days. He turned up suddenly late in the evening, just as they were done with the cooking and were about to eat. He looked exhausted. Paru tried to catch his eye, but he gazed studiously at his food. Champabai had something on her mind too. She seemed to be summoning the courage to speak to Paru. "I talked to Babubhai today," she said finally. "We searched the hut, where your dear mother lived. As you said, there was nothing there. Are you sure she did not leave any money in her effects, in your clothes, perhaps."

"I don't know," Paru replied stupidly.

"Would you have any objection if looked through your things... myself?"

"No."

After supper, Champabai laid out Paru's clothes on the floor and carefully examined each item. She methodically went through Paru's mother's knick-knacks, then through each of her mother's clothes, which Paru still kept. Champabai checked every sleeve, every hem. Uncle looked on interestedly.

"Well," he said, when the search concluded. "That is that." He stood up, yawned, and stretched elaborately. "I am extremely tired today. I will go to bed now. Please do not wake me up in the morning," he ordered his wife.

Champabai was re-examining the hem of Paru's mother's *ghagra*. "Okay," she said absent-mindedly.

"I will be sleeping right here in my bed till the sun is up," Uncle emphasised, looking at Paru. Champabai's little boy stepped on a pot filled with leftover *dal* and spilt it over his foot. The boy started bawling. Champabai looked up and yelled perfunctorily at him.

Paru woke up early the next morning. She was out in the fields with Champabai, working at the crack of dawn. The hours stretched by. Paru gradually worked her way until she was a whole field away from Champabai. Suddenly, she stopped, and ran back to the village.

Uncle was waiting nervously for her. "Do you have that seven *rupiya*?"

"Yes!" Paru replied breathlessly. "I hid it."

"Good!"

"Did you... did you..."

"Yes. There is a rather good dance class in the City. I think I know where it is. I had to make quite a few inquiries. That is why I am so tired."

"How much... how much does it cost?" Paru asked her heart pounding.

"It costs twelve *rupiya*," Uncle replied.

Paru's heart sank.

"You must not tell her," Uncle said anxiously.

"No... no! I won't tell her."

"You promise!"

"Yes, yes! Uh... what should I not tell her—"

Uncle held his fist out. He opened it. There were five bronze coins in his palm.

"But that's... your money."

"We will add it to your seven. Then we will get twelve!" he said, pleased with the miracle of adding numbers.

"But... it's yours, I can return it," Paru mumbled.

"No, no, no! You must not return it! If you do, she will find out. I do not want her to find out!"

Paru could not believe her eyes. It seemed a miracle was happening right before her eyes. Was it Ganpat's cow? She leaned forward and hugged Uncle. Uncle stood awkwardly as her arms encircled his bony form with her passion. "You must not tell her!" he said again, sounding a little terrified. "Promise me you will not tell her!"

"I will die before I tell her!" Paru replied. She remembered something. "Uncle! Uncle! What about the money for the bullock cart!"

"Ah, yes!" he was reminded. "I have already arranged for the cart."

Paru started to cry.

Paru is walking down her street. It is the hour just before dawn, and the street is at its most silent. The frantic flirtation of the early evening gave way to love-making in the late night, and now even that has concluded. It is the time for people to actually sleep, for whores to be returning home.

Paru slows down before rounding the corner. She peers cautiously through the shadows, as far down the street as she can see. There is a movement at the far end, a shape against a wall that is not perfectly still. It is hidden under the shadow cast by a house and Paru cannot make out what it is. Her hand strays towards her knife. She decides to advance cautiously down the street keeping to the sides. She disappears into the shadows. She is all but invisible. Slowly, cautiously, she advances until she is almost upon the shape. It moves a few times. Paru can now discern what it is.

Two lovers. They appear to be doing it while standing up. Late birds. There are soft cries from the woman.

The large room that Paru shares is dark, but there is enough starlight from outside to navigate over the sleeping forms. She notes with satisfaction that her things are untouched.

June 1605

It is the first *Diwani Khaas* since the return. Formally and impeccably dressed, the courtiers stand silently, mindful of their strict hierarchy. At the back of the court is an addition — a line of twelve ceremonial guards. They are accompanied by two musicians with horns. Asaf Khan looks unhappy.

Jahangir presides at the apex of the court. He nods his head slightly. The horns blow a loud fanfare. Four of the ceremonial guards step forward and to the side creating a gap in the centre of the line.

Revealed in the gap is Nur. She is magnificently dressed in a red and gold *burkha*. A light, golden veil covers her face. The bandage that holds her wound together is made up of matching red taffeta. It is barely visible under the burkha and veil. As the fanfare continues to play, she walks to the throne and climbs the steps until she stands one level below Jahangir. She bows deeply, and looks down.

"As Emperor of Hindustan," Jahangir announces, "and Ruler of its far-flung dominions, I appoint you, Mehrunissa, Minister of

Special Counsel to the King. You shall follow in the tradition of Birbal, my father's advisor. It is my hope that you will bring to the post the same wisdom and high-mindedness that was so typical of the great Birbal."

Jahangir looks at Nur's bowed head. "You may lift your veil."

Nur lifts the veil. She looks up at him.

"I command you to turn around and face the men."

Nur turns. She moves her gaze slowly around the court, looking into the faces of each of the men.

"You shall work with these men as their equal," Jahangir commands. "They will not give you any less credence, because you are a woman."

Nur gazes without expression at Itimad Ud Daulah.

"Nor will they do you any favour, because you are a woman."

She looks at Mahabat Khan. Then her gaze shifts to Asaf Khan. He is clearly suffering. He looks away. Nur's gaze comes full circle, back to Jahangir.

An attendant carrying a jewel box on a velvet cushion climbs the steps to stand behind Jahangir.

Jahangir and Nur's eyes meet briefly. "There will be a public announcement," Jahangir says, looking around at the *Diwani Khaas*. "But I wish to tell the members of the Private Council myself — I have asked Mehrunissa if she will marry me. And she has accepted. As is allowed by the wisdom of *shariyar*, I shall court my future wife and speak to her respectfully from a distance for the period of our engagement. Which will be four months."

There is a murmur of approval from across the room.

Jahangir reaches behind him for the box and takes out a magnificent necklace. From a slim gold chain that scintillates with tiny diamonds and topaz stones, hangs an enormous pendant. The pendant is different from Paru's jewel, and outclasses it utterly. At its centre is a perfect, large ruby, perhaps the largest ever seen. It is supported by three large diamonds, sparkling with inspired workmanship. The whole is set in gold casing, studded with emeralds and diamonds.

Jahangir allows himself the barest of smiles. "It is worth more than a hundred thousand *rupiya*."

He puts the necklace around Nur's neck. "As Emperor of Hindustan... And as a sign of my love for you — I confer upon you the title of..." Jahangir pauses, "Nur Jahan! Light of the World!"

The courtiers burst into spontaneous applause.

Nur looks down, her classical features expressionless and perfectly cast, while inside she is a sea of roiling emotions.

It does not take long for Nur to adapt to the *Diwani Khaas*. She is the most vocal of the ministers and often has to be silenced. Asaf Khan assumes a mantle of statesmanship, running the Private Council with restraint and rarely voicing his own opinion. He says little to Nur.

It is at a session, a month later, that Jahangir's gaze seems particularly stern. Asaf Khan clears his throat to speak, but he is stopped by a movement made by Jahangir. He has produced a document. Jahangir has had a scribe write it out with special care. He now unrolls it with a show of importance. Unbeknownst to the assembly, the document is a bridge. It is a bridge across the chasm. A bridge of such perfection and beauty, it covers the chasm completely. It is as if the chasm never existed, because justice triumphs over all, and with its brilliance the chasm can be buried and forgotten forever. The emptiness that haunts Jahangir deep inside the chasm will be replaced forever with the beauty of this document. This document will define the brilliance of his Kingdom — not just now, but when people look back a thousand years from now.

"In the past month," Jahangir commences, "I have been turning my thoughts to the notion of justice. What is justice? It is a happiness brought upon a people by the laws that govern them.

Gentlemen, we have but to look around us to see that the laws of nature have given us a world of infinite beauty. One day in the near future I intend to take all of you on an expedition of the jungle floor. I want you to see for yourselves the perfection that has been wrought by these laws in even the most inconsequential patch of grass deep inside the jungle.

"The laws of man can but hope to emulate the laws of nature. They can only be a poor copy. But it is my duty as the ruler to strive for justice in the same way that Allah has accomplished beauty and perfection with his laws of nature. It was with this in mind that I swiftly dispatched that... wretch, who is my son, and his seditious friends. It was my desire for justice. I wish to establish such a high standard of justice throughout this realm."

The courtiers regard Jahangir with dark foreboding.

"I have had inscribed on this document Twelve decrees. I have put much work into them. From now on, these decrees will be the supreme law of the land. No advocacy, no exceptions shall be allowed to overcome them. They shall apply to all persons at all times... without exception. They shall apply even to myself."

Jahangir takes a minute to gaze commandingly into the eyes of each member of the *Diwani Khaas*. They tremble.

"Before I finalise the decrees I would like this Private Council to think about them and to advocate any changes that may reasonably apply. But once we have made them public, they shall remain as they are — pillars of justice. Supreme, pure, and beautiful.

"I shall read the decrees to you now." Jahangir casts his eyes on the unfolded document. The courtiers think they can hear it crackle. "First," Jahangir says, "all petty fees and taxes that landowners levy on tenants for their own personal profit shall be lifted.

"Second, on remote roads frequented by bandits, the landowner shall be compelled to build a shelter and a mosque, and to dig a well for the comfort and safety of travellers who cross his domain."

The courtiers wait. The worst is surely for the last.

"Third, no one, not even soldiers of the realm, shall be allowed to open travellers' packs, or search any person's property without my express permission, which may only be obtained by petition and for good reason.

"Fourth, when a man dies within the realm, be he infidel or Muslim, his property is to be turned over to his heirs.

"Fifth, the sale of wine, liquor and intoxicants of any sort shall be forbidden." Jahangir looks up at the courtiers. "I say this in spite of the fact that I myself commit the sin of drinking wine intemperately. Once the decrees become public, I have resolved to reduce my current intake from twenty cups a day, to five or six. And thence gradually to none." Jahangir pauses for a moment, to reflect on this arduous course.

The courtiers are waiting for the bad news.

"Sixth," he says. "No one's house is to be used for the quartering of troops.

"Seventh. I expressly forbid, from this moment on, the cutting off of any person's ear or nose for any crime whatsoever."

"Eighth. The revenue collectors of royal lands shall be forbidden from seizing the land from tenants or from cultivating it themselves.

"Ninth. The revenue collectors of royal lands shall not intermarry with their tenants.

"Tenth. In each of the cities of the realm, I order free hospitals to be built and physicians appointed for the treatment of the sick. All expenses are to be paid for from the Royal Treasury.

"Eleventh. I command that the slaughtering of animals for meat be forbidden." Jahangir looks around at the room. "The vast majority of our subjects, being Hindus, already have a great reverence for animals and do not eat meat. I see no reason why the rest of us cannot follow their worthy example.

"Twelfth. I order that the ranks and lands bestowed by my

father upon his servants and loyal followers remain as they are, except to be increased where the servant or loyal follower deserves merit."

Jahangir has concluded. He looks up. "I now throw the discussion open to the floor."

There is silence in the *Diwani Khaas*. The puzzled courtiers search the decrees for the trick, the catch, the bad news they have been dreading. There seems none. Did they hear right? No one dares speaks. But there is a little surge of relief that seems to flow warmly between the seated men and throughout the corners of the court. Outside, the birds are chirping.

A small cough echoes through the *Diwani Khaas*. It is a woman's cough. "Your Majesty, you did say the decrees are to apply to all persons at all times, without exception in the realm."

Jahangir looks warily at Nur.

"I think that reasoning will give the decrees great strength and legitimacy among your subjects," Nur opines.

"Good," Jahangir replies without expression. He looks around at the other courtiers.

"Your Majesty..." Nur persists.

"Yes."

"If you forbid the killing of animals for meat on all occasions, does this mean that we shall have to cease the royal hunt? Or that we shall no longer be able to enjoy a lamb *biryani*?"

Jahangir stares at Nur. "We shall have to take that into consideration. When we finalise the decrees. Are there any other questions?"

No one speaks.

At night there is a harem entertainment. The hall is brightly lit. Eight girls dance a fast, earthy composition, its choreography freely extemporising in the *kathak* style. Ritu leads, at the centre of the line of dancers. Against the wall, behind the girls, are the musicians — two *tablas* playing in mind-defying synchronism, a sitar, a *sarodh*, and miscellaneous strings.

The dancers' skirts flare out as they spin. Their waists are exposed, their blouses see-through. About forty royals, minister, officers, harem crowd the hall. Asaf Khan is present with one of his wives, looking formal and a bit out of place. Mahabat Khan has stationed himself in the first row, looking on with well-meaning interest.

Jahangir sits at the centre with Nur. On the carpet in front of him is a row of wine cups. In one hand he holds the mouth-piece of a hookah, in the other, a cup of wine. He blows out a thick, stream of hookah smoke and takes a sip from his cup.

As if accidentally, the girls are dancing in a perfect straight line which advances menacingly towards their audience. They spin rapidly three times, and dance with their almost bare backs to the audience. They execute some pleasing patterns. Then they spin rapidly again three times and return again to dancing with their backs to the audience.

They spin a third time. A flock of white doves bursts out of their hands with a great flapping of wings.

Jahangir watches, stopping in mid-puff. He hands the hookah to Nur. The doves fly back and forth through the room. The people laugh and duck.

A dove lands in front of Mahabat Khan. Mahabat Khan picks it up, looking up in exaggerated anticipation at the girls. The girls are swaying their hips in synchronism. All of them have intense come-hither looks. Tied to the foot of the dove is a tiny silver box with a note. Mahabat Khan struggles to open it. He reads the note. He looks up and smiles at Ritu.

Ritu comes up to Mahabat Khan and dances for him. Her feet move with stunning speed on the floor, her anklets going *chhumm, chhumm, chhumm.* She edges closer and closer. She straddles his legs. She descends slowly to his level, her body writhing with desire. She opens her mouth, tongue curling.

Nur takes a puff from Jahangir's hookah, watching Ritu with interest.

A dove wanders over to one of Jahangir's ministers. He picks the dove up and opens the silver box tied to its foot. The minister opens the note and beckons to the girl dancing to the extreme left of the line. The girl goes over to the minister and dances for him.

Ritu presses her body close to Mahabat Khan. Deliberately, Mahabat Khan runs his hands over her waist, down the sides of her thighs. He places a hand purposefully on each of her buttocks. She presses her breasts to his chest. Jahangir downs his cup of wine in one gulp, watching approvingly. Wine dribbles down one side of his mouth and down his shirt. Ritu runs her lips over Mahabat Khan's face and neck, moving her body rhythmically. She nips his neck. She licks it, going down toward his chest.

The girl who was dancing for the minister parts her legs and stands over him. Slowly, she descends to sit on the minister's lap. She moves her body rhythmically, against his.

Jahangir squeezes Nur's hand. Nur lets smoke out of her mouth. He looks at her.

"How is my Light?"

"Shining," she replies with a smile.

Ritu has her breasts exposed. She is on top of Mahabat Khan passionately moving her body against his. He lies flat, running his hands down her naked back. The girl making out with the minister uses her tongue to play with his mouth.

A dove, a late bird, lands in front of Jahangir and walks busily about. One of the girls still in the line, looks expectantly at Jahangir. She edges closer. Jahangir looks down at the dove. He looks up at the girl with an exaggerated display of temptation. He picks the dove up. There is a silver box tied to the dove's foot. Jahangir opens it. There is a tiny note inside. Jahangir unfolds it with some difficulty, using his finger-nails. He makes a show of reading the note, which contains the girl's name.

He chucks the note aside and stands up to join the girl. He dances close to her, doing a creditable *kathak*. The party-goers hoot with anticipation. The rest of the girls, who are still dancing in line, surround Jahangir and his newly acquired *amour*. They edge even closer. The courtiers shout their encouragement.

Jahangir trips over his own feet, colliding with one of the girls, and falls abruptly to the carpet. He lies flat, looking up at the high, ornate ceiling, his head buzzing. He spreads his arms out and decides not to get up.

The girls dance around and over him waiting for a cue. Jahangir grabs two of them by the hands and drags them down. They crowd over Jahangir, kissing and caressing, rubbing their bodies with his.

Nur looks on unaffected. She appears to be enjoying herself. She blows a smoke ring with Jahangir's abandoned hookah.

Jahangir's arm emerges from the tangle of bodies, signalling for a cup of wine. There is no response at first. Jahangir waves his arm insistently. An attentive official walks up to Jahangir's row of previously-filled wine cups and delivers one into his hand.

Jahangir downs the cup carelessly. Wine slops down his neck and onto his shirt. He flings the cup across the room, hitting a wall. He pulls a girl over on top of him. Jahangir's arm emerges from the pile of bodies yet again, waving for another cup. The official delivers it as before.

Nur stands up to leave. She smiles at the assembly.

An *amir* sitting not far from Nur stands up with her. "Begum, will you not take His Majesty to his room?

Nur's smile is sporting. "Oh, he's quite capable of looking after himself," she replies equably. She turns and leaves.

Jahangir lies on the floor blissfully looking up at brilliantly-carved ceiling as the girls work on him.

It is late evening, well after the *Diwani Khaas*, when the meeting is called. It has some of the feel of the previous meeting when Khusrau rebelled; but there is not the same panic, or the sense of things flying apart. Jahangir is seated on a divan facing Itimad Ud Daulah, Asaf Khan, and Nur. A single cup of wine stands filled and ready by Jahangir's side. The hall lights have been neglected through the long day and some of them have gone out. The conversation is overcast with gloom and shadows.

"How far have these stories spread?" Jahangir asks.

"All through the city," Itimad Ud Daulah replies, a look of deep concern on his face. "And to Delhi... and perhaps to Lahore..."

"These are bad stories."

"I think so, your Majesty. It is only a matter of time before she is discovered. She could start a rebellion. And I am concerned this time..." he hesitates. "This time... we may not have your subjects on our side."

There is silence as this sinks in.

"We have to find her quickly," Jahangir says.

"And quietly," Asaf Khan adds. "They think she is a Prince born of Shiva. And that she is preparing for a great battle."

Jahangir looks accusingly at Itimad Ud Daulah. "You failed to catch her."

"It was a first attempt, Your Majesty. At the time, I did not realise how quick she is."

Jahangir picks up his cup and takes a modest sip.

Nur looks on impassively. She catches Jahangir's eye. "What does the Minister of Special Counsel advise?"

Nur is silent. It looks as if she is not going to answer at all. Finally she speaks. "The Minister thinks that she should be appointed to capture the Third Prince."

"Impossible!!" Asaf Khan says hotly. "I object your Majesty—"

Jahangir cuts him off by raising his hand. "Why do you say that?"

"Your Majesty, this is not an endeavour where we can use the force of State to advantage. This... Parvati Devi I sense that she is subtle and clever. She thinks like a woman. So do I."

"Your Majesty this is outrageous!!" Asaf Khan storms. "The Minister knows nothing of this business! She has no knowledge, no experience—"

"Prime Minister!" Jahangir looks coldly at Asaf Khan. "How long has it been since you and I embarked on this venture?"

Asaf Khan is silent, rebuked. He stares miserably in front of him. Then he decides to make a last effort. "Your Majesty, I urge you! We have only this one chance! If she should escape, we could have another war!"

Jahangir turns to Nur. There is a dangerous fire in his eyes. "The Prime Minister is right. If we do not have the Prince's head very soon, it will be yours."

Nur takes a deep breath. "It would be foolish of me to think otherwise, your Majesty."

Asaf Khan is seated at his table in his new quarters at the fort — Birbal's former palace. He is attempting to prepare for the mountain of questions and petitions at the *Diwani Aam* tomorrow. But he is distracted. His thoughts drift away, and he has trouble returning to his stack of papers.

There is a movement at the door. Nur stands in front of him. "Brother," she says. "I need your help."

He looks at her in surprise.

Nur and two guards ascend the staircase leading up to the empty jail cell. It is situated at the top of a one-storey structure built into the fort wall. It overlooks the moat far below. They reach a tiny landing that faces the solid wooden door of the cell. The door has a barred window through which one can look inside. Nur peers through the bars. The prison is a little cavity in the rock, seven feet by seven feet.

Nur stands facing the door of the cell. She touches the lock. She looks over the stone parapet down into the moat below. In the green water she sees a crocodile make a sudden white splash and drift towards shore. A second crocodile emerges from the water and pulls itself onto the muddy bank. A third floats just below the surface.

Nur looks down intently.

The guard notices her interest. "She will be safe here, Begum," he says.

Nur glances up at the guard. Without replying, she turns and descends the staircase.

At the courtyard-level there is a larger landing, where the guards normally have some room to make themselves comfortable. Nur alights onto this lower landing and departs wordlessly.

The sun is bright. With his usual scowl, the Snake Charmer uses his wooden scoop to shovel charcoal into a jute sack. A shadow falls over him. Suddenly there are more shadows. The Snake Charmer looks up. It is Bhir Das, accompanied by several soldiers. The Snake Charmer springs up. Two of the soldiers grab him. A soldier hits him hard in the stomach. He doubles over.

Sita Devi emerges from the hut. She sees the men and screams. She tries to run. Three soldiers rush at her. Sita Devi dodges, but one of the men easily catches her. She struggles and screams as the men hold her down. A trooper puts his hand over her mouth. Sacks descend roughly over the heads of Sita Devi and the Snake Charmer. They are trussed up tightly and slung over the troopers' horses.

The troopers ride with their captives to the fort's gates. Nur stands on the fort wall watching the road. She hurries down to meet the arriving troop.

Paru is hustling on Jaan Chaal, a surprisingly tony neighbourhood notwithstanding its name. The street itself is long and winding. Elegant residences are interspersed with traders' shops and a set of old barracks, now doing duty as flop-houses.

The city guards come by regularly to disperse hawkers and prostitutes, but the girls have learned to time their presence, so as to do business safely. In keeping with her policy of not being seen close to where she lives, Paru is many blocks from home.

She is with three other girls. It is mid-afternoon, but there is brisk traffic. The street is narrow and dusty. On either side are shops and doorways. A bullock cart laden with hay threads its way slowly past the pedestrians.

A girl approaches a large man with well-formed biceps. "Want to have some fun, strong man?" she calls.

Another girl blocks a man's path. "Hey, hero! Want to fuck?"

Paru hangs back, leaning against the doorway of one of the flop-houses. A man walks by. He glances surreptitiously at Paru. He cannot take his eyes off her. He walks some feet ahead. He stops, as if he forgot something. He looks back at Paru scratching his head. He turns around and walks past her again.

Paru regards him with amusement. The man stops and looks at Paru, smitten. The other girls hustle loudly. Paru smiles at the man.

Sita Devi walks by on the opposite side of the street. Her head is covered with her *odhni*. Her eyes dart sideways trying to watch the street. She sees Paru, draws her *odhni* tightly over her head and face, and hurries past.

The man smitten by Paru still stands in the street trying to make his decision. Paru watches him as he struggles.

At the fort's gates, a phalanx of one hundred swordsmen and mounted archers comes pouring out. They are led by Asaf Khan. The troopers thunder over the drawbridge, over the red cobbled road, and out onto the street leading from the fort towards the city centre.

Some blocks away, the captain with the elaborately-curled moustache is leading a separate troop of twenty men down a side-street. The men are headed for Paru's home at the whores' boarding house.

The troopers led by Asaf Khan establish themselves at an intersection of Jaan Chaal, blocking it. There are so many soldiers, it is difficult for them to manoeuvre. "We should not be seen!" Bhir Das shouts. He stands on his horse. "BACK! BACK everyone!" The troopers quickly withdraw on either side, keeping the crossing clear.

Sita Devi arrives along Jaan Chaal. She breaks into a run. She looks at Bhir Das and nods.

"I am going to the other end!" Bhir Das shouts to Asaf Khan. He points to Sita Devi. "She knows what she looks like!" Bhir Das hastily splits off with a troop of thirty men. He departs with them along the intersecting street amidst a clatter of noisy hooves.

Bhir Das's troopers storm through the streets and alleyways, effectively circling Jaan Chaal to reach its other end. On arriving, they start a sweep up the Chaal. A portion of the troopers position themselves across the road, two deep. The rest dismount and begin a house-to-house search. Bhir Das walks deliberately along the centre of the street. The troopers burst into the flop-houses, shops and homes on either side, ransacking and searching. Whores protest and scream. Any young girl who might bear the remotest resemblance to Paru is dragged outside for Bhir Das's inspection. He shakes his head to each one.

The captain with the curled moustache has reached the street where Paru has her home. The troopers ride rapidly up to the entrance of the whores' boarding house and block it. Two men kick the door open. Ten of them storm in. They grab the four women they find inside and drag them outside before they can even open their mouths to protest. Inside the boarding house, the soldiers rip, tear and smash, searching thoroughly through the women's belongings.

A trooper notices Paru's things arranged neatly around her mattress. He kicks at the pile of knick-knacks on top of the mattress. Her *lota* goes flying, landing with a clang. Her over-abundant clothes are arranged in neat piles on the side of the straw mattress. The trooper pulls at the clothes and scatters them across the room. There is still a pile of clothes on the floor. He kicks it.

Something falls out. It is the scroll. The trooper dives at it. He opens it up officiously. Unable to read, he rushes outside and hands the scroll to the captain with the curled moustache. The captain unrolls the scroll reverently. He stands for a long time in the sunlight in the middle of the street reading every word. He holds it up to his troops, parading it in triumph.

On Jaan Chaal, Paru and the other prostitutes are hustling, unaware of the approaching soldiers. The hesitating man still stands, looking at Paru. "Want to have some fun?" Paru calls helpfully. The hesitating man gives Paru one last regretful look and walks on. A man carrying a battle-mace in his belt is approaching. Paru moves to come in his way. "Hey, soldier!" she calls. "Where are you going?"

The soldier pauses. He looks at Paru with interest. "How much?" he demands.

"I'm expensive," Paru replies playfully.

Paru is jerked abruptly as Pithu grabs her hand and pulls her away. "Come on!" Pithu snaps. She is covered in her noblewoman's *burkha*, in sharp contrast to the suggestively-dressed whores.

Paru lets herself be pulled. "What... where are we going?" she says.

"Home!" Pithu replies.

Pithu walks so fast, Paru has to run. "What home?" she asks, confused.

"Our home." They come upon Pithu's covered carriage. "Get in the back!" Pithu orders. "I don't want those bitches to see that you're a prostitute." The carriage starts clattering rapidly along Jaan Chaal.

Paru feels the luxurious fittings inside the carriage in bewilderment. "Why—" she asks flustered.

"Why what?"

"Why are we... going home?"

"Because I thought... You're my friend. I want you to come home with me."

"But I'm the one..." Paru's voice is small, hesitant. "I keep saying there are men trying to kill me."

"I believe you."

"You believe me?"

"Yes. I believe you." Pithu flashes her a mysterious smile.

There is silence in the carriage. "Don't worry," Paru says at length. "I won't ask you to help me find them again."

The carriage comes to an abrupt halt. The women look up, distracted. Pithu sticks her head out of the window. The road on which they were riding is crossing a slightly broader street. "What's the matter?" Pithu calls out to the driver. The carriage is attempting to turn into the broader street. But it is blocked by a large mass of threatening soldiers. A mounted captain has intercepted the carriage.

"Why is the road blocked?" Pithu asks the captain apprehensively.

"State business," the captain responds. He glances back at Sita Devi and Asaf Khan, who are watching the encounter.

Sita Devi shakes her head.

The captain points up Jaan Chaal past the crossing. Pithu nods, careful not to offend. The carriage clips-clops across the crossing past the soldiers standing on either side.

It is a few minutes before Bhir Das appears with his troop, having completed his sweep of Jaan Chaal. "She's gone!" he yells in alarm. "Did anyone get through?!"

"Only the carriage," Asaf Khan responds.

"That wasn't her," Sita Devi says.

"The carriage! There was a carriage?"

"Yes—"

"She was in the carriage! Come on!"

The orders are shouted. The troops split, half of them charging up Jaan Chaal in hot pursuit of the departed carriage, the rest attempting an intercept by circling around.

Further up, Pithu's carriage clip-clops serenely along the almost-deserted street. This is the tonier end of Jaan Chaal, with no whores hustling, and only a smattering of passing pedestrians.

Paru has been quiet. "What you said..." she hesitates.

"What?" Pithu prompts.

"That I'm your friend."

"Yes."

"Say it again," she requests.

Pithu takes Paru's hands in hers and leans forward. She looks into Paru's eyes. "I'm your friend," she whispers.

The tears roll down Paru's cheeks. Pithu hugs her. Paru grabs her fiercely, her thin grip needy and yearning. Pithu feels her small body in her arms. It seems she will never let Pithu go. They hold each other for a long time.

"I can't," Paru say wiping her tears.

Pithu looks at her.

"I can't come," Paru says.

The carriage comes to an abrupt halt. The horse whinnies.

"What now!" Pithu sticks her head out of the carriage window.

She stiffens. The street outside is blocked by scores of mounted soldiers. Their bows are stretched, the arrows bristle, matchlocks are trained — directly at them.

Pithu looks at the massed troops in shocked incomprehension. Paru reaches for her knife.

"Get out of the carriage!" Bhir Das shouts.

Pithu looks back into the carriage at Paru. Paru puts a protective hand on her arm. "They've come for me. Do what I tell you."

"Your life is worth a feather!" Bhir Das calls. "Get out of the carriage!

"Go," Paru tells Pithu. "They are going to kill me."

"Paru—"

"You need to get away from me!" Paru says urgently. "Go!"

Pithu sits, hesitating.

"Go!"

Pithu steps slowly out of the carriage.

"Stop!" Bhir Das shouts to Pithu.

Pithu freezes.

"Parvati Devi!" Bhir Das shouts. "You, in the carriage! Come out with your hands away from your weapons!"

The carriage is still, silent.

"Parvati Devi! We know you are the Third Prince! Step out of the carriage!"

Pithu turns slowly to Paru, "The Third Prince?"

Paru looks uncomprehendingly at Pithu.

Pithu puts her hand over her mouth. "The Third Prince!" Pithu repeats incredulously. "Paru, you are *the Third Prince*?!"

"Parvati Devi!" Bhir Das shouts. When I give the order, our men will let fly. Your friend will die instantly. And you a few seconds later. Come out with your hands showing!"

The street is silent. A clump of straw lying between the carriage and the troops stirs in the slight breeze.

Bhir Das looks at the men. He draws his breath to give the order.

Asaf Khan raises his hand to stop him. "I want her alive."

The carriage is still.

"Parvati Devi!" Asaf Khan calls. "If we give the order, a hundred arrows will fly out of our bows and kill your friend. But there is a chance she can walk out of here alive. You should think about that."

Inside the carriage, Paru is slumped forward holding her head in her hands.

"Come out with your hands showing!" Asaf Khan shouts.

Paru steps out of the carriage. Her hands are stretched out far away from her body. "Let her walk to you," she calls, her voice calm. Her eyes meet Bhir Das's. "Or, I will get you through the heart." She motions with her head to Pithu. "Go!"

Pithu looks at Paru, the tears welling up in her eyes.

"GO!"

Pithu walks reluctantly towards the men. She looks back at Paru.

Paru glances at the carriage driver, who has been sitting fearfully on his perch. "Him too," she calls to Bhir Das. Asaf Khan nods. The driver scampers to safety.

Asaf Khan lowers his hand and murmurs an order. Twenty troopers charge the short distance to Paru. Two troopers in the lead dive off their horses throwing Paru violently to the ground. In a single motion a trooper rips her knife-belt off. They shove her face down into the dirt. A trooper places the full weight of his knee onto the back of her neck. A second trooper kneels on her back pinning her hands in a tight grip. Two more troopers grab Paru's legs. She is almost invisible under the pile of soldiers.

A trooper produces a set of chains. She is held tightly, while her hands and feet are chained.

Asaf Khan's horse towers over Paru and the tight knot of troopers. "By order of the Emperor," he proclaims, "I place you, Parvati Devi, under arrest for treason. For the crime of sedition against the Emperor. And for spreading false rumours under the guise of the Third Prince."

"I am not the Third Prince!" Paru manages to get out, through the manhandling by the troopers.

Bhir Das holds up the scroll. "Then what is this?"

Paru looks at the scroll in consternation. "You stole my scroll! You bastard! You stole my scroll!" A trooper hits her savagely across the face. Her head moves sideways in stunned pain. "You stole my scroll!" she cries, recovering, as the troopers prepare to move her. "Why must you take everything? Why must you take everything?"

Asaf Khan looks around urgently. He notes several passersby standing at the edges of the amassed troops. "We need to cover her up!" he commands. "We do not want an uprising in the streets."

A palanquin consisting of a small, bamboo cage has been brought. Paru is stuffed roughly into the cage. The thick door is slammed shut, barred and locked. A large black cloth is placed over the cage. Covered by the cloth, the palanquin is secured onto a horse-drawn cart. The cart starts off down the street. Troopers ride on all sides obscuring it from view.

A small knot of people gathers to watch the procession as it goes past. The people are passive, quiet. The black cloth that covers Paru's palanquin cues a larger blackness, a gloom that settles over the City. The gloom pervades despite the bright afternoon sunlight.

Pithu follows the palanquin at a distance, her heart filled with dread and blackness. "The Third Prince," she mouths silently to herself as she sees her friend depart in the covered palanquin to her death. "The Third Prince."

Nur stands alone in the courtyard into which the fort's gates open. She already has the scroll in her possession. She watches as the horse cart carrying the palanquin covered by a black cloth enters the fort. Twelve troopers ride on all sides, ready and alert. The cart stops in the middle of the yard. The captain in charge of the troopers comes up to Nur.

"Where is the Honourable Prime Minister?" she asks.

"He has gone to inform his Majesty."

A look of contempt for her brother crosses Nur's face. She goes up to the palanquin. She lifts a corner of the black cloth and peers into the cage.

Paru lies on her side, bound by the chains. She looks like a hunted animal.

Their eyes meet. Nur appraises Paru curiously. Paru stares back defiantly.

Nur holds up the scroll. "Is this yours?"

"Yes," Paru replies.

Nur becomes conscious of the captain standing to the side, listening. "Then you are the Third Prince?" she says.

"I am not the Third Prince," Paru spits out contemptuously.

"Then what is this? You have read it, haven't you?"

"I cannot read," Paru replies.

Nur draws her breath in sharply. "Do you know what this says?" she asks.

Paru shakes her head.

"How did you get this?" Nur demands.

"It's mine!" Paru replies fiercely.

"How did you get it?"

Paru is silent. "My mother gave it to me," she says at length. "She is dead. You cannot hurt her."

Nur's demeanour betrays suppressed excitement. She glances at the waiting troops. Then abruptly her manner becomes more deliberate. She straightens up.

"There is no doubt that you are the Third Prince," she announces coldly to Paru. "You are guilty of treason against His Majesty. There is an old murder... and a list of crimes too long to relate. I will plead with his Majesty to make your execution swift and merciful."

Nur drops the cloth back. She walks away quickly.

Paru sits listlessly on the floor of her jail cell. Its position high in the fort wall exposes it to the sun. In the afternoons, the walls bake. A stream of hot sunlight comes in through the barred window. Paru sits away from it. The heat makes her sleepy, and she closes her eyes for forgotten periods. She asks the guards for water every time they appear. Sometimes they remember, and sometimes they do not.

On the first day, the guards stood outside the door and peered at her through the bars with a mixture of curiosity and fascination. They were doubly impressed by her good looks. Paru closed her eyes to shut them out. But then she found she could use their fascination to get water and other favours. So she was more civil, going so far as to reward one of them with a smile. She asked for a fan with which she might stir the hot air, but they grew apprehensive and baulked at that.

In the gaps between falling asleep in the heat, passing out from thirst, and waking up on the stone floor to ask for water, Paru's thoughts flow every which way and meander like the river outside the City. So she is the Third Prince. She still cannot believe it. What a joke! Except this joke has landed her inside this tiny cell, from which she cannot escape.

No wonder those men were so persistent in wanting to kill her. If she is the Third Prince, she is supposed to rise up from the land and defeat the great Taraka. That must have been threatening to someone. She had wondered where her assailant got all his men from. She had thought there might be someone big behind him. Well, apparently there was. Is. The great Taraka. She was threatening Taraka. So, who is Taraka? Who are these people, anyway? Why don't they leave her alone! Paru lays her head on the stone floor and puts her arm over her face to try to shut them out.

Then again if she is the Third Prince, does that mean her father is a prince of some kind? Perhaps a high-up one. She remembers a phrase from that Street Orator, who is always haranguing people in the *bazaar*. "Taraka would usurp the rightful rulers of the land." Is she a 'rightful ruler of the land'? And is that because she is descended from her father, the high-up prince? And then if her father is a prince, then her mother... Paru sits up in amazement.

"I used to be princess once!" her mother laughed as she worked long hours in the fields. "We were not always this poor."

"You're a princess with eleven grey hairs," Paru informed her. But the joke did not go down well. When Paru called her a princess again, her mother showed irritation. Embarrassment almost. It made them seem pompous and silly to their new relatives, she told Paru. And then the joke was forgotten, and Paru never thought of it again... not even when she and her mother had their secret meetings to see the jewel. The jewel! That is how she came to possess the most expensive, the most amazing jewel in the entire village. Because her mother was indeed a princess! How stupid Paru had been! How stupid, stupid, stupid! And how clever her mother, how precise, to separate the different worlds to which Paru belonged, to spare her the pain, to protect her.

The two guards are lounging on the lower landing when Nur suddenly appears. They spring up. Nur holds the scroll in her hand. She sweeps past them. "Stay here," she commands. She ascends the stairs rapidly by herself.

Nur blocks the light from the barred window. Paru's eyes are closed. Nur stands silently watching her. It is some time before Paru senses something different about this watcher. She opens her eyes. She takes her time sizing Nur up. Nur for her part seems to be studying Paru.

"You say that this scroll belongs to you," Nur says hesitantly. "And that you have never read it. I thought I would read it to you."

Paru tries to hide her surprise. "Who are you?" she demands.

"You will learn by and by. Would you like me to read this scroll?"

Paru tries to look indifferent. "Yes."

Nur takes her time opening out the parchment. "It is a marriage proclamation," she informs Paru. "It says, 'On this day of grace, twentieth of Jumada, in the year 998, let it be joyfully proclaimed... the marriage of his Grace, the Emperor Akbar...'" Nur pauses. Paru is looking fixedly at her. "'...to Kashibai, daughter of one Karan Singh, may Allah the all-Knowing and all-Powerful bless this divine union...' There are more words... 'Blessings from the Quran...'"

Paru's heart is beating fast. She tries to maintain her composure as she looks at Nur.

"Your father was the Emperor Akbar," Nur says. "And you are the Third Prince."

There is a long silence. "The Emperor Akbar," Paru says mechanically.

"Yes."

"My father was the Emperor Akbar?"

"That is correct."

"Wasn't he a high-up prince of some sort? Because, I'm a Prince."

"Prince is not the right word," Nur replies. "He was the Sun King. The King of Kings. He was in fact the Emperor."

Paru stares at Nur. "Are you joking?"

"It says so in your document." Nur holds the scroll open, so that Paru can look at it through the bars. "If you could read it. Look," she points. "Here is the word. That is your father's name, written over there. It is your scroll, isn't it?"

Paru nods. She is as white as a sheet. When she speaks her voice is barely audible. "Didn't the Emperor Akbar just die?"

"Yes," Nur replies. "There is now a new Emperor."

Paru rocks her head back and forth, as if she needs to learn this fact and make sense of it. "So he is dead."

"Yes."

"You're sure."

"Of course I'm sure! The Emperor Akbar is dead."

Paru is silent. Nur stands patiently.

"I will not be able to tell him then," Paru says.

"Tell him what?"

"That she loves him."

"Who... loves him?"

"My mother. Who else?"

"Oh."

"She could never forgive him. For something he did. That she never told me about. That is why she did not go back to see him. But she loves him... loves him still. And I was the one to find him. And tell him."

"Well. I am sorry... to have given you such bad news."

Paru looks at Nur. "Can you please go?"

To Paru's surprise, Nur nods. She turns and departs down the stairs.

Paru lies down on the floor and stares at the ceiling. She is stunned. Numb. She feels nothing. Her father, who was never there her entire life, whom she had to find, to discover the goodness in him, because her mother thought there was goodness in him. Dead. Gone, all gone. She will never be able to know him. Suddenly, she laughs. All this regret... didn't the Palace Lady say she is going to be executed soon? What is the point? How can she even find her father now, who cannot be found in any case? Sometimes the strands of destiny seem to lie just loose and unheeded; the worthless end-points of a large and futile tangle. The only thing that seems to matter is what her mother wanted. It was her drive, her caring. It was what she wanted for Paru and, indirectly, for her father too. It was for her that they had to do it, both of them.

Now it will not be. Paru experiences a surge of anger towards her father. More to the point, she has always been upset at him, but it is at times like these that the anger really surfaces. Where was he all these years? Why did he not come back and look for them? His own wife and daughter. And an Emperor at that! Men are such shits! A popular sentiment among the whores at the boarding house. But there is truth to it.

The stone floor cools. The bright sunlight coming in from the window turns from harsh to mild, to pleasant, to dark. In the darkness, Paru dreams she is standing with her mother outside the fort, while the Conqueror with the Mole conducts his massacre inside. Her mother described it so well and so many times, she thinks, drifting off into sleep, it was as if Paru was there.

The flames crackle and rise up into the sky, amidst sparks and explosions. Paru and her mother can smell the smoke from where they stand. The entire fort is ablaze. They can hear a human roar from the fort, which sounds like the roar of battle. But it is in fact the collective shouts of pain and terror mingled with the madness and debauchery of the invading soldiers. When a woman commits *sati* by jumping into the flames, the act sounds poetic only in principle. In reality, a hideous involuntary scream emerges from her lips. The writhing, the burnt flesh become too unbearable to witness. Through the collective roar they can hear the screams. Paru puts her hands to her ears. Her mother covers Paru's hands with her own. Everyone, everyone they know is being killed inside, and all Paru and her mother can do is stand helplessly by.

She wakes up because she is cold. The night is unusually chilly. She has nothing to cover herself with, other than the clothes she came in. She can see stars through the little barred window. She rubs her hands over her arms and lies shivering on the floor, waiting for morning.

It was foolish of her to ask the Palace Lady to leave. What if she does not come back? But something tells her she will. When will morning come? It seems to take forever, but at length the sun is up and she is a little warmer. The soldiers come by and slip her some rice and water. She tells them she was cold at night and she needs a blanket. They laugh and walk away. She has almost given up hope of seeing the Palace Lady again, but then in the late afternoon she reappears at the small barred window.

Paru has not forgotten her complaint. "I was cold last night!" she says accusingly. "I need a blanket to cover myself."

Nur nods. "I will tell the guards."

Paru regards her appraisingly. She knows something is up with this one. All this kindness must come at a price.

Nur hesitates. "Is there anything else I can tell you about your father?"

Paru laughs. "Anything else? Yes! What was he like?"

"He was the Emperor Akbar," Nur says simply. "He was the greatest ruler in living memory. The wealth of these lands, the vastness of his dominions has never known an equal in the history of the world. Not only was he very powerful, he possessed that rare ability. He was a genius in the very art of ruling. He made his subjects happy. There are few lands that can claim—"

"No! What was he like?"

Nur stops to think about Paru's question. "He was a large man," she says slowly. "Handsome, in the way that men with a strong character are handsome. It was said that the mole on his lip made him even more attractive to women than if it had not been there." Nur smiles to herself, recalling. "When he entered a room, he seemed to fill it with his laughter. And his noise! It was always a celebration. You felt safe with him. And he missed nothing. No matter how small the thing you did, he always remembered it and asked you about it the next time he met you."

Paru's eyes are filling with tears.

"And he had an eye for the women. Oh, how he adored them! He worshipped them like goddesses. And he was like you! He could not read."

The tears roll down Paru's cheeks. She wipes them with her hands and when this proves inadequate uses her sleeves. Softly, she asks, "Does the Prime Minister have my jewel?"

Nur starts. Her mind races. It is some time before she can reply. "No," she says measuring her words. "It is the Grand *Vazir* who has your jewel."

Paru looks away, lost in a reverie. Minutes pass by in silence. Nur stands at the door, bracing herself, and Paru wanders back and forth inside the cell, occasionally glancing through the bars at Nur.

Finally, Nur says that which she has been thinking of for many days. "Tell me," she says. "This may seem strange to you, and it will of course never happen. But, if there was a key to this door... and a horse waiting outside the gate... and you had a chance to ride into the street. And to show yourself to the adoring crowds... In some distant city... as the Third Prince..."

Paru stands close to the bars, her eyes wide.

"...and if there was an old general many miles east of here. A general who served your father. And who has no particular liking for the present Emperor — the new one. And if this old general could raise an army to follow you and support you... what would you do?"

Paru looks at Nur with amazement. She searches her face for facetiousness — a trick, a joke perhaps. But, no. Nur is serious. She turns away to hide her confusion. "You think I can be Emperor?" she says finally, with a little ironic laugh.

"You are Akbar's direct," Nur replies simply. "He was twelve years old when he was crowned King of a rag-tag Mughal army. You have an advantage. You are sixteen. And you can seduce men."

"You really believe I could be Emperor?" Paru asks incredulously.

"The *bazaars* of Hindustan want to believe in you," Nur says. "Delhi... Lahore... Kabul... the stories have spread far and wide. They all want to believe in you. They dream of a great and just king... a God, like your father. Would it not thrill them to know that they have a Queen? A wise, strong, beautiful Queen! They dream of an Empire of the Sun. A beacon to the world... of justice, wisdom, riches... they dream."

Paru is silent for a long time. She paces with greater intensity, coming up in frustration against the close walls of the cell. The seconds flow by in the warm afternoon air. Nur stands patient, unmoving. She turns to face Nur. She takes a deep breath. "This is a large question," she says gravely. "I have never thought of such a possibility in my entire life, not even in make believe. I now need some time to think about it. Will you please leave me by myself?"

"You do not have a lot of time," Nur tells her. "With every hour your certain execution approaches. It may be tomorrow, it may be the day after. I believe you are safe for one night. Tonight. I will return for your answer in the morning."

Paru clutches the bars of the window and watches Nur's back as she descends the stairs.

But, it is easier than Paru had imagined. Scarcely an hour after Nur's departure, one of the guards brings her a blanket. Paru sits on the floor luxuriating in its softness. The thoughts came softly and lightly. They require almost no effort. She reaches her conclusion quickly. And then there is nothing to do other than sit with her blanket and muse over the enormity of what Nur has just told her.

Her mother... damn it! So simple and cheerful on the outside, so deep inside! Paru is angry at her. But how could she have done anything differently? Paru feels overwhelmed. Life is a strange beast! She feels dead inside. There are no more decisions to be made by her. She just has to let it unfold. She is calm. Dangerously calm.

To her surprise, she sleeps well. She is up at dawn and sits with her blanket around her shoulders with that terrible calm she has acquired. She sits, waiting for Nur. It is not long before she hears her coming up the stairs. It is as if the last twenty hours had not been. Paru takes her time putting her blanket aside and rising to meet Nur at the barred window.

Nur searches her face. "Have you thought about it?"

"Yes. And you want to know the answer," Paru says.

"Yes."

"What I would do if I could escape from here, and there was a horse waiting for me outside the gates, and the people took me for their Third Prince."

"Yes."

"I would turn my horse around and find this Grand *Vazir* of yours who has stolen my jewel. And I would slash his face, till he gave it back to me. Then I would disappear — as far away from you as I possibly could, Palace Lady!"

Nur recoils as if slapped. It is a few moments before she can collect herself. "You disappoint me," she manages.

Paru does not answer. She turns her back on Nur and stomps away from the window, only to come up against the opposite wall.

"And what persuaded you to come to such a foolish conclusion?"

"You did. You said my father had a mole on his lip."

"What does your father's mole have to do with your conclusion!"

"Everything. I have been a fool my entire life. My own mother played me for a fool! She told me she was running from the Conqueror with the Mole. And she told me to find my father, in the hope that I would grow to love him. But, I had no reason to think they were one and the same person. You told me. For that, I must thank you. Whoever you are, Palace Lady, and whatever your purpose, you have done me a great service."

"That is good then. Now that you know you are truly the Third Prince it is your turn—"

"No!" Paru interrupts.

"—your destiny calls you in your father's footsteps."

"I would rather die tomorrow, Palace Lady, than follow in my father's footsteps! My father killed my mother's family! She told me how it happened. She told me! Her whole family, our whole village. Ten, twenty, hundred villages! Killed in one day! Killed by my father! My mother stood outside the fort and wept. And the fires rose up to the sky. The sky was orange, my mother said. And she could hear the screams of the burning women. And her burning brothers, and her burning sisters, and her burning father, and her burning mother! I was fourteen years old when she died, but even on that day the memory haunted her. She endured years of hardship and poverty fleeing the forces of the Conqueror... or so she told me. But now that I think of it, she was just fleeing from him. From who he was. And you want me to be like him!"

"But you will not do what he did."

"I will not? How do you know that, Palace Lady?"

"I know that you would be a fool to turn away from your destiny."

"Destiny has its own shape!" Paru retorts, her eyes blazing. "How do you know that it is my destiny?"

Nur tries to calm herself by taking a deep breath. "I think you are just afraid of what it holds for you. Afraid of being at the head of a huge Empire. Are you afraid?"

"Yes."

"Afraid to lead an army against the present Emperor?"

"I can always do that," Paru retorts scornfully.

"Then what are you afraid of?"

"I am afraid of who I will become, Palace Lady. Because I will scarcely mount that horse outside the Gate, than I will be faced with a choice — kill ten thousand, or be defeated."

"And you are afraid of being defeated?"

"I am afraid I will kill the ten thousand."

"That did not stop your father. He had his eye on the greater good."

"I am not so proud, Palace Lady, as to believe that in the end I can create a greater good. My soul does not desire it. My father was different. And he was a lucky man. He was lucky indeed — if in the end he had no regrets for all the horrors he committed."

"Then who would you rather be, if you would not follow in your father's footsteps!"

"Myself! I would be myself. Just the way I am! I have to get my jewel back! And find my father! And tell him my mother loves him—"

"And your father is dead. And you will be put to the sword in a day—"

"And then... and then... my destiny is to dance! That is who I am! Those are the promises I made. To my mother and to my Uncle..."

"Uncle! Who is Uncle!"

Paru smiles. "He is a man who gave me five *rupiya*, once."

"As Emperor you can get fifty thousand *rupiya* and give it back to him!"

Paru shakes her head. "You do not understand."

Nur is feeling increasingly nervous and irritated. This is not going the way she had imagined. "You are only making excuses," she says. "You would rather die like a coward, than face your true destiny!"

Paru is silent. She paces about the cell, her insides in a knot. Suddenly she gives a little, knowing laugh. "This is not about me, is it, Palace Lady? It is about you. It is your dream. Your plan. Your horse outside that gate. I am only a creature in your dream. Like the horse! Then how long do I have?"

Nur can barely contain her anger. "You are an ignorant! pleasant! girl! Do you think I need to do this! To be kind to you? Do you think I have no other means?"

"I know this, Palace Lady — that there are two kinds of people in the world, those who are true to Shiva, and those who will only pretend. Until the day comes that those who pretend see a chance to increase their own personal glory. And then they will change who they are, these other people. You are such a person, Palace

Lady. I can see it in your eyes."

"You know nothing! You little HORROR! It was your precious mother who betrayed your father in the first place! Why do you think she married him?! To set him up! To be ambushed and killed! Why do you think she was running away all those years? Because it was her crime, in the first place!"

Paru is as white as a sheet. "You do not say bad things to me about my mother, Palace Lady!"

"I will say whatever I want to you, you little... rat! I will decide how you *die*, whether you will be put to the sword or be ripped apart by horses! I will decide whether you get food, or water, or heat, or cold! I will change your past, if I have to! You have not the *slightest idea* of who I am, or what I can do!"

Paru stares at Nur for a long time. "How do you get all that... power, anyway, Palace Lady? Do you fuck the Emperor?"

"*Yes!*" Nur spits back. "As a matter of fact, *I do!*" She turns violently away and departs down the stairs. Before she is tempted to kill me, Paru thinks to herself.

It is late afternoon at the *Diwani Khaas*. Jahangir struggles with the faint remains of a hangover. Nur sits a little apart from the men, as is now the custom. Asaf Khan stands at his side-table sorting through his papers. "Next," he says. "Your Majesty was to decide the fate of the prisoner Parvati Devi."

"We had decided she would go quickly," Jahangir says. He turns to Itimad Ud Daulah. "Put her to the sword tomorrow."

"Your Majesty," Nur interrupts.

Jahangir looks at her.

"The sword is too kind. I urge a more severe punishment."

"Why would you do that?" Itimad Ud Daulah protests.

"Sedition is a serious crime, your Majesty. When word leaks out from the palace of her death, as it surely will, we would like to send a strong message, to the *bazaar*."

"What punishment do you suggest?" Jahangir asks.

"You are the master of these things, your Majesty. All that comes to my feeble imagination... perhaps, bury her alive?"

Itimad Ud Daulah looks unhappily at his daughter.

Jahangir smiles wickedly. "I will give it some thought."

"To move on—" says Asaf Khan.

"Your Majesty," Nur interrupts.

Jahangir turns to Nur.

"It vexes me greatly to think that none of you have taken the trouble to talk to the prisoner."

"Talk?"

"She has a bigger following than did Prince Khusrau. She poses a greater threat. But now that I have captured her, none of you seem to show the slightest interest in her. My brother was all too eager to report the good news to you—"

"I had an equal part in her capture!" Asaf Khan retorts hotly. "If not a bigger part!"

"Well then, why have you not visited her?" Nur demands.

Jahangir watches, mildly amused.

"What would be the purpose—" says Asaf Khan.

"The purpose? The purpose would be to find out how she eluded capture for so long! The purpose would be to discover who her friends are. And if those friends are helping her even now to plan an escape—"

"How dare you talk to me like that!"

Jahangir raises his hand for silence. Nur is about to respond, but stops herself.

Jahangir looks coldly at Nur. "The Minister shall refrain from criticisms of her elders."

Nur lowers her head, rebuked.

"But there is something here I had not thought of," Jahangir says. "I am remiss not to have... talked to this prisoner, as the

Minister of Special Counsel puts it. I shall make a visit."

"Thank you, Your Majesty. Your Majesty! If you would be so kind..."

Jahangir turns wearily to Nur.

"I was going to suggest a picnic," Nur says hurriedly. "The jail cell in which this prisoner is kept is in a remote part of the fort. It is quite pretty there. There is a red-and-brown bird that visits every day. And I cannot tell if it is the Indian *chakur* or the red spurfowl."

"This court has no more favours left, Minister," Jahangir replies. "You have used them all up." He turns to the assembly. "We shall see the prisoner. And we shall have a picnic at the same time. And we shall look at this bird that is so tormenting the Minister of Special Counsel."

Paru's guards lounge on the bottom landing. The duty is boring. Ritu approaches, leading a good-sized goat by a rope. She finds an iron ring in the wall, where she proceeds to tie the rope firmly.

"What are you doing!" one of the guards demands.

"There is to be a party," Ritu says. She starts walking away.

"A party? Who's coming!"

"His Majesty."

The guards stiffen. "What? When?"

"This afternoon," Ritu replies without looking back.

The guards are overwhelmed. They stand apprehensively, looking about for surprise visitors.

It is ten minutes before Ritu reappears. She holds a flask of wine and two cups. "Begum said you boys can have some fun before the big shots arrive." Ritu hands the flask to the first guard. He cannot believe his luck. "Thanks!" he says gratefully.

Ritu turns and departs. The other guard is looking wistfully after Ritu's almost bare back. "Hey!" he calls. "Can we have more fun than just the wine!"

Ritu walks away, cold, sexy.

"Hey! Come back here!"

The guards pour the wine, fumbling with the cups and the jug. After a while they feel uncomfortable standing, so they sit next to the steps. The mid-morning sun is hot. A soft drowsiness descends on them. The first guard tries to look straight ahead. But, he has difficulty keeping his eyes open. The courtyard and the walkway seem to rock back and forth in front of him. He leans heavily against the bottom step for support. The second guard has already made himself comfortable, using the bottom step as a pillow.

When Nur appears some twenty minutes later the guards are fast asleep. She glances at the goat, which is still tethered to the wall. Nur steps over the sleeping guards and climbs the steps to Paru's prison.

It is noon when a group consisting of Jahangir, Asaf Khan, Itimad Ud Daulah, and attendants gets ready to make its way from the *Diwani Khaas* to Paru's prison. The attendants carry cushions, fans, carpets, and wine. A much-anticipated and larger set of attendants is to bring the picnic banquet. Jahangir looks around for Nur. "Begum has gone ahead to make arrangements, Your Majesty," the head attendant informs him. Jahangir looks displeased. The procession makes its way along the walkways towards Paru's prison.

Nur stands outside Paru's jail cell. She blocks the sunlight streaming in through the barred window. Paru looks up apprehensively.

"I have something to show you," Nur says with a smile.

A wild hope that it may be her jewel flashes through Paru's mind. She goes to the window.

Nur hands her a heavy metal object. It is a short tube that bends at right angles and broadens out into a handle. The broad part has some wood and embedded ivory with carvings. Paru's face falls. She holds the object by the tube. She hands it back to Nur through the bars. "What is it?"

"It is like a matchlock," Nur says with a wicked smile. "Only smaller. You can hide it in your clothes." Nur holds the pistol comfortably by the handle. "You hold it like this," she says, her finger on the trigger. "You squeeze this... and it can blow a hole through a man's head."

Nur points the pistol at Paru's head. "Or a woman's."

It takes a second for Paru to understand what Nur is going to do. Her eyes widen with shock, as she realises she is about to press the trigger. Nur looks at Paru with calm purpose. Her finger starts squeezing down on the trigger. The hammer moves back. Paru closes her eyes and cringes, bracing for the shot.

BANG! The shot fires. Paru jumps. The pistol is enveloped in smoke. Paru feels nothing. Is this how death feels? She opens her eyes. Nur is still standing in front of her. Is she dead or alive? She passes a hand over her head and chest. Maybe she can feel the shot. Nothing. She seems to be alive. She looks more closely at Nur. Nur is calmly reloading. She is examining the lock on the door of the jail, which has been shattered.

Nur fires again at the lock. Paru jumps. The jail door swings open. Nur steps back to give Paru space to come out. Paru looks at Nur, her heart pounding.

"Come on!" Nur says. "There isn't time."

In a split second, Paru decides. She lunges at Nur, trying to grab the pistol. Nur moves her hand out of the way just in time. She falls backward with Paru on top of her. Paru half raises herself and punches Nur hard on the face. Nur's head bangs on the stone floor. She is stunned. Paru twists Nur's evading hand and gets the pistol. Paru attempts to stand, pistol in hand. She is almost at the head of the stairs. Nur half-rises and lunges at Paru's legs grabbing them from behind. Paru falls headlong down the stairs. Nur hangs on to her legs. The two go rolling over each other down the stairs.

They come to a stop halfway. Nur releases Paru's legs to attempt to get her hands. Paru whacks the pistol across Nur's face. Nur cries out loudly in pain. Blood emerges from the cut on the side of her head. Paru escapes Nur's hold and tries to fly down the stairs. Nur launches herself at Paru from behind and above. She collides with Paru in mid-air, grabbing her around the shoulders. The two fall forward, rolling head over heels, almost bouncing, down the stairs.

They come to rest on the bottom landing. They lie still for a second, next to the sleeping guards. They are both winded, in pain. Paru's *odhni* is halfway up the stairs.

Paru tries to get up. Nur grabs her hair and punches her face. Paru swings the pistol a second time into Nur's face. Nur yells with pain. Paru twists and frees herself from Nur's grip. She stands. Nur starts to get up.

Paru points the pistol at Nur's head. "Stop!" she shouts. Nur launches herself at Paru. Paru squeezes the trigger. It clicks uselessly. Nur drops Paru, landing on top of her. Paru's head hits the stone floor. She is stunned. The pistol drops.

Nur sits astride Paru and punches her face forcefully. "I am trying to help you!" Punch! "You stupid—" Punch! "good for nothing," Punch! "whore!" Punch! Blood pours out of Paru's nose. She looks as if she is about to pass out.

Breathing heavily, Nur looks down at her. A large bruise is developing on the side of Nur's face where Paru whacked her with the pistol. Blood streams down from the earlier cut. She stands. Paru rolls slowly onto her side, trying to get up. Nur kicks her violently in the stomach. Paru groans and doubles up in pain. "That's for crossing me!"

Nur kicks her again, unexpectedly, gratuitously. Paru grunts with pain. "And that's for shooting a pistol at me!"

Jahangir and his entourage are making their way towards Paru's prison. They hear the faraway sound of a pistol shot. Jahangir looks up. It is followed by a faint cry from Nur. The members of the entourage are electrified. Asaf Khan urgently whispers to one of the attendants. The attendant departs at a run. The procession picks up the pace.

"Hurry!" Asaf Khan says nervously. They are almost running.

Nur walks over to the fallen pistol. She picks it up and starts loading. She looks over at Paru. "If you want to see your jewel ever again, you will do exactly what I say! Come on! Get up!"

Paru struggles to regain her senses. "What did you say?"

"What?"

"About my jewel."

"I have your jewel. And I will throw it into the moat if you do not do exactly as I say. Now get up!"

Paru struggles painfully to her feet. Nur walks to the goat and unties it. "Follow me," she says. Paru follows, tentative, obedient. Nur leads the goat to the edge of the courtyard, where the stone parapet overlooks the moat. Nur points downward and fires the pistol. Paru jumps. The goat lies dead.

"Take your clothes off," Nur says.

"Clothes?"

"Yes, your clothes. Take them off! Hurry! They will be here any minute."

Paru gingerly removes her *choli.*

Nur snatches it from her. "Everything! Come on!"

Paru starts taking her *ghagra* off. Nur slips the sleeves of Paru's *choli* over the dead goat's front legs. Blood from the goat covers her hands and stains her clothes. She secures the *choli* around the goat.

"Your pants," Nur says. She slips Paru's *ghagra* over the goat's head. Paru stands naked in front of her. She hands Nur her harem pants.

"Where is your *odhni?*"

"On the stairs."

"Go get it!"

Paru runs naked back up the stairs. Nur uses the rope to tie the *ghagra* securely around the goat. She places the goat's hind legs through Paru's pants, and pulls the pants up around the goat.

Paru returns with her *odhni.* "Why?" she says holding the *odhni* out.

"What!"

"Why are you helping me?"

Nur knots the *odhni* around the dead goat's blood-stained head. She looks up at Paru. "You are more use to me alive, than dead. Now come on!"

The goat is fully clothed. Nur picks up one end. It is heavy. "Pick up the legs!" she urges. Paru picks up the goat's hind-legs. They struggle with the carcass and place it on top of the wall.

Nur takes a deep breath. "Now listen carefully!" she orders Paru.

Nur sits on the stone parapet overlooking the moat. A stream of sticky, drying blood flows down the side of her face to her clothes. There is a dreamy look in her eyes as if she is about to pass out. Behind her the sky is light with haze from the afternoon heat. The Yamuna River curls in the distance, disappearing vaguely into the soft horizon. There is blood on Nur's hands and clothes. She is by herself. Paru is gone. The goat is gone.

She hears the sound of running feet. Jahangir and his entourage burst into the courtyard. The pistol lies on the ground some distance from the parapet. Paru's two guards lie drugged and unconscious at the bottom of the steps.

"What happened!" Jahangir exclaims.

Nur does not reply. She looks away, staring absently at the horizon. Asaf Khan has a sudden thought. He charges up the steps to Paru's cell.

"Mehrunissa! What happened!" Jahangir begs.

Nur turns slowly to look at Jahangir. "I failed," she tells him.

Her eyes look dazed, faraway.

Asaf Khan is on the top landing looking hurriedly around. The cell door is ajar, the lock broken. The jail cell is empty.

"What are you saying? What happened?"

"You said it would be my head or hers, your Majesty... she is gone. It is my head."

"Gone!" Itimad Ud Daulah repeats.

"She had help... from outside. The guards were drugged. She had a pistol." Nur feels the cut on her face, with her fingers.

Jahangir looks at the pistol, still lying on the ground. Asaf Khan is back.

Nur examines the blood on her fingers.

"I tried to stop her..." Nur says. "She is very quick."

"Which way did she go!"

Nur makes a curious motion with her head — over the parapet and into the moat. "I may have killed her."

Jahangir, Asaf Khan, Itimad Ud Daulah rush to the parapet. They stare intently at the moat far below. The water is a bright green. Paru's clothes float on the surface. Emanating from her clothes and spreading outwards into the water is a red cloud of blood. Two crocodiles thrash around, finishing off the last of a good meal. A third crocodile swims from the bank and snaps sharply at something underneath Paru's clothes.

Jahangir's face is red with emotion as he looks down at Paru's clothes and the spreading cloud of blood in the water.

Nur gazes bleakly at the horizon. A slight breeze ruffles her dishevelled hair. She looks curiously at the men staring over the parapet. "Is she dead?" she asks tentatively.

No one replies.

A troop of fifty soldiers rushes onto the courtyard. They quickly surround the group, weapons at the ready. The captain approaches Itimad Ud Daulah for instructions.

Jahangir continues to stare down at the water in the grip of an intense emotion.

Nur gets off the parapet. She looks around, her arms outstretched, waiting to be arrested. But Itimad Ud Daulah does not give the order.

Jahangir turns and walks away from the parapet, lost in his thoughts. The others follow. When it becomes apparent to Nur that no one is going to arrest her, she starts to follow the group. She walks in evident pain.

Jahangir stops and looks behind. He waits for her and holds his hand out. Nur limps slowly towards Jahangir.

Agra Fort, 1606

Hamida Begum likes the courtyard that adjoins the deserted hall at the far corner of the harem. Its broken down, overgrown look causes it to merge back into nature, and its earthiness appeals to her. It reminds her of the years in the desert with her husband, the Emperor Humayun.

The year has taken its toll on her and her bones are stiff with the cool of the winter months. She walks slowly and infirmly across the courtyard, escorted by Nur. Nur carries her usual low seat and cushion.

Nur looks fresh and beautiful. Six months have passed since Prince Khusrau's rebellion and the subsequent escape and death of the traitor Parvati Devi. Nur's wounds have almost healed.

Hamida Begum finds herself headed into the shade cast by the hall's roof. She changes course towards a spot where it is bright and sunny. She stands looking at Nur. Nur puts the seat down in the sun and places the cushion on it. Hamida Begum sits.

"I will get your tea," Nur says. She disappears for a few minutes and returns with a tray of tea servings. She pours Hamida Begum a cup.

"Did you make it yourself?" Hamida Begum asks suspiciously.

"No, Begum."

Hamida Begum tastes the tea tentatively. "It's good," she says, reassured. "Well, Mehrunissa. I hear you have done quite well for yourself! I hear the Prince is going to marry you."

"Yes, Begum... Emperor."

"What?"

"He is now the Emperor."

"Ah, yes."

Hidden behind a stone grill inside the deserted hall, Paru watches the scene. She stares hungrily at Hamida Begum, as if she cannot have enough of her.

"Well?" Hamida Begum demands. "How is he treating you? Is he any good?"

"He is everything I could wish for, Hamida Begum," Nur replies.

Hamida Begum is not fooled. "I always had my doubts about that boy," she says thoughtfully. She sips her tea. "Emperor-Shemperor!" she says suddenly. "There has never been anyone like my Shah Baba!"

Watching from behind the grill, Paru smiles a little smile.

"But I don't want to offend you. Now that you are going to marry this new Emperor."

Nur is amused. "You cannot offend me by saying that, Hamida Begum."

Paru clutches the stone grill, absorbing every part of Hamida Begum as she sips her tea.

Paru enters the darkened room tentatively. It is daylight outside, but the curtains have been tightly drawn across the big, airy doorways of Ruquiya's chamber. A single shaft of daylight sneaks through the curtain and falls across the low bed where Ruquiya is seated. She is so still, Paru wonders if there is anyone in the room at all. Ruquiya's hair is white. The last few months have not been kind to her. "I do not go out much," she says by way of explanation.

"You wanted to see me?" Paru says nervously.

"Yes. Come. Stand here by the light."

Paru stands as instructed. Ruquiya looks appraisingly at her face for a long time. She reaches out and holds Paru's wrist, as if to steady herself. The tears well up in her eyes.

"As a rule, I see no one these days," Ruquiya tells her. "But I had to see you. There is something I have to tell you."

Paru steals a glance at Ruquiya's face.

"I witnessed your father's wedding. I was sitting on a horse, hidden behind some trees. He and his new wife... your mother... did not know I was there. To be honest, I was consumed with rage and jealousy. I hated your mother at that moment. So, when she started to run from him and the shots rang out, I was happy. I could see your father's marriage to her breaking up in front of my eyes. But there was something, a detail — I told no one about. I did tell him, though, finally, before he died."

Paru looks directly at Ruquiya.

"When your mother ran from your father, she grabbed his hand and tried to pull him with her. At the last minute she decided that she was going to save him. He was too stunned to follow. He just stood there, looking like a big oaf. Then the fireball landed and Sipahsalar, his General, was killed, and he was distracted by that. He released his own hand from hers. And then she ran..."

Ruquiya is lost in thought. "She could not bring herself to betray him."

Paru nods slowly. She never doubted her mother. But it is good to know from this lady just the same.

Ruquiya smiles. "I am glad I could make you happy."

Paru nods.

"You may go," she says kindly.

The harem entertainments have changed subtly over the last two months. They are no longer as raucous and unpredictable as they used to be. Instead, there is an emphasis on fashion and on high art. The clothes the dancers wear are at once startling and enhancing. The dances too are more formal, but without losing their touch for interesting choreography. It is an open secret in the fort that this is because of the sweeping hand of Nur.

The musicians tonight are an ensemble that has been successful for some time — two *tablas* playing in synchrony, a *sitar*, a *sarodh* and miscellaneous strings. The music is deliberate, textured, thoughtful. The hall is brightly lit. It is festooned with long, brightly dyed sashes, hanging across the cavernous ceilings — Nur's touch.

Nine girls dance together in a line. Their costumes are stunning, grandly colourful. The dance seeks to delight with surprising turns of choreography rather than with the girls' sexuality. Ritu leads. She dances centrestage, confident and beautiful.

Paru dances one next to the last, from the left.

At the opposite end of the hall sits a packed audience. Jahangir and Nur sit up front. A small amount of carpet space separates them. Asaf Khan and Itimad Ud Daulah sit immediately behind with their wives. Mahabat Khan is in the far corner at the back of the hall, whispering something to Malika Jahan, who sits very close to him.

A loud buzz rises from the audience. The royals and courtiers are not especially attentive, inspite of the artistry of the show.

Jahangir has been drinking since early afternoon and is now dead drunk. He has his usual row of cups lined up in front of him. He finishes off a cup with a single swig and puts it down on the carpet, taking a moment to make sure it balances. He tries to gather himself to watch the performance. Nur inhales smoke from a *hookah*. She is watching the dancers closely.

Jahangir notices Paru. He interrupts himself, suddenly fascinated. Paru dances, perfectly-groomed, expressionless. Jahangir stares at Paru.

Mahabat Khan's face is close to Malika Jahan's as she whispers animatedly to him.

Jahangir gazes at Paru, transfixed. Nur lets the smoke out from her mouth. She is a little stoned herself, and her eyes have a glazed look.

Jahangir leans over to Nur. He taps her on the shoulder to get her attention. "Who is that girl?"

"Who?" Nur asks.

Jahangir points to Paru. "That one."

"Which one?"

"The one... on the left. Not that one... the one next to her."

"Ohh!" Nur smiles, realising that Jahangir is pointing at Paru. "That's the new girl. She's very talented. She can dance with snakes." Her eyes flicker towards Jahangir. "Poisonous ones."

They watch Paru dance. Jahangir continues to look bemused.

"Beautiful, isn't she?" Nur says.

"I do not like her," Jahangir replies.

"No?"

"I feel I have seen her somewhere before."

Nur shrugs. "I just got her. From a distant village."

Jahangir watches Paru. "She is certainly not beautiful!" he says petulantly.

"No?"

Jahangir attempts to focus on Paru, as if he cannot come to terms with the way she looks.

Paru turns to look directly at Jahangir. Their eyes meet.

Jahangir scowls back.

Nur takes a puff from her *hookah*. Something occurs to her. She leans over to Jahangir. Her mouth is next to his ear. It looks as if she is about to put her tongue in, but no, she only intends to speak.

"Think of her... as your sister."

The music and the party chatter seem very loud to Jahangir. He continues to stare unhappily at Paru.

Afterword

It is hard, today, to appreciate the large space that the Mughal Empire occupied in the world of the 1600s. In terms of land mass, it was relatively modest. Akbar's Hindustan bordered Iran in the northwest, included present-day Afghanistan and Pakistan, swept across the lion's share of India, and went as far east as Bengal, including present-day Bangladesh. In the northeast it braved the Himalayas, to push up against Tibet. In the south, it had a contentious border with three hold-out kingdoms, Ahmednagar, Bijapur and Golconda. All told, the Mughal Empire was smaller in land-mass than its two rivals at the time: the Persian Empire and the Ottoman Empire. But what it lacked in area, it made up for with its people. The historian John Keay reports that the population of Akbar's Hindustan is estimated at about a 100 million people.[1] By contrast, all of Europe at the time was 40 million, and the population of Great Britain could not have been more than five million.

Paradoxically, this large population was the source of Hindustan's wealth. An ancient, unbroken tradition of village handicrafts reached its zenith during the Mughal era. Villagers produced not only food from the abundant, fertile land but village factories, born of family-run local enterprises, produced fabrics, dyes, metalwork, jewellery, weapons — anything imaginable, with a level of artistry and innovation that are still admired today.

Akbar's genius was to create structures and liberties for his subjects that turned this industry into the most explosive, longest-sustained economic boom the world had known. Artisans flourished.[2] A bustling middle-class grew. Stone-cutters and architects reached a level of sophistication that permitted them to create the joyful facades of the Agra Fort and of Fatehpur Sikri. A generation later these skills would evolve to create the Taj Mahal. An adventurer in the employ of the Persian Emperor could hope to triple his salary by traveling to India and switching allegiance to the Mughal Empire.[3]

To be sure, this wealth did not do much for the average Indian peasant, who then, as now, lived in poverty. The Mughals wrote the book on exploitation. About the only things that can be said in mitigation is that the lot of the Hindustani peasant was similar to that of peasants all over the world at the time, and it was probably better than the grinding poverty of some rural areas of India today. Two factors contributed to this. Land was still plentiful, and the price of food as a proportion of the cost of living was higher. Hence, produce from rural areas comprised a significant part of the economy and fetched a good price.

Not the least of Akbar's leaps was his edict of *suhl-i-kul*, or universal tolerance.[4] "Let not difference of religion interfere with policy, and be not violent in inflicting retribution," he advised his son Murad when appointing him governor of Malwa.[5] Hindu tradition, which by its very nature is inclusive of different sects, had already made the Indian sub-continent among the most tolerant places in the world at that point in history. Akbar's enshrinement of an active and inquisitive multiculturalism into state policy created a fluidity and an emphasis on merit in Hindustani society that undoubtedly contributed to its economic success. In the words of William Dalrymple, "...as Mughals and Hindus visited the same shrines, followed the same holy men and began to intermarry... the dialogue between the rival religions reached its climax, the two cultures finally fused into one and flowered into a civilisation of breathtaking beauty and perfection."[6]

Ten thousand miles away, shivering European nations watched the moving feast that was Hindustan and yearned for a piece of the action. In 1600, the English, envious of the flourishing Portuguese trade with India, formed the East India Company of London for the express purpose of developing trade in the Indian subcontinent.[7] Two years later, the Dutch followed suit. The foreigners brought gold and silver bullion (which they took from the New World), and exchanged it for cottons, silks, dyes, furnishings and "spices".

It was in this bright, hopeful world of contrasts, of genius and vanities, that the events of this novel take place.

There was no such person as Paru. There was a Siege of Chittor[8], and there is enough evidence of Akbar's sexual effusiveness that a dalliance with a local woman during the long, hot years of the Siege was not out of the question. Consider this from Jahangir's diary: "Three months after my birth, my sister Shahzada Khanim was born of one of my father's serving-girls."[9] Akbar's sexual adventures extended not only to his wives but to a loosely-defined harem said to have contained 300 concubines.

The Siege of Chittor ended in 1568, which is about fifteen years earlier than the events of the novel would have it. Paru would have been too old. As the novel describes, when the Siege ended, the sati fires within the fort could be seen by the soldiers below.[10] Akbar's army did indeed massacre the forty thousand peasants living inside the fort — a lasting stain on his career. It is not known if he later regretted this action on his death-bed.

Prior to Akbar's becoming ill, relations between Akbar and Jahangir were not good. As touched upon briefly by Khusrau in the novel, Akbar was wont to becoming intensely irritated with Jahangir, while Jahangir displayed a stubborn disregard for his father's directives.[11] This antipathy, and a sense of insecurity about his succession to the throne led Jahangir to march against his father with an army of "30,010 battle-ready horse" from Allahabad towards Agra. The rebellion was put down without bloodshed, although not quite as I have described it. The real Akbar did it with letters, persuading Jahangir to turn back, with some astute, unstated brinkmanship.[12] Jahangir's murder of the Writer, Abul Fazl, followed, more or less as I have described it.[13]

Since there was no Paru, the characters in the novel closely associated with her did not exist either. Paru's mother is fictional, and Akbar did not marry her or give her his turban pin. Pithu and the Snake Charmer are, of course, fictional.

Following Akbar's illness, a meeting did indeed take place in which the nobles were summoned to help choose a successor. It was initiated by Man Singh and by Akbar's half-brother, Aziz Koka.[14] In the history books it is called simply a "meeting", and not a Choosing, as I have named it. There were two candidates: Jahangir and Khusrau. The meeting-initiators must have been taken aback when the nobles chose Jahangir. Perhaps the nobles were caught cold and found Khusrau to be too radical a choice. I have been able to find nothing more than a cursory mention of this meeting in my sources, and therefore its flow in the novel is fictitious.

On the other hand, Jahangir's visit to Akbar's death-bed, where the dying Akbar gave Jahangir the nod, did indeed occur. When Akbar finally assented, with a slight movement of his head, the assembled ministers confirmed Jahangir's succession with the royal robes, turban, and the sword of Humayun, as described.[15]

Aside from the invention of Paru, my other big license has been to bring forward the events leading up to Nur's engagement to Jahangir. In the novel, Nur and Sher Afghan find themselves stationed in Bengal somewhat earlier than the real date, which was 1606.[16] As in the novel, Sher Afghan killed the officer, Qutub Uddin, in an encounter marked by misunderstandings. Sher Afghan's subsequent murder remains a mystery. One theory has Jahangir secretly instigating the murder out of a variety of motives, one of which could have been an incipient and unreported liaison with Nur. However, unlike the novel, there is no record of any suspicions of the real Nur having had a hand in Sher Afghan's murder.

Between 1606 and 1611 Nur and Jahangir must have had only a passing awareness of each other. The first record of a full-blown romance was at the Navroze* celebrations of 1611.[18] Jahangir did indeed encounter Nur in the Mina Bazaar, as reported in the novel. The historical account has Jahangir "...gazing upon her unveiled face" and falling in love. I found this too facile to make interesting reading. Better to have a conversation filled with private conflicts arising from earlier liaisons. After all, no one really knows what they said to each other.

The game of fire-polo at Nagaricin was real,[19] as were the elephant fights in which Akbar forced Jahangir to take part. In her great character-study, *Nur Jahan*, Ellison Findly suggests that one factor motivating Jahangir's drinking may have been "to encourage in himself a personal recklessness large enough to compete with the courage and fearlessness of Akbar."[20]

Jahangir's scientific bent, and his interest in all manner of natural phenomena is well documented. His diary is sprinkled with observations of the plant and animal life of India. Some of these would befit a modern naturalist. "...Also there is the *seoti*, a member of the *keora* family. The *keora* usually has thorns, but the *seoti* does not. Its color is yellowish, while the *keora* is white."[21] Bamber Gascoigne describes how, over a period of many months, Jahangir closely observed and recorded in his diary the details of two cranes mating and giving birth to chicks.[22]

---

* For the Zoroastrian aficionados, this is the very same Jamshedi Navroze celebrated by the Parsis, and by people of Iranian cultural roots the world over. The Mughals celebrated it for eighteen days. The custom was brought to India from Persia by Akbar in 1582. In the preface to his wonderful translation of the Jahangirnama, Thackston Wheeler describes how the Mughals used two calendars simultaneously, the Persian and the Islamic.[17] Here are the days that Wheeler lists for the days of the Persian calendar: Farvardin, Urdibihisht, Khurdad, Tir, Amurdad, Shahrivar... and on!

Making Nur's romance with Jahangir occur six years earlier gave her the opportunity to play a swashbuckling role in Khusrau's revolt, which led eventually to her entanglement with Paru. In reality, Nur was not present during the revolt. Historians have characterized this event as a minor skirmish, which Jahangir easily won. But a reading of Jahangir's diary shows that the revolt perturbed him greatly, and he played an active and anxious role in putting it down. The sleepless night of confusion, when it was not clear which direction Khusrau had gone, did indeed occur. "God willing, when day broke, I myself would set out," Jahangir wrote in his diary.[23] Two *amirs* loyal to Jahangir encountered the rebel army at Sikandra and hastened to Jahangir to "...report that Khusrau was headed at a gallop for the Punjab. It occurred to me that he might have pulled a feint and actually be headed in some other direction. Because his uncle Raja Man Singh was in Bengal, most of the court servants thought he would be there."

It was not Nur who rode to the Lahore citadel to close its gates, but Dilawar Khan. By chance, Dilawar Khan, who was apparently headed south to Agra at the time, encountered the rebels in Delhi. "...when he heard these things he had his sons cross the Jumna [to inform Jahangir], while he himself, like a good soldier of fortune, decided to gallop with the intention of reaching the Lahore fortress before Khusrau got there."[24] On reaching the fort, "Dilawar Khan entered the citadel with a few men and began to fortify the towers and ramparts."

The biryani was real. When the battle was almost upon Jahangir's forward guard, "Muizzulmulk had brought me a pot of biryani and I was about to partake of it with gusto when news of the battle arrived. No sooner had I heard it than I took one mouthful for good luck and mounted, although I was very desirous of eating the biryani."[25] Jahangir was preempted from taking part in actual hand-to-hand combat (to the relief of his men), when "news of victory was received".

Although the real Nur was not a part of putting down the revolt, the daring actions attributed to her in the novel are not out of character. The example most often cited of her boisterousness is one I find somewhat distasteful. She is said to have killed "four tigers with six bullets" while mounted on an elephant and encumbered by the veil.

A more interesting story took place in 1626, towards the end of Jahangir's reign.[26] Jahangir was all but disabled from illness. Mahabat Khan staged a coup and held Jahangir captive. When news came of the coup, Nur found herself on the opposite side of the Jhelum River from Mahabat Khan and his troops. Nur and Asaf Khan (who, for the moment, were allies) decided to stage an ill-conceived attack by attempting to ford the river. On the opposite side stood five thousand battle-hardened Rajputs under Mahabat Khan's command. Nur led the charge on her elephant, accompanied by her daughter, her grand-daughter and a nurse-maid.

From the start, things went wrong. The ford was worse than expected, with deep pits of water. The river was swollen, and the forces quickly got separated. Soldiers, horses and elephants drowned. The Rajputs from the opposite bank rained arrows upon the attackers. The nurse-maid was hit in the arm with an arrow. In mid-current, Nur removed the arrow, staining her clothes with blood. She emptied four quivers of her own arrows into the forces on the opposite bank. Incredibly, the party made it across, only to be captured by the waiting troops.

The story has a satisfactory conclusion. Some months later, while still in Mahabat Khan's captivity, Nur and Jahangir managed to organize a counter-revolt. This was helped in no small part by their enduring popularity in the countryside, which allowed Nur to quickly assemble an army of her own to oppose Mahabat Khan[27].

In the novel I have greatly relaxed the Mughal custom of *purdah*. Women of high rank did not expose their faces in public. Even within the confines of the forts and palaces, where men outside the immediate family could be present, the women had to be veiled or sit behind the *purdah*. Bamber Gascoigne relates the example of a "European doctor" who was called upon to attend a royal lady in the harem. A large shawl was placed over his head and he had to be led into the presence of the sick lady by the hand.[28] When the Emperor traveled, royal ladies rode on elephants with covered howdahs whose windows were covered with gold mesh. Mounted servants carrying large canes rode ahead to clear the road of possible men who might cast eyes on the royal personage. Nur could not have ridden open-faced on horse-back through the countryside. Nor could she have attended the *Diwani Aam* unveiled, as the novel would have it. The real Nur, even at the height of her power, ruled from behind the *purdah*.[29]

The *purdah* restrictions did not apply to women of lower rank. Dancing-girls at the palace entertainments were open-faced, and, judging from the paintings, quite open-bodied. Paru was free to wander the streets of Agra as she willed. Prostitutes were common;[30] to the extent that Akbar sought to regulate prostitution, by restricting it to certain parts of town.[31]

I agonized much about those "streets" that Paru walked. What did they look like? How did common people live in the cities? Historical narratives are typically sparse in such details. Luckily, I did discover some clues, mostly from the accounts of travellers across the sub-continent during the Mughal era. Father Antonio Monserrate, for example, journeyed from Goa to Agra, at Akbar's invitation, in 1579. Of Agra, he wrote, "Agra is a magnificent city, both for its size and its antiquity."[32] Also, it had "beautiful gardens". Describing Delhi, he wrote: "Delhi is inhabited by substantial and wealthy Brahman, and of course by a *Mongol* [Mughal] garrison. Hence its many fine private mansions add considerably to the magnificence of the city... rich men construct for themselves well-built, lofty and handsomely decorated residences."[33] Passing through a nondescript town called Sironj he noted, "Many of the inferior classes in the town live in small and round huts. Indeed nowhere else in the region are such miserable hovels to be seen."[34] Jahangir himself wrote of Agra in his diary, "Most people have constructed three- and four-story buildings, and the congestion is so great that one can scarcely pass in the lanes and the markets."[35]

Khusrau's defeat and capture at Lahore were followed by Jahangir's famous retribution,[36] which took place more or less as I have described. The one difference is that Khusrau was forced to ride through the streets of Lahore while the rebels were staked, not around the polo field at Nagarcin, on the outskirts of Agra. Bringing the rebels' punishment back to Agra, allowed it to be connected to Paru.

The Twelve Decrees were real.[37] In even detailed histories of Jahangir, the Decrees are considered to be so insignificant, as to deserve scarcely a mention. I find them nothing short of astonishing. Consider the era in which Jahangir lived: Barely sixty years earlier, Henry VIII had ordered his last execution of a wife, Catherine Howard. The reign of Elizabeth I, which followed, was hardly as golden as is typically suggested. It was marked by the serial execution of Catholics and the hounding of Catholics with punitive levies and forced conversions. No slouches in the area of conversions, the Catholics were in the middle of their own world-wide Inquisition. Portuguese soldiers in the colony of Goa went AWOL into the Indian subcontinent, to escape the Inquisition, as much as to earn higher salaries.[38] In 1605, the year that Jahangir enacted his Decrees, the English Bill of Rights was still 84 years into the future. It would be passed in 1689. And the US Constitution was a full 185 years away.

Yet, consider Jahangir's Third Decree: "No one was to open merchants' packs along the roads without their permission and consent."[39] This is a fair prototype of the Fourth Amendment to the US Constitution. And Jahangir's Sixth Decree, "No one's house was to be used for the quartering of troops" uncannily predates the US Third Amendment, without the latter's exceptions. As for Jahangir's Tenth Decree, it has an eerily modern ring: "In large cities hospitals are to be built and physicians appointed to treat the sick. Expenses are to be covered from the royal demesne." Could it be that the emissaries of the English, Dutch and Portuguese trading companies who, over the years, had direct contact with the great Mughals, assimilated ideas from Hindustani governance and carried them back to their home countries?

I simplified the Eleventh Decree, which forbids the killing of animals for meat. The actual Decree provides a graded formula for moving Hindustan towards vegetarianism one day at a time. It was not followed through because Jahangir balked at the thought that it may restrict hunting. But, what a far-reaching law for a nation to adopt!

Progress is not linear. We are not automatically superior to our predecessors. If we care to look back through the halls of history and understand where we came from, it is possible that our vision becomes a little more stereoscopic. As we see people engaged in conflicts that mean nothing to us and yet display a passion and heroism that humbles us, perhaps, just perhaps, we can be persuaded to abandon our own conceits of the moment and learn something from the wisdom of the ages.

Notes

1. Keay, p. 320.
2. Keay, p. 323.
3. Gommans, p. 95.
4. Fisher, Preface by William Dalrymple, p. xvii.
5. Gascoigne, p. 128.
6. Fisher, Preface by William Dalrymple, p. xvii.
7. Keay, p. 323.
8. Gascoigne, p. 90-92.
9. Jahangirnama, p. 37.
10. Gascoigne, p. 92.
11. Gascoigne, p. 122.
12. Jahangirnama, Preface, p. 9.
13. Jahangirnama, Preface, p. 10.
14. Gascoigne, p. 126.
15. Gascoigne, p. 126.
16. Findly, p. 27.
17. Jahingirnama, Translator's Preface, p. xiv.
18. Findly, p. 35-36.

19. Gascoigne, p. 95.
20. Findly, p. 78.
21. Jahangirnama, p. 24.
22. Gascoigne, p. 132.
23. Jahangirnama, p. 49.
24. Jahangirnama, p. 52.
25. Jahangirnama, p. 55.
26. Findly, p. 267.
27. Findly, p. 271.
28. Gascoigne, p. 162.
29. Gascoigne, p. 160.
30. Hansen, p. 33.
31. Gascoigne, p. 108.
32. Fisher, p. 49.
33. Fisher, p. 55.
34. Fisher, p. 45.
35. Jahangirnama, p. 22.
36. Gascoigne, p. 135.
37. Jahangirnama, p. 26.
38. Fisher, Preface by William Dalrymple, p. xiv.
39. Jahangirnama, p. 26.

Selected Bibliography

Keay, John. *India – A History.* Harper Collins Publishers and Harper Collins Publishers India, 2000.

Fisher, Michael H. *Beyond the Three Seas – Travellers' Tales of Mughal India.* Random House India, 2007.

Gascoigne, Bamber. *The Great Moghuls.* Harper & Row, New York, 1971.

Thackston, Wheeler M, translation. Jahangirnama: Memoirs of Jahangir, Emperor of India. Oxford University Press, 1999.

Findly, Ellison Banks. *Nur Jahan, Empress of Mughal India.* Oxford University Press, New York, 1993.

Gommans, Jos J. L. *Mughal Warfare: Indian Frontiers and Highroads to Empire 1500-1700.* Routledge, New York, 2002.

Narain, Brij, Sri Ram Sharma, translation. *A Contemporary Dutch Chronicle of Mughal India* (by Pieter van den Broecke). Susil Gupta (India) Ltd. Calcutta, 1957.

Hansen, Waldemar. *The Peacock Throne.* Holt, Rhinehart and Winston. 1972.

Author's Note

This is a work of historical fiction. Many of the characters and incidents described in this novel do, in fact, have a basis in history. For others, I have exercised the novelist's license to invent.

In the Afterword at the end of this book, I have attempted full disclosure and pointed out the aspects of the story that deviate from the historical record.

For Rashna